Believe in yourself!

Analiesa

In Desperate Search of Peace

By Analiesa Adams

In Desperate Search of Peace

Copyright © 2015 by Analiesa Adams

Cover by

Acknowledgement

My thanks go to the two people who have always believed in me, no matter what the circumstance, and encouraged me to be creative in whatever format makes me the happiest—my mother and my son. Both are wonderfully steadfast in their own way, witty, and a true blessing to have in my life.

Table of Contents

Chapter 1

The loud crash of the front door bounced off the walls of the nearly empty living room jerking Lisa out of her exhausted sleep. Disoriented at first, she struggled to make sense of where she'd woken up, the immediate awareness of danger eminent.

Oh God, not again, please make this stop, she pleaded in silence.

She didn't know if God listened to her or not. He didn't appear to pay attention, no matter how often she prayed.

Bedcovers flew to the floor as she kicked them off and leapt to her feet. A cold sweat of panic formed on her forehead and trickled down her face. She tried to take a few deep breaths between the shallow quiet ones as she struggled to listen for any noise indicating the location of the intruder. The sudden rush of adrenaline made it impossible as the thunderous rhythm in her ears roared like ocean waves slamming against the breaker during a hurricane. If her heart pounded any harder she would pass out for sure.

Fooled by the dark, she thought she saw movement outside of her door. She pressed her back against the wall hoping not to be seen by the intruder. She blinked hard, trying to focus her tired eyes against her shadowy surroundings. The gentle sway of the curtain she used as an enclosure to the linen closet became clearer to her, disturbed by the sudden influx of air into the apartment. She made out the low curses being muttered by the intruder in the other room.

Her stomach did a somersault. *He's here.*

"Where the hell are you?" The expected familiar shout from the other room brought the hackles up on the back of her neck.

Matt came again in the night, just as Lisa knew he would, this time much sooner than any of his break-ins before.

How on earth does he keep finding me?

She waited a second, hoping for the sounds of someone coming to help. A couple of healthy weight lifters from across the hallway had agreed to keep an eye out for her. They'd told her if she ever needed anything they'd be there for her. Although, she remembered the second part of their offer had been delivered with a wink and smirk from them both.

Damn it! Someone must have heard that! Where are they now?

Evidently, she couldn't count on anyone to rescue her. No use in waiting around, if she were to get out of this alive, she'd need to act fast.

Lisa slid along the dingy bedroom wall she kept purposefully clear of any obstacles and peered around the edge of the bedroom doorjamb.

She gripped her most important belongings close to her chest, stuffed inside the backpack ready at her side at all times. An uneasy shake of her hand couldn't be stopped as she instinctively reached down to the front pocket of the sweats she wore. The lump of keys taped inside the front pocket with duct tape remained in place. If the keys were all she took with her, at least she might still possess a fighting chance to reach her car in time to get away.

"What's wrong with the damn lights?" Matt screeched, stumbling through her small dark living room.

She would recognize his voice anywhere. Every day hoping she'd never have to listen for his garbled speech again, yet here he was, close enough to send a cold tremor down her neck.

His pattern of breaking in at night had taught her to switch the electrical panel off before going to bed, for this exact reason. Darkness had become her friend. A tool of survival in this awful life she lived, playing cat and mouse—God how she hated being the mouse.

Her stomach rolled and twisted. The brief thought of throwing up to ease the pain crossed her mind. No telling what might happen if she came face to face with him again tonight. Visions of the last time he'd come, when she'd permitted him to get too close, flitted past her in waves increasing her anxiety tenfold. He'd been coherent enough to grab onto her. Still able to feel his clammy hands grasping the bare skin of her arms, his putrid breath in her face, she brushed her hand across the sweat beading on her forehead.

She knew she was damn lucky back then. His weakened state allowed her to escape from his grasp and flee from the repercussions of his toxin-induced fury. A sudden shiver of dread flew over her, like the frigid winds whipping through the icy arctic tundra.

Tonight she may not be so lucky.

Focus, Lisa. Don't make the same stupid mistake, she reminded herself as she took the first careful step out of her room.

As she slithered against the wall, she stopped to listen. Matt cussed, tripping over the cheap coffee table she'd found at a garage sale. The loud thud and splintering of wood added to the racket disturbing the calm of night.

3

"Damn it, Lisa, I know you're here. Don't hide from me. You fucking whore, get out here. Stop this shit."

His ear splitting squeal wasn't a good sign. She could tell he was on a current high. The draft from the open door carried the gaseous stench from his clothes through the air past her nose, making her gag. Memory of their previous encounters suggested the potency of the rancid odor meant he'd no doubt used not too long ago, making him much more volatile.

A quiet hiss from a nozzle filled the now silent room. She'd been through this enough times to recognize the sound came from some type of toxic substance, like butane or starter fluid. The cheap hardware store fix of choice, which he often carried with him in order to keep his high going strong while on the move. She knew she didn't have much time before his behavior would turn brutal and abusive, and she didn't want to be around when that happened.

Hard to hear over the sound of her heartbeat, she strained to listen for the perfect moment to escape. She could tell the chemicals must be torturing Matt's throat when he began a hacking cough that proved he still lay on the floor. She hoped he'd be incoherent enough from the last huff to allow her to slip toward the back of the apartment without catching sight of her.

The sudden silence caught her attention. *Good, maybe he's passed out*.

Lisa held her breath and moved past the hazy shape of Matt's body, barely visible through the living room archway. He lay in an unmoving heap where her coffee table used to stand.

A grating of metal-on-metal made her cringe when she opened the kitchen windowpane against the cold night air. She sucked in a quick breath. The irregular skitter of her heartbeat went

4

unnoticed when she glanced back to see Matt struggle to sit up. He lurched to his feet, still disoriented by the dark.

"Bitch, I knew you were here," he barked, the vicious undertones making her shudder.

Lisa heaved herself and her backpack out of the window. Her throat caught on a scream, hot tears springing forward, when Matt reached out to grab hold of a small patch of her hair just as her toes reached the wet grass below. He yanked her head backward, and his other hand searched for another handhold, crossing her face with wretched smelling fingers. Wrenching her head forward hurt, but caused him to lose his tentative grasp, and with a quick twist she vaulted away from the building. She slid to her knees as her foot slipped on the overly wet patch of grass next to the leaking water sprinkler. Her heart tumbled to her throat with an erratic beat when she heard the footsteps behind her getting closer and closer.

"Come back here you bitch. You're mine. You hear me, you're mine. I won't let you get away this time."

Frantic, she pulled herself up, the driving force of terror about to overtake her sense of control. She wanted to run. To keep running until she reached safety, but what would be safe when a madman was chasing you? She made herself focus on reaching the car, each step bringing her nearer to survival. The blanket of damp grass shifted into the sharp sadistic rocks of the small parking lot, and they cut deep into her tender bare feet, causing the hot panic filled tears to roll down her cheeks.

She gasped for air, as she yanked open her little red Ford Pinto, and jumped in slamming the door shut at the precise second Matt caught up to her. Her twisting contortion to reach the lock behind her wrenched the tightened muscles in her side, and she cried out in pain. To her relief, the lock engaged at the same time he

5

tugged on the handle. He began cursing, the wrenching sound of the door handle rattled, the car rocking back and forth with the force of his attempts to gain access.

Matt's dirty and unshaven f ace, pressed up against the glass beside her, was a mere semblance of what he once used to be. The feverish pounding of his fists on the driver's side window muffled his shouted curses. As she started the engine, she saw him glare at her with such hatred it brought the tears out with a renewed vigor. As if in a dream unable to move, she watched as he ran around the front of the car to the passenger side door and reached for the handle. She realized—this was no dream—it was a nightmare.

Oh God, did I lock that door? Please, let it be locked.

Lisa jerked the gearshift backward, the grinding moan of the mechanism indicative of an unsuccessful connection. Frenzied turbulent waves of nausea in her stomach threatened to come up, so she swallowed hard and tried again. The loud stripping of the gears didn't matter much to her right now as she shoved the stick into reverse and tore backward in a spew of rocks. Her front fender swung around throwing Matt to the ground on his backside. If she ran over him or the cars around her, she didn't care.

As she skidded out of the parking lot, she recognized Matt's van parked at the curb, the nondescript gray color fading into the concrete building behind it in the hazy night air. She shuddered, knowing the contents of that van would be revolting, a memory she wished she could forget. Something no decent human being should ever have to see.

"Oh please, please don't let him catch me," she prayed aloud, taking the next corner at an unsafe speed.

She'd prepared for this day, and hoped it would pay off. Every place she'd ended up, her steps to plan out the most complicated route out of the city proved to be her saving grace at times. Denver had been no different. The myriad of one-way streets, and multiple lane thoroughfares turned out as one of the hardest she'd ever planned. If he succeeded in following her, she might be able to lose him in the confusion.

Her head swam with the longing for peace. The fear she lived day in and day out a reminder of how things used to be before Matt. If only she could go back home to the life she'd been working so hard to achieve. She'd worked hard after earning her fine arts degree for the teaching degree she knew she could count on to make a living. She'd studied in the wee hours of the night while her mother slept. The time during the day monopolized by her mother's failing health issues. Although she'd ended up placing her in a care facility, she'd spent all her free time assisting her mother with anything she needed. She'd promised her father on his death bed she wouldn't leave her mother's failing memories to the care of strangers—and she hadn't, until she'd met Matt.

Now, no matter how much she wanted to, she couldn't go back to her dream of a calm peaceful life being an elementary school art teacher. Matt made sure she understood if he ever found her he would kill her. The restraining order she'd placed on him did no good. Police could never find him. He lived in his van, and moved from place to place. She never knew when or where he would attack, making it impossible to catch him. He might be an addict, but was smart enough never to be picked up by the law. Otherwise, they would have hauled him off to jail for violating the order.

Until she could figure out a way to get him and the police in the same place at the same time, she was forced to live this life of exile. The problem was finding the right place, the right people to make this happen. She'd had no luck so far.

Denver, she'd thought, the perfect place to hide. Much farther than she'd ever ventured before, but obviously not far enough. This time, she needed to go farther, much farther. To the end of the earth, if that's what it took.

She jammed her foot on the accelerator, her hysterical state restrained as she tried to remember her careful plans to get away. Her glance flickered back-and-forth between staying on the road and her rear view mirror, both actions equally important to her next decisive move.

The frosty early spring temperature caused uncontrollable shivers as the chilled sweat trickled down her back in rivulets of fright. Each time she caught a glimpse of headlights she pushed harder, sped a little faster. Her heart racing in terror of the one thing she was deathly afraid of—her ex-fiancée.

* * * *

Breathing easier, it seemed as though Lisa once again escaped Matt's tirade. Miles posted with relentless continuity on the odometer as she forced herself to stay awake. Darkness turned to dawn, daylight turned into darkness once more. Dazed and unaware, except for the need to keep going, she watched the trees pass by while the mountainous climb taxed her aged car to extreme limits.

She had to keep going. There was no other way.

The dim light of morning crested again through the haze of an early fog that hung close to the ground as she traveled West on I-90. Lisa began to wonder where she'd driven, then spotted a sign posted on an upcoming railroad overpass. She figured she was still in

Washington, but had no clue where she was at the moment. Through her weary blurred sight, she made out the words 'North Bend' as she went under the tracks.

"Where the heck is North Bend?" Lisa groaned, followed by a huge yawn.

She wasn't sure where she was going, and didn't much care where she ended up, as long as he didn't find her.

After a few minutes, her eyelids weighed heavy over her vision again. The need for sleep more evident as the repeated sound of her tires hitting the reflective lane markers startled her awake.

A blue highway indicator, which read 'Rest Area – 1 Mile Ahead', came up on the right, and she sighed in relief. She kept trying to open her eyes wider to stay awake, yet her vision hazed over with an involuntary sleep seeping over her in subtle waves. Barely making the cutoff, she gave a silent prayer of thanks, and pulled into a parking space under the lamppost closest to the restrooms. She squinted, searching the empty parking lot for danger.

A ghostly white mist hung eerily under the bright light feeding out into the nearby dark shroud of evergreens. They stood like menacing giants out of a fairy tale her mother once read to her, which she never had liked. Spooked, Lisa considered heading back out to the freeway, but pure exhaustion prevailed. The need for slumber, now more important than any fear she could conjure up in her mind about her surroundings, had a strong grip on her consciousness.

She took one last glance around for safety. Her slight tremble at the thought of what might be lingering amidst the fog made her laugh.

"Get a grip, Lisa. It's all right. They're just trees."

Although she'd locked her doors before, she checked them twice then reached back for the head rest and afghan she kept in her back seat. She fluffed the worn stuffing of the pillow without much effect, and crammed the padding behind her head against the window. As she kicked off the shoes she'd slipped on at the first chance she had at a gas station, she gave a sigh at the relief from their constriction. Those flats she kept in her emergency stash in the trunk had come in handy. She tried to find the best place to relax, and grumbled at the uncomfortable upright seat position she considered necessary in case she needed to start the car in a hurry.

Her hand brushed against the homemade key chain she'd made for herself hanging from the ignition, and she pulled the keys out to bring the unique shape closer to her face. In the macramé knots between two pieces of plastic, she'd encased a small picture of her parents, the only one of her father she still owned.

Tears welled up as she gazed at the images from a much earlier time. Her mother appeared to be in her twenties, her father in dress uniform as they held on tightly to one another. The figures were almost too small for any clear detail, but the love between the two stood out without question. She held close the memory of her youth, watching her parents remain solid in their love throughout every twist and turn of life.

Her father had always been her stronghold. She could always count on him to help her work through her problems, no matter how small. Ever since he'd passed, she longed for the safety and security she'd depended on—especially now. Now she had nobody to depend on but herself, and sometimes that just wasn't enough.

A sigh escaped her lips as she gave a kiss to the memory of her parents. Without fail, before she closed her eyes, she said a little prayer in hopes one day her dreams of having the same type of bond between two people would come true for her too. She'd read once if you truly believed something, it would happen. Right now she needed to believe in something, no matter how unrealistic it seemed.

Peace and love were the most important things to her, neither of which belonged to her at the moment. Undoubtedly, peace was a given. She couldn't think of anything she wouldn't do to end this hell she'd been living. Love, a little more tricky—no guarantee it would happen, and no telling whether she would ever meet the right person. Now, looking toward the future was her only means of mental fortitude, she had to believe someday, somehow, she would come out of this to claim the life she longed to possess.

She didn't ask for much, but every day she prayed for a relationship similar to what her parent's had found in each other. Her dream to somehow discover a steadfast companion to share the ups and downs, a true best friend to enjoy even the smallest things with, and secretly she hoped would all be rolled up into a magnificent lover to fuel her innermost passions. She figured asking for everything couldn't hurt.

The daydream of peace and happiness made her smile as she forced the thought of the never ending life of fleeing from place to place from her mind.

When she pulled the afghan up close to her nose the faint scent of her mother's perfume comforted her enough to drift off into fitful bouts of rest. The fantasy was lovely for a time, but soon her dreams were filled with shadowed gruesome monsters. The same recognized fears she fled during the daytime became distorted visions during sleep, haunting her with an ever present heart-wrenching need to run.

Lisa shifted in a fretful turn to another position, when all of a sudden, a loud tapping noise jolted her awake. She sprang forward, defenses engaged, her hand ready on the keys in the ignition. Eyes wide, yet still blurry, she tried to focus on the figure outside of her window. Through the condensation collecting on the glass, she made out the form of a heavyset person a short distance away. His action of standing with arms to his side in full view put her at ease. He didn't appear as a threat. At least not the one she was so desperate to avoid.

She rolled the window down about an inch, just enough to be heard. "Yes?"

The colors of a uniformed employee became clearer, as he came closer to her window.

"Ma'am, I need to ask you to move your car away from the building. If you require sleep, Area C is where you need to park. The morning rush is about to hit. All vehicles at an extended rest must follow the rules." His polite professional attitude, accompanied by the straight line of his lips, told her he took his job very serious. "Anything over a four hour period, we ask you find lodging in the next town."

"I'm sorry, I didn't realize." Lisa muttered realizing she had a serious need to stretch her legs and back anyway. The sitting position had taken a toll on her cramping muscles. "I'll use your restroom and be moving on."

The glimpse at her watch told her she'd only been asleep for about two hours. She yawned, still exhausted.

I can probably last a little longer now, she deduced judging her alertness. *Coffee, I definitely need coffee.*

She waited until the man moved away from her vehicle to sweep up some trash by the garbage cans. In a swift movement, she opened her door and peered from side to side.

Did he follow me? Is Matt hiding somewhere, just waiting to grab me?

Out of the corner of her eye, a movement startled her. Her heart palpitated with the trepidation she carried with her everywhere. She searched the trees carefully, her hand held ready on the keys. She blew out a breath of relief when a crow flew back out of the trees carrying something in its talons. Always on the lookout, never able to relax, her need to stay alert had become a part of her she didn't like.

The only other car around was a small VW Bug that pulled up as she spoke to the uniformed attendant. A young college-aged woman had turned off the engine, but remained seated speaking with animated gestures to someone on her cell phone. Lisa glanced over when the woman jumped out and sprinted toward the restroom, her sandals clapping loudly against the asphalt.

As Lisa stepped onto the cold hard pavement, she winced peering down at her bare feet. She reached back into the front seat to pull out the white canvas slip-ons and pushed them back on with a grimace. The soles of her feet were still sensitive from her flight through the unyielding gravel the night before last. She looked down, shaking her head at her appearance. Her pants were a loss. From her knees down, dried mud stained the material with dark brown and green grass splotches. Unfortunately, the act of brushing the excess dirt off only left a nasty mess.

Disgusted, she wondered for a brief moment whether she should change her pants with the extra set of pants she kept in her trunk. The heavy sigh that came tumbling out proved the effort to carry out this action seemed more than she was willing to take. She was too tired to care what she looked like anyway. When she found a place to stay, she'd stop at the first Laundromat and make the swap there.

At the restroom mirror, Lisa's grim expression stared back at her from the reflective image. Her hair scrunched to one side, and the dark circles under her eyes made for a ghoulish sight. Almost as if she'd left her makeup on overnight. Though, she hadn't worn any for weeks, as money was so tight she couldn't afford such luxuries. With a yawn, she ran her fingers through her twisted curls without much result, wishing she'd grabbed her hairbrush from her backpack.

The other woman stepped up to the sinks and turned on the water faucet, pouting at her own reflection. Her image revealed a perky young girl, with short-cropped blond hair, and what Lisa thought was way too much eye shadow.

"You've got really pretty hair." The girl grinned as she finished washing her hands and fluffed her own locks. "I wish mine would curl like that."

Lisa smiled. "Keep what you've got. Curls aren't all they're cracked up to be. They can be a real pain sometimes."

"Yeah, but the guys really love them. They must be chasing after you all the time."

"Something like that," Lisa chortled, and broke into a fit of laughter, the stress and her exhausted state making the woman's statement way too funny all of a sudden.

In obvious confusion to the outburst, the girl gave a forced smile, gathered up her purse and hurried through the door.

"You definitely need some caffeine," Lisa told herself viewing the baggy black marks under her eyes again.

As she stood in line for coffee, she eyed the other people in the cramped area, making sure none of them were a threat. A teenage girl glared back at her with obvious disdain. She said something in the ear of the older woman standing next to her, who turned around to take a quick glance at Lisa. The older woman grimaced, and nodded in agreement to the comment, as she stepped toward the counter for her coffee.

Lisa didn't know what earned such contempt, but a wave of embarrassment settled over her, and she faulted herself for looking so appalling in public. When a draft of cold air brushed past her as another person came in for some refreshments, she pulled her arms closer to her cold body. Holding her head low, she felt exposed and vulnerable all of a sudden.

Although, the dollar the rest-stop charged for a small Styrofoam cup of coffee was outrageous, when she brought the cup closer it smelled like heaven to Lisa. The taste, however, a bit less satisfying than she'd imagined. As she sipped the steaming liquid she wrinkled her nose. It tasted a bit like stewed socks. She decided against eating the free cinnamon roll they offered with her purchase, but wrapped it up in a napkin and tucked it away for later snacking. The thought of eating something now didn't sound like such a good idea. Her stomach still churned, whether from hunger or tension, she wasn't sure.

Besides, she needed to get moving.

As she walked toward the exit, a road map caught her eye on the far side of the wall. She pulled out a chart of Washington and realized she still didn't have a clue where she'd driven.

"Excuse me," she prompted the attendant behind the desk.

The elderly man lowered his newspaper and peered at her over his reading glasses. He continued to stare at her as he took a sip of his own coffee. Apparently, not everyone here had the same work ethics as the attendant she'd met earlier.

"Would you show me where we are on this map," she asked, not wanting to sound as dumb as to say, *Where am I?*"

He frowned, pointed to a spot on I-90, and turned back to his paper. Following the direction she'd been traveling, Lisa traced a line down the highway where it ended not far from North Bend at Seattle. From there she'd need to decide whether to head North or South on I-5.

Her heart lifted when she saw she was getting closer to the coastal waters. She'd always wanted to visit the ocean. Books and movies could only go so far to describe the grandeur of what she imagined she would feel standing in the presence of one of God's greatest creations. Enthralled with the idea of fulfilling at least one of her dreams, she was determined to keep moving in the direction she'd started, and decided to drive South, then continue West on Highway 12. This route would take her toward the Pacific coastline, as far West as she could possibly go.

That sounded like a fine idea, lost to the world, living out her life peacefully combing the beach for seashells.

* * * *

Lisa drove for what seemed like hours. As she got closer to the coast she stopped for a time in Hoquiam, unable to travel any further. The need for sleep had taken over once again. So, she pulled into a small parking area overlooking the bay, to take what she

16

thought would be a short nap. This time, total exhaustion won its mischievous play on her senses and she passed out uninterrupted for a four-hour stretch.

She awoke charged with a new strength to keep going. As she munched on the small snack she'd set aside, she studied the map again. The ocean side town of Ocean Shores, she'd originally thought sounded to be a nice place to stay, might not be the best choice. Right on the coast, there would probably be more people and more activity than she felt comfortable in being around. For safety reasons, she changed her mind and decided to head north on Hwy 101 toward the Olympic Mountains. Perhaps she would discover an enjoyable place close enough to the ocean, yet sufficiently tucked away from any tourist traps where she might be more easily tracked.

Maybe this time Matt wouldn't be able to find her.

The radio didn't seem to work for long, so instead of listening to the scratchy talk radio station she'd found she drove in silence. Everywhere she looked there was a beauty in her surroundings that she loved. She knew the greenery held an abundance of life. The lakes, forests and sporadic meadows she'd passed were sure to have what she'd dreamt of for some time. An urgency to discover their riches began to stir deep down. She knew this was a place where she could explore her artistic side, a place to relax and enjoy the smallest pleasures of life. It had been so long since she'd had the chance to sketch. It felt as if a piece of her was missing. The only piece she had left that brought her joy.

Contentment seemed to settle over her, and she smiled, though the loud rumble of her stomach persisted, this time with a sharp pain. Unsure of her next stop, she attempted to quiet the annoyance with a stale bag of popcorn from her stash of emergency supplies. Although, used to not eating much for long periods of time, she realized she needed to stop soon. The lightheadedness from not eating had started to affect her driving reactions.

She glanced from side to side and laughed. Out in the middle of nowhere, there was nothing but trees on both sides of the road. She'd have a hard time finding someplace to eat an actual meal. So she grabbed another handful of popcorn and stuffed the dry leathery kernels into her mouth.

As if by magic, a small restaurant sign caught her eye pointing east one mile to a town with the name of Lake Duchess. Her stomach growled at the mere thought of good food, and made her decision an easy one. Turning down the side road, the afternoon sunshine filtered through the tree limbs onto the pavement. She felt as if the glow pulled her along like a welcome mat, enticing her to discover the wealth of beauty wrapping its arms around her.

'Maggie's Bar and Grill' was proudly displayed over the log cabin archway of the restaurant when she pulled into the parking lot. Thrilled that the structure overlooked a gorgeous view of the lake, Lisa stepped out of her car in awe of her surroundings. In the late afternoon sun, the bold crispness of the air surprised her. An amazing freshness of recent rainwater, mixed with the musky aroma of the forest, filled her senses with a ray of new hope.

At this hour, there were no other customers around, as it was a bit late for lunch, and too early for dinner. The heavy wood door creaked and she entered with soft timid footsteps into the old-fashioned restaurant. She stood stationary for a moment, her backpack dangling from her fingers, not sure if she should find her own table or wait to be seated.

"Take a seat, I'll be out in a minute," shouted a gruff female voice from somewhere in the kitchen.

For safety measures, Lisa sat in a booth at the far window, close to the back door, in case she needed to escape all of a sudden. Remembering her unsightly appearance, she tucked her legs under the table, hoping nobody would notice.

The peaceful lakeshore's beauty drew her breath away, causing a sting of tears to form at the back of her eyes. Excitement rose up when she spotted the regal pose of a blue heron perched on a fallen log alongside the waterline. Her fingers itched to sketch the scene for a reminder of what could be someday. She almost reached for the artists pad in her backpack, but decided against sketching something so beautiful on an empty stomach. She was sure it would come out distorted. But, oh, how she wished for this exquisite scene to be hers, forever.

"Quite a view isn't it?" stated the same voice she'd heard from the kitchen, now at her side.

Lisa glanced up to find a solidly built woman in her fifties, her reddish tinted bun drawn up to the top of her head with wisps of gray filtered throughout.

"It's beautiful. So peaceful," Lisa responded, a wistful smile pulling at the corners of her mouth.

"That it is," the woman said with a decisive nod. "I'm Maggie. I don't have the specials made up yet, but I can throw something on the grill for you. What can I get you, dear?"

"Um…I'm not sure, what do you suggest?"

"I make a mean Reuben sandwich. I'll toss some potato salad on the side. You look like you can use it," Maggie said, obviously not too shy in checking this out-of-towner over once or twice.

"That would be wonderful, it sounds delicious." Lisa glanced toward the desert case, and her stomach rumbled again at the thought of a slice of the moist cake she'd spotted on her way to the table.

"I'll throw in a piece of that carrot cake you're eyeing, no charge."

"Oh, I can pay." Lisa assumed she must be a mess for the woman to make the assumption she was short on cash. She was, but she didn't want anyone taking pity on her, she would pull through one way or another.

Maggie took a hard look at her again, making Lisa a bit more uncomfortable. Nodding her head in silence, Maggie walked back into the kitchen. When she returned, she set down the biggest portion of food Lisa had ever seen in her life. The huge sandwich took up most of a dinner plate, split in half with a heaping mound of potato salad in the middle.

"Enjoy. Holler if you need anything else," Maggie said with a smile that warmed Lisa's heart.

Baffled at her ability to fit the end of the sandwich into her mouth, Lisa marveled at the wonderful flavors of corned beef and sauerkraut, mixed with Swiss cheese and sauce. The gloriousness melting with each bite she took.

She'd found absolute heaven.

The next mouthful had juices running down her chin, and a smile plastered across her face. She knew her mother had taught her better manners, but she didn't care.

All of a sudden, the front door swung open and smashed against the doorstop with a bang. Surprised, Lisa inhaled sharply, unsure of what to expect. She almost choked, swallowing hard as she sputtered with the gulps of iced tea she took to wash the food down.

A picturesque view of a small town sheriff appeared in the doorway. He ducked his head as he walked in, his frame almost too large to fit through the entrance. He wore the state colors, a dark green jacket open at the front over light brown pants, sporting a crisp crease from thigh to ankle. His matching shirt fitted nicely over the best well-toned physique of a man Lisa had ever had the pleasure of seeing, in person at least.

"Is that you, Sheriff?" Maggie called out from the kitchen.

"Sure thing," he responded. The bass intonation of his voice covered Lisa's senses, like a deep sexual massage. The sound seemed to tug at her from the inside, making her crave the chance to hear more. Lord, she hoped he would speak again. She had to memorize his effect on her for future fantasies.

When she realized he'd caught sight of her from his peripheral vision, she tried to turn away, but couldn't. He slowly shifted his position and paused, looking straight at her, though his eyes were covered by the shadow of his hat.

The Sheriff reached up to tilt the brim forward in acknowledgement then removed the covering from its resting place. He stood too far away for Lisa to determine the true color, but his eyes were unusually bright, his expression speculative.

She stopped breathing when their eyes met, and an unusual sensual energy ran a rampant course through her body. She drew in a quick breath as a sudden impression settled over her. Somehow, somewhere, she knew this man. His eyes glittered, intent with a similar recognition of her, as the corners of his mouth hinted at a smile. Her heart began to flutter as if they'd just engaged in a spiritually erotic dance, like the reckoning of two souls joining together in this lifetime.

They were meant to be lovers, that she was sure. In another time, another life perhaps, but she longed to know him again, in this life. Her inner consciousness of this man made her tremble with an immediate anticipation she sadly could not acknowledge. She wouldn't be around long enough to find out.

Matt would see to that, she was convinced.

He broke the gaze to turn his attention to the hat he held in his hands. With a sigh, she allowed her eyes to wander. It didn't hurt to look. He was handsome, no doubt, with some American-Indian ancestry in his blood. His thick dark hair lay against the tanned skin of an outdoorsman, cut close at the neck with a bit of a wave on top, enticing her to run her fingertips through to sense the difference in textures. The strength of his shoulders, apparent underneath the jacket, tapered down to what she imagined would be a washboard stomach. Her fingers began to tingle as she visualized running her hands down that perfect body.

He brought his gaze back up to her, a slight grin appearing on his lips, as if he knew exactly what she was thinking. She forced herself to tear her gaze away. The thump of her heart climbed up a notch, but she couldn't stop her thoughts from racing forward. How could she? Heat rose up to her cheeks as she found herself fantasizing about the surprises she might find below his waistline.

Oh my God! What are you thinking?

Who was this man to evoke such a quick physical response? Though for some reason, she longed to be in his arms—to feel his skin against hers, to know him in the most intimate way—all from the mere meeting of their eyes.

Maggie came through the kitchen door whistling a familiar tune, and plopped a brown paper bag down on the counter. Hands on her hips, she stood as if expecting something big in return.

The Sheriff's attention stayed briefly on Lisa, the enticing smile shining bright in his eyes. Then he turned to the woman in front of him.

"What do I have to do to get a hug around here?" the image of pure male deliciousness asked.

"It's only for the asking," Maggie replied with a well-practiced answer to the obvious little game they'd played before. She swung forward and gathered him into her arms in a bear hug revealing the strength of the love between the two.

Oddly, this made Lisa want to join in, as if she belonged. She could almost feel the love between the two wrapped around her in the strength of their arms. Sadly untrue, her fantasies were getting the best of her. She attributed this to the fact she'd been unable to share in the intimacy of even a simple hug for so long she was starting to create outrageous stories in her head to placate her yearnings.

That explains what just happened with my little sexual daydream. Right?

She'd have to ponder that thought at a later time. For now, she needed to get a grip before she did something really stupid like make a fool of herself by jumping up to join them.

"Night shift again?" Maggie pulled away from the hug and patted his arm.

"Bobby's out sick. You know, every time little Joshua comes down with something Bobby comes down with the same thing. I think it's all in his head." Snatching up the bag Maggie had set on the counter, he placed the hat back over his shiny black hair, adjusting the perfect fit. "Stay out of trouble Maggie. I'll be back tomorrow."

"You be safe out there."

"I'm always safe." He turned again to bow his head slightly toward Lisa then disappeared as swift as he came.

Lisa took in a deep breath and let it out slow, not being able to help but feel as if something with extreme importance just walked out the door.

Chapter 2

Lisa gazed out the window, uncertain about what had just happened. She'd never reacted that way, to any man. Not even her ex-fiancée, when he'd been right.

Minutes later, she still felt the heat sweeping her cheeks. Like tears, she tried to brush the evidence of her response to this man away with her fingers as Maggie made her way to Lisa's table.

"Are you all right?" Maggie asked her brows furrowed.

"Yes Ma'am." A bit embarrassed, Lisa pulled her glass to her lips and took a sip, avoiding Maggie's eyes.

"Hmm," Maggie responded. "Do you need anything else—more iced-tea?"

Already full and satisfied, Lisa contemplated the amount of food still left on her plate. She figured the remainder of the sandwich would last her for at least one more meal.

"No, but I'm going to need a to-go box. And I think I should have you put the cake in the box too."

Although she would take a couple of bites of the tasty treat to satisfy her craving, she needed to leave the rest for her breakfast the next morning.

When Maggie came back, Lisa had her wallet on the table as she counted what cash she had left. Her checkbook lay open showing where she'd calculated her remaining monies. She needed to find work—soon. There had been one more day left before picking up her most recent paycheck, one of several she would never see.

The exhaustion of her flight-or-die life surfaced, and she found herself wanting to lay her head down to cry. This couldn't continue much longer. Relief had to be in sight, somewhere. Prayer and hope were her only methods of survival. She had to keep believing an end would come soon.

Lisa scooped up her wallet, fearing Maggie would pick up on her destitute financial situation when she set the Styrofoam boxes in front of her.

"Where you headed?"

Here was a question she didn't know how to answer.

"I'm not exactly sure at the moment. I guess I'll know when I get there."

She wouldn't hide anything, she answered as honestly as possible.

"Need a job, honey?" Maggie sat down like an old friend in the chair across from her.

Drat, she must have seen my bank balance.

Quickly thinking over her current financial outlook, Lisa considered her options. She might take a job long enough to put some cash in her pocket again. Then she'd move on when the time was right, before it became a necessity.

"Well…yes, I could use some work."

Maggie looked at her with intensity then made the decisive nod Lisa had seen before.

"Ever work at a coffee house?"

"If you mean an espresso stand, yes, I've worked as a barista before. Is there one of those around here?"

That would be easy enough. She would definitely pick up a few dollars in tips.

"You can call it what you want. The Coffee Hut is down a couple of blocks, closer to the highway."

"Oh, yes. I think I saw the little stand as I drove in, right outside of a residence?" Lisa asked.

"It's home to me."

"Do you own the Hut too?"

"Sure do. I do what I can to pay the bills and keep folks happy around here," Maggie beamed with pride. "I imagine you need a place to stay, too. I've got a studio over the garage you can use."

Lisa found Maggie's matter of fact character a little disarming, though she was grateful for her offer. This would solve a few of her immediate problems.

"You don't even know me. Why do you trust me so quick?"

"I'm a pretty good judge of character. You need help, and so do I. Becky quit a few weeks back to move down to California with her Mom. This early morning shift is killing me." Maggie put a hand to her back and made a show of rubbing fiercely.

"It's awfully kind of you. Thank you so much." Lisa, humbled by the outright trust this woman was willing to offer, gave her a soft heartfelt smile. "What time should I start?"

"You'll show to work no later than 4 a.m. We open bright and early at 4:30. Get in and warm things up for the run of the early morning truckers and regulars, then be here at the restaurant at 8:15 for the breakfast run. I expect you can wait tables as well," Maggie paused for a show of Lisa's acceptance. "Susan will take over for you at the coffee shop after she gets Joshua to school. I'll expect you to stay until the lunch crew gets set for their shift. There are times you'll have overtime, there's no avoiding it. I expect my workers to be on time, and willing to work. Does that work for you?"

She saw Maggie watched her as if she waited for a refusal, but Lisa was overjoyed to have landed full time employment this quick. Relocating as often as she did, she usually had to settle for part-time positions, doing anything and everything she could get.

"Yes Ma'am."

"Good."

Maggie unhooked from her belt a heavy key ring and plopped the monstrosity onto the table. She searched for a moment, then found what she looked for, and began the task of pulling the key off of the ring. She placed it in front of Lisa and stood up.

"There's the key to the room. The access is on the backside of the garage. Go get yourself settled in. Towels and linens are in the hall closet. You're welcome to use the washer and dryer in the garage, too. Just don't' use the last of anything without telling me first."

Lisa couldn't believe she was so lucky. "Thank you Ma'am."

"If you need anything else, you can go to the market across the street here. Tell Helen to start a tab for you until your first paycheck, she won't have a problem if you say I told you it would be all right. I'll meet you at the stand in the morning. We'll take care of the particulars after you get here tomorrow."

Maggie rattled off the instructions as one used to being in charge.

"Yes Ma'am. Wait, how much do I owe you for lunch?" Lisa asked as Maggie began to walk back to the kitchen.

"First off, my name is Maggie. Maggie McTavish. Use it. Don't worry about paying. Today's lunch is on me."

"I'll pay, but I appreciate your offer," Lisa responded, not wanting to take advantage of the situation. She started to pull out the last of her cash.

"Proud too, I see." Maggie gave her another hard look. "I like that, but I don't offer very often. Most everything you get from me is because you've worked your tail off. So you better take it while you can." The expression in Maggie's eyes told Lisa not to argue. Then, as if not expecting any question to her actions, she turned to walk back to the kitchen.

"Thank you Ma'am…Maggie. I hope I don't disappoint you."

That brought Maggie to a full stop. She surprised Lisa by saying over her shoulder, "You won't."

* * * *

Lisa caught on quick enough to the new environment. The coffee stand wasn't much different than any other she'd worked in before. Relieved the comfortable size of the little building had enough room for two people to move around without bumping into each other, she hated the tiny shoebox kind where moving from side-to-side would only result in sloshing coffee on her shoes.

She'd never been formally trained, but once she'd mastered a triple shot, skinny peppermint mocha, with a caramel twist, she figured she had the gist of the basic makings of most drinks. Although, why anyone would order a drink like that and still call it low-cal, she'd never understand.

The truckers hit the stand pretty heavy during the early hours. Maggie stayed as a back-up through the rush to help her with her first morning. Lisa recognized a leader when she saw one. She noticed, as they drove up, her employer made everyone feel special by greeting them with their first name and some personal comment or question about their job or family. They in turn all talked to her as if she were their mother.

The male customers eyed Lisa as Maggie introduced her to them, appearing very interested in the new blood. Lisa couldn't tell if they were concerned with her worthiness to work for Maggie, or whether she might be a potential mate for a lonesome trucker. She wasn't sure if she should be flattered or offended.

Lisa caught the raised eyebrows and the slow grins as the truckers followed her movements around Maggie in the small space. Although they never spoke outright, she knew an unsaid sexual innuendo when she saw one.

Maggie sent the last one off, with a chuckle and turned to rinse the stirring spoon off. She raised her eyes and chortled when Lisa drew her brows together in question at the obvious looks the last trucker had given her.

"Oh, don't give them a thought. They gawk at all my girls that way," Maggie glanced toward the clock and clucked her tongue.

She began to gather her belongings. "You've got everything covered here. Six o'clock hits and I've got to head over to the restaurant to prepare for the breakfast bunch. I've told Susan to come a bit early so you can get your paperwork settled."

Maggie took hold of the doorknob, tins rattling as her girth brushed against some empty canisters on the countertop beside the door.

"Maggie?"

"Yes?" Maggie turned her head impatiently toward Lisa. "Come on girl, out with it. I've got to be on my way."

"Would you mind too much if I kept the door locked when I'm here alone?" Lisa asked for her own safety and sanity, unsure of how well her request would be received.

Maggie peered at Lisa with her eyes squinted in contemplation of the request. The slow nod came without question.

"Nobody here will bother you. They'd have hell to pay if they did." Maggie paused, her eyes fixated on Lisa. "But, if you need to, go ahead and lock the door. I'll tell Susan to knock before she comes in."

* * * *

The sun began to burn through the haze in the East with a lazy awakening. Throughout the morning, every little noise made Lisa jump–the slam of a car door, the bark of a dog. By this time she knew Matt hadn't followed her, but the chance still existed he would show up sooner than expected. So far, she hadn't found a place safe enough to call her own. Every place she'd landed, within a few months he would show up again, which made her doubly sure she hadn't seen the last of him yet.

She'd begun to think the constant worry of not knowing far outweighed any actual confrontation. At one point, she'd thought she knew him. Well enough to say 'yes' to his proposal of marriage. Then she'd found out the truth about him. He wasn't the strong creative man she'd fallen in love with – it had all been an act.

The problem was, his addiction had taken control and he'd become so unstable she didn't know what he'd do when he did find her. He'd stopped listening to her, or caring about anything else. Now, since he'd changed, she couldn't take the chance she would be able to talk any sense into him. How do you reason with someone that wants you dead?

The sound of an engine pulled into the drive-thru, the purr of the motor almost silent. Lisa peered out the window before opening the slider. She couldn't be too safe, but the blue and red lights on top of the car allowed her to relax her tensed jaw.

"Morning, and welcome to The Coffee Hut, what can I get started for you?" she asked, brighter than she felt.

Upon closer inspection, she found the handsome face of the Sheriff gazing up at her. His eyes appeared bolder than she remembered, still causing her heart to skip a beat, their color taking her by surprise. They were the brightest green she'd ever seen, the contrast between his well-tanned skin and dark ebony hair making them even more vibrant.

"Welcome to you. I didn't get a chance to introduce myself yesterday. I'm Ryan Jacobs, 'Sheriff' to most people."

His voice melted over her like a bar of chocolate. Lisa experienced the sudden urge to move in close to taste his silky sweetness. She had to shake herself free of the mental image of following through with her fantasy by drawing his mouth to hers to devour.

Lord knows, I'd love to, but I'm sure that wouldn't be a good idea, she thought, a slight wariness popping up. There were reasons a relationship with someone in the law wouldn't be a good idea right now.

"Thank you sir, I'm glad to meet you. My name's Lisa, I'm new here, but…but you already know that," she stuttered.

"What brings you here to Lake Duchess?"

Lisa hesitated a minute before she answered, pretending to clean up a spot on the countertop. What did you say to the hottest guy you'd ever met, who also held the town's law and order in his hands?

Oh, I'm here for a quick buck and hope I won't cause too much damage on my way out, she thought. *Right, why don't I just wave a red flag?*

She had to be honest without giving too much information. "I was passing through and couldn't leave this breathtaking place. So I decided to hang around for a while. I hope you don't mind," she said, her voice breaking and somewhat breathy.

An increased anxiety began to surface, and she felt the hot explosion of a liar's blush paint her cheeks. She didn't lie, but her statement wasn't the full truth either.

As she spoke, Ryan appeared to observe her every movement, making her extremely self-conscious. Unsure if he'd been sizing her up on his gauge of most or least probable for illegal acts, she glanced away, uncomfortable with her slight mistruth.

When she glanced back, his steely stare had turned warm, the gorgeous color of his eyes inviting her trust. His gaze held her captive for a moment, banded by the unexplained secrets still present between them.

"No, not at all, we welcome all to our humble little town here in the Olympics."

Finding words, or at least the right words, became difficult. "Um…thank you, Sherriff."

A van pulled in behind the Sheriff's car, and Lisa sucked in a quick breath ducking back into the hut. She peeked around the window to inspect the new arrival. The duskiness of dawn had lifted. Yet, the moisture in the air created a misty fog now floating above the ground, which made the detail of the vehicle and driver harder to determine.

Lisa pulled back even further, the familiar brisk beat of her heart starting as soon as she realized the van's undistinguishable color could easily be Matt's. Her hand went directly to her pocket to locate her keys, and she twisted her head to make sure the bag she kept packed remained in the chair behind her.

Although her first instinct to flee surfaced, she decided to double check before bolting out of there without proof. So she peered around the edge of the window and took another glance at the man inside the van.

The driver of the van rolled down his window and poked his head out. Lisa took another deep breath, this time with relief.

"Hey Sheriff, how's it going?" the older man called out, his long graying beard waving in the breeze.

Sheriff Jacobs stuck his hand out the window to give an acknowledgement. He called back, "Doing fine, Beatty, just fine."

When Lisa's attention came back to her duty, she realized the Sheriff hadn't taken his eyes off her. His intent gaze caused a shiver to run down her back.

"What can I get you Sheriff?" Lisa asked trying not to show any sign of discomfort.

"I'll have my usual," he replied as he glanced away, his attention distracted by the stats of a highway traffic accident blaring through the car radio.

Lisa kept silent, not wanting to intrude on police business. He shot her a quick look as he scribbled on a tablet on his dashboard. Her blank expression must have triggered his response.

"Oh, sorry, simple enough for me, a 16 oz. shot in the dark, light on the cream."

As Lisa made his drip coffee and extra shot of espresso with quick expertise, she found it hard to concentrate very long with the handsome Sheriff so close. She stole several glimpses of him, her calm veneer jostled as she found him staring right back at her.

Her breath came quick, and the unexpected excitement bubbling up from inside made her yearn for more than the mere look she got from him. The physical affect he had on her bore cause for her to remember though. Desperate to soak in the structure of his face and the form of his body, she tried not to gaze at him at length. Lord knew she wouldn't be able to get to know him any better, but it didn't hurt to memorize his handsome roughness. She had nothing better to remember. No doubt he would pop up in later hot and heavy dreams, and not just her daytime fantasies.

"How long you plan on staying?" he asked, placing the coffee she handed him in the cup holder under his right hand.

Ryan's question didn't surprise her. His matter of fact manners meant he didn't mess around with politeness when it came down to business. Her honest answer she hoped would not raise any more interest in her reasons for staying.

"As long as I need to, Sheriff," she responded, her mood sinking a bit, though she appreciated the protective position for his community. "Don't worry I won't cause any trouble for you."

"Good to hear. I don't put up with much of anything," he paused, his gaze a bit unsettling, as if he waited for his words to sink in. What caught her attention the most was the depths to the green swirling pools of his eyes changed as he continued an intent focus on her. "You have a good morning."

"You too, Sheriff, I expect I'll be seeing you around."

Lisa stood perfectly still, frozen by the expression on the Sheriff's face, the singe from the heat she experience traveling to her cheeks. Then he narrowed his eyes for a moment, and dipped his head in agreement and pulled out onto the main road. She swallowed hard, and attended to the next customer's needs, but the flutter in her stomach took some time to subside.

His eyes had drawn her in, like a moth to a flame. A look so intrinsic yet so dangerous. If given the chance she didn't know whether to run or be burned.

The rest of the morning went by without much activity. Lisa figured the majority of The Hut's success came from the early morning business. A few townspeople came by to check out the newcomer in town. They would chat and try to pry information out of her, until Lisa began to tire of their incessant questions. Hopefully tomorrow people wouldn't be so inquisitive of her background and why she was there.

She jumped at the loud bang at the back, and a female voice called out her name asking her to open the door.

A young woman, Lisa guessed in her early thirties, entered in a flurry. Her short strawberry red hair flew around her face in the slight wind that had kicked up outside. Her arms were packed with supplies and she whipped them onto the counter with ease before turning to face Lisa.

"Hi, I'm Susan, you must be Lisa. I am so, so sorry. I couldn't get away any quicker. My daughter Shannon had a science project she had to bring to school with her today, and my baby Joshua is still sick. I would have gotten here earlier but I couldn't find anyone to look after him. He's so particular about who stays with him. You know how it is, they want their mommy. I finally found Mrs. Peters. She said she would be glad to sit with him. She's a little older, but Joshua seems to have taken to her," Susan rattled on as she unpacked the bags from the market.

Lisa stood amazed at the speed in which Susan relayed the information as she put the items away, like a whirling dervish, twirling around to her own beat.

"No problem. I'm glad to meet you. I can't stay. I've got to get over to the grill."

"Oh, that's right. I would have taken the job, but I can't work full-time, not with three kids running me crazy. It's all I can do to keep this morning job. But this helps to feed the family." Susan stopped momentarily to take a breath. "You better get going. Maggie doesn't take too kindly to lateness."

Lisa had grabbed her bag and stood at the door, unable to get a word in between Susan's life story. She started to say goodbye, but snapped her mouth shut when Susan pushed her out the door with a motherly 'shoo'.

* * * *

Maggie made a point of glancing down at her watch when Lisa bustled into the restaurant and rushed toward her. She'd barely made it in time for her shift start time. Maggie motioned for her to follow her into her office in the back.

"I'm sorry. I tried to get here as quick as I could."

Maggie appreciated the fact she didn't throw her co-worker under the bus. She knew Lisa would be late. Susan called to tell her about her awful morning.

"You're all right. Take a seat." Maggie pointed to the folding chair across from her. On the table in front of her, a pile of paperwork waited for Lisa to fill out. "I'll need a copy of your driver's license, and social security card. Damned Fed's even control us out here."

Lisa retrieved the requested items from her wallet and handed them to Maggie, who studied the cards to ensure they were legitimate.

"Ohio? You've come a long way girl, got any family in the area?"

Maggie's curiosity was peaked, and she wanted the whole story.

"No Ma'am, I don't."

"Why then would you come all the way out to the farthest point of nowhere? Running?"

The girl's guilt filled eyes and the bright red blush rising to her cheeks sufficed to tell Maggie she'd guessed right.

"Anything I need to worry about?" she asked, Lisa's continued silence disturbing her a bit. "Are you running from the law? If so, you'd better keep going. Sheriff Jacobs will put the pieces together soon enough, and he won't be too nice when he does."

"No Ma'am, I'm not in trouble with the law," Lisa assured her with a defiant shake of the head.

Maggie noted the color had drained from her face. Something in the girl's eyes told her this wasn't altogether the truth. She may not have broken the law, but the guilt returned with the slightest frown to her brows as if a part of the story was yet to be told. She didn't know what it was, but she'd get the truth from her.

"But if my being here will stir up all these questions, maybe I should go." Lisa rose to her feet and started toward the door.

"Sit," Maggie barked out the command and waited for her to respond. Lisa stood at the door, staring at Maggie. The handle to her backpack was gripped so tight in her hand her knuckles turned white. Maggie's intuition told her the girl was torn by a need to escape the interrogation, and some internal debate she was having with herself.

Lisa sighed and sat back down, her head lowered in resignation. Maggie knew her persistence had paid off. She would talk.

"You're not lying to me. Are you girl?"

Lisa seemed offended. She sat up straight and her eyes met Maggie's.

"I don't lie. I never have and I don't intend to start now." The confidence in her statement confirmed Maggie's belief she told the truth, at least to the part she'd revealed so far. "Don't worry, I won't cause any problems. If I even think something might happen, I'll be out of here quick. I'll pay my rent weekly in advance, but I can't promise to stay. I might need to leave in the middle of the night."

The suffering in the girl's eyes broke Maggie's heart. Her voice softened, "Who's after you, honey?"

Maggie saw the tears spring into Lisa's eyes when the girl turned her face away to regain her composure.

"There might be a chance he'll find me if I tell you, so I won't. It's better that way. He's someone who doesn't need my whereabouts. If I think he knows where I am, I'll leave."

"How long have you been running?" Maggie, impressed by Lisa's strength of composure, had the feeling she was more afraid to ask for help than anything. Though, her willingness to keep her troubles to herself, where most people would drag everyone into their mess, was certainly commendable.

"Almost four years now. So I would appreciate if anyone comes asking about me, you'll let me know, but you won't tell them I'm here."

"Have you gone to the authorities?" Maggie asked wondering if the girl was just running scared.

"I tried a while back. Didn't do any good, the only thing they said I could do is file a restraining order. Problem is, if I sit and wait for someone to come to my aid, I'd be dead. He doesn't give a lot of warning when he makes the decision to move on his threats."

Maggie watched Lisa take in a breath and exhale slowly, as if finally releasing the knowledge of a long-standing burden. Lisa drew one hand across her forehead and rubbed at her temple. As her gaze returned to Maggie, she saw the girl straighten her torso with a feigned fortitude, and folded her hands in her lap.

The poor thing is exhausted, Maggie thought.

"I'm not the law, but I'm pretty sure more can be done for you. Check with Sheriff Jacobs he'll tell you what to do."

Lisa's nod was weak. "I'll consider doing that, but I'm not sure what good it would do. Either way, unless he has someone available to monitor me day and night the chance is I'll be caught by surprise if I don't keep moving."

"Sounds to me like you need a place where eyes are all around you–someplace where the neighbor's dog can't piss in the woods without someone knowing."

Lisa chuckled at Maggie's reference. "That would be a good place to start."

"You've found it. Lake Duchess is that place," Maggie said without hesitation and matched Lisa's long query filled gaze, and saw the tears well into her eyes again.

"I hope so, Maggie. I sure hope so."

* * * *

Ryan sat at his usual table, against the wall with a full view of the restaurant. Early lunch business was good today. He noted the regulars were there. Pat and Lucy Hawkins, the owners of the horse ranch off Grady Way, sat involved in a serious discussion. Old man Beatty belted out a hearty laugh at something Tina said when she served him his biscuits and gravy.

The Crenshaw twins were out of school now, and made a habit of coming in for a good home cooked lunch to avoid the heat of the noon-time sun on their outside activities. They would go back out to fish the lake when the tree shade drifted onto the lakeshore by mid-afternoon. Then stay on the lake until evening set in, before bringing in their catch for the day to sell at the market for some extra spending money.

A couple of folks, from off the highway, seated and enjoying a bite to eat before heading to their final destinations, were of interest. Though, the new barista/waitress Maggie took under her wing was the one person who captured Ryan's attention.

His eyes followed her competent movements from kitchen to table and back again to serve her customers. Seated in her zone, she was forced to move back and forth past him, each time she would pass with a shy smile and a dip to her head, her eyes averted. As she greeted her customers, her soft genuine interest in what they said struck a chord within him, as did her underplayed natural beauty. She'd pulled her bountiful curls back into a ponytail to keep them out of her eyes and the dishes she served.

The response she received from the townspeople stirred up his curiosity the most. A fairly easygoing bunch as a rule, they were somewhat reserved around strangers, but the true and wholesome quality surrounding her seemed to put everyone completely at ease.

Yet every time the door opened, no matter what she was doing he watched her twist around to face the door, a brief second of fear shooting across her face. On several occasions, her hand went down to her pants pocket, checking for the unknown item he'd seen her check for once before.

Her actions were at best curious to the untrained eye. Obvious to him, he knew she was a runner, both from her actions and the answers she'd given him earlier that morning.

"Have you checked her out yet?" Maggie asked as she took a seat across from him in the booth.

Their daily lunch chat would be more interesting today than most days.

"Yeah, I ran her last night." He picked up his sandwich for another bite. "The car she purchased in Illinois. Plates were changed in Kansas City, claimed they were stolen."

"Last name on the license is Roberts, coming up for renewal in January," Maggie offered pieces of information to complete the puzzle. "It was issued in Ohio, three years ago."

They both watched as the new waitress made acquaintance with the Crenshaw twins.

"What did you pull?" Maggie questioned.

"Car's registered under Henning, probably bought from one of those quick-shot used car dealers."

"She's got covering her tracks down pretty good."

"Did she talk?" Ryan asked, knowing everyone talked to Maggie. She could get you to spill it, even if you didn't want to.

"Didn't give me any details. Said she's running from someone—a man. But she wouldn't say who. Told me she won't let anything happen to cause any problems."

Ryan nodded, and continued to follow Lisa's movements as she walked from table to table offering to freshen up the customer's coffee. He hadn't seen her stop moving since he came in. Her clothes were worn, though clean. She had no signs of any wear and tear on her face, such as nervous unhealthiness with drugs. The only thing he could say about her was she looked tired.

In her pale face he saw the hardened endurance of someone who just kept going, no matter what. At times, her actions seemed almost mechanical, as if she were determined to make it through another day. There was no question she'd been on the run for a very long time.

A young woman came through the door, her two children fussing and crying about one thing or another. She appeared frazzled.

"No, sweetheart," the woman said, "this isn't where Grandma is, we're not there yet. You said you were hungry, we're going to get something to eat." Brushing her hair from her eyes, the woman tried to locate a place to sit.

Behind the young mother came a young couple sporting fresh sportswear, apparent vacationers on their way to one of the more trendy resorts on the coastline. They scrutinized the place as if judging the quality of the food by the cleanliness of the floors.

"I better get back to work. Next batch for lunch is on their way in." Maggie rose out of her seat to place the customers in what Ryan knew she considered the best seating arrangement for their needs. She gave the high society pair to Tina's side of the floor, and sat the mother and her children across from him to Lisa.

He continued to observe, and became quite captivated as he saw a softening of Lisa's eyes and voice when she spoke to the children. She was able to settle the two children down with her calm patient voice. In opposition to the agitation they displayed coming into the restaurant, they became quiet and attentive to her every word.

As he'd watched her during lunch, he'd found she possessed a level of empathy not many had the patience for, nor could easily master. Her mannerisms showed a style of communication rare to someone of her profile. Her actions with everyone here, no matter what age, indicated her ability to truly listen and respond in a deeper, more connective way than he'd expected.

The moment he'd set eyes on her the day before he'd found his extreme curiosity about her unsettling. Something deep inside prompted him to know more, and not because it was required of him to hold peace and order in his town. For some reason, she'd stirred up an unquestionable hunger, both physical and emotional, something he wasn't sure could be easily satisfied.

Before their meal was served, the two children became antsy again, and began to spar with each other. They threw questions at their mother, one after the other, and Ryan recognized the woman's answers had become more clipped than before. She appeared to be on the brink of tears.

Coming forward to freshen up the woman's coffee, Lisa asked politely, "Would you mind if I showed your children the 'Incredible Jumping Frog'?

With this simple statement she received the undivided attention of both children, their inquisitive eyes pleading with their mother to say 'yes'.

"Anything to settle them down," she said with a weak smile.

Lisa knelt down to the children's level and tore an order ticket off the top of her pad. Ryan's interest was equally peaked.

"Watch me carefully, so you can make one for yourself next time," she told her eager audience.

As Lisa began to fold the paper, Ryan glanced and caught the mother raise her hand to her face to brush away the start of tears he'd seen surface earlier.

"I understand you are off to visit Grandma. You must be really excited," Lisa said to the children. Ryan saw her glance at the woman, and knew she must have seen the tears as well, and had addressed the children in conversation in hopes to give the poor mother a few moments to gather her composure.

The varied answers from the two youngsters told him this trip hadn't been planned.

"Daddy couldn't come with us. He had to stay home," pouted the younger of the two. "Mommy said he didn't want to see Grandma."

The young mother, obviously aghast at her child's honesty, rushed to clarify. "Mommy said he couldn't visit with her right now, but he might come later. Daddy works very hard, he doesn't have time." Her lips trembled with the effort of keeping her emotions in check.

Lisa reached out and placed the frogs she made for the kids on the table in front of them. Luckily, she'd had the sense to make two. Otherwise, Ryan could envision a war breaking out between the siblings.

"Look here, if you press on his tail like this, he jumps," she said showing them how they worked. "You can have a contest to see who can make their frog jump the farthest."

Lisa rose from her kneeling position to stand, the two boys engulfed in this new activity.

"Thank you," the young woman said, the reprieve appreciated, expressed in the small smile Ryan saw her give Lisa. She hesitated then went on to explain, "Their father is a good man. He just doesn't seem to understand what's most important," she said looking at her moppets having fun in their attempts to make the paper creations jump. "He thinks money is the answer to everything. We never see him anymore."

Ryan, touched by the pain in the woman's eyes watched as Lisa bent down and gave her a hug and a kiss on the cheek.

"I'm sure he will figure things out soon. There's no way you couldn't miss these two," Lisa responded soft enough for the boys not to hear through their state of excitement. Ryan, trained to focus his attention, was able to pick out her words fairly well even though her face was turned from him.

The woman sniffled and nodded her head in agreement. "I know. I just hope it's soon. I can't do this much longer."

Lisa gave her an extra hug and reached out to help one of the stubborn frogs to jump for the younger boy.

"Order up, Table 12," called Maggie from the kitchen.

"That's yours. I'll be right back with your meal."

As Lisa placed the plates in front of the hungry family, Ryan let his eyes rest on the shapely figure before him. Small in stature, she was perfectly shaped in all the right places. Her full hips seemed to beg to be touched, as did her firm plump breasts under the dark blue t-shirt she wore that clung close to her curves.

Ryan berated himself for the directions his thoughts had taken him. He needed to stop this and treat her as he would any other unidentified individual. Strictly professional interest was all he could allow. He knew he shouldn't luxuriate in thinking anything more than courteous friendship could be started. But there was something about her that made him crave so much more.

She turned and caught his gaze, and dipped her head shyly as she moved off to tend to her other customers. The prettiest color rose to her cheeks when their eyes met, which made his blood rush to places he'd rather it hadn't.

When he was done with his lunch, Ryan got up from the table and made his way to the counter to pay his tab. Lisa had just finished up with another customer at the register.

"How was your meal Sheriff?"

"Always the best, you can't get any better than Maggie's around here."

Lisa's fingers brushed his lightly as she reached out to grasp the ticket he held. The strong sensation of sexual interest crossed his mind, yet again, when the light blush bloomed on her cheeks. Her eyes, the color of cinnamon, remained on his for a brief moment longer than he expected. The quick rise and fall of her breasts against the snug apron told him she was thinking the same thoughts. He felt tongue tied, unable to come up with anything to say.

"Pretty impressive, with that little frog thing you made," he said as he reached into his wallet. "What do you call that anyway?" Placing the money on the counter, he finished his thought mumbling, "I always get the word wrong. Comes out sounding obscene," he said more to himself than to Lisa.

Lisa laughed a bit, her blush deepening even more. "It's called origami. It's an old Japanese form of art."

He found himself unable to keep things purely business. Her laugh brought an odd sense of pleasure to him he couldn't explain. He wanted to hear it again.

"Aren't they known for something else? Kamikaze…no, that's not right. It's something I imagine you wouldn't want to try around children. What's it called? I never get that one right either."

She laughed outright this time. He enjoyed playing with the innocence surrounding her. A grin came slow to his face, and he couldn't help but be mesmerized by the rosiness of her cheeks. This time she met his gaze and held it with sparkling amusement of her own.

"Kama-Sutra? Yes, well, that's another form of art for adults only, but was founded by the Indian Hindu culture not the Japanese."

Interesting, she's quick and educated too. Her knowledge intrigued him. She piqued not only his professional curiosity, but his unprofessional interest as well, in a way he knew wasn't good. He had no intention of becoming involved, especially with a woman obviously here for only a short time. He needed to move the conversation back to neutral ground.

"Aren't you the smart one? Where'd you learn to do that?" he asked motioning toward the table where the children played happily jumping their makeshift toys at each other.

"I taught fourth grade art for a while. You have to come up with all kinds of things to keep their little minds active."

"Sounds like you really enjoyed it. Why'd you quit?" Now he was trying to pry for another piece to the puzzle he'd begun to fit together.

She looked at him briefly, as if sizing up the reason for his question. She sidestepped the question by saying, "Things happen, Sheriff. We can't always do what we love to do."

Lisa viewed her other customers beyond him. An uncomfortable expression in her eyes came up quick, and Ryan knew she wasn't ready to open up to him, yet.

With a tenseness that hadn't been there before, she stated, "I need to get back to my other tables. Have a good afternoon Sheriff. I'll be seeing you around."

He nodded. "That, you will."

He remained a moment longer to follow her movement back to the tables, watching the easy sway of her feminine curves. Her unique beauty, not strikingly so but underplayed and simple, spiked a pure sexual awareness that bothered him. It was as if he already knew her.

There was an unsaid message between them, of that he was certain. The smile in her eyes when she looked at him created a feeling in his gut he thought he'd lost forever. Something he wasn't sure he wanted to revive.

Then again, it had been a while since he'd had the pleasure of a woman's company. Perhaps, if she stayed around long enough, he'd have a chance to explore this feeling further and find out whether he wanted to do anything about it.

* * * *

Lisa sat on the back deck, her head pounding almost as bad as her feet ached. She'd been working non-stop since four in the morning. For a small town business, Maggie's pulled in a constant stream of hungry customers. They were short staffed today, so she and Tina volunteered to stay through until the dinner shift came to take over at 4:30. She was exhausted, and imagined twelve hours on your feet at such a fast pace, would wear anybody out.

The burger and fries she ordered for her first meal of the day smelled awesome. The effort to lift her hand and bring the nourishment to her mouth felt almost too much to ask. She sat limp and unmoving in her chair, looking out over the lake as the sun came down to meet the far shore.

"Can I join you?"

Lisa glanced up to find Tina, ready to chow down on her own burger.

"Certainly," she said taking her feet out of the chair across from her.

Tina sat and glanced briefly out to the gorgeous view in front of her, then dove in to take her first bite of food.

"Mmm...Maggie makes the best burgers." Tina's mouth was full, yet she didn't have any problem talking through the food. "You going to eat that, or let it get cold?" she asked eyeing Lisa's dinner.

"I'm going to work on it. I'm a bit worn out for my first day on the job."

"What? That?" Tina asked raising her eyebrows. "That was nothing. Last winter we had a storm so bad Maggie and I had to work forty eight hours, by ourselves. We were the only ones to make it in to work. We slept in our sleeping bags in her office. Wouldn't think there'd be as many customers, but seems everyone still made their way out here, even if they were on foot. I'm just glad she's closed on Sundays, otherwise we'd have worked three days straight."

Lisa laughed at Tina's animated way of telling the story through mouthfuls of her burger.

"No, I guess I don't have anything to complain about then, do I?"

"You'll get used to it."

"I suppose I better take advantage of these free meals."

"Believe me. You'll need them, especially as hard as you work. I couldn't believe you didn't take lunch today. We were busy, but I would've covered for you, all you need to do is ask," Tina replied with a long slurp from her soda.

Everyone she'd met so far in town had the same good natured willingness to help. Humbled by this experience, Lisa nodded but remained silent, as she gazed out over the water. She glanced back to the table when Tina pushed her plate away and sat back in her chair.

"Whew, that was definitely worth waiting for." She rubbed her stomach, in a male show of appreciation. From Tina's display of mannerisms, Lisa expected her to belch as well.

Taking a small nibble from her burger, she had to admit, like the Reuben she'd enjoyed before this was the best burger she'd ever tasted.

"So, where're you from?" Tina asked.

Lisa paused to finish the next bite she'd taken. Dabbing her lips with her napkin, she needed to delay long enough to figure out how she wanted to answer the question.

"Originally, from the East Coast, but you could say I'm kind of a traveler."

Tina stared at her for a moment. "So, you don't really want to say." Lisa was surprised at her boldness. "That's all right. You don't know me from Adam. I suppose you'll tell me when you're ready."

Looking out toward the setting sun, Tina turned to face Lisa and placed her hands on the table.

"There's some saying you won't be here for long. I told them it's none of their business, and we should let you know you are welcome here at Lake Duchess."

Lisa was drawn to Tina's strength and boldness. She wished she could be truthful and tell her everything.

"I'm not sure how long I'll be here. Sometimes there's no telling."

The feeling of uselessness began to creep over her again. Running had become the only way of life for her.

How long can I keep this up? The nagging question surfaced quite strong this time.

Tina rose from her chair and gathered her dishes.

"I'm here when you need to talk." Tina offered. Lisa watched as she started to walk away, then turned around and came back. "There's something my Grams always used to say. She'd tell me, 'No matter how bad things seem, remember I'm always here for you.' I'd like you to think of me in that way. No matter how bad it might seem, you can always come talk to me. I may rattle on a lot, but I can listen real well too."

The tears welled up into her eyes as Tina spoke, the good heartedness touching her down deep, and she sat for a moment before answering.

"You're too kind," she whispered, turning her face away, not wanting to cry.

"You remember what I said," Tina stated firmly.

Lisa kept her eyes hidden, as she felt the first tear fall. She nodded silently, and listened to the retreating steps of her newfound friend.

Chapter 3

A little bell at the top of the door jingled happily when Lisa stepped through the shop's entrance. The slightest hint of lavender in the air brought to mind a soft caring female friendship,   something she hadn't had in such a very long time. The shop proprietress, arranging soaps and perfumes on the back shelf, glanced up and gave Lisa a smile and a wave of her hand.

"Good morning!" the woman called out. "I'll be right with you."

Not having shopped for new clothing in the last few years, Lisa looked around the place with interest. This was definitely different from the thrift stores she'd frequented. Viewing her financial situation earlier that morning, she would have preferred to purchase used clothing, but according to Maggie the closest Goodwill was located some thirty miles away, much too far to travel for such a small purchase.

As she glanced around, the contents of the racks and shelves didn't seem to fit the ambiance that had invited her in. This women's clothing shop obviously catered to the necessities of a small town – a small town with many requirements. The expected dresses with frills and colors, designed to attract the opposite sex, were displayed in the front windows with an artful flare. The springtime pastels drew her attention as she sauntered through their appealing nature.

Outdoor garments made up a good portion of the main floor. In the far corner, she found what she needed in an area she would call a workwoman's section, which sat directly across from an array of bathing suits. Even the hardy attire appeared womanly as the entire store had a definite feminine flair with its interwoven décor of bright colors and frills.

Having escaped with the limited amount of clothes she kept packed away in her car for emergency use, she'd discovered her one pair of jeans were close to shreds in certain areas. They wouldn't last much longer, and the sweatpants she usually wore to bed were not appropriate for work.

Heaven only knows what kind of damage new clothes will do to my wallet.

She headed toward the heavier styles of the work clothes required for long wear and comfort, and went straight for the price tags.

"Hello, my name's Roberta. You're Lisa, right?" the shopkeeper said from behind her.

Lisa turned as the woman, in her early-thirties, came up to stand beside her. The dark haired woman was so petite Lisa couldn't imagine being as pregnant as she was, her rounded belly creating the appearance she would topple forward at the slightest movement.

"Yes," Lisa replied, not sure what to make of the woman's instant connection to her identity. She had asked Maggie earlier where to find the closest shop. Curious how Roberta had found out so quick, she wasn't used to the idea of everyone knowing everybody else's business.

"Don't worry, I'm not a psychic. Maggie told me you'd come by today. She thought you might need some things for work."

Lisa gave her a smile and glanced at the pants she'd considered purchasing. She held up the price tag again, thankful they were within her budget. She needed one or two more pullover t-shirt type tops as well. Comfortable with a flexible purpose of work and or casual wear, and anything easily folded for quick transport were her best choice.

"You might want lighter wearing pants than those. Lake Duchess is pretty warm in the summer. We're high enough in the mountains not to be unbearable, though some days can be downright uncomfortable."

"I don't know, I think I'd better stick with what I'm used to," Lisa said, eyeing the sleeker styles with cautious interest.

Roberta waddled over to another isle where a much lighter grade material in different styles and colors hung.

"These here are awesome. I own a couple pair myself. They're so comfy I wouldn't give them up for anything."

Roberta glanced back at Lisa with a studious look, and with expertise pulled a few pairs off the rack in the correct size, and handed them over to her.

"Try these on. You'll understand what I'm talking about."

A few minutes later, Lisa viewed her figure in the dressing room mirrors. The pants had a full cut around the hips which flattered her small waistline, causing her to smile with feminine approval. Something she hadn't experienced in quite some time. She had to admit they were unusually comfortable compared to the stiff jeans she normally wore.

Pulling the tag up, she groaned at the price. These were definitely way beyond what she was able to spend. Her check for one week of wages wouldn't be enough. Even though her expenses were low, she'd promised Maggie to pay her rent every week in advance, leaving her a limited amount for the rest of the week.

"I appreciate your help. These are so nice," Lisa said handing the pants back to Roberta, "but I think I'll have to stick with the other ones."

"Cash a little tight? I understand. Maggie told me to start you an account. She said you'd be good for it," Roberta replied, holding them out again to tempt Lisa's reasoning. "No problem if you do or don't."

Maggie apparently had her hands in everything around town. Lisa did accept the ability to use the account at the market, only because she needed to get a few personal items and some food for her every day living before her first paycheck. Now she needed to draw the line. She'd learned if she couldn't pay for something in cash, then she didn't need the item that badly. Although grateful for everyone's willingness to trust in her, they didn't understand her situation. If she left in a hurry, she may not be able to pay her debts, and she wouldn't let that happen.

"Thank you so much, I appreciate the offer. I'm going to stick with these and pay cash," Lisa replied, bringing forward a pair of the jeans and two t-shirts she could afford.

The purchase of these clothes would almost deplete the last of the money in a debit account she used for her phone payment and the occasional expenditure for these types of items. She needed more things, but the usual transfer of trust funds wouldn't be available again until the end of the month. So she'd have to be content with what she held in her arms.

Roberta shrugged, set the pants aside on the counter, and made her way back to the register.

"Whatever you like, but tell me if you change your mind later. We help each other out. Life's hard enough without adding more pressure. When you need something, I'd bet anyone around here would be willing to come to your aide. We're just that way."

Lisa, astonished by the benevolence of this small town, felt like she'd stepped into another world.

"Thank you Roberta. I appreciate everyone's generosity. You don't find goodwill so often these days. You are all very unusual."

"Well, we might be a little behind the times out here, but we've kept what's important." Roberta said with great confidence.

"Yes, you have," Lisa agreed pulling the debit card from her wallet.

* * * *

It had been a little over a month and Lisa was beginning to relax a little. She stared at herself in the mirror. The bags under her eyes were starting to lighten up, and the natural color had returned to her cheeks.

Not looking half bad, she thought as she pulled her hair from around her face to fasten it in the back with a tie.

As she went through the morning rituals, she made sure her keys were in her pocket and her cell phone clipped to her belt. Ready to head out she remembered one more thing she needed to do and reached under the sink to get a small container to fill with water.

When she opened the window, the cool mountain air met her in an instant jolt of refreshment as the unique earthy pine filled fragrances played happily with her senses. The small indulgence of a couple of Marigolds she'd allowed herself to buy from the market greeted her with their sunny faces and made her smile. Reminded of a time she'd spent with her mother in their garden back home, she touched the bright yellow petals with the tip of her finger. For a moment, Lisa held close to her heart the memory the soft blossom evoked of the love and care of her mother's touch. And just as her mother had instructed, she tested the dryness of the dirt in the window planter before dousing the flower roots with water.

Still dark, Maggie's porch lamp threw a hazy blanket of light over the yard and driveway. A slight rustling of leaves came from the bushes beside the house. Startled, Lisa jerked her head toward the sound, a knot forming in her stomach. To her surprise, the tiniest of fawns appeared and wobbled over to her mother a few feet away. The doe stood in total silence, aware of the movement from the window. Yet not perceiving any impending danger the deer lowered her head again to nibble a tasty tidbit.

The sheer beauty of the moment etched a lasting impression into Lisa's memory, as if the scene were set for her eyes only. The fawn nuzzled its mother as the doe bent her head again to savor the early morning dew on the fronds of the grasses. So silent and peaceful, they grazed for a few minutes then moved on to the next delectable plant.

She remained locked in silence watching the scene when a sudden awareness hit hard. The peace she'd dreamed of surrounded her. This was the tranquility she'd searched for so long. There was no better place to be than this small corner of nowhere amidst the profound simplicity God had intended. This was where she wanted to belong—this was home.

The next realization came tumbling forward, jerking her back into reality, smashing head-on into the nirvana she'd just found. Tears stung the backs of her eyes, blurring her view of the picture of perfection.

This is a fantasy world, not mine. How long is Matt going to leave me alone this time?

Saddened, the reticent depression slipped from under the cover tried to hang onto, returning once again to cloud her visions of hope. She closed the window with a quiet click, resigned to the fact this dream wouldn't last forever.

* * * *

Matt's fingers shook as he maneuvered the mouse to click on the correct browsed address. He stared at the computer screen, waiting for it to load the website he'd requested. He knew the impatient tap of his foot, and the drumming of a rhythm on his knee with his free hand, were as detestable as talking in the quiet library. He didn't care. He'd do what he wanted.

He hated waiting. Everyone and everything had him waiting for something.

Lisa was the worst. He'd had his fill of waiting on the damned woman. No more. This was the last time. Next time he caught up with her she'd stay, no matter what he had to do to make it happen.

Matt pulled out his wallet and frowned at the last three dollars he owned. He'd spent the last of his cash on the ride back home from Denver. He needed more for this next trip, wherever the hell Lisa had ended up.

Time to go see Mom, he thought. She was always good for a few bucks. The money she'd given him the last time hadn't lasted very long. He hoped she'd had enough time to save up some more for him.

There were three other people at the computers next to him. Each engaged in their own project. The woman next to him had what looked to him to be a resume in front of her. Lot of good those did. Nobody wanted to hire someone who listed one part-time job as a janitor at the local bar and lead guitar player for their in-house band as the only source of experience.

He ignored the rude glances from the people who sat around him. The young woman beside him leaned farther and farther away from him. He stared back at her as she glared at him making an unintelligible sound. Just for fun he smiled and leaned in closer to her. She groaned and shoved her papers into her bag, hurrying off with her hand covering her nose.

He snickered. Yeah, okay. He knew he needed a bath. He hadn't gotten around to it yet.

As he waited for the website's slow connection to come up, he pulled a ragged slip of paper from his worn out wallet.

"Where the hell are you this time?" he muttered.

He typed in the answers to the secured site questions, cursing as it returned with an error. Again, he tapped in the numbers to the account and the password. Chemically induced nervous energy made him squirm in his chair as he waited for the secured website to finally produce what he wanted.

A daily check of the bankcard usage hadn't produced anything since the last time he'd seen Lisa. Day after day he sought the answer to his question, with no result. But he hadn't been able to get to the library for over a week now, so he hoped there would be a change.

Her patterns were predictable. She wouldn't use the card for a while, and then all of a sudden purchases would show up, one after the other over a spread of a couple of days. That meant she'd stopped someplace.

"Bingo!" he yelled out.

A few days prior, charges had been posted from some place called 'Roberta's' and 'The Market', a couple of days apart, in an area called Lake Duchess. Angered by the fact he'd missed out on a whole week of planning, he banged his hand on the desk, swearing as pain shot through his overly sensitized fingers.

The librarian stood up from the research desk, and made a not so quiet hushing sound.

Matt held up his hand in acknowledgement. "Yeah, okay. Sorry," he growled, writing down the information he needed on a slip of white paper.

"Lake Duchess, where the fuck is that?" he let out very loud, ignoring the rules again.

He glanced up as the librarian came up beside him. She stepped away with a soured look on her face, and raised a hand to her nose. "You need to stop talking in the library. It's not allowed, you know that."

A quick rage swept over him.

"Get out of my face woman," he belted out. Who the hell was she to tell him what to do? "Cunt," he mumbled under his breath. He looked up at her authoritative expression and ducked his head down toward the keyboard.

Then he remembered the not too pleasant last time he'd disobeyed her, she'd called the police on him. That little incident had ended him up in jail for a couple of days. If he didn't need to find what he was looking for so bad, he'd tell her to her face what he thought of her and risk being thrown out.

"What did you say?"

Matt looked up. The indignant woman glared at him from behind the thick eyeglasses she wore, her bloodshot pale blue eyes bulging out like a toad's.

Shit, she heard me. Better think of something fast.

"I said I'm hunting for something. Don't have a cow."

Unstirred by his behavior, the librarian whispered, "Matthew Aaron Caine, don't talk to me that way. You know better. If you don't stay quiet you know what will happen. Do you want that?"

He grunted at her in response and went back to what he was doing. As she continued to glare at him, he acquiesced with, "I'll be quiet."

"See that you are."

He nodded solemnly, knowing how to get his way with Ruth. He'd known her since he was a child. She'd been at the library forever.

"You have ten minutes left on your time. I suggest you finish up with what you are doing," she stated firmly as she moved back to her desk. "And if you plan on coming back, I want you to clean yourself up first. You're a disgrace."

Matt gave her the finger from under the desk. Lucky he didn't need to come back.

He signed out of the bank website and opened up the geographical mapping program.

Hmmm...Lake Duchess, Washington? Shit, over twenty-five hundred miles. That's going to take some big bucks, he thought to himself.

Where the heck would he find that kind of cash?

Fuck. Dad.

He grimaced and shook his head. This wouldn't be a good visit with his parents. Not that it ever was. Things never turned out the way they should. He hoped his father would listen to him this time.

God, I don't want to do this, he thought, the familiar nagging need to escape from it all washing over him, as it had all his life.

Better to be prepared for the worst.

* * * *

Tina sat on the steps of the restaurant's back porch with Lisa, her shoes off, rubbing her left foot carefully. Lisa smiled up to the tree leaves moving about in the sunlight, their gentle clapping filtering down around her.

"I shouldn't have worn those new shoes when I went dancing the other night. Damn things gave me a blister." Her short curly blond hair played with listless whimsy in the afternoon breeze.

Lisa had grown quite fond of Tina over the last few days. Hard working and generous of her time for anyone in need, Tina's lighthearted attitude was refreshing and somewhat contagious. She found herself laughing more than she had in months, maybe even years. Tina's saucy attitude and ability to brighten everyone's day was precious to her.

Close to her own age, Lisa imagined Tina to be a kick in the pants as a best friend and buddy. She found herself wishing she could take her with her when she had to leave.

"Dancing? Where the heck can you do that? Out at the Hawkins barn?" Lisa kidded.

"That's right, gotta dust your shit kickers off every Friday night around here!" Tina howled. "No. Redford's isn't very far. Pretty cool place to hang out. We all head out on the weekends to relax and have some fun. Depends on who they can get, but sometimes there's live music, and karaoke too. Dancing, food, drink – pretty much anything they've got is great."

"Who all is 'we all'?" Lisa asked, curious to the group Tina hung around.

"Me, and a few of us here around town, you've met most of them. The Crenshaw twins, when they're back from college. John and Darlene come sometimes, if they can find a sitter. I try to get Shawna and her sister Colleen to come out. I don't know, just anybody I can get to come with me. Heck, even the Hawkins come out sometimes."

Lisa tried picturing this group out having fun – could be pretty lively. "Sounds like fun."

She hadn't ventured out to do anything fun in so long. Live music was her favorite. So much passion and talent flowed off the stage from the musicians she'd seen, inspiring her own creative talents. Though, her heart sank as she remembered her last experience had ended in disaster. When she'd met him, Matt was one of those passion filled musicians.

Gazing out over the lake, Lisa's thoughts traveled to a place and time when she'd been so happy, taking for granted the freedom she enjoyed. It hadn't lasted long enough. Everything she'd ever known had been swept away by the delusions of a madman—the same passionate guitarist she'd once enjoyed watching.

"Hey, I've got an idea. Why don't you come with us on Friday night?" Tina yelped out, turning in excitement to face Lisa.

Dragged back to the present, Lisa looked at her friend, not comprehending her words. "What?"

"Come with Richard and me out to the Lodge on Friday. You'd have a great time."

Lisa thought it over quick and shook her head 'no'. A night out on the town sounded awesome, but she envisioned this to be a place where she couldn't see what was happening around her – too many people with dark, unfamiliar surroundings. What if…?

"Come on, I'm not taking no for an answer. You're coming with us." Tina bounced down the steps to the grass. After a long hard day on the floor waiting tables, Tina's energy amazed Lisa.

"I…I don't have anything to wear. Payday isn't 'til Friday. There won't be enough time," she said, searching for reasons not to join them.

"No problem. You and I are about the same size. You can borrow something from me." Tina danced around in joy like a teenager. "This is going to be so much fun."

"I don't want to intrude on your date with Richard. Maybe some other time," Lisa tried again, knowing soon she would run out of excuses.

"Date? You've got to be kidding." Tina bent over laughing. "Richard's my brother. Please. He'll probably drag a bunch of his friends along. You've got to come save me from boredom."

"I don't know…maybe."

Her noncommittal answer was apparently not what Tina wanted to hear.

"I might be able to get Ryan to come too," she said raising her eyebrows in question. "I saw how the two of you look at each other."

A ferocious heat rose up to Lisa's cheeks. She didn't think anyone had noticed her inability to take her eyes off the Sheriff. Horrified, she didn't want Tina to force anything. Especially something she couldn't start in the first place.

"Please don't. I wouldn't want him to think I was making the first move."

"Oh, geez…A little conservative are you? All right, I'll leave it to you two. Promise me you'll go. Please, please, please…"

Lisa was hard pressed to come up with another excuse. She found it almost impossible to say 'no' to Tina. "I will if I can, but I can't promise. Something might happen and I won't be able to."

"Nothing's going to come up, believe me, nothing ever happens around here." Tina bounded up the stairs. "I'll go through all my clothes and find which ones would look the best on you. Come over to my house later this week and try some of them on."

Lisa sat for a moment after the bundle of energy left. She'd been hit by a hurricane, and only hoped she could hang on to her sanity from the bounding force called 'Tina'. Excitement began to creep over her with the idea of going out to have fun. An activity she hadn't considered in a long time. Before now, this would be out of the question, at least by herself. Maybe being with a group of people might not be so bad.

She didn't like to make promises when the chance still existed she wouldn't be able to follow through. The exact reason she didn't make friends, or get involved again with lovers. She never knew when she'd have to leave. There was no way of knowing. The possible outcome of what might, or rather would happen sooner or later went against good reasoning. Leaving without a word was the ultimate to break of hearts—of others, as well as hers.

Lisa frowned. Better she not get too involved with anyone. She'd go out this one time, but she needed to limit forming any more personal relationships, no matter how much she found herself wanting to call this place her home.

A sudden fatigue began to creep forward, the solemn loneliness of reality settling over her. The inevitable depression she battled day in and day out, from the first day she'd escaped Matt's tirade, lingered in the shadows ready to take control.

Soon she'd be forced to move on and start again someplace else. If asked, she wouldn't be able to explain how deeply this lifestyle had affected her. Never settling down, unable to form friends or close relationships, living a life of fear had worn tremendous holes in her physical, emotional, and spiritual self.

The same guilt niggled at her conscience. Maybe Matt would stop if she corrected the wrong she'd done him. She'd never stolen anything in her life. She knew the ring belonged to his family, but she'd sold it and had actually been glad to get rid of the thing. Now she wished she still had it in her possession. How on earth was she ever going to get it back?

Besides, the ring had been given to her as a promise, and that promise had been stripped away without any sign of remorse from him. He'd thrown it all away for his preferred choice of a good time. Sooner or later, that choice would cost him his mortality, and she'd feared if she stuck around it would cost hers as well. She'd acted out of desperation to survive. A desperate need caused by his actions. Nobody would fault her for that, would they?

There had to be a way to put an end to all of this, but she hadn't figured out how yet. Helplessness invaded her mind, causing an inability to form a constructive thought. She felt as if she couldn't function anymore.

She dragged herself to her feet and headed toward the door. The best solution right now was to go back to her room and take a nap.

* * * *

The temptation to finish what was left of his last tank of propane had been too much to handle. After leaving the library, Matt found an out of the way spot to feed his craving and forget the world around him once again.

70

He didn't want to have to ask his father for help, knowing the chances of his agreeing were almost impossible, but he had to try. Maybe he'd catch him on a good day.

Taking a couple of days to dry out, Matt craved another huff of anything he could get his hands on so bad his head hurt. He couldn't cave in now though, it was time to try and straighten up before his visit to his parent's house.

The usual spot for his shower worked out well today. The state park facilities hadn't caught on to his ruse of pretending to be an overnight camper. He'd pulled out his cleanest clothes, and hoped the slight odor of his past propane use would dissipate before he arrived.

If it wasn't for the money, he wouldn't have come at all. His grandmother's trust fund and the occasional odd job he got to pay his expenses didn't seem to be enough these days. He used to be able to make it through to the next distribution without any problems. He didn't require a lot, but he'd spent more chasing after Lisa than he ever had before. This would be the last time he'd come begging his father for anything. Once he caught Lisa, everything would change. He had to do this.

As he stood now at the front door, his heart pounded, unsure if he would be able to go through with another confrontation with his father. His mother was hard of hearing, so he sucked in his chest and knocked hard. Not detecting any noises from inside, he banged the knocker again. The loud shouts of his father from the back room reverberated throughout the house and beyond.

"Get the damn door woman!"

"Ok, ok, hold your horses," Matt's mother yelled back. The sound of her feet shuffling toward the door stopped, and Matt figured she peered out the peephole as she usually did, so he made a funny face.

The door yanked open and she gathered him into her arms, squeezing tight. "Matthew, my dear, oh my goodness!" she exclaimed.

"Hey, Mom," he said, never really understanding her excitement at seeing him.

"Come in." She ushered him into the front room. "Sit, sit. Let me get you some nice cool tea." She rushed out of the room, leaving him very uncomfortable on the front settee.

Matt rose to his feet and walked around the room. Nothing had changed. Everything was exactly where he'd remembered before he left home. The front room, where he now stood, had been off limits to him as a child. His mother's fanatical tendency to keep this room free of any dirt or disorder always baffled him. As he looked around, the plush navy carpet beneath his feet and the ivory on ivory paisley patterned furniture felt out of place with the rest of the house as he remembered.

Everywhere else had a warm, lived in feeling, his favorite being the kitchen. It had been the only time he spent with his mother. Watching her cook dinner for him and his father every night had been a special time for him. That was before the accident.

A chill ran down his spine as he realized what this room represented for his mother. This room was the stark image of his father as a police officer, held suspended in time, as if who he'd turned into had never happened.

On the mantle, he stared at his father's awards and badges. He recollected the nights he'd snuck downstairs to gaze up at those keepsakes, their impact overwhelming him as he regarded the words on each one, just as they did now. The symbol of 'courage' and 'honor' was what his father represented to him. As difficult as his father could be, Matt refused to believe otherwise.

He'd been taught to love and respect his parents, or there'd be hell to pay. He loved his mother without question. She was sweet and gentle, unlike his father. He loved his father too, in a different way. Matt hadn't understood his father's harsh punishments growing up, but he attributed that to the injury he'd received while on patrol. Matt forced himself to forgive him for his injustices.

The photograph in the middle of his father standing regal and proud with his fellow officers in full-dress uniform was the image Matt preferred to remember.

The rustle from the kitchen drew his attention away, and he heard his mother's answers to the shouted questions from his father.

"Who's at the door?"

"It's Matthew, dear."

"What does he want?"

"I don't know, Frank. I haven't talked with him yet."

"Find out what he wants and tell him to get the hell out."

Matt's stomach churned. His father hated him. He'd never been good enough for him, no matter how hard he tried.

"Now be nice," his mother fussed.

The next muffled words were undistinguishable, but Matt knew from experience his mother was trying to calm Frank down. She'd always been on his side, the go between him and his father.

She hurried back in holding a glass full to the brim with her special sweet tea.

"Here you go, sweetheart," she said leading him back around to the settee. His mother sat on the footstool in front of him.

They talked for a few minutes about nothing in particular. She asked about a job, which he had none, and a girlfriend, which he wasn't sure how to answer. He'd never told them about Lisa. There wasn't much to tell. They'd met and he'd fallen in love with her. He asked her to marry him and gave her his Grandmother's ring. She'd said 'yes', and that's when everything fell apart. The bitch had left him.

So, he liked to get high, so what.

The conversation with his mother paused, and he took a long sip of the sweet tea he loved so much.

"Now why don't you tell me why you've really come to see us?" she asked, direct to the point, as she always did.

Matt squinted sheepishly down at the glass in his hands. He'd never get any money if he told her what was really going on. He'd have to lie. He hated doing this, but couldn't figure out any other way to accomplish what he needed to do.

Besides, the inheritance was his. The money belonged to him. He despised the fact his father had been given the control of when the funds should be released to him.

"I need an advance on next quarter's distribution."

His mother hissed out a breath. "Oooh, I'm not sure that's possible. He's still upset about that other thing, sweetheart. Your father can be stubborn, and he's in one of his foul moods today."

"I need to get to…to this…this gig in Washington," Matt stuttered not wanting to lie to his mother, but knew he had to in hopes she wouldn't see through him. "It's for the big time, Mom. The 'Bandits' are going up to play for a big music festival where the record studios find new talent. This is big. Really, really big," he claimed, overemphasizing the importance to cover up his dishonesty.

His mother gazed at him for a moment then reached out to grasp his hands. She held them in hers and fixed her gaze on his slim fingers. He saw the slightest shake of her head and wondered what she was thinking. He squirmed wishing he'd remembered to clean his fingernails.

"I'm not sure he will part with anything, but you can go in to ask if you'd like." She stood and glanced back at him. "I'll see what I can pull together for you in case he doesn't budge."

She stared at him a moment longer, then abruptly left him in the front room to gather the courage to go in and face his Dad.

He reached up and smoothed the frazzled top of his head, of which the strands of his naturally thin hair had become fewer and fewer as time and his chemical abuse wore on. Standing tall, he marched into his father's study.

Frank sat in the easy chair at the far corner of the room. Matt saw him adjust his weight on the seat cushion, one leg propped up on the footrest. The other, a steel framed limb used in place of the one he'd lost on duty, rested motionless on the floor. His father's physique had turned from sturdy and muscular to the unkempt vision of a man who no longer cared. The stained shirt he wore barely covered the bulge of his stomach, and an unshaven face showed the stubble of a couple days growth.

"What do you want?" he asked gruffly, in acknowledgement of his son's presence.

Matt shuffled his feet, and tried to stand strong in the face of his father's rejection. He always felt so childish in front of his father.

"Hi, Dad, how's it going?"

"No."

"No? What? You have no idea what I want," Matt retorted.

"You want money. You're not getting any."

He could feel the tips of his ears get hot, and the blood rush to the surface of his skin. "Grandma gave the fucking money to me," he shouted. "Why won't you give it to me? It's my damn money."

"Get the hell out of here," Frank shouted back, and turned up the volume of the baseball game.

Matt took in a slow breath. He knew this hadn't started the way he'd wanted. So he tried again.

"Look Dad, I just need a draw on the next quarter. I've got to get to Washington for a…for a gig."

Frank didn't even look at him. The grunt he gave his son was his answer. His father had never understood his love of music, but Matt dug the hole a little deeper and tried to make his appeal sound more important.

"We're going to sign with a big record company out on the west coast. All I need is enough for the trip out."

The lie felt sticky on his tongue.

His father looked him over once or twice then turned his attention back to the television set. "No."

"Why the hell not?" Matt yelled at him, his fury coming fast to the surface.

Frank wheeled around, his face reddened by his returned anger.

"You're a thief and a no good excuse for a human being. Now, get out and leave us alone."

Matt's rage bubbled even harder. Yes, he'd taken the ring without his father's permission, but that didn't make him a thief. He couldn't tell him he'd asked someone to marry him, he wouldn't believe him anyway. She was nowhere to be seen. He'd find her, and prove to his parents he'd had a good reason. Then what would his father have to say?

"I told you I didn't steal it. I'm just using it for a good purpose. You'll see." If he brought Lisa back, then they'd believe him. They'd see he was good enough. "I need the money to show you."

"Your poor dead grandmother was very specific in what I should give you. That ring was supposed to be for a very special person. Someone I'm sure you'll never find in this lifetime. At least I have some say over the money. I can't imagine why she ever left you anything, but for some reason she loved you." Frank paused to catch his breath, years of inactivity causing his distress.

"At least someone did," Matt grumbled under his breath. He'd show him.

Frank grasped hold of the cane he kept at the ready, and rose unsteady to his feet.

"Until you crack down and get a job and make something of yourself you won't get any more than the quarterly allotment you already get. And if the decision were up to me you wouldn't even get that."

In a feeble attempt to change his father's mind Matt argued, "I do have a job. I play for the 'Bandits' and we...we've got a chance to make it big," he said pushing the lie out there even further.

"Look at yourself boy. You're nothing but an addict. That's all you've ever been and ever will be. By the looks of you I can tell you've been snortin' that shit again. Get the hell out of my face," Frank shouted in disgust, advancing toward his son.

Matt wasn't sure what Frank would do if he stayed any longer. He may have a bum leg, but his father might still be able to beat the crap out of him, as he had once or twice before.

He bolted out of the room hoping his father wouldn't follow. When he reached the front door his mother stood waiting and shoved a paper bag into his hands.

"Here, this is all I could find. There's only a couple more days until the first of the month, this should be enough until then. I'll keep paying for your phone. Now, go on before he gets out here." She shook her head as she stared into his eyes, and then pulled his face down and kissed him on the forehead. "I'm not sure what this is for, but I pray you take care of yourself. God be with you."

His mother had seen through him. Her concern for him made him grab hold of her for a hug. He wished he could stay and talk with her, to tell her of the surprise he would bring back to her soon.

Until he could present her new daughter-in-law to her, he had to stay quiet. Otherwise, he'd be the same looser he'd always been. He'd show them both.

He hesitated for a second, but the sound of his father's uneven gait on the wooden floor scared him, and he flung open the door to escape his father's wrath once again.

Back in his van, Matt opened the bag.

"Woohoo! Way to go Mom," he shouted as he feathered his fingers through the bills. Hundreds and fifties, mixed with twenties and tens, littered the bottom of the bag.

His mother always pulled through for him. He didn't know why or how, but she always did.

Chapter 4

Although still on edge, Lisa soon began to relax. She had a good feeling about this place. Maybe Matt had finally decided he'd had enough of chasing her all over the country.

God, she hoped so.

She took each day one at a time, delighting in the little things each day brought to her. One of her favorite things was the short walk to the restaurant in the mornings. Today, the early morning chatter from the birds overhead enlightened her outlook while she enjoyed the briskness of the clean fresh air. A pair of chipmunks made her laugh. They scampered across her path, battling with each other over a pine nut, gleeful enough their scuttle might have been just for the sake of playfulness. This glorious feeling played over her when she started to believe for a moment she could partake in the same lightheartedness, if given the chance.

Even though the inevitable need to flee still hung over her like a storm cloud ready to let loose at any time, she still believed in living in the moment. She chose to hold on to the dream that one day all of this could be hers to keep.

As soon as she imagined she could forget her troubles for just a moment, a vehicle pulled up behind her and slowed. Her heart jumped in her chest as she turned around to see a van, but the glare of the sun off the windshield obliterated her view of the driver. She swallowed hard and walked faster toward the restaurant. There was still a good fifty feet before the driveway, so she jumped the drainage ditch almost slipping as her foot caught the edge of the grass. She felt the pounding quicken through her veins as she all but ran to the front door. An ache in the back of her throat pulsated with each breath she took.

The van pulled into the parking lot, too. She heard the driver's side door squeak open and slam shut. Just as she reached for the door handle, the voice of a man called out to her.

"Hey, Miss Lisa, nice day ain't it?"

She looked behind her, and the mass forming in the pit of her stomach dropped like a rock, making her somewhat queasy.

Beatty, it's just Beatty. Oh, thank God.

Stopping a moment to catch her breath, Lisa turned and gave him a smile and a wave of her hand, and pulled open the heavy wood door. Inside, her heart continued to thud in her chest as she hurried to the back to hang up her coat. She placed her backpack once again within reach if she needed to get out. Always ready for anything. She had to be, just in case.

She glanced toward the clock on the wall, thankful that she'd arrived a few minutes early for her shift to take the opportunity to call the care center where her mother lived. Without fail, she had to make that call on the first of each month, no matter where she ended up.

"Maggie, can I use your office to make a call on my cell? It's a little quieter in there."

Maggie flipped a stack of pancakes on the grill and glanced up to meet Lisa's eyes. The curious expression on Maggie's face seemed to Lisa as if she'd posed a larger question than the simple use of her office.

"Go ahead honey. The extra key is above the door on the sill. Make sure to lock it back up again when you're finished."

"Thank you. I'll only be a couple of minutes."

Lisa couldn't remember a time when Maggie had locked her office door before, but who was she to question her boss's actions?

As she stepped through the doorway, what she saw explained everything. Laid out on the desk were the cash receipts of the day before. Maggie had apparently been distracted by some early morning customers and hadn't completed the daily deposit ticket. Stacks of bills lined one side of the desk according to denomination. The change, not yet counted, sat in a pile in the middle. An efficient ticker sheet showed at what point she'd stopped her tally, awaiting her return to finish.

Lisa, stunned by Maggie's trust in her, shook her head. Not many would have risked so much at stake. If Maggie only knew the things she'd done, she wouldn't have let her come in here. She didn't deserve Maggie's faith. In Lisa's humility, she swore to herself she would do whatever she could to earn that trust for real.

She took her cell phone from her pocket and made the call to the Marshall Care Center.

"Hi Shelby, this is Lisa Hill. How are you this morning?"

"Lisa, I was looking forward to talking with you today."

"How is Mamma doing?"

"She's doing very well. We had a small period of recognition the other day. Her nurse was looking at a photo album with her and she started telling her stories about you as a little girl. She recognized the pictures of your father too. This period wasn't long, but made us hopeful this new medication Doctor Lang put her on will help with the memory loss."

The tears welled in Lisa's eyes. "That's wonderful. I wish I had been there to see her."

"She asked about you. She wanted to know where you were."

Trails of tears began to flow down her cheeks. "I'm sorry Shelby. It's been way too long. I just haven't been able to get away."

"I've told you this stage of her condition is kind of a guessing game, dear. There's no guarantee she's going to be as coherent as this when you can make it." Shelby's tone didn't reprimand, but the truthfulness came only too clear.

"There isn't any way right now. I've told you it's difficult to explain. I promise I'll be with her as soon as I can."

"Don't wait too long. I'd hate for you to miss those few chances she has to remember."

"I won't, I promise." Guilt plagued her daily for not being with her mother. "Were there any additional expenses we need to take care of this month?" She could do nothing more at the moment, but she swore to herself she would make up for it. The clock on the wall struck the top of the hour, and her extra time before starting her shift had come to an end. She needed to clear up her business and get to work.

"Nothing to add to the regular amount, but don't forget next month the rates are going to be adjusted and our bank accounts are going to be consolidated with the home office accounts. So we'll need to go over the changes then."

"I'll call you a couple of days before the end of the month to get everything straightened out. Thanks for the reminder." Lisa paused for a moment. "Shelby, give my mother a hug and a kiss for me, would you?"

"Of course, dear, just remember what I said."

There was no way Lisa would forget she'd failed to keep her promise to her father. She should be there, every step of the way with her mother. She would never forgive herself either.

Lisa proceeded to make the transfer of funds from the annuity account her father had set up for her mother when his own failing health had determined an impending early death. They'd seen the beginning stages of her mother's Alzheimer's condition worsen, and he'd wanted to make sure she would be taken care of after his passing.

Some time ago, she'd come to grips with the fact in a figurative sense she's alone now. Cancer took her father from her, and her mother's failing memory was slowly being stripped away, leaving her an almost empty shell at times. Although sad, Lisa was grateful her mother didn't know anything about what she'd been forced to do to save her own life over-and-over again over the past few years.

While there was still time, Lisa transferred the small amount she received for handling her mother's affairs to her own account. At times, those few dollars had been the only money she survived on between jobs.

She brushed the tears from her face and locked the door behind her, replacing the key as requested. When she passed by the kitchen doorway, she stopped to watch Maggie expertly flip an omelet with one hand and turn the hash browns with the other.

Without even looking at her, Maggie said, "They're starting to pile in, you better get out there." Lisa continued to stand for a moment longer. Maggie glanced over, "You need something? What's the hold up?"

Humbled, Lisa didn't know how to say what was in her heart, but she needed to say something. "Thank you, Maggie."

This caused Maggie to look up and connect with Lisa directly. The slow nod of her head acknowledged the meaning of those simple words, and she went back to flipping pancakes.

There was no need to say more, Lisa was sure Maggie understood exactly what she meant.

* * * *

Lisa looked forward to Ryan coming to the coffee stand every morning. This morning he hadn't shown up, which was unusual. But when she came out to the dining area, his presence was unmistakable.

Maggie was right. People had started to pile in. A small group waited to be seated. Tina hadn't had a chance to get to them yet. Ryan stood behind them talking with the very pregnant Roberta, who'd brought her gaggle of kids in for a good breakfast at Maggie's.

Lisa realized he wasn't in his uniform. This was the first time she'd seen him in anything different. Dressed casually, he appeared the same as any other man would, yet for some reason his clothes fit differently on him. The form fitted jeans shaped against his thighs leaving not much to the imagination. His sleeves, rolled up to reveal the sinewy muscles of his forearm, and the broadness of his shoulders filling out the button down shirt implied no question as to the toned abdomen beneath. He stood like a model waiting for the chance to bust out of his clothes to unveil his prowess – or at least that was how Lisa found herself imagining him.

She caught his returned gaze, the twinkle in his eyes made it obvious he was aware of her intent review of his body. His slight grin disconcerted her a bit, and she knew she'd been caught ogling the view. She was reminded of their first time they'd met, where without the need for any physical contact the simple meeting of their eyes stirred up feelings of an intimacy she longed to realize.

He laughed as Roberta leaned toward him and turned her face away to make a comment. Lisa felt what she'd said must have been directed at her, as Roberta avoided making eye contact when she turned back around. The sound of his voice made Lisa's heart flip in her chest and reminded her of the dream she'd had the night before. Though the deep melodious undertones of his voice were not the only things she'd had in her dreams. She felt herself blush at the thought.

Every time he came around, she seemed to act like a schoolgirl with a crush. All sorts of fantasies began to play in her head about what being his girl would be like.

Girlish dreams she'd never have the chance to experience. Walks in the park, sharing an ice cream cone, lying under the stars in the backyard…making out in the backseat of his car. She berated herself for such foolishness and approached the group with as much maturity as she could muster. Tina rushed in front of her with a smile, to usher Roberta and her group to her side of the restaurant, giving Lisa a little nudge toward Ryan as she went.

"Sheriff, how many in your party this morning?" Lisa asked, not sure who would be joining him for breakfast.

"Just me," he said quietly, his expression turning more serious as he gazed into her eyes.

She stood, unable to move. His presence flooded her senses with his power, and an unforgiving sexual need she couldn't deny. To try to brush the awkwardness away she turned to lead him to a table. "You're not in uniform today. Are you taking a day off?"

"I take a day once in a while. But, always on call," he said indicating the phone at his hip.

She placed the menu on the table and turned to step away, but came closer to him than anticipated and realized he'd stopped right behind her. His freshly showered scent caused an erratic flutter to her heart. She raised her eyes up to his face to discover him gazing down at her. Without a word, he reached with his fingertip to brush a lingering tear hidden away in her lashes.

"You've been crying," he said, his voice gentle and his eyes soft with kindness. "Is everything all right?"

All activity in the room seemed to stop suddenly, as if there were only the two of them present, standing within arm's reach of each other. Lisa had to refrain from acting out the need to lay her head on his shoulder, and wrap her arms around him.

The compassion in his voice made the tears sting behind her eyes. She stepped away quickly, and turned around to straighten the napkins and silverware on the opposite side of the table. There was no sense in another lie, she didn't need to cover up the reason she'd been crying.

"I called about my mother this morning. She's been in a care facility for many years now."

The genuine concern in his eyes pulled at her heart. "Is she okay? Is anything wrong?"

"No, she's fine. She has Alzheimer's and they think she might be having some breakthroughs. I wish I could be with her is all."

"Why aren't you?" This time the question prompted too much information, so she sidestepped.

"I told you before we can't always do what we want."

The narrowed eyes indicated his kindness had turned into analysis. "And sometimes we are blind sighted to being able to solve our problems."

Lisa had nothing to say in response. His reply stopped her short.

Could it really be so easy? Is there an answer to this hell I've been living and I just can't see it?

"I'll give you a chance to decide what you'd like and I'll be back to take your order," she said softly and turned away.

The effort to walk away from him was hard. Lisa so desperately wanted to talk to someone. Something about him made her crave the warmth and closeness of another person. She wanted to open up and tell him everything, to climb into his embrace and soak in his exuding strength and confidence. She wondered whether her choice to walk away had been the right one, whether keeping quiet was really the best thing to do.

A few minutes later she came back to take his order. She'd needed to regroup, and thought perhaps now she might be able to handle a conversation without breaking down.

He checked the screen of his phone as she poured a refill on his coffee.

"I guess you never really get time off, do you?"

"Things aren't always lively around here. Bobby can call if matters get out of hand."

"Any plans for the day?"

"Some of the usual, I suppose, maybe a little fishing or some work around the yard to get ready for next winter."

Lisa realized she'd never asked whether he was married, and didn't know Tina well enough to be sure she would have offered up the information. She wasn't even sure why she wanted to find out all of a sudden.

"I guess the misses has a load of those things for you to do?"

An odd expression crossed over his face, but the smile returned. "No, no misses, just me and Pluto."

"Pluto?" Lisa asked, her interest in the obvious pet name she hoped would cover up the fact she was unmistakably happy he didn't have a wife.

"My bloodhound or more specific a redbone coonhound, he looks like one of Disney's characters."

"Hence the name," she smiled at the surprise on his face. He apparently hadn't thought she'd recognize this small piece of trivia. "So…" Lisa glanced down, interrupted by the buzz of her cell phone in her pocket.

Her stomach twisted in a knot. The only one who should use this number was the Marshall Center. She pulled the cell quickly from her pocket and glanced at the number on the Caller ID.

Everything spiraled around her, and she had to breathe in deep to stay in control. Her heart began to pump hard, and the knot in her stomach clenched with vigorous force.

The name on the phone ID was 'Matt'. Oh God, he'd started again. Somehow he'd tracked her number again.

Compelled to remain calm, she didn't take long to come back to the present moment, though her thoughts were on what her next moves needed to be. She shoved the phone back into her pocket again and pulled out her order pad. As she glanced back up, the cool green pools of scrutiny in Ryan's eyes met her.

If she wasn't careful, he would start asking questions. The way she felt now, there was no doubt she'd spill her whole story, before weighing the outcome to her confession. But if she continued to stare into his query filled eyes, she might convince herself her first instinct to flee might not be the right choice.

That was just foolishness though. If she didn't take the first action it might be her last. There was no way she would let Matt get to her, at least not willingly. She had to stay ahead of him without fail. She didn't believe it was as easy as telling Ryan what had been happening and it would all go away. Was it?

Besides, the danger of telling him was either his legal duty to uphold the law would prevail and he'd have to lock her up for stealing, or he might be so taken by her story his compassion would get him involved and then she'd be risking his life as well. Not to mention her heart. She couldn't handle either scenario. Either way, she didn't have the heart to allow anyone to get so close to her. She had to figure out how to end this craziness on her own.

She took a second to settle her nerves, but his eyes followed her every move, almost as if he cared about her, which stirred up every nerve she had any hold over.

Lord, how I want someone to care for me.

Annoyed with the weakness he seemed to stir inside her, she tried not to show any change of emotion on her face.

"Everything all right?" he asked.

"Fine. What can I get you Sheriff?" She hated her clipped answer. She wouldn't allow the turmoil the call had stirred up to become evident, but by the looks of it Ryan expected some type of response. Her throat tightened up on her. Her heightened emotions played with her ability to stay in control. She couldn't answer him.

She knew this first call was only a warning sign, Matt hadn't found her, he'd only found her cell number. Months might pass before he found her again. Then again, it could be days, she never knew.

"Steak and eggs, medium rare on the steak, extra hash browns on the side and whole grain toast," he said without blinking.

"Coming up in a few," Lisa said with efficiency and walked away as quick as possible, the frustrated pound of her heart reverberating in her ears.

Throughout the breakfast hour, several of the same calls startled her. No messages yet. The buzz of the incoming calls set her on edge. No indication of where he might show up next. Lisa went over in her mind the patterns of previous encounters with Matt. He would make these calls while he was high, incoherent to anything except what he'd set his mind to do.

Before all of this started, she'd confronted him, and he'd sworn he was unable to remember what he'd done or said. She didn't dare answer the call and tell him what she thought of his harassment. She'd tried before, and ended up so distraught by his babbles she refused to put herself through the pain again.

Even with the frequent change of her cell phone number, somehow he'd find her new number and track her down again. She didn't understand how he accomplished finding her. She'd done everything she could think of to escape. The whole mess made no sense to her.

Ryan left after he finished his breakfast, but she was aware he'd studied her while he ate. Every time her phone would vibrate, it was as if he had a sixth sense, and he would scrutinize her actions even more carefully. Out of habit, she found herself glancing at the screen of her phone to make sure the call wasn't anything more important, only to be reminded of her tentative hold on her emotional control.

At the end of her shift she put the last of her tips in her pocket and headed toward the back. Her phone began to vibrate again in her pocket. Distracted in her own thoughts, she passed by Tina without looking up.

"Who the heck keeps calling you?"

Lisa turned to where Tina counted her tips on the countertop by the register. She shoved the phone back into her pocket, and pretended to straighten the menus in their slot.

"Not sure, must be a wrong number," she said in an attempt to sound innocent.

"Hmm…Ok, still not ready to talk I see." Tina finished up her tally and stuffed the dollars into an envelope. Her eyes flashed at Lisa in unconfirmed acknowledgment of her real situation. "Remember what I said. I'm here for you, honey. Tell me when you'd like to sit down and talk."

Tina walked away from her with a confidence Lisa wished she possessed herself. Halfway to the door, Tina turned around and kept walking backwards toward the exit.

"Listen, come by this evening. We should decide what you'd like to wear tomorrow night."

Lisa stumbled over the thought of going out as planned. She really didn't think she should now. "I…I don't think I can. Why don't you go on without me?" She felt so childish.

Tina stopped and came back to stand in front of her. Her self-assurance lighting every step she took.

"Didn't your Mamma ever tell you not to let the bully win? You can't keep doing this to yourself. You'll come with me tomorrow night if I've got to hog tie you and throw you in the truck bed. And, you're going to have fun."

Tina was heated, and Lisa didn't dare disagree at the moment. If she had to she'd beg to be let out of her commitment at the last minute. "What time do you want me at your house?"

"Six, and don't be late. We've got a lot to go through." Lisa nodded as Tina began to leave again. Before she crossed the threshold, Tina shouted over her shoulder, "There's nothing to worry about. I'll protect you."

Lisa almost believed she could.

* * * *

Packing up the papers strewn across the desk in front of her, Lisa blew out a heavy breath of defeat. She'd spent the afternoon making phone calls trying to track down the engagement ring she'd pawned, but came up with nothing. She figured that if she could find the ring, she would find a way to get it back and somehow get it to Matt. Then maybe he would stop following her. She hoped.

The piece was unusual, with a diamond at least a carat, surrounded by natural sapphires of an extraordinary teal color in an antique setting. This ring had an obvious history tied to the craftsmanship and was worth fifty times more than she'd gotten for it. The problem was she couldn't remember the name of the pawn shop or the exact city she'd been in when she'd run into trouble and it became necessary to find a way to survive. She felt pretty sure it had been somewhere close to Chicago when her car broke down and she'd been forced to purchase another one. There had to be over a hundred shops listed, and so far none of them had record of any such ring having been purchased or sold in the last two years.

Lisa folded up the map she'd been staring at for the last hour wondering where she should go this next time she'd need to leave. She stood and gathered the necessary belongings she never let leave her sight and put them into her backpack.

The decision to go out dancing hadn't been easy, but she needed to allow herself this one night of freedom, and act like a normal person would at her age. If she didn't, she'd begun to think she would go crazy. She might as well be one of those poor people who get so caught up in their own miserable existence that they never share in the love and laughter going on around them. Never enjoying the benefits of a full adventure filled life. She frowned. Fact be known, she was one of those people.

It was time she took a step toward a normal life, no matter how small the baby step. Sure, there would be a chance she'd be caught unaware, and she'd considered that aspect. However, the timing was all wrong. The only way Matt could be so close would be if he knew where she'd headed in the first place. She had a few more days left. Of that, she was sure. By that time, she'd be long gone.

She headed out to walk the short way down Main Street to Tina's house in the balmy early evening breeze. The day had been a warm one, unusual she'd been told for this early in the year. As she strolled through the town, the cool air against her cheeks revitalized her spirit, and she began to daydream about what life in a small town would be like. She could hear the activity of children outside playing games, their laughter floating in happy abandon with her as she walked. One of the elderly frequent diners from Maggie's passed by on the opposite side of the street. He gave her a toothy grin and a genuine greeting she'd expect of a friend. A warm feeling spread over her from her heart outward, something she hadn't been conscious of for a very long time.

As Lisa passed by a small rambler to her right, she recognized one of the deputies outside in the front yard playing catch with his son. She realized the little boy must be Joshua when her co-worker, Susan, raised her hand and waved from the front porch. She smiled and waved back. The melancholy thought dancing through her mind o grasp onto this feeling of freedom forever.

She watched the two in the yard, giggling and laughing over a dropped ball. The young father scooped his son into his arms and blew triumphant loud noises against the little boy's bare belly. She let out a long sigh of resignation, and started walking again down the sidewalk, broken over time by the effects of weathering. The same brokenness of her own life lay out in the path in front of her. Love and laughter, the two most important components of life was the glue to fix those cracks, but they were way out of reach for her. Oh, how Lisa longed for them to be hers as well.

The leaves of the trees rustled in the wind around her, whisking a breath of fresh life into her as she continued her journey toward Tina's house. If she continued to feel sorry for herself, it would only kill what strength she had left in her spirit. She had to believe somehow, some way, there was an end to her current circumstance. The solution just hadn't presented itself to her yet. Or had it?

Her thoughts moved naturally to the mysterious Sheriff Jacobs. She found it hard to dismiss the attraction she had for him. It couldn't be ignored, at least not very easily. Every time he stepped into a room, an odd sensation would pull at her from inside, as if she belonged at his side. She had to stop herself from giggling whenever he spoke to her. If she let herself feel it, the giddiness he caused equaled nothing less than glorious. The contagious sparkle in his eyes drew her in, to be filled with the delicious taste of man. He seemed able to lift her heart, to disperse all her fears and woes in the brief meeting of their eyes.

She laughed out loud. All of this was nonsense. She hadn't even so much as touched him, though none of that seemed to matter.

"What's so funny?"

Ryan's voice scared her so much it felt as if her heart leapt out of her chest. He'd come from nowhere, appearing beside her like a vision from her dreams straight into her path.

"Don't do that! You scared me to death." Lisa looked around, "Where did you come from?"

"If I told you then you'd know one of my favorite hiding places. I can't have that."

"Sneaking up on people is kind of creepy, even if you are the Sheriff," Lisa said pretending to be offended, when really she was excited he'd joined her on her walk.

"What were you laughing at?"

She wasn't sure what to say. Her dreams it seemed had gotten her into trouble. "I'm on my way to Tina's to try on some clothes for Friday. I was just happy, that's all."

"Tina and Friday night? You must be going dancing."

Obviously nothing was a secret around here. Now she'd have to tell him, she had no choice.

"Tina asked me to join her and her brother dancing with a few other people. I'm not sure who yet."

"Up at the Lodge near Forks?" Ryan asked, more as a statement than a question. He apparently knew the place well, he didn't need confirmation. "I hear 'Anything Goes' is playing this weekend. They're a great band."

"Oh, I hoped there would be live music," Lisa exclaimed. "There's something different about live music. It seems to get your blood moving."

Ryan smiled at her comment and stopped walking. She glanced back and realized he stood outside Tina's house. Embarrassed she'd almost missed her destination Lisa wished the end of the walk hadn't arrived so quickly.

"I hope you enjoy your clothes fitting." He paused and took what seemed to be a long thoughtful study of Lisa. His green eyes mesmerized her. "Maybe I'll see you up there."

Lisa couldn't seem to think, so she shook her head in agreement and started up the walkway. She stopped and turned around. Ryan was walking back in the direction they had traveled.

"Wait," she called after him. He turned around. She had to ask, "See me up where?"

The slow smile that came to Ryan's face made her heart flutter.

"The Lodge," he called back.

"Oh," she said more to herself than anyone. She hadn't expected him to want to come with them. Not knowing what else to say she waived at him and turned to knock on Tina's door.

Tina apparently had been waiting for her. The door opened immediately, before Lisa had a chance to put her hand down. Tina stuck her head out the door and looked from side to side. Stopping at the retreating backside of Sheriff Jacobs she let out an exclamation of joy.

"What did I tell you? I knew it. I knew he liked you." She pulled Lisa into her front room and gave her a hug.

Lisa blushed furiously and tried not to smile too fast. "I don't think that means he likes me. He said he might be there is all."

Tina took Lisa by the hands and danced around in foolish circles. "You don't understand. Ryan doesn't go out. He never goes to the Lodge. Believe me he wouldn't go unless he really, really liked you."

All of a sudden, Lisa felt a little foolish herself and the giddiness began to return. "Do you think so?"

Tina replied with an exaggerated expression. "Yeah, ask Maggie, she noticed his goo-goo eyes too."

Lisa wasn't sure what to say. She shook her head in disbelief. "You're both full of dreams. I don't think you've seen any such thing." Though, her response was noncommittal, inside her heart leapt for joy.

Tina raised her eyebrows at Lisa. "Umm hmm…C'mon, we've got some dresses to try on." She pulled Lisa by the hand into the back bedroom.

On the bed, a dozen dresses of various shapes and colors had been flung in disarray. In the chair next to the closet door, at least another half dozen lay sparkling in the light. Through the open closet doors, clothes were packed so tight Lisa was amazed Tina had taken these out already. She gazed at the dresses then turned toward Tina, her eyebrows raised in question.

"All right, so I'm a clothes horse. I can't let the perfect dress go. Besides, who wants the same old clothes on a body like this?" Tina flaunted her pretty shape in front of the mirror.

They both burst out laughing when Lisa took a models pose next to her silly friend.

For several hours, they went through all of the clothes Tina had pulled out. Each one needed to be judged and rated on how they fitted on Lisa's figure.

Is this sexy enough? Is this the right color? Does this choice show off my curves in the best way? Does it fit in all the right places?

Finally, they decided on a simple shimmering sequined peach colored summer dress with spaghetti straps and a V-cut back. The color brought out the reddish tints in her naturally curly hair, the bodice hugged in the right places, and the length showed enough leg, not to mention the little slit that invitingly displayed a touch of thigh.

"What about shoes? I don't suppose you have anything but those things, do you?" Tina asked indicating the one pair of beat up tennis shoes Lisa wore. Lisa shook her head, feeling like a cumbersome bother. "Well that won't do. Wait…here," Tina said pulling out several boxes from her closet, throwing them with wild abandon into the corner until she found the right one. "I was saving these for something special. You're about an eight, same as me, right?"

Lisa nodded truly amazed at the blessing her new friend had turned out to be.

From the box, Tina pulled a stylish pair of sandals, the perfect height for dancing. She handed them to Lisa, and they both agreed as soon as she put them on they looked astonishing.

Later, they sat on the floor, the discarded garments all around them, with two spoons and a half-empty carton of Reese's Peanut Butter Cup Ice Cream.

"You'll knock his socks off," Tina said diving in for another gigantic spoonful. "He won't know what hit him."

Lisa laughed. "I haven't had this much fun in…forever!"

Tina shook her head. "You don't get out much, do you?"

"I can't believe I'm even doing this." Lisa had forgotten all of her troubles, intent on the joy of the moment.

"Well, you better get used to it. This is only the start for you," Tina gurgled over the spoonful of ice cream she'd shoved into her mouth.

Lisa leaned her head back against the bed, and smiled her shy heart full of hope.

"Do you really think he likes me?"

Chapter 5

Lisa jerked back to reality as her phone began to vibrate from her jacket pocket on top of Tina's dresser. She let the message go to voicemail, saying a silent prayer the message wasn't from her mother's care center. That would only be bad news.

She grimaced and pulled the phone out of her jacket. As suspected, Matt's name popped on the screen, and the optimistic attitude she'd had a few minutes earlier shifted in a dismal direction. Her deluded hope drifted back into her own personal cold hard reality. The truth to the matter was, no matter whether Ryan liked her or not, she'd never be able to explore this connection they had with one another.

"All right, I've had enough of this bullshit. Who the hell is calling you?" Tina prompted, and not to kindly.

Lisa was unable to speak. The disconcerting crash of being brought down out of the clouds so quick deadened her response, and the answer to the question evaded her. The phone began to pulsate in her hand again. She stared blankly at the screen as the name came into view. Matt.

Tina held out her hand. "Give me that thing."

Lisa peered into Tina's eyes. Her evident concern caused every emotion Lisa held inside to tumble forward, threatening the thin layer of control she still possessed to burst through.

"Give me the phone," Tina said with force.

Numb, Lisa handed the phone over to Tina.

"When did you listen to your calls last?"

"Umm…this morning, I guess."

"Did you erase them?" Tina asked fumbling with the buttons on the phone. When Lisa nodded, Tina slowly placed her hands in her lap. "Since then you've got fifty-two calls and fifteen texts on here from the same person. Want to tell me? Who the hell is this Matt?"

Lisa lost all control. Hot tears sprang up like the geyser pressure of a hot spring coming through a fissure in the ground. Sobbing, she struggled to rise to her feet to leave. She couldn't let herself break, at least not when someone would witness her true devastation. She felt Tina pulling her back. Drained of all energy she flopped back down on the floor and wilted.

Tina gathered her into her arms. Her consoling words would have been calming, if only Lisa could believe them.

"Everything is all right. You're here now. Nobody will hurt you. I'm not going to let anything happen to you."

For a few minutes, Lisa continued her uncontrollable sobs muffled against Tina's shoulder, until finally reduced to an occasional whimper. Tina reached back to grab the tissues off the nightstand behind her.

"Here, sop up some of this mess you've got going on."

Lisa laughed at Tina's comical way of saying 'enough'.

"I'm sorry. I guess I needed to let go," she said annoyed at her inability to hold herself together.

"We all need to cry sometime, and seems like you've been holding back for a long time." Tina sat back, her brows knit together. "So, spill the beans. What's up with the calls?"

Lisa realized, no use in keeping her secrets quiet any longer, Tina wouldn't leave this alone. She'd be at her every hour of every day before she let her out of explaining this breakdown. The concern of her new friend pulled a need to talk from her she hadn't realized existed. She trusted Tina. Her strength of character motivated Lisa to reveal the reason for her taciturn actions. Even if nothing good came from her disclosure, the time had come to admit the wrongful actions she'd committed and those Matt continued on doing. Maybe going to jail wouldn't be so bad. At least Matt wouldn't be able to get to her.

"I'm not sure where to start." Lisa plucked and twisted the tissues she held in her hand. "I guess everyone in town is aware I've been running from someone."

"Yeah, people have been talking about you showing up here all of a sudden."

"I've been running from Matt for about four years now."

"Wow. Four years, man, how've you kept going?" Tina shook her head in disbelief. "Where did you guys meet?"

Lisa hadn't told anyone about Matt. Her friends from before didn't understand her actions. For some reason she believed Tina would. Normally, she left the bright beginnings of their relationship tucked away. Remembering the way things had started with Matt hurt.

In her mind, she went back to the smoke filled nightclub as if she were there. The lights, the energy of the dance floor, and the band on stage were still so very clear.

"My friends wanted me to go out with them to the club where this new rock band called the 'Bandits' was playing."

"You bet, I'd be there," Tina speculated.

"I'd been trying to qualify for the full time position at Sherford's, and I really needed to get out and relax."

"Sherford's?" Tina asked.

"The eastside elementary in my hometown," Lisa answered, pausing to blow her nose one more time. "Anyway, we drove into Columbus to get to the club by nine to get a table. When we walked in, the band had started playing this upbeat rendition of some tune I've heard before," her brows furrowed for a minute. "I can't remember what now."

"So where was Matt?"

"Matt is the lead guitarist for the Bandits. He stood center stage, the lights overhead streaming down over him." Lisa stopped, envisioning her experience that night. "He was awesome. You had to be in the room to understand what I'm talking about. He's not much to look at, but when he plays he's so full of energy, so full of life. He glowed, like the music poured through him into his hands. I'd never seen or heard anything like him before."

"I knew a drummer like that once," Tina commiserated.

Saddened by the memory of how he'd affected her, she raised the tissue to her eyes to dab away the forming tears. "He looked up into the crowd straight at me. I think I fell in love with him in that instant."

The tears began to run down her cheeks again, she brushed at them impatiently.

"Somehow I got back to meet him at the break and we started this whole thing."

"Tell me what happened next." Tina leaned forward taking Lisa's limp hand in hers.

"I guess we fell into what's called a whirlwind romance. He swept me off my feet. So generous, so full of character, he really had me fooled. At first, I believe I did love him. He made it so hard not to."

"So, how long were you two in love?"

"We dated exclusively for about three months, and out of the blue he asked to move in with me to spend more time together. I'm not sure why I agreed, I should've never let him stay. I knew nothing about him, other than he was driven to play the lead guitar like a genius. He couldn't stop talking about how he would make a name for himself in the music world. He's kind of obsessive about the music thing. Like his playing was the answer to all his problems." Lisa paused to reflect on the past. "I can see now all the mistakes I made. I feel so stupid."

Tina reached out and squeezed her hand. "My Grams used to tell me, mistakes are what we learn from, without them we'd be to innocent to survive in this world. Anyway, go on. Tell me what happened after he moved in with you."

"I'd been hired on full time at the school by this time, and came home one night after a particularly challenging day. The light from the fireplace was glowing and all these candles were lit around the room. On the coffee table there were two glasses and a bottle of wine. He'd done things like this before, so I thought it was another one of his nights for me to remember."

"Sounds like a dream come true. I'd give anything for a guy to treat me like that," Tina exclaimed.

"I thought I was dreaming, because all of a sudden he got down on one knee and proposed to me." Lisa gave a weak smile in memory of the way in which he'd asked. "It all happened so fast. I was so stunned I said yes. It was a mistake, I never should've agreed. I mean, I'd never met his mom or dad, they might be ax murderers for all I know."

"Oh my God, so he's your fiancée?"

Lisa nodded. "I guess I was so infatuated by the drama of being asked to be someone's wife I didn't see the reasons why it wasn't such a good idea."

"I don't understand. Why are you running from him?"

"Right after that he started doing really strange things. He'd be gone for days at a time and wouldn't tell me where he would go. He drank heavily when we were together. His moods would be all over the place. One minute he was the happy guy I'd fallen in love with, the next I'd have to lock myself in the bathroom because he'd be drunk and mean. It was like he'd turned into a totally different person."

"Regular Jekyll and Hyde isn't he."

Lisa nodded. "Finally, he confessed to me he'd been hiding something from me from the start. He's an addict. I just happen to run across him on a dry spell, and he'd started to slip back into his old ways."

Tina's eyes widened with the revelation. "Something like cocaine or heroin? Can't the police pick him up for doing those?"

Lisa shook her head. "He doesn't do drugs. He says hard drugs are way too expensive, especially when he can get the same high from other things."

"So what does he use?"

"He huffs inhalants."

"He sniffs paint and hairspray? Isn't that something kids do?" Tina raised her eyebrows in disbelief.

"Those are the simpler types you've heard about in the media. I've done a lot of research. Seems huffing isn't just what kids do. Kids are easier to pick up on because they can't control their use or hide the affect as well as adults."

"I'm trying to think of other things he'd use. I imagine all kinds of things."

"Mostly propane, but he uses whatever gas he can get his hands on."

"Ick, that stuff stinks. What? Like those big tanks on the side of the griller outside? Wouldn't a tank last a lifetime?"

"Not really. I've seen him go through a full tank in about three days."

"Whoa, doesn't that kill brain cells? He's got to be dumber than a rock right now," Tina said incredulously.

Lisa nodded. "Honestly, I don't understand why he's still alive." Lisa was so tired. She rested her head behind her on the bed, and said with a feeble sigh, "I just wish he would leave me alone."

"Did you tell him how you felt about what he's doing?"

"For a while, I actually thought I'd been brought into his life to help him stop this nonsense. I tried getting him to stop, to get some help, but he thinks he can stop at any time. He thinks his music is enhanced by the experience. He says he's not hurting anyone, so he doesn't think there's any problem."

"I don't understand. Why is he chasing you?"

"I'd finally had enough of it and told him I wanted to end the relationship. He begged and pleaded with me, but when I wouldn't give in he went storming out and was gone for over a week. I thought he'd left for good. I even started boxing up his belongings. Then I started getting these phone calls from him. He's got this fantasy in his head I belong to him. He believes we are meant to be together, and I'm wrong for leaving him." She took a deep breath. "Among other things, he threatens to kill me if he gets his hands on me. He's come close several times, but I've been able to get away."

"Can't you put him away for harassment or something?"

"I've tried. The only thing I've been able to do is get a restraining order on him." Lisa wiped her nose with the tissue. "A lot of good a stupid piece of paper does though. I'd be dead before anyone got to me. I'm actually lucky to still be alive. He came at me once with a crowbar."

"Geez," Tina exclaimed, her eyes widening in shock.

"Yeah, that was a night I'll never forget."

"So you've been running from him this whole time." Tina put her chin on her bent knee, tracing circles in the carpet with her finger. She looked up to Lisa's frown and shook her head. "You must really hate him. I know I would."

Lisa took a moment to ponder the assumed response to what she was experiencing. She gave a half-laugh and gave Tina a weak smile. "You know, that's what you would expect. But I don't. Not really."

Tina raised a speculative eyebrow and asked, "Why on earth not?"

Shrugging her shoulders, Lisa wasn't sure how to answer at first. She thought about her father's teaching about life, and how she knew he'd have told her we should love each other and treat others with respect and kindness, no matter how much they didn't deserve it.

What was that saying he always used to tell me? Do unto others as you would have them do unto you.

"You know, I know down deep he's a good person. He's just gotten lost in the world he's fallen into. He really needs to get some help. If I could figure out a way I'd make it happen for him. Thing is, he just won't listen to reason."

"That's for sure," Tina snorted. "So what are you going to do?"

Weary, Lisa's despondency began creeping back to settle over her again. "I haven't figured it out yet."

"I don't understand how he keeps finding you. There's got to be something you do telling him where you are."

"I can't figure it out. I wish I knew."

"You don't deserve this. Nobody does. We're going to figure this thing out. Trust me, I don't give up easily."

Tina's fortitude breathed fortitude into Lisa's spirit, though she felt undeserving of such loyalty. If she were to do this right she had to come clean.

"Look, there are some things I've done in the last few years I'm not very proud of doing. I've tried to correct them all when I can, but I'm not as innocent as you may think."

Tina straightened up and threw a questioning glance at Lisa. "Really, like what?"

Lisa rolled her shoulders, and turned her face away, ashamed of what she was about to say. "Do you remember a story in the news about a year ago about a waitress receiving a huge anonymous tip in the mail?"

"Yeah, in Iowa somewhere, wasn't it?"

"Cedar Rapids," Lisa offered softly.

"She'd been fired from her job for taking the bartender's tip jar. A couple weeks later she gets a couple hundred in tips and an anonymous note saying the person who sent it knew she hadn't taken the money. Funny thing was, the tip jar showed up the same day at the restaurant with the missing cash still in it."

"I sent her the money. I was the one who stole the tips."

Tina's jaw dropped.

"I couldn't get her job back for her. But there was no way I would let her pay for my misdeed." The expression on Tina's face confused Lisa. "That's not the first time I've had to take something that wasn't mine. I've paid them back, all but this last one."

"Remind me to watch my tips better," Tina quipped, then shoved Lisa's shoulder playfully. "Just kidding, you must've had good reason to do those things. Which one is left?"

Lisa paused for a minute to figure out if she should tell Tina about the ring. If she told her it would get back to Ryan, and she didn't know if she was ready to go to jail yet. She had to find the ring first and make some type of attempt to get it back, then maybe she'd show her good will in making a wrongful act right again.

"Another debt for having done the wrong thing," Lisa offered in hopes Tina wouldn't ask too many more questions.

"So, this is one of those things you aren't ready to tell me about yet?" Tina asked, a clear disappointment dulling her eyes.

Lisa could only nod, and glanced away.

"You can come to me with anything," Tina stated in a firm voice. "I hope you realize by now I'm not going to judge you for something you've done wrong. If you need my help, let me know."

The need to straighten this out on her own pressed against Lisa's need to tell her new friend the whole story. She knew if she were to be right with herself, she had to take care of this last thing on her own, no matter how long it took. Grateful for the support Tina was so willing to give, she gave her a hug.

"Thank you. I will."

Lisa rose to her feet and stretched. A weight had been lifted from her shoulders. Being able to talk helped her mood to lighten. Sitting back down on the edge of the bed, Lisa had to tell Tina the next part of what this all meant.

"He's started calling again, which means he's about to get on my trail. I'm not sure how long this time will take for him to find me, sometimes only a matter of weeks. I've got to be ready to move at the slightest reason. If there's any indication he's close, I'm out of here."

Tina jumped up and started to pace the floor. "Nuh-uh, that's not going to happen this time. You're sticking to your guns, and finally stand up to this asshole."

Lisa shook her head. "Easy for you to say, you're not the one in fear for your life."

"We've got to find Ryan. He can figure out what to do."

Lisa put her head in her hands, she had to think. Did she really want him to immediately bring herself into a professional category of victim, in need of his protection and skill to figure out how to solve her problems? She would of course need to divulge the truth to her own criminal activity, no matter how risky to her life with an unmarked record. This for sure would put a mark against her, eliminating all possibility of working with children again. It definitely would not be a good start to a romantic relationship, if any possibility existed for one. If Ryan helped, she'd rather it be because he wanted to, not because his job required him to protect and serve the interest of the public.

She stood again and placed her hands on Tina's shoulders to keep her from moving back and forth. "Tina, you've got to promise me you won't tell Ryan, not yet. I'll tell him when the time is right. Just not now, okay?"

Tina stared at Lisa for a minute and ended in rolling her eyes. "All right, I know what you mean. You don't want to become the needy woman begging for help. You've got to get a little more substance under your belt first." She stamped her foot on the floor. "But, damn it, don't wait too long. I'm not sure I can keep this to myself too long. You've got to have help figuring this out. I'm not going to allow you to fly in the middle of the night because you're too proud to ask for help."

* * * *

The next morning, Ryan sat at his usual table for breakfast. As his gaze followed Lisa's movements between her customers, he couldn't figure out he was so fascinated by her. She was a big bundle of trouble, for sure. Not only was her whole life a mystery to his sense of right from wrong, his reaction to her presence threw all kinds of questions into the mix. Who was she? And why the hell did she make him feel this way?

He wanted to protect and to serve, but for all the wrong reasons. She was the only thing he thought about all day, and she even came to him in his dreams at night. If he was honest with himself, he'd never felt this way about a woman before, not even Tess. He needed to figure out what made Lisa different from other women.

He'd thought he was done with any type of close relationship with a woman, except for the occasional fling. Something about Lisa made him want for a different type of courtship. One which would lead to the very thing he was determined never to experience again.

His thoughts were halted by a familiar interruption.

"Ryan, do you have a minute? I really wanted to tell you about something that happened the other day. You wouldn't believe who called me. She was the last person on earth I thought would call. I mean, she knows the way we all feel about her after what happened. Can we sit and talk?"

Not surprised by the source of this string of questions, statements, and comments coming all in one breath, Ryan looked up to find Susan, with Joshua in tow.

He indicated his approval with the upward extension of his palm toward the seat in front of him. "Good morning."

Without having to say another word, Susan settled herself and her little one in and launched into another string of words that if he didn't listen carefully enough he might miss something.

"I wouldn't come bothering you like this, but Bobby said he thought you should know. She called me out of the blue, like nothing ever happened. Like I would really want to still be her friend after what she'd done. If you ask me, she's up to no good. And I'll have you know I'd tell her that straight to her face. No good I tell you. I won't have anything to do with her. Not now," Susan's expression was almost comical. Her eyes were wide as if in shock, her never stopping mouth was turned down into a frown, as if horrified by her words.

Ryan would have found it funny if he didn't dread who he thought she referred to in her ramblings. His fist clenched in his lap. "Who called?"

"Tess, who else would I be talking about?"

He waited for his reaction to hit him, but nothing happened. Interesting, the mention of her name didn't tear him apart like it used to. He only wished he didn't have to think of her again. She'd made her decision, and so had he. Tess didn't exist as far as he was concerned. He had better things to think about.

Susan continued to ramble on about every word Tess had said in their conversation. Ryan tried to listen, but his thoughts began to drift off as he continued to watch Lisa and Tina talking, and laughing candidly with the Hawkins. Lisa held the coffee pot in her hand. She turned toward him and their eyes met. What Susan was saying meant nothing to him. Lisa on the other hand held all of his interest.

He raised his coffee cup up and Lisa turned to pardon herself from the conversation with the Hawkins. She walked toward his table their eyes locked, and all he was able to think about was the astonishing physical union he'd experienced with her in the dream the night before.

"She was asking about you. I told her you were doing fine without her. She wanted all the details. You know, if you were still Sheriff, if you ever bought the house on the lake, if you were seeing anyone. She really has no business in asking, and I told her so right out," Susan chattered on as Lisa poured Ryan's cup of coffee.

He glanced up at Susan. "I'd appreciate it if you would not discuss anything about me and my life with her. Tell her if she wants to know something she should ask me herself."

Ryan's attention had wavered from Lisa for only a moment. As she began to leave, he reached out and grasped her hand. A tingling sensation ran up his arm, straight to his groin.

How on earth does she do that?

Lisa looked startled. She stood stiff, her body tensed as if waiting for punishment for something she'd done.

"Did you need something Sheriff?" Lisa asked glancing around the table. "More cream?"

"No, thank you." He glanced at Susan hoping she would get the message he wanted to talk with Lisa alone. Susan started to say something more about what she thought of Tess's call. Ryan's eyes caught hers and she stopped in mid-sentence, and scooted out from the table.

"I should get back to work." Lisa moved out of Susan's way.

"Stay, we need to talk," Ryan insisted.

Both Susan and Lisa looked at him as if he were out of his mind, both for obvious different reasons. Ryan could almost hear the tongues wagging at the gossip table behind his back. It took a moment, but Susan seemed to snap out of her transfixed state before Lisa.

"Oh, well, I've got to get going anyway. Joshua and I need to go to the market. We've got a big dinner planned for Daddy, don't we?" Susan said as she picked up her little boy. "I've got to go ask Maggie about the birthday cake."

"Tell Bobby 'Happy Birthday' for me, and I'll see him at the station tomorrow."

"All right Ryan, have a good day. See you Monday morning, Lisa. Have fun this weekend."

Ryan caught the tail end of the smirk Susan gave Lisa as he pulled her over to sit down across from him. Why was it all the women around town seemed to know what he had on his mind before he even thought to tell anyone? It was as if they were all mind readers.

He wasn't exactly sure what he was going to say to Lisa, but he needed to find out more about her and what made her have this affect on him.

"So, tell me a little about yourself."

"Excuse me?"

"You are a mystery to all of us. Why don't you tell me about you," he repeated.

Lisa glanced around the almost empty diner, appearing to be very uncomfortable. "I really should freshen up everyone's coffee. I'm working now, maybe we'll talk later."

"Tina can handle this," Ryan stated, grasping the coffee pot and holding the carafe up to where Tina could see it. He knew she'd understand what he meant.

"Got it," Tina shouted from across the restaurant, a huge smile plastered across her face. He'd never be able to live this request down. Tina would be all over it.

Lisa stared at him as if he'd asked her the most outrageous of questions. He waited in silence. She wiggled in her seat like a ten year old, and frowned at him. No matter, he was drawn to her anyway. For some reason, he couldn't get out of his mind the look he'd envisioned on her face in his desire filled dreams. He craved her gaze for him to be the same in real life, no matter how dangerous to his self-proclaimed destiny to live alone.

"I don't understand. What do you mean?"

"I want to know you."

"Why?" Lisa queried, apparently confused by his interest.

Ryan shook his head. "For the life of me, I can't figure out why I've got this feeling about you…" Lisa stared at him as if he were out of his mind.

From the kitchen, Susan hurried out and rushed up to the table. Her little boy squirmed in her arms, begging to be put down. "Oh, by the way, I forgot to tell you Tess mentioned she's thinking about moving back to Lake Duchess."

That got a small twist of the stomach from Ryan. He grimaced then nodded, still staring into the gorgeous depths of Lisa's brown eyes. Lisa's expression changed. Confusion turned almost instantly into an accusation of sorts, as if he'd done something wrong.

"Nice to know, thanks for telling me."

"I'll come tell you about it if I find out anything else," Susan offered, putting the active child's feet on the floor. "Come on Josh, let's go get dinner."

Ryan stared back at Lisa, feeling almost as if he should be ashamed of having talked about another woman. This was absurd.

"Who's Tess?" Lisa questioned, once Susan had left them to talk.

He blew out a breath of frustration as this was not what he wanted to get into at the moment. "She was someone I was involved with I'd rather not talk about, much like the life you keep under wraps yourself."

When Lisa straightened her back and stuck out her chin, just enough to be defiant, Ryan thought maybe he should have handled that better.

"Well, then I guess we don't have much to talk about then, do we?" Lisa retorted.

"Look, I don't want to get into it right now. What I really want to know is…"

Ryan was cut off by Maggie's loud bellow coming from the kitchen doorway.

"If you want to sit there all day I'm going to clock you out. Get to work girl, there's things to be done around here."

Lisa got up from her seat and started to walk away. Ryan reached out again and grabbed her hand. She stopped and glared at him.

"We're not finished with this conversation," he stated with firm authority.

"We'll see," Lisa said flatly and pulled her hand from him.

How did that go so wrong? Ryan wondered as he watched her walk away from him.

Chapter 6

The Lodge, nightlife hotspot for the more adventurous, Lisa found took much longer to reach than she'd expected. They'd been driving for what seemed like hours, when Tina finally turned to the right over a small waterway with a huge cedar log sign engraving simply stating 'Redford's'. Their destination was tucked away, in a place nobody would venture unless they had already found out about the resort. Near Forks, at the base of the Olympic Mountains, set high on the cliff side, a quaint cabin structure building looked over the rushing water of the Sol Duc River below. Soft flood lights strategically placed illuminated the beauty of the evergreens and bountiful colors of the flowering bushes all around them. Lisa may have enjoyed the view more if a cramp hadn't been forming in her leg since a few miles back.

"Not too far? That was a serious road trip," Lisa groaned as she and Tina got out of the car.

"You're used to city driving, where everything's within five minutes. Out here, an hour or more is about your normal drive to just about anywhere," Tina laughed.

Lisa pulled her backpack out of the car, the habit of bringing her treasured belongings wherever she went not easily broken.

"You're not seriously going to bring that ugly thing in with you, are you?" Tina asked with a distasteful glance at the bag.

The backpack definitely didn't match the mood of the evening. Nothing of her former self would. She felt a little like Cinderella, poor and destitute one minute a princess the next.

"I'm sorry. I guess I'm not like most people. I'm more comfortable having my things next to me."

Tina frowned, then her eyes brightened and a huge smile came to her pretty red lips. "Well, tonight we're going to throw all caution to the wind, and forget everything but having fun."

Sounded like a wonderful idea, but Lisa wasn't so sure she should take the risk of leaving her things behind. What if…?

She watched as Tina took some items from her small clutch and shoved them into her pockets. She walked over to hand the purse to Lisa along with the keys to the Isuzu.

"Tell you what – get what you absolutely need and hang onto this tonight. Here's the key to the car. Leave your bag and keep the keys. If you need to escape, take the car with you, it's more reliable and quicker than your feet."

"How would you get back home?" The incredulous trust of Tina shocked Lisa. Why did people trust so much around here?

Tina put a hand up to bounce her pretty blond curls, and winked at Lisa. "I think I might convince someone to give me a ride home."

"You're so bad," Lisa giggled.

"You know it! Now let's go have some fun."

They were greeted by a huge open fireplace in the middle of the front lobby, separating the check-in from a lounge area outfitted for comfort. Huge deep cushioned couches in browns and gold to match the rustic mood were brightened by orange and red throw pillows with the occasional blue or purple thrown in to give a splash of character. Ottomans and authentically carved end tables had been scattered about to serve as a place to set a drink or two.

The bar at the far side of the lounge reminded Lisa of an old western movie she'd seen once. Mirrors lined the wall behind the bearded stout bartender, upturned glasses lining the shelves beside every possible choice of alcohol she imagined. While he made his customers drinks, the bartender's gusty laugh filled the room as he chatted with them.

The warm air of the friendly setting smelled faintly of wood smoke, pipe smoke, and the deep scent of liquor. Lisa followed Tina, pulled along by the drifting atmosphere, to the right of the bar into the large area. She figured this must be the most popular dance venue on this side of the mountains. By the looks of it, Lisa could tell this room also served as the restaurant during the day, and was magically transformed to fit the ambiance of the nightlife crowd – of which there were more than she'd expected.

Little white sparkling lights swirled around posts and lined the edges of the walls and ceiling, combined with the dimmed main lights bringing a romantic quality to the old-fashioned rugged room. In one corner, a small bar had been set up to serve well-drinks for their thirstier customers wanting to get back out on the dance floor. People milled around the area, laughing and conversing with neighbors and long time friends.

Tables lined the log walls and dotted the floor between the four support poles in the center. In the opposite corner to the bar, a stage and dance floor displayed the main entertainment for the evening. The band, already in full swing, had brought everyone to their feet. Loud shouts came from behind her and Lisa turned sharply, relieved to find a group of people at the dartboards and card tables that stood in the far corner.

Her attention was drawn away from the glitter by the huge open glass doors at the far end of the room. They stood proud, surrounded by floor-to-ceiling windows draped sparsely in little twinkling lights. She moved toward the doors as a nice cool breeze ran across her shoulders, and she slipped past the crowd to stand at the entrance to an impressive split log cedar porch. From her viewpoint the edge of the steep cliff was visible, feeding to the river below by a tree covered ravine. Moonlight sparkled along the water's surface as it flowed westward toward the coastline.

As she stood engaged by the romance of it all, she heard a constant low rumble over the music inside. She stepped out further onto the deck and realized they were not so far away from the river, the sound she'd heard coming from the water crashing over crevices and rocks unearthed by its erosion-causing force. She breathed in deep, the crisp clean air cleansing her mind of the murky existence she endured. Lisa turned back, to the crowd mingling and enjoying themselves, and smiled.

Tina was right it was time to have some fun.

All of a sudden she was brought back to her vivid reality by a loud shout very close to her. A young man, a few feet from the door in front of her, waved an enthusiastic arm to someone who had just entered the club. She cringed, realizing she still needed to be careful, and glanced around to find the quickest exits. Out the back where she stood now, and down the porch would be the most difficult. Two other exits, where they had entered the building and one she noticed near the main bar by the restrooms would be the ones to use. Her preferred choice would be the one by the restrooms which gave her the better opportunity to disappear if she needed.

More at ease after having scoped the place out, she found Tina motioning her toward a table close to the dance floor.

"Here, this is the best spot. I can't believe I found a table in this crowd." Tina pulled out a chair and threw her jacket down. "I'm going to get a drink, you want one?"

"White wine is fine for now," Lisa replied surveying the space around their seats. The dance floor held enough space for a dozen or so couples at any one time, unless you wanted to dance in the aisles, which some had taken advantage of already.

"Todd. Todd…Come give me a hug." Tina yelled out over the din of music toward a young man coming in their direction. "Where have you been? I haven't seen you in ages."

Lisa could tell Tina was no stranger to anyone here. She shook her head as Tina made her way back to the bar. A variety of men, some young and some older, made their way toward the vivacious woman for their special greeting.

Lisa, disappointed Ryan hadn't arrived yet, soon forgot as she was whisked away to the dance floor. From that point on the dancing never stopped. She had no chance to sit and rest her feet. One after another of the eligible partners asked her to dance, some more than once.

Winded, she needed to catch her breath. As she stepped off the dance floor, one of the young men who danced with her before tapped her on the shoulder and pointed toward the crowded floor. She shook her head and smiled politely, but she had to say no. Her lungs were screaming for some fresh air. She searched the crowd for a pathway to get to the porch, and caught sight of a man standing against the doorpost. She didn't need for his face to be uncovered to know who belonged to the sleek mysterious figure.

He wore all black. The jeans fit him to perfection, molding against every curve of his muscular thighs. His button down shirt

125

opened at the neck with the sleeves rolled halfway up the forearm. The Stetson sat low enough to cover his eyes, but she'd become familiar enough to imagine the delights she would find beneath. He tilted his head in acknowledgement of her recognition of him.

She couldn't seem to move. The mere presence of him knocked the air out of her lungs. She stood still as he came toward her.

"You've been busy," he murmured, taking off his hat, to reveal the bright sparkling eyes she wanted to drown in every time she peered into their depths. "The boys have taken quite a liking to you."

He must have been there for a while.

Doesn't he realize I wouldn't waste my time with anyone else?

She had no interest in anyone but him.

Irritated Ryan hadn't made himself known before now, she tried to act indifferent to his statement, though his slow smile made her heart flutter.

"That's what you come here to do isn't it? Dance and have fun?" she responded, with a dry sarcasm in an attempt to throw him off the fact that she was thrilled by his being there.

"For some," he said, the familiar grin wavering at his lips. He moved closer to her, his innate power enveloping her senses.

"And what do the others come to do?" Lisa asked somewhat breathy.

He lifted his eyebrow in response and shrugged his shoulder.

"Did you bring a date?" Lisa asked as she looked around to see if anyone was coming to join him, still unsure whether he'd really come to see her. Then she remembered why he'd caused her some concern the day before. "Is Tess here with you?"

"No, I came alone." His terse response made her look up, his eyes were steely hard.

This made her even more curious. "Who is this Tess? Should I be worried she's going to come run me off?" Lisa looked around a bit nervous at the thought. Trying to seem nonchalant, she grinned up at him. "I don't want to butt into a budding relationship."

Ryan didn't seem to be very amused. "Not very likely," he muttered, glancing around the room.

"Really, who is she? Everyone around town is talking about her. Seems you two had something going on and she's coming back to reclaim it."

Their eyes met in a stand-off of sorts. She questioned whether she should even make the effort tonight. He'd visibly stiffened, with a fierce control on an anger swirling in his eyes, as if unsure whether to divulge any secrets. He glanced away for a brief minute then brought his gaze back to rest on her.

"All right, since you won't leave it alone, I'll tell you. Tess and I were engaged to be married a couple of years ago. She had second thoughts and called it off. I have no idea why she's decided to come back, but frankly I don't care," he retorted, his jaw tensed, lips thin and angry.

"Oh," Lisa said wondering if he jumped too fast. High anger usually meant high emotions. She furrowed her brows and glanced up to his face. "I was just asking."

Ryan was looking out to the crowd on the dance floor, and he made a slight stretch of his neck and took a long deep breath. She could tell there was something going on in his head, but didn't dare ask. As they stood in an uncomfortable silence the current fast dance music ended and the band slid into a soft smooth song calling for intimate contact to be made.

He turned back to her, a smile returning to his eyes and held his hand out to her. For a moment, she gazed up into his eyes then realized he'd asked her to dance.

"Now this is my type of music." He grasped her hand in his, the touch of his hand sending a thousand visceral tingles to run up her spine.

Lisa followed Ryan out to the dance floor unable to do otherwise. A few couples had already gotten close, and he pulled her against him, their bodies falling into step with one another. If she'd thought she couldn't breathe before, this rapture took the need to breathe swiftly away. At every point of contact a heated energy generated an unquestionable sexual excitement within her body. His thighs brushed against hers in a way to make her think of the long nights of passion she'd dreamt about since seeing him for the first time. Her cheek came up against his shoulder, and she peeked up to his strong profile. She took in a quick breath, the fragrance he wore intoxicating her even further.

His fingers trailed down her spine along the openness of her dress causing her to quiver inside with the unexpected touch. Lisa pulled herself closer to him, wanting never to let go. He in turn pulled her tighter, sliding one leg between hers, for the most intimate contact possible. There was absolutely no question as to what they both were experiencing.

They stayed locked in each other's arms, barely moving, through the next two slow dances. As if the whole world had frozen in time around them, with the only constant being the fire building between them.

Lisa became aware everything started hopping around them again and she stepped away with reluctance. The band's rendition of "Mustang Sally" had everyone on their feet again, ready to dance.

Ryan took hold of her hand and led her out into the coolness of the night air. She moved toward the edge of the deck a bit embarrassed at how wanton she'd acted on the dance floor.

Partially to cool off, she flipped her hair back over her shoulder in hopes he'd notice how she looked tonight. She'd pinned her hair up on both sides away from her face, leaving the curls to flow in abundance down her back. The swish of the hair against her shoulders reminded her how bare they were under the slender straps.

She sensed him come up behind her, his form shadowing the filtered glow from the porch lights. The subtle musk scent she'd grown to know as Ryan wrapped around her as if he'd taken her in his arms. Too aware of his body, she turned and drew in a quick breath. He placed a hand on either side of her on the deck railing, without a word his intimate act made her knees weak with anticipation.

His eyes, serious now, revealed an inner battle of wills. He stared at her for the longest time, appearing mad, but his body language told her otherwise.

"I don't know who you are, or why you've come to Lake Duchess, but right now I don't really care."

Lisa didn't even know what he'd said. All she knew was she had to taste those lips that teased her will to be strong every time she heard him speak.

As he bent down, he pressed his body against hers. Reaching up with one hand to grasp her neck in his palm, he brought his other arm around her waist to draw her even closer with a quick firm motion. His control of her was welcomed as she began to melt against him. His eyes bore into her soul as he brought his lips down to claim hers, which sent all mode of thought out of her head.

She brought her arms up to wrap around his neck, and feathered her fingers through his hair, searching for the textures she'd fantasized over. The close cut of the hair against his neck faded into a thicker smoothness making her wish they were someplace dark and quiet, where she would run her fingers all over his body.

The heat of his breath caressed her cheek in the cool night air, his lips seeking for more from her, and she gave without hesitation. She opened for him, and he took the lead. She'd never been kissed quite like this before. Sure, she'd been French kissed before, but this seemed different – as if he demanded more than a kiss. He pressed her for an answer to an unspoken question, and she responded back with everything she had. Her heart pounded so hard, by the time he lifted his head from hers she thought for sure he would hear the thunderous beats, too.

The anger in his eyes had dissipated to a low smoldering, causing Lisa to crave the taste of his lips against hers again. He still held her close, and as he traced a line down her cheek, he followed his finger with a nip of his teeth at her jaw line.

"I've wanted to do this since the first time I saw you."

"Me too," she said, wanting to kick herself for sounding so lame. "I mean, you…" she said sounding even lamer. "I mean…you know what I mean…" Unable to form a clear sentence yet, she let the words drift away.

Ryan grinned at her, his eyes sparkling in the moonlight as he glanced over her shoulder.

"That must be why I can't keep my hands off of you," he said indicating with a nod of his head behind her. "Look, a full moon."

She turned in his arms with her back to him and was glad he kept her close, his arms wrapped around her waist. The full sphere of the moon shone bright against the darkness of the surrounding heavens, like a cool reverse version of the sun during daylight.

"You smell so good," he whispered in her ear sending voracious tingles throughout her body, to hover over her abdomen tempting further action.

Ryan began to nibble on her neck below her ear, making her want to surrender all inhibitions. She leaned her head back against his chest, not sure if she would be able to take much more. With the quickened rise and fall of his chest his breaths became heavy against the wet kisses on her neck, the heat of it against her skin igniting every possible sexual response within her.

Before tonight, Lisa never imagined he felt the same way about her. Now absolutely no question existed. She started to think she must be asleep. This had to be one of those lifelike dreams she would wake from, only to wish for the fantasy to be real.

"Hey, why don't you two get a room?" A familiar voice joked from behind.

Shocked back to reality, Lisa stepped out of Ryan's arms begrudging the intrusion. She would have stayed as long as he'd wanted. He immediately raised his leg up to hook the heel of his boot on the deck railing as Tina came up next to them to lean against the railing, her back to the beautiful landscape. He flashed a quick grin at Lisa, and she wondered what he was thinking.

"Hey, full moon. Better watch out the vampires will come out to get you."

"Don't be silly," Lisa muttered trying to pull her composure back together.

"No joke. This town's known for their neck biters. Some movie was filmed out there in the bushes, and now people come all the time to seek out the freaks."

"I'm sure I can handle the freaks, in whatever form they come in," Ryan mumbled staring into the crowded club behind her. Lisa peered over her shoulder, wondering who he was talking about. His gaze seemed to be intent on someone. Her nerves began a slow rise to the top when she realized she hadn't been paying attention to anything around her. Better keep her eyes open, she didn't want to be surprised.

"You two seem to be enjoying yourselves." Tina laughed when Lisa gave her an exasperated glare. "Too bad I can't do the same," she pouted.

"I thought you were having fun, seems like you know everyone here," Lisa said as Tina waved to someone inside.

"Oh yeah, but they're all so boring. Michael came tonight." Tina wrapped her arms around herself and hugged. "He and I've had this thing going on for a while now. He is so dreamy."

"Dreamy?" Ryan asked as he rolled his eyes at her.

"Oh, stop," Tina shot back. "You wouldn't understand."

Lisa was amused by their exchange, like brother and sister. She let out a soft laugh at Ryan's bemused expression.

"Anyway, he asked me to go party with him after, but I told him I can't. This isn't really the kind of party I'd want to take someone else along."

Tina looked directly at Ryan, indicating Lisa with a motion of her head.

Lisa frowned. "He can't bring you back home?"

"No, he's got to work tomorrow. There wouldn't be enough time for him to get back. I'd need my own wheels."

"I'll bring Lisa back home with me." Ryan responded without hesitation.

Before Lisa was able to open her mouth to respond, Tina jumped up from her resting place and gave Ryan a hug from behind. Tina peeked around his shoulder and gave Lisa an animated wink.

"Awesome. You're a life saver. Ryan, you're the best."

Lisa realized Tina had planned this whole thing out. She wouldn't call her on the ruse now. Not wanting to make her friend out to be the conniver that she was, Lisa would address this with her later, not in front of Ryan.

"Keys please," Tina said reaching her hand out. "Keep the bag. I've got all I need in my pockets. I'll put your backpack in Ryan's truck."

Lisa dug into the clutch and brought the keys out. As she placed them in Tina's hand, she pulled her close and whispered in her ear, "You are in so much trouble. We're going to talk about this later."

The mischievous grin on Tina's face was unmistakable as she waved the keys around in the air.

"Have fun. Later!"

Then all of a sudden she disappeared as if she'd never been anywhere near.

Lisa glanced up to Ryan, his expression as surprised as hers.

"I wonder if anyone has ever told her she's as transparent as a window?" he chortled.

Lisa had to laugh. He'd seen right through Tina as well.

Ryan expression turned serious again and he reached out to run his fingers down her bare arm, their eyes met and her stomach began to flutter again.

As if on cue, the clutch in her hand began to vibrate, the buzz clearly audible. Ryan's eyes narrowed at her as she pulled the cell from the bag, but she had to make sure the care facility wasn't calling about her mother. All evening she'd tried to ignore Matt's incessant calls, but it couldn't be done effectively for very long.

Stuffing the phone back into the purse, Ryan's expression made her very uncomfortable, and the doubts began to surface again.

What am I thinking? I know better. How can I start a relationship with Ryan – with anyone? I don't even know if I'll be here tomorrow.

Without explanation, she shook her head. "I think you better take me home."

The drive home was a quiet one. Ryan noted Lisa's immediate withdrawal from him, as soon as the call came through on her cell. He'd been there when she and Tina arrived at the Lodge, but stayed out of sight wanting to survey her in another environment and find out how she carried herself with others. Her immediate check for exits and the intense scrutiny of the people already in the building had been expected. This appeared to be her constant mode of operation. Deep down he saw, in between the nervousness, a happy, carefree woman crying out to be let free.

What struck him hardest was the way she looked tonight. He'd never seen her in anything but a pair of jeans and a t-shirt. Even that was enough for him to want more of her.

Tonight she'd literally transformed into a goddess, the radiance of her inner and outer beauty only enhanced by the change of clothes. The shimmering essence of her deep brown eyes and the hints of golden flames in her hair were brought out by the peach colored hue of the dress clinging perfectly against the curves of her body.

He'd had to work up the nerve to move through the swarm of admirers to ask this Aphrodite for a dance. The more he watched her dance in the arms of another man, the more he realized he wanted to be that man. When she'd finally ended up in his arms on the deck, he'd lost himself for a few minutes. Lost in what could only be described as a moment destined to happen.

Her lips begged him for the kiss ever since the day he'd seen her at Maggie's. Something about her pulled at him in so many ways he couldn't decide which one to act on first. Curiosity to find out who she really was, the need to protect her from what she feared, a definite sexual chemistry he'd sensed from the start – each with their own level of need.

Tonight though, no question existed in his mind as to which one held priority. He needed to touch her and to have her next to him, in the closest way possible. That's why he'd waited for the slow song to come up before making her aware of his presence. And from that moment on he'd no intention of letting her go.

Maggie's back bedroom light turned off quickly when they pulled into the driveway. He had no doubt she'd been worried and waited for Lisa's return.

"Thank you so much. I appreciate you bringing me home," Lisa said nervously, and reached for the door handle.

"Hold on there," Ryan said, grasping her hand in mid reach. "You must not be used to having a gentleman around."

Lisa smiled and gave a sheepish shake of her head.

"I've been taught whenever you take a lady home, you open the door and walk her to her door." He sensed her unease with his actions, yet he had no intention of doing anything but treat her as she should be treated. Beside the fact, he wanted to check things out and make sure everything appeared safe.

At the top of the stairs, Lisa's hands shook as she fumbled with the keys, so he took them from her hand and reached around to unlock the door. He stayed for a moment where he was, her back pressed against him, fighting the need to gather her into his arms again. She didn't move away from him, but someone had to make the first move, so he opened the door to let her enter.

Lisa flipped on the light before stepping through the doorway and took a quick glance around, as he'd expected her to do. He didn't see anything out of place, and she apparently didn't either. Ryan set her backpack down against the wall, and she tossed the clutch on the stand beside the door. She turned toward him and came square up against his chest.

Ryan had been thinking of their kiss on the deck all the way home. Some time had passed since his last encounter with a female, but he swore something was different about her kiss. He was bothered his reaction to her had been so strong, and he wasn't exactly sure why he'd kissed her in that way. With Tina's interruption, he hadn't been given the chance to find out.

Now with nobody to intrude, he needed to determine what made him feel so out of control. He stood for a moment, her body pressed against his, one arm extended to keep her from moving away. At first, she stood stiff, as if unsure how to act. She held his gaze steady, a touch of indecision flashing from under her the long lashes. He heard an exasperated breath escape her through her lips and she began to soften her stance against him.

He searched her eyes for something, anything. She didn't appear to be scared. Sometimes his size became disconcerting, overpowering those around him. Her gaze captured his curiosity, pleading with him in a way for something more.

Slowly he bent his head to claim the lips he swore called out to him. Her immediate response excited him. She grasped the moment, and pulled him closer to her, not waiting for him to push any farther and took as much as she gave back in the impact of her kiss. He felt an inner passion surface in her, the heat at maximum blast pouring through her embrace, as if she'd been starved of intimate contact and found it necessary to drink in as much as possible at each opportunity.

He couldn't help himself, his kisses became more insistent and he began fondling her round curves from behind, pressing her body closer and closer to the immediate erection she'd prompted from him. The moan that came from her throat was like the call of the wild, her inner beast responding to him without hesitation. Her hand came up to explore his chest, the other to grasp his neck and pull him down to her eager lips.

Again, the phone buzzed with an incoming call. He almost didn't hear, but she stiffened slightly in his arms, and he knew something was wrong. She continued the kiss though he knew her attention no longer stayed intent on him. The phone beeped with a message and began buzzing with another incoming call. This time he wasn't able to ignore it.

Pulling away from her was harder than he thought. He had to get things straight with her, here and now. He didn't let her go, but placed his forehead on hers. He took a minute to sort out his thoughts. Everything had jumbled together into this bundle of passion called Lisa.

"Who are you?" he whispered, not yet able to catch his breath.

Silent, she closed her eyes and shook her head as if talking to herself. Then her eyes opened and darted away from him when the phone began to beep again. At that point, he knew what he had to do.

He carefully took her by the shoulders, and pulled her away from him. The expression on her face almost tore him apart. The exhaustion buried deep among the folds of anguish, and what looked to be the pain of rejection, resonated over her face.

"Until you tell me what is going on, I can't help you Lisa." Her continued silence disappointed him. He walked toward the door and stopped, with his back toward her and his hand on the door jam in front of him. She'd stirred things up in him he didn't know still existed. He hadn't felt this way about anyone in a very long time—if ever.

Turning back around, he took a very long look at the woman in front of him. She stood in silence. Now instead of being full of life and exploring the moment as she had a few minutes before, her head hung low in surrender to her situation.

"I want to know you better. There's no question we have something between us." He waited for her eyes to come back to him. When they did, they were full of tears, ones he wished he hadn't caused. "Until you can come forward to tell me who you really are and what's going on, I think you know you can't expect me to continue."

Lisa shook her head slowly. The pain he saw in her eyes tore him apart.

He turned back to open the door. Before he stepped out he stood for a moment looking out into the dark tree covered lawn.

"It's your choice what you do. I'll be waiting."

Chapter 7

Lisa didn't sleep at all. Remnants of her conversation with Ryan, the emotions he'd aroused with his kisses, and the nightmare of the life she'd been living for so long kept drifting in and out of her dozing state of mind. She rose several times throughout the night to sit with her feet dangling from the side of the bed, dazed and staring at the wall.

By daybreak, her image in the mirror disgusted her. Dark circles had formed under her eyes again, and she felt like hell. Not caring to go to any trouble, Lisa pulled her hair back from her face into a ponytail, the curls cascading down the back of her neck like a waterfall.

At some point during the night, she'd made up her mind. She finally understood what she needed to do. The words of Tina caused her to take a real hard look at what she had been doing.

'Don't let the bully win,' was something her mother had taught her. Naturally quiet, Lisa learned at a young age to stand her ground and not be intimidated by the rougher, more aggressive, people around her. Although some enjoyed having a mean nature, most acted like bullies because they hadn't matured enough to figure out how to get their way in any other method.

'You're not going to fly in the middle of the night because of your pride.'

Tina's words kept playing over and over in her mind, which made her stop to scrutinize her own actions. What she thought was strength might very well be her egotistical pride not willing to be seen as being weak.

Other than basic survival, the necessity to take care of others before thinking of her own personal needs had become a natural way of life. She couldn't remember ever asking for help. Through college, she'd taken care of her father in his failing health, without much help from her mother, whose waning memory took her far from the present day.

She may have shown strength then, but now she admitted to herself she really did need more help from people around her. Just like now, an abundance of resources were at her fingertips, yet she hadn't taken advantage of them. If that wasn't enough, she'd met the most amazing man. They had one hell of a chemistry going on between them, and if she believed strong enough, it could turn into something more.

If what she'd discovered with him didn't show her this was the time to do something about her situation she didn't know what would. He was right. She knew they couldn't continue without her telling him the truth. The whole truth, even if it meant putting an end to the start of something she felt promised something wonderful. She prayed her efforts to make things right with the people she'd wronged would hold some weight with him—and maybe, just maybe, he would have a way to put an end to this nightmare.

Lisa took one last look in the mirror and grimaced. She mumbled to her reflection, "Better you find out how he feels now. You're going to fall hopelessly in love with him and then have to tell him you lied straight to his face—a perfect way to start."

The risk she took in telling her true story was minimal to the suffering she now endured. So what if she went to jail for theft and never taught children again. She had to believe she could find other ways to support herself and be just as happy. But it was time to change. She couldn't keep doing the same thing over and over again. If she didn't do something soon she might as well sign herself into a mental hospital.

Today was her day off, a good day to carry out what she'd decided on doing. As she packed her artist tablet and pencils in her backpack, she noted the change of clothes rolled up in the bottom. Her new frame of mind prompted her to take them out then almost immediately she changed her mind. She wasn't ready yet to let go. Not yet. She might still need them.

The walk to the Sheriff's office was pleasant enough, though her stomach churned the whole way there. She kept going over in her mind how she would tell Ryan what he needed to hear.

Should I just blurt it out, or slide into my explanation with a little bit of finesse?

As she walked toward the station, she saw Ryan's patrol car parked out front, and the open door revealed he sat behind his desk. One foot propped against his knee with a book open in his lap. It was a huge with a bright green cover. It appeared to be a textbook of some sort—not something she'd imagined he would read.

Her steps caused the gravel under foot to grate, and he looked up from his book to watch her as she came up the steps.

She saw he wore jeans over a pair of dirty work boots. Not the usual attire for being on duty. Inside the doorway, she stood in silence, unsure of how to phrase her words. His intent gaze was analytical, offsetting her original approach.

Ryan didn't say a word, but he closed and placed the book on the desk in front of him. Lisa glanced at the title and thought the subject matter a little unusual for him to be studying. 'Indigenous Plants of Washington State' reminded her she really had no idea what his personal life was like, and she wondered what he'd planned to do this afternoon. Her gaze came back up to meet his eyes and her stomach fluttered again. Their eyes locked and she sensed he already understood everything without her having to say a word.

Quick to clear her throat, the words came to her, not in the smooth confident way in which she'd practiced them. Rather, she blurted out what she needed to say in a rushed disclosure.

"My name is Lisa Hill. I'm originally from Columbus, Ohio. My Bachelor's degree is in the Fine Arts and I have a Master's in Education with an emphasis on art."

She stopped to take a deep breath. Ryan continued his silence, and leaned back in his chair to wait for her to continue.

"I grew up in a small town in Ohio. My father passed away seven years ago, and my mother is at the Marshall Care Center in Columbus for a latent stage of Alzheimer's disease. I've had to leave my home because my ex-fiancée has been chasing me for the last four years. He wants to kill me. I've barely escaped with my life a couple of times, and he just keeps finding me. He's on the trail right now." Lisa swallowed hard, and paused before stating the hardest part. "I need...I need your help to figure out how to stop him."

She didn't know if she could continue with the next part. Out of breath and growing more emotional with each confession, her tears flowed steadily down her cheeks, which made it hard to make out Ryan's expression. He didn't move so she began to believe she should just turn around and leave, but she knew she had to say the rest or just plain give up on all hope.

Gravel seemed to gather in her throat as she forced herself to continue. "I've had to do some things…" She gulped down hard and balled her fists together. "I've stolen money, and pawned the engagement ring for my own personal gain, which makes me a thief. I've given it all back, all except the ring. So I expect you'll put me in jail now."

Still no movement came from Ryan, so she held out her hands, wrists together, and waited with tears coming hot and heavy. Maybe he really was going to lock her up. She couldn't tell.

He arose and moved toward her, only to close the door behind her and gather her into his muscular protective arms. She pressed her face into his chest, soaking in his strength. The fresh scent of clean clothes and the soap from his recent shower seemed to bolster her new sense of hope.

Yet still confused, Lisa muttered, "Aren't you going to put me behind bars where criminals belong?"

He gave a soft laugh. "No, not unless you tell me you've done something far worse." She raised her face to look up into his eyes. His brows furrowed. "You haven't, have you?"

Lisa shook her head vehemently and shoved her face back into his shoulder.

"Your thievery, as you put it, was done out of my jurisdiction. Besides, it sounds as if you've made amends. In terms of the engagement ring, was it given to you willingly?"

Lisa nodded and peeked up again. He had an odd smile in his eyes, though he kept a somber face, just like her father would when he was about to lay out punishment for something she'd done.

"Did the person who gave the ring to you ever ask for it back?"

"Well, no." Lisa straightened up, fully engaged in where Ryan had taken this conversation.

He seemed to consider her answer, and then glanced down. She waited, her breath shallow, in anticipation to his next words.

"Then, it seems to me it was yours to do with as you wished. Other than perhaps a small moral implication, I'd say there is no wrong in what you found yourself having to do because of his actions."

The air in her lungs swooshed out all at once. Did he really mean what he just said?

Ryan continued, "However, if you ever do anything like that here, I will have no qualms in locking you away. Understood?"

"Yes, sir, I do." Fully chastised, Lisa bent her head and clasped her hands in front of her.

Oh my God, does this mean I'm clear of any legal repercussions?

Tears of relief started to trickle down her cheek. The guilt she'd built up began to slowly drift away. He was right though, morally she still needed to make this last wrong right. She wouldn't stop until she found that ring and gave it back. She wanted no hidden ties to Matt.

Ryan pulled her against him and placed his chin on top of her head, and then all of a sudden he pulled away from her placing his hand under her chin to lift her face up.

"Is that why you've never gone to the authorities? Because you thought you'd be put in jail?"

She nodded her head, and gave a small sniffle.

He shook his head and pulled her back against him. "I can't imagine how keeping a clean record is more important than having him put away. I'm sure the judge would have taken a close look at the circumstances and ruled in your favor."

"I didn't know. I couldn't risk it."

"Why?"

Lisa clasped her hands together, "Because all those years of hard work would have been put to waste. No school would willingly place their students at risk by giving a teaching position to someone with a legal record. I'd never teach again."

"What made you change your mind?"

Did she dare tell him he'd been the reason? She'd had enough, and he'd given her what she needed to make that change, even if it meant sacrificing her dreams. Unsure of what she should say, she shrugged her shoulders and hugged him closer.

Ryan moved back far enough to place his fingers under her chin and bring her face up close to place a tender kiss on her lips. The compassion in his eyes took her breath away. She grasped hold of the moment and wrapped her hand around the back of his neck to pull him down for another kiss. Words escaped her, but she made sure to pour her heart into the kiss, to show him how thankful she was for his understanding.

He was the one to break the contact and placed his hands on either side against the door behind her, lowering his forehead down to hers.

"You don't give a man a chance to think straight, do you?" he said with a soft laugh. "We'll explore that side of things soon enough. For right now, we need to talk about this problem you've got."

She didn't want to let go, afraid he would rethink his position if he heard the details of her sordid past.

"You're going to need to let go so we can talk," he said, but she shook her head and pressed her nose back into his shoulder.

"All right then," he appeased. With her arms still tightly wrapped around him, he picked her up and sat down on the bench along the wall. Comfortable on his lap, her legs dangled, his size making her almost like a young girl in her father's lap.

"Why don't you tell me more about this fiancée who's been chasing you?" Ryan asked as he settled himself for a long explanation.

"Ex-fiancée," Lisa corrected to make sure he understood her position. She then recanted what she'd told Tina, giving a little more detail on the progression of her relationship with Matt. She kept checking Ryan's reaction at certain points, but his expression never changed. She appreciated the professional side of him was hard at work gathering the facts, though she hoped he didn't conduct interviews like this one too often.

"Huffing propane?" he asked in the same manner as Tina. "That is really quite unusual. Although, I suppose propane has the same effect as butane or gasoline. I've read about inhalant use, but haven't had any occurrences to deal with during my service time."

"Believe me you don't want to. Especially involving someone you care about."

"No, I imagine that would be difficult." Ryan gave her a squeeze. "I wonder what would make someone take to breathing in something as nasty as propane."

"He said it was easier to get and had a longer effect. I think he said he can still feel it in his system for up to a month."

"Must be hard to hold down a job," Ryan speculated.

"He claims that's why he can't get a job, especially if it requires a blood test."

"No job? So how does he survive? He must get spending money from somewhere." Ryan's brows furrowed.

"He said once that his grandmother left him some money that he gets every once in a while. Other than that he does some odd janitorial and yard work type jobs, nothing that lasts for very long. Once in a while the band he plays in gets money for a gig or two. I guess he makes just enough to fund his habit." Lisa said with a small sniffle. The tears had stopped, though now her nose had started to run.

"Very convenient," Ryan grimaced. "Doesn't sound like he brings in enough consistently to pay the rent, so where does he live? He doesn't live at home with his parents, does he?"

"No. His dad apparently kicked him out a couple of years before I knew him." Lisa looked down at her clasped hands. The knuckles were white against her cold hands. She let go of the hold and mentally shook off the tenseness she felt settling over her. She took in a deep breath and let it out slow.

"Where was he living when you met him?"

"Said he'd been staying at his church's shelter for about six months, but I didn't find this out until after he'd moved in with me. When he doesn't have a place to stay, he lives in his van. I really thought he was just an unemployed musician, in search of a better life."

"Sounds like he had you believing all sorts of things," Ryan shook his head.

"He told me later the church had kicked him out a couple weeks before he moved in with me. Supposedly, they didn't like his lifestyle. I thought he meant his night life and playing non-Christian music in a band at bars and clubs. Now I think he meant he'd started using again, and they couldn't put up with that lifestyle."

"No doubt," he concurred and reached down to grasp one of her hands in his.

Lisa stared down at their joined hands for a moment.

"Is it true because gas is a legal substance he can't be picked up for possession or for his personal use to inhale the stuff?" she asked, suddenly realizing she had a chance to prove something she'd always wondered.

"That's a tricky question. It's true, however if the user's actions become violent, or in some way endangers others around him, then he can be picked up for those reasons."

"Oh," she said, almost resigned again to not being able to do anything about her situation. "The only thing I could ever get was a restraining order on him for the threats he made. Thing is, I figured he'd break in to kill me before the cops would get there to save me."

Ryan was silent for a moment. "When did you last talk to any official about his actions?"

"I don't know, I guess back when he started to harass me. They told me the law stated the harassment order could be employed and they would wait for him to break the ruling."

"When was that?"

"I'd had the locks changed, but he broke into the apartment."

"Was he still living with you?"

"Well, not really. After I'd asked him to leave when I broke off the engagement, he'd been gone for over a month. I boxed up his things and waited for him to pick them up, but he never did. Then he broke in one afternoon when I was at work, and he was still there when the cops arrived. Luckily my neighbor saw him break the lock on the door and called 911. Matt told the officer he'd lost his keys and wanted to get his stuff."

"So he's been taken to jail for this already. Surprised he wasn't kept in longer," Ryan stated with his brows furrowed.

"He'd never been picked up for anything serious, and this was before he'd started the harassing calls and the restraining order. His dad was apparently on the police force for many years, so the judge slapped his hand and told him not to do it again. The thing is, he can be so convincing when he wants to be."

Lisa pulled a tissue from her pocket to dry the remaining tears on her lashes.

"You could have had him charged with burglary."

"But he didn't take anything."

"Doesn't matter, breaking and entering is burglary in every state I know."

"The cops told me what he did was called a domestic dispute and the only charge would be harassment, so they suggested I file the restraining order on him."

Ryan shook his head.

"Even after the threatening phone calls, they still said the restraining order was all they could enforce. Then if he was caught, they would only impose a monetary punishment. Lot of good that would do, he doesn't care about money and he doesn't have any anyway."

"A criminal prosecution is hard to get in these cases, frustrating for both the victim and the legal officers I imagine. I understand most departments funding is pretty scarce and the allocation of manpower to prove this type of thing is almost nonexistent. "

Lisa nodded her head sadly, only too aware of how limited her options were. The familiar exhaustion began to set in again.

"When I broke things off he told me he wouldn't let me go, and we belonged together. He said he would never leave. After he'd been taken to the station when he broke in, he told me I shouldn't have gotten the law involved, and I needed to pay for what I'd done."

Ryan took a deep breath and nodded. She watched as his eyes became hard and narrowed, as if he was all too familiar, and she wondered if he had a personal connection with a situation like hers.

"One night he broke in and came after me with a crowbar. I swear he looked as if he were about to kill me. Luckily, I got away from him." Lisa closed her eyes and shivered in memory of that first time she'd let him get close enough. "He still leaves messages saying he plans to kill me, and details of how he's going to do it."

"If you had gone to the authorities then they would pick him up for violating the order, with an intent to harm, and burglary, which would carry a stricter punishment."

"I did, but they told me they weren't able to find him and I should go stay with someone. After a couple of weeks they suggested I move, and if anything else happened to give them a call."

Ryan shook his head. "I hate to say it, but they probably didn't keep trying after that first night."

"So, I guess I can't do much now." Lisa raised her hands to rub vigorously at her face. Not seeing beyond what she continued to believe as her impending fate, her newfound relief seemed to crash around her.

"Not necessarily," Ryan said gripping her a little tighter when she tried to move from his lap. Lisa caught his gaze had locked on the edge of his desk at a picture, its frame tilted away from her. "I'm not as restricted here as they may be in the bigger cities. We can figure out some way to take care of this—the right way."

"How?"

Ryan allowed Lisa to stand, and he rose to walk over to his desk. With a gentle movement, he picked up the frame and gazed at the image it held then placed it back down and turned toward her.

"Sooner or later he'll make a big mistake—one that will cost him his freedom. I'll be there to catch him." He walked to her and put his hands on her shoulders. "I'm sworn to protect all people, especially the inhabitants of Lake Duchess. You are no different. You live here now. I will do whatever needs to happen to keep you safe." Then a little twinkle began to glimmer in his eyes. "Besides, you are a special interest to me. I need to keep you unharmed."

She rose up to her toes to press her lips against his. The heat from the returned kiss reminded her of the unspoken passion between them—of things yet to come, or at least Lisa prayed feverishly would happen. She took the lead to convey her feelings for him as well. There was no denying the connection they had between them. His kisses became more insistent as he pulled her closer. Her inner response to him overpowered all other thoughts.

Again, Ryan stepped away and took in a deep breath. He kept his distance and reached up to caress her cheek with the palm of his hand. "I think we better put a hold on that for a bit longer."

Lisa wanted nothing more than to get closer, much closer. This, however, was neither the time nor the place to carry through with what seemed to be her body's one track mind. So she moved over to his desk and raised the picture he'd picked up earlier. A beautiful woman of Native American Indian decent, in her late twenties, was dressed in simple attire. Her glorious long black hair covered her shoulders, and with pride in her eyes, her hands were placed on the shoulders of a young boy who stood in front of her. Lisa peered closer and saw the resemblance right away. The young boy was Ryan, and the young woman his mother.

"She's beautiful," she said in earnest. "Does she live here in the area?"

A slight cloud passed over Ryan's face, and Lisa noticed a brief sadness along with it. "No, she passed away when I was young."

"Oh, I'm so sorry. What about your father, is he still here?" she questioned finding herself wanting to know more.

A darker cloud hung over his expression. "He's at the state penitentiary."

"Oh," she wasn't really sure how else to respond. His closed attitude showed he didn't want to go into any more detail, so she delayed asking any more questions.

She glanced away, the silence a bit uncomfortable. Without any warning, her stomach made a loud grumbling noise. Surprised, she placed her hand over her tummy and raised her eyebrows. She hadn't even thought about eating since her quick lunch the day before.

Ryan reached out to grab her hand. "I think it's time for breakfast, don't you?"

All of a sudden, the door burst open, and a woman of questionable taste came through the door. The first thing Lisa noticed was the array of short ice blonde hair, curled in short little ringlets all over the woman's head. Next was the ungodly amount of dark make-up she wore around her eyes. She looked as if she were about to pop out of her tight bright red spandex top, and shorts that had been cut off just a little too short for a woman of her age.

"Ryan, have you heard? My baby's coming home. She's coming back to us! I rushed all the way home from Hawaii when she

154

called. I can't believe it, she's finally coming home," the middle-aged woman squealed as she rushed toward Ryan.

The woman pushed Lisa out of the way with the wiggle of her hips between the two of them she wrapped her arms around Ryan, and placed her head against his chest. Lisa backed away her legs coming into contact with the desk. No place left to go, unless she crawled on top to save herself from being squished. Luckily, Ryan managed to peel himself off of the gregarious individual and stepped back.

"Angela," he acknowledged. Lisa could see his eyes shuttered any type of emotion, as was his voice cool and bland.

"Didn't you hear me? She's coming home to us. You must be excited," the woman exclaimed reaching out to shake his arm in her ring-encrusted fist.

She caught sight of Lisa in her peripheral vision and turned slowly to face her, making an obvious show of looking her up and down. Her lips curled, accusation written all over her face.

The woman turned back to Ryan. "Who's the tramp?"

* * * *

"Shit, I need a drink or a huff," Matt groaned and reached over to the passenger seat to search for the bottle of liquor he'd purchased a few miles back.

There were only a few sips left. Swerving to his left as he opened the lid, the driver of an oncoming car blasted his horn.

"Fuck you too." Matt threw him the finger and slurped down the rest of the whisky. He tossed the bottle into the floor with the rest of the trash. The music from the radio played so loud it was amazing

155

he'd even heard the horn. Tapping his hands on the wheel in rhythm to the music, he wished he could make a stop to put an end to this constant crap running through his head.

What he needed was his favorite Fender guitar back. At least then he could draw some of this frustration out of his system. He longed for the feel of the strings beneath his fingers. There was nothing much like it. His Fender was the most important thing in his life.

He'd get it back. His former band members couldn't hold his baby hostage. Okay, so he'd busted up a couple of their amps when they told him he wasn't in the band any longer. So what? They deserved it. That didn't give them the right to lock his baby away until he paid for the damage.

The drive alone for such a long time was hard. For once he wished his brain would just stop working. Matt laughed. The only way to do that is die or huff another tank of shit. That would do it.

But he didn't stop to huff because doing so would delay his getting to Lake Duchess. No way. He couldn't allow that to happen. Not again. He had to find Lisa. Fucking whore—he'd teach her a lesson, too.

Images kept flashing through his mind, increasing with every hour he drove. So real and painful were the memories that he screamed out, wanting them to stop. In the past, he'd tried exercise, physical exertion, reading, and television, anything to take his mind away from the horrible scenes. But nothing worked—nothing but huffing the crap out of some propane.

His eyes caught sight of the white tank in the back of the van. The temptation seemed to call out to him, to beg and plead for him to take a whiff. The result of giving in always paid off. It would do him right. It always did.

He tried to ignore his need for the total serenity the stuff would give him. If only he were to pull off somewhere and surrender. He forced himself to stare at the road in front of him. There were times he wished some magic pill would make it all go away, but none of that shit worked either. Once his mom had taken him to the doctor and they gave him a drug to clear his ability to bring up these horrible images. They weren't worth the money she'd spent on them. The side effects caused this lethargic sensation that seemed to last forever. Weeks after he stopped taking the medication he still had no desire to play the guitar. It just wouldn't come to him—the drive was gone. He didn't want to do anything but sit in front of the television allowing the pictures to run on and on in front of him.

At least with the propane everything would disappear. A euphoric happiness would settle over him. Nothing else mattered. Sure, he'd pass out off and on, but that was part of the high. When he needed to come back to reality, within a day or two he would be back to normal and could go on as if nothing had happened. The problem was he craved the effect. The stuff had started to command his every move, and he had a hard time staying away.

God how he wanted a tank right now.

He caught a whiff of something putrid and made a face. Smelled like rotten Chinese food. Must be the Mongolian beef he'd picked up a while ago. He'd wondered where that had ended up.

Garbage was nothing new. Since he'd been kicked out of the band, he'd been living in his van again. The effects of which had started to pile up in the back. Time to make a stop somewhere and empty the trash, it didn't matter where, just someplace to dump the stuff.

He was used to this life. He moved from place to place every night so as not to be picked up for vagrancy. Though he'd found, if he chose to park in dark spaces at parking lots of stores open 24 hours, there was less chance of his vehicle raising attention. Security at those places were not as interested in something that showed no activity. Once he got his bottle of wine, he'd settle in and drink himself to sleep for the night. Though huffing had to take place in vacant lots or covered areas where there was a better chance of not being found as sometimes it could last for days. Roaming had become a way of life for him. Between drinking for a day or two, and huffing propane-which could take up to a week-Matt lived his life not caring from one day to the next what happened to him.

Music was special, though. Unfortunately, the natural high he got from that was short lived. Playing the lead on an awesome piece like his Fender brought up sensations of power and excitement. It made him feel a joy that was unmatched by anything.

That is until he'd met Lisa. She'd made things different. Now all he thought about was her. To be with her again was everything he wanted. She'd made him hope again. She'd made him want again.

He'd screwed that up too, and she'd left him. Bitch had no right to leave him. She was his. He'd given her that damn ring, and now she'd made him look like a no good thief to his father.

A car passed on a straightaway and Matt looked down at the couple inside snuggled together, the girl's head resting on the driver's shoulder. It reminded him of his goal. He was going to get Lisa back. She would be that girl with her head on his shoulder. A smile drifted across his face.

Yeah, that's what it's all about.

All of a sudden his fantasy turned ugly as he envisioned Lisa snuggled up to the young man in that car. Fury boiled under the surface and he felt an unmatched anger spring up from his gut. She'd better not be with anybody else. He wasn't sure what he'd do if he found her with some other guy.

Pounding his hands against the dashboard, he yelled at the top of his lungs, almost running the van off the side of the road.

"You bitch! You're mine. I'm going to get you for this."

Chapter 8

Ryan came into Maggie's to search for Lisa. There hadn't
been much time to see each other, and he discovered some news he
thought she should hear. He'd also been debating whether to ask her
something.

Angela called out to him, her bright neon pink bangles
flashing against her sunshine yellow dress, waving her hand at him
as he came through the door. For a split second, she reminded him of
her daughter, Tess—God forbid. Earl, her husband, sat across from
her his nose pointed toward his plate with an intent purpose. She
continued to rattle on about something to him, and he obviously was
not paying much attention. He was a quiet man, hard worker, and
good father. Ryan never had understood what he saw in his wife. He
gave a soft laugh.

*But then who am I to judge, I fell for his equally flamboyant
daughter, didn't I?*

Ryan politely waved back, but sat on the other side of the
restaurant in hopes she wouldn't come bother him again about Tess.
Angela had been a nuisance ever since she got back into town. Tess
this and Tess that. He was sick and tired of hearing Tess's name pop
up everywhere.

He looked around the serving area. Lisa wasn't anywhere
that he could see. Tina was at the register with a customer, so he set
his cup on the edge of the table to wait for her to bring some coffee.

Lisa had been busy at the restaurant most of the time. He'd
been side tracked by a call he'd gotten by the attending doctor at the

160

prison. When he'd gotten the call he'd been at Maggie's house the night before, doing a check for any unusual activity. Lisa's fears had not been taken lightly, nor were his promises to keep her safe. He would have spent some time with her, but needless to say, his attitude was far from companionable after the call, and he'd gone back home.

His father had been involved in a fight with a fellow inmate and wounded by a makeshift weapon. The wound wasn't a mortal one, but Ryan being the closest immediate family member, was called to be given the update. He hadn't heard from his father in over ten years, and was surprised something of this nature hadn't happened sooner.

Maggie came out of the kitchen, took one look at him and grabbed the coffee pot. Too early yet for the restaurant to be busy, after filling his cup she came over to sit with him for a minute.

"How are you doing?" she asked.

"Fine," he replied aware of her real question.

"Heard about the fight," she stated.

Ryan lifted his chin in acknowledgement of her knowing why he was out of sorts.

"Have you heard any more about Howard?"

"No, and I don't care if I ever do again," he said honestly.

"I know, but he is your father. You should go see him."

"I told you before, he might be part of our family, but he's no father to me. I have no interest in hearing what he has to say."

"He wants to see you."

"No."

"I've been meaning to tell you," Maggie looked out over the tables. "Last time I talked to him he told me he's been pretty involved in the ministry at the Chapel. Says he's been facing his demons and has asked the Lord for forgiveness. Now he wants to ask for your forgiveness as well."

Ryan's response was a shake of the head and an undeterminable sound.

"I know how hard this is for you, but think about going up some time. Here, he sent this to me to give to you—said I'd find the right time to give it to you." Maggie suggested as she pulled a folded up letter from her pocket and handed it to him.

Ryan stuffed the paper into his shirt pocket. He took the letter out of respect to her, but had no intention of reading the contents. Maggie waved to Lisa as she came through the door with a load full of produce in her hands. He nodded toward Lisa, who smiled and blushed prettily at Ryan in response.

"Produce truck didn't come through this morning. Said they broke down on 101 near Shelton. If they don't get up here by morning I'm going to need to drive into Forks to pick up some supplies. Helen will too. The market's going to run short, and then nobody will have anything to eat around here."

Lisa came back out of the kitchen and smiled again at Ryan. He smiled back, his gaze lingering.

"You two got something going?" Maggie asked, her eyebrows rising with interest.

"Maybe," he said at the brief knowing nod and Maggie's expression. He figured this wasn't the last of this subject.

"Did you check out her story?"

"Yeah, everything checks out. She was born in Columbus, and lived there up until about four years ago. She has a Master's in Education and was employed by the local elementary school. About the same time she left, she filed a restraining order on her ex-fiancée, Matthew Aaron Caine, requesting protection from harassing calls, and the usual distance of 150 feet. Looks like they took about six months to serve him from the time she filed. Then all records of her residence in that city drop off."

"I could have told you she was telling the truth," Maggie said with her expressive nod. "She doesn't lie."

"What makes you say that?" he questioned, putting his coffee cup on the edge of the table. He hoped Lisa would come to refill the cup as he watched her come back out of the kitchen, but she turned to the opposite side of the restaurant. He'd sat down in her usual area, though now he wasn't sure if he was in the right space.

"She told me so," Maggie responded. If she believed in her, it must be true.

Tina pulled the coffee pot off the counter and sauntered over.

"Haven't had you sit at my tables in a while Sheriff. Not since Lisa came into town."

Nodding, he replied without commitment, "Been a while."

"Lisa and I switched up today, thought we would mix things up a little bit. Wouldn't want anybody to get bored," she said winking at him.

He nodded, though he could tell she was leading up to something. There was no mistaking Tina's mode of operation.

"Who are you taking to the BBQ?"

Ryan met Maggie's perceptive glance across the table with one of his own. "Don't know I've asked anyone yet."

Tina topped off his cup and threw a pointed glance over to where Lisa seated the Crenshaw twins, laughing over something one of them said.

"If you thought about asking Lisa, you might be too late. She has quite the bunch of admirers."

Maggie shook her head at Ryan. "Tina, why don't you mind your own business? I think the Sheriff can ask who he wants in his own time."

"I just thought I'd say is all," Tina said with feigned offense. She turned her attention back to Ryan and said in a more proper tone, "What can I get you Sheriff?"

"I'll get his order up for you, don't you worry about it." Maggie stood with authority. She turned to Ryan and said in a firm voice, "We'll talk later."

Ryan knew she would make what he wanted to eat he didn't even need to say. He watched as Lisa walked toward him passing Tina who gave her the thumbs up.

Shaking her head, Lisa approached Ryan. "I'm sorry. I bet Tina is pestering you about me somehow. Forgive her. She's only trying to be a good friend."

"That's all right. She reminded me I needed to ask you something."

"Oh, really? What?"

"Every year Lake Duchess has a BBQ and Chili Cook-Off. Our neighboring towns are all invited to join in. It's coming up on Saturday."

"The twins were telling me about their smoked fish they bring. Sounds like fun."

"How would you like to go with me?"

Lisa's eyebrows rose, "You mean like a date?"

"Yeah, something like that," Ryan responded, intrigued by her surprise.

Lisa looked around nervously. "I…I don't know. I might have to work. Saturday's busy. I'm sure with all the extra people coming into town Maggie's going to need me here."

He smiled. She was a newcomer for sure.

"That's the one day out of the year Maggie's is closed. She provides all the burgers and ribs for the BBQ. She takes one day out of the year where she doesn't have to cook all day long. You might need to work a shift at the Coffee Hut, but we can work around that."

"Oh, well I guess I could go with you," she said with a shyness he found endearing.

"It's a date then."

"It's a date." Lisa grinned, her eyes twinkling. "I better get back to my tables."

Ryan reached out and took her hand in his as she turned to go. "I needed to tell you something else. I did a check on the name of Matt or Matthew Caine. There are no outstanding warrants for him. However, he does have a long laundry list of minor infractions."

"So there's really nothing you can pick him up for unless he does something wrong?" Lisa asked her eyes diverted from his.

"Not at the moment. I've put a BOL out so we'd be notified if he is in the area."

"BOL?" Lisa asked bringing her eyes back up to meet his.

"Be On Lookout. It's a code used for different agencies to keep the lines of communication open for someone of interest. Too bad you can't remember his license plate number though. I've had some trouble locating his registration to any vehicle. I could only give a generic description of a dirty 1980's gray van and his personal information. Either way, I'll find a registration if he has one."

"I think he bought the van from one of his band members. I remember him saying something about having to get the title transferred." Lisa's eyes were locked on their joined hands.

Ryan hadn't let go of her hand yet, he'd wanted to give her as much reassurance as possible. He gave her slender fingers a light squeeze.

"Don't worry, I'll figure this out."

She glanced into his eyes, a hint of anxiety beneath her long lashes. Ryan wanted to pull her down to kiss her, but knew it wasn't time yet to show that much affection in public. His holding her hand would be enough to start all kinds of rumors flying around town.

"Don't forget Sheriff, I'll be watching you," Angela called out from near the front door, reminding him of her insistence that he and her daughter were still involved.

Suddenly, a crash at the front entrance caused Lisa to jerk her hand out of Ryan's to bring it up to her throat as she swung around to face whatever might be coming her way.

"You crazy old coot," shrilled Angela as old man Beatty tripped over the threshold and almost ran her over. She gathered herself together and scurried out the door behind Beatty.

Lisa backed up, looking from side to side in search of the quickest escape route. Her chest rose up and down in quick panicked breaths, and Ryan could tell she was scared out of her wits. He'd jumped up at the ruckus, and now pulled her into his arms to protect her from any approaching danger

"Sheriff, Sheriff…they're gone. All my babies are gone. Those dirty Charlie's stole my Gin again."

A strong stench of alcohol wafted toward them. With a wild-eyed stance, his old green fatigues askew, Beatty spotted Ryan and stumbled toward him.

Slurring his words heavily, he said, "You gotta do something, Sheriff."

As Beatty got closer, Tina came forward to help. Ryan transferred Lisa carefully to Tina, and grabbed hold of the drunken man before he fell to the floor.

"Everything is okay, honey. Poor old fool Beatty's gotten into his Gin again. He thinks he's back in Vietnam," Tina consoled.

Ryan looked back at them, the full weight of the half-conscious man pulling him forward. "I'll take care of Beatty. Tina, make sure Lisa's all right. Lisa…" he paused for her attention to come up to him, "Don't go anywhere."

He waited for her to confirm she understood. Her slow nod and darting eyes showed she was still slightly shocked.

"Maggie, Beatty's back at it again. Get the coffee going," he yelled over his shoulder as he half lifted, half dragged the large man to one of the booths. Propping him between the table and the back of the bench, he was able to lean him against the wall without falling over.

"You got to get 'em Sheriff. They'll take everything. Them thieving bastards took my babies," Beatty garbled, leaning forward to see Ryan better. He closed one eye, squinting through the other. "Damn it, there's two of you again."

"OK, Beatty. You sit here and drink some coffee." Ryan took the cup from Maggie and set it in front of the old man. "I'll go check things out. Maggie's going to make sure you drink this coffee."

Beatty grumbled into the cup taking his first sip. "Them Charlie's took my food too. Took me all summer to catch 'em damn fish," he said slamming his hand down on the table, his coffee splashing out onto his hand. "Damn it Maggie, can't you keep this cup from moving?"

Ryan turned and raised his eyebrows nodding his head in answer to Maggie's questioning look. He'd heard what Beatty had said and this new occurrence posed a question to him as well. He walked to where Lisa sat precariously on the edge of a seat. She looked as if she were still ready to bolt. He knelt down in front of her, coming eye level with her sitting position.

"Are you all right?"

Lisa nodded peering over Ryan's shoulder. "Just surprised is all."

Ryan took Lisa's hand in his. Her fingers were cold and shaking. "Old Beatty has his demons. He does this every once in a while. We're all pretty used to it. I'm sorry, I should've warned you."

"Who's this Charlie he's talking about?" she questioned watching Maggie and Beatty squabble over the coffee cup.

Ryan didn't need to see the activity, he knew Beatty argued over drinking the coffee, while trying to convince Maggie the Viet-Cong were camping out in his back yard.

"That's what they called the enemy during the Vietnam War." Ryan brought her attention back to him by rubbing her hands between his. He smiled at her softly. "Look, I need to go check something out. Are you going to be here when I get back?"

She nodded, her smile returning. "I don't have anywhere else to go."

* * * *

Maggie heard the door open. She came out of the kitchen wiping her hands on the apron tied around her waist. In uniform, Ryan stood with his hat in his hands. His gaze searching for the one thing Maggie assumed was of interest. Lisa.

"She's down by the lake," she said throwing a knowing glance his way. At the end of the day Lisa had gone down to the lakefront after work, as she had all week long. Maggie walked to the windows with Ryan close behind. "She's been down there quite a bit lately."

Lisa sat on a log, an artist's tablet on her lap, a pencil in her hand. She drew for a minute, then glanced up, and back down to her paper. They watched her furious strokes as she sketched the object she'd caught sight of across the water, the passion she held flowing from her spirit onto the page.

"Has she shown you any of her work?" Maggie asked aware of Ryan's intent focus on the girl.

Ryan shook his head, and his voice softened when he answered, "No, I haven't had the chance yet." Maggie stared at him for a moment and realized his feelings for the girl had advanced into something more than a casual interest.

"She's quite the artist—could be a professional if she applied herself. Needs to settle down so she can concentrate on what's important to her." Maggie emphasized her words by nodding toward the scene before them.

Ryan's answer was another nod, and replied, "Went to check out Beatty's place."

"And…"

"Someone's been there, just like he said. His storage was broken into and the freezer trashed. Took most everything, what they didn't take was left on the floor to rot in the heat."

"Think he could have done this himself? He gets pretty weird in those episodes of his."

"No not this time. I found smaller footprints, not the same size as his, fresher too." Ryan scratched his chin. "His usual stash of

Gin's depleted, he might have gone through that…but the grill hoses had all been cut and the propane tank is gone."

"Are you going to tell her?" Maggie raised her eyebrows.

Ryan paused then shook his head. "Not yet. Not until I've got proof someone around here isn't the one causing trouble."

Maggie nodded. "Smart. Still, you'd better keep an eye on her."

"Plan on it."

Maggie watched as Ryan headed toward the back door. Without a doubt, she knew he would do everything in his power to keep the girl safe.

* * * *

Ryan walked down to where Lisa sat. Not wanting to scare her, he cleared his throat as he approached. She turned around, shielding her eyes from the sun with her hand.

"Hi, I thought that was you." She smiled, the sparkle in her eyes melting his heart just a little bit more. "What do I owe for the pleasure of your company?"

Scooting over on the log, Lisa patted the place next to her for him to sit.

"Maggie told me you're pretty good at this drawing stuff. I thought I would come down and find out for myself." Ryan sat as gently as he could, not wanting to disturb the log or her artist's tools on the other side of her.

"She's being way too kind. I do this when I get a little time. Drawing helps me to relax."

His gaze fixed on her face. He could watch her for hours. Nothing else mattered, but the two of them. When she glanced at him again the prettiest color rose to her cheeks, which caused a ripple of heat to run down his torso.

Damn. How does she do that?

"May I?" Ryan asked as he held out his hand toward her paper. Lisa hesitated for a moment, and then handed the tablet to him. He studied each of the first few pages carefully, not missing a detail.

"This is amazing," he declared softly. "You've brought everything to life on paper. Here, this one, I'm sure Harold had to be posing for you."

"Harold?"

"The blue heron—I'm surprised he let you get so close." The dimensions of the image appeared as if she sat only a few feet away from the majestic bird.

"He didn't actually. I've learned this process to convert the depth and size of any object to any focus or distance for the particular depiction I might prefer."

Ryan continued to scan through the drawings. Landscapes and still life filled the pages, with a few portraits. Each had a story to tell, an awe-inspiring beauty portrayed by the hands of its creator. The landscapes were obviously from different parts of the country. He imagined he held in his hands a part of history from the path she'd been on in her forced travels.

"How'd you manage to keep these? You must've had to leave on short notice most of the time."

"I learned early on to keep what is important with me at all times. My pens and paper, I keep in the backpack you've seen, along with a small change of clothes and my wallet."

She reminded him of something he'd meant to ask before. "You wouldn't by chance have a photo of this Matt, would you?"

Lisa shook her head, "No, I never had one of him. Oh, wait…" she exclaimed and reached down to grasp her backpack and pulled out another tablet, similar to the one he held in his hands. Flipping through quickly, she handed the tablet to Ryan. "Would this work?"

The full portrait displayed a young man, posed in the middle of playing an electric guitar at the front of the stage. His action captured so candidly, Ryan almost believed the wild riffs of the melody he played sounded off the page. The face of an animated man stared back at him. Small in stature with an odd flare to the style of clothing he wore, his hair—a little on the long side—was caught in mid-air as it flew about in response to his energetic motion. His facial features were thin—almost gaunt—which spoke of his addiction for themselves, but it was the glare of an uncaring intensity she'd embodied on the page that caught Ryan's attention. A look he'd seen once before.

"Quite the character, isn't he?"

Not exactly the word he would have used for him, Ryan's impression of the man was marred by the recognition of whom Matt had turned out to be—an abusive addict with criminal tendencies. Ryan flipped through some more pages, one caught his eye. The closer profile would help his search, though he was bothered by the expression she'd caught in several of the portraits. A soulful, almost tragic representation in Matt's eyes reminded him of his father— someone he wished he could forget.

"May I take one of these? I can post the likeness with the BOL for a better response."

She nodded as he removed the picture. She glanced away and sighed. "I don't look at these very often. They make me sad to remember him with such potential. The band members told me his talent was unmatched by anyone they'd ever run into. They'd even begun to talk with a recording studio the last time I saw him." She shook her head. "He really had so much going for him. I might still be by his side if he hadn't started using again."

Ryan sat for a minute, unsure of how to deal with the way this made him feel. A little puzzled by his immediate jealousy, he tried to pull himself back to being the professional.

"I understand all addicts show similar outlying addictive behaviors. Were you aware of anything?"

"Not at first, but you're right, after a while I started picking up on some strange things. He always seemed to need something in his hands. There wasn't a time he wasn't either drinking something or smoking something. He would get nervous and obsessive if he didn't. I told him I didn't like it, so he switched between cigarettes and pot, but nothing ever seemed to settle him down."

"Classic signs," Ryan confirmed.

"Damn it, I should've seen the signs before we got as far as we did. Then maybe none of this would be happening."

He watched a flock of coots, startled by a nearby noise, take off over the surface of the lake then circle around to land again in the water.

"I just don't understand. Why in God's name would you get involved with him in the first place?" Ryan asked.

"You know, I've asked myself that many times." Lisa glanced away from him, regret painted across her face in broad-brush strokes. "I was drawn in by his dynamic personality. It was like his fever for the music he played spilled out to me in a way I found irresistible. For a while he showed me a side of him that is buried deep inside wanting to come out. "

"But why did you stay with him after you found out who he really was?"

"I don't know. I guess maybe I wanted to be needed again. With my dad gone and my mom being taken care of at the home I'd started to feel like nobody depended on me anymore. I thought he'd been brought into my life for me to help him change. The problem was he didn't want to change bad enough."

The reference to her troubles stirred up her unease again, and Ryan watched as she started to pick at the small hole in the knee of her jeans. He reached out and took one of her hands in his, the response to his touch the same as her kiss—full of need and ready to accept any comfort he was willing to give. Her fingers instinctively intertwined with his and she let out a soft sigh.

"Do you really think we can put an end to this?"

Ryan looked down at their hands, warm contentment spreading through him. He squeezed gently and glanced back up to find her gazing across the lake with a wishful expression.

"You know, if you'd asked me a couple weeks ago I would've told you I'd do my best to help." Lisa's eyes came up to meet his, a slight misting at the edges. His heart swelled unexpectedly. "Now I'll tell you…we better, because I have no intention of letting you go anytime soon."

Chapter 9

Lisa almost couldn't contain her excitement. All morning, a flurry of activity bustled around town. The BBQ was no doubt the perfect social event for Lake Duchess. Everyone knew each other, and she was pretty sure she'd met all the locals. She expected no awkward silences, standing around with nothing to say to each other. Not with this group.

Maggie took advantage of the use of her staff to marinate the ribs and prepare all the fixings she volunteered each year to bring to the function. The chili cook-off contest entry was her baby. She'd won the last five in a row, but they were bringing a special guest to judge this year's variations on the dish.

Unlike before, this year the event committee decided to keep the judge's identity a secret until the very last minute. And apparently Maggie was not used to being kept out of the loop. She'd flitted about the kitchen the last few days, in a tizzy about who the judge might be. She was the keeper of all the secrets of this little town, and voiced her opinion that this was unacceptable.

Lisa yawned and took a sip of the Americano she'd made herself. She'd had trouble sleeping the night before, and hoped once the movement and activity started for the day she would wake up fully.

She watched as the next customer pulled up to get a coffee. So far, everyone that morning had been in a festive mood, asking if she was planning on being there. She recognized the woman in the grand white Lincoln Continental right away. Angela Burns rolled down her window, and glared up at Lisa. Her hair was in curlers, which she'd tried to cover up with a turban wrap, though one had escaped out the back.

"Well, well. You make coffee, isn't that special."

The hackles on Lisa's neck went up. She didn't like the woman, but that didn't mean she could be rude.

"Yes ma'am, what can I make for you?"

Lisa almost laughed out loud when Angela said, "A skinny-peppermint-mocha, with a caramel twist, and an extra shot of peppermint. I'm watching my weight you know."

As Lisa made the drink for her, the woman continued to glare at her. At one point she almost asked Angela what her problem was, but decided against any further prompting of conversation.

When she handed Angela her drink, the woman put a hand to her over indulged mascara encrusted lashes and boasted, "You know, my daughter Tess is a beauty consultant. I taught her everything I know, and now she's making a real living at teaching others how to put on their make-up."

It was so hard for Lisa to keep from the loud guffaw that threatened to come out. If Tess followed in her mother's shoes, she was in need of another job.

"How nice for her," she said as polite as possible.

Angela stuck her head out the window and spat out, "I know you think you've got your hands on Ryan, but she's going to be here in a couple of days, and you'll be heartbroken. They are still an item, so I suggest you keep your paws off of him."

Ryan had told her how he and Tess had been involved for a time, but there was no chance of anything starting up again. If he hadn't told her the woman was half-nuts, she might have taken what she said to heart. But by the looks of it, she was just a hopeful mother trying to protect her daughter's interest.

Lisa raised her eyebrows at the woman and watched her pull the Lincoln out onto the road. She shook her head and had to laugh. If Tess was anything like her mother, they would be quite an amusing pair.

* * * *

Ryan came by the Coffee Hut at the end of her shift to pick her up for their 'date'. Lisa didn't know how to treat the affair. Was this truly a date, or just going to a public event with a friend? She wasn't sure.

Trying to prepare for either case, she wore one of her new pair of jeans and a flattering camisole and sweater set Tina loaned her, casual enough not to appear as if she thought of this as an official date. Just in case, she gave her neck an extra splash of the last of her favorite perfume. The expensive small bottle she'd purchased lasted her almost four years. Secretly, she hoped the day would turn out to be worth her splurging those last few drops.

Susan arrived a few minutes earlier, rushing as usual.

"I'm so sorry. Joshua had a fit before I left. He wouldn't let go of my leg. He said he wanted me to go with them to the 'Q'," Susan said with a misting of the eyes. "Thanks for staying so long. I'm so glad Maggie said we can close down at two. I'd never hear the end if I didn't get to join Joshua and Bobby today."

179

"No problem. I needed the extra hour. Not working at the grill today put me short. At least now I'll have a little extra for emergencies."

A heavy knock on the door caused Lisa's stomach to jump in anticipation. She recognized the sound—definitely the hand of Ryan Jacobs.

When she opened the door, she couldn't have been more pleased. Her eyes were drawn to his muscular build, accentuated by the crisp lines of the fitted denim shirt, seeming sexier than usual. Her breath caught in her throat, unable to believe this handsome man was there to pick her up. Overwhelmed by his presence she tried not to stumble down the stairs as he stood back a ways to allow her to exit the little building. In his hands, he held a small bouquet of daisies, the expression on his face uncharacteristically shy.

"These are for you. I thought you might like them."

He didn't look directly at her when he said this, and she wondered if he was as pensive about the day as she.

"Thank you Ryan, they're beautiful." Taking the flowers from him, she kissed him on the cheek. "I'll go put these in water up in my place. Then we can get going."

"All right, things are probably getting started right about now. I'm sure Maggie's got the grills going already. I think I can smell the ribs," Ryan said lifting his face to the air drifting past.

When she returned he reached behind her to open the door to his truck, and bent further to draw in a deep breath of her perfume.

"My God, you smell good." He took another breath and stepped back from her. "If I do that again, we might not make the barbecue." The twinkle in his eyes confirmed she'd made the right choice.

"I think Maggie would send out the dogs if neither one of us showed up." Lisa laughed, purposefully tempting him by leaning into the truck to place her bag on the floor. As she turned back around, she saw her action had done exactly what she'd hoped. His eyes devoured her, their color deepening in the stormy connection she felt they shared.

Ryan groaned. "You do any more of that and I won't care who she sends after us." He placed his hand on her waist and pulled her to him, his lips landing on hers. The adrenaline rushed through her so quick, the kiss full of so much passion, Lisa was ready to forget all cautions and pull him up the stairs to her room.

He again showed his self-control and pulled away from her. His eyes darkened to an emerald green, and he murmured, "Soon...very soon."

* * * *

A few minutes before, Matt had pulled off the highway onto the exit road pointing toward Lake Duchess. There was more traffic than he's expected and he almost pulled off to the side of the road to wait for some of it to let up before venturing much farther. Signs posted along the highway and down the side of the road boasted this day as being the event of the year and the best chili on the peninsula. His stomach rumbled at the thought of a good meal. The crap he'd been eating lately hadn't done much to ease the hunger. The fish he'd taken was all gone, or at least what he could eat before it went bad on him.

As he drove behind a car full of kids in the back seat he wondered if he would see Lisa again. He'd figured out where she was staying the last time he came into town. She'd stepped out of the little red Pinto she'd just about run him over with in Denver, and headed up the stairs of that garage with some bags in her hands. Lucky for him she hadn't seen him.

He had to wait for the right time to grab her. He'd been watching her for a couple of days straight. Trouble was she always seemed to have somebody around her. If it wasn't someone where she was working, it was some cop sitting close by. There couldn't be anybody around to stop him. He wouldn't risk all this time and effort to end up in jail somewhere.

The most recent huffing binge still whirled in his head, and he felt invincible. He'd have her soon, very soon. Didn't care who he had to go through to get to her, he just needed to figure out the best way to do it.

The stop and go traffic pissed him off. Swearing at a car that pulled in front of him, he just about ran into the back of them, just for the sake of running into them. But he had to keep it cool. They were coming up on the little coffee hut and garage where Lisa worked, and from where he now sat behind the other cars he had a side view of the building. The sweat from the effects of the propane he'd huffed the night before poured down his forehead in little salty rivulets.

He blinked furiously, wiping away the gathering moisture on his brow, and saw there at the back of the coffee stand stood a man, a very large man, with his hands around Lisa's waist. The man bent down and placed a kiss on her lips. He recognized him as one of the officers he'd seen hanging around Lisa the last few days.

"You fucker," Matt yelled out, barely able keep from driving off the road and into the man where he stood. "Keep your hands off my woman."

His heart gave him a thunderous beat as he watched the two become more intimate. Lisa was kissing the guy back. "Bitch is cheating on me, too," he exclaimed. "Oh, you're going to pay for this big time, Miss Lisa."

Traffic started to move, which forced Matt to go forward at the same time Lisa turned to get into the man's truck. Matt ducked down in his seat, hoping she wouldn't see him. As he slammed his fist into the dashboard, he swore at the pain and pulled off the arterial to a side road to wait and watch. This wouldn't work if they were behind him. He needed to see where they were at all times.

"Fucker is dead meat," he said as he watched the Sheriff's truck pass by where he waited.

* * * *

The park at the lake buzzed with activity. Lisa was happy to find all types of activities for the kids and smiled in excitement. This reminded her of the festivals she'd been to back home, but homier with not as many people.

Off to one side, cheers filled the air as the younger crowd competed valiantly in an informal softball game. A stray ball tumbled toward them and Ryan picked the rolling object up and tossed it back to the young man running in pursuit.

Elderly people sat comfortable in their lawn chairs, talking with friends who stopped by to chat. Lisa saw a couple of booths where locals had their wares out for sale. Jewelry, yarn crafts, fresh vegetables, homemade jellies and jams, and the soaps and candles she hoped to check out later.

A large group of children, all seemed to be chattering at once. Tables were set out with what appeared to be some pots of paint and objects Lisa imagined would be used as art projects for the kids. Her favorite place in the world, she longed to be right in the middle of the chaos.

As she walked with Ryan toward the picnic area, community members gathered around the grilling dogs and burgers, in wait of their turn for the campsite delights. The ribs slow cooking to perfection, created the savory scent of roasting meat that hung in the air. It made her mouth water as the lid to a smoker was lifted to turn the delicious racks of beef and apply more sauce for a rich more flavorful taste.

In one area, contestants to the chili cook-off had begun to assemble their entries, and Lisa saw Maggie directing traffic, as was her usual method of communicating.

"I'm going to find out if Maggie needs any help. You want to come with me or is there something else you want to do?" Ryan asked.

Lisa turned toward the activity at the art table again. She looked up at Ryan who smiled back.

"I think I'll go check out what's going on the kids."

"I thought so." Leaning forward he laid a simple, yet expressive, kiss on her lips. "Don't forget about me."

"I don't think that's possible," she said as he walked away.

At the art table, a disorderly amount of activity was afoot. Lisa found two young women, apparently out of their comfort zone, trying to handle the requests from a dozen or so kids. She watched as they rushed between children, not at all prepared to handle the complexity of the task at hand. Lisa couldn't tell if they were part of the solution, or an added ingredient to the problem.

"Need a hand?" Lisa asked without hesitation.

"Do we," one of the younger women exclaimed.

Lisa walked into the center of the tables and held out her hand. "Hi, my name's Lisa."

"Katrina," said the one free for the moment. "That's Sheila," she offered up for the other woman intent on painting something on the cheek of one of the children. The woman raised her hand and waved in response to the introduction.

"I can't believe Megan quit her job just before the fair. She's the one with all the art knowledge. We volunteered to help out, but I don't think either one of us knew what we were getting into," Katrina said jumping to grasp the neck of a paint bottle about to be spilled.

"I used to teach art at an elementary school. Would you like some pointers?"

"That would be awesome. The closest I've come to anything like this is painting Easter eggs at my house, with only five kids."

"What are you doing here?" Lisa asked wanting to make sense of the chaos.

"At the moment, over here they are attempting to build candles from wax beads. This one with watercolors we wanted to help create greeting cards. Sheila is doing face painting…" One of the children who'd had his face painted crossed between them, the image on his cheek unidentifiable. Lisa couldn't tell if the animal was supposed to be a horse or a very short giraffe. "And as you can see, it's not turning out too well."

Sheila walked up wiping her hands on her apron. "Hey, I said I would give this a try. It's a lot harder than it looks."

Lisa stood thinking, in search of the best way to sort out the mess they'd gotten themselves into.

"Here, why don't you two concentrate on the candle making and the greeting cards, one on each project? Line the children up one behind the other, and only handle two at a time for each activity. That way you can direct better and have them be happier with the end product. Let me do the face painting. I have a talent for that sort of thing."

"Sounds like a good plan," Katrina said agreeing with Sheila's apparent relief.

Within minutes, a productive order came out of the amassed confusion prior to her arrival. Lisa showed Katrina a much easier way to control the wick of the candle in the container as the children poured the beads in colorful waves, which made all the difference in the world. She demonstrated to Sheila and a few of the kids a way to produce a recognizable picture, if that was what they were after. Otherwise, a splash of color here-and-there was perfectly acceptable for watercolors.

"Hey, maybe you should apply for Megan's position at the middle school."

Still unsure of what the future had in store for her, Lisa was stunned at how quick she was ready to agree. This would be a perfect job for her, but she answered without commitment. "Thanks, I'll check it out."

Already a line of six children waited for their faces to be painted when she sat down at her station. Some she saw had come back, wanting to discover what the newcomer had in store for them.

"What's your name?" She asked the shy young boy at the front of the line.

He looked back to where his mother's attention was drawn to a younger sibling. "Billy."

"What would you like on your face, Billy?"

"I dunno."

"Hmm...what did you learn about in school last year?" she asked, grasping for straws. Judging his age, she guessed, "Did you learn about the jungle?"

With his nod she asked, "Were there tigers and lions?"

He nodded again. "How would you like a Bengal Tiger on your face?" Bingo, she'd guessed right. His face lit up and he nodded again happily.

This she could do without question. She was overjoyed with the pride she received from the look on Billy's face when he peered into the mirror at the perfect image of Shere Khan from the Jungle Book. He started to hop around in glee, chanting something she thought sounded like the name of the tiger. Before she could ask him if he liked the image, he ran off in excitement to show his mother.

The next little girl stared at her quietly. "I don't want anything yucky like a tiger," she announced pointedly. "I want a flower. I want a pansy on my cheek." She pointed specifically to the very spot she wanted the design to be placed, and stuck her face out for Lisa to get started.

Lisa laughed. She hadn't had this much fun in years.

* * * *

Ryan watched from a distance the order Lisa was able to maintain with the children. It seemed as if everything fell into place as soon as she'd stepped foot into the art arena.

"She's pretty amazing if you ask me."

He glanced over his shoulder to find Tina's gaze toward the children's activity. She stepped forward to stand beside him.

He didn't need to say anything. They'd known each other long enough, he had no doubt Tina would go on to say what she'd come to say. So he merely nodded, his eyes fixed on Lisa.

"You know she's nothing like Tess."

This caused him to raise his eyebrows. "I'm not sure I asked for the comparison," he said not bothering to hide his rudeness.

"She was born for a small town like this. Just look at her. She is overjoyed with the task of painting butterflies and pansies on those happy little faces. She's dreamed of a place like this."

"What makes you say that?"

"She told me."

Ryan watched as Lisa herded some children around to engage in another project. The smile on her face unforgettable, she was definitely in her element.

"Tess was an idiot Ryan. She left you at the altar to go follow some outrageous dream of making a big splash in Hollywood. Last I heard she's selling makeup to tired housewives in search of an easy lift." Tina came around to face him. She made sure he looked her in the eyes. "What she didn't realize was she lost the best thing she'd ever find in this lifetime. Everyone knows she was never good enough for you."

Ryan had gotten over Tess a long time ago. He stared at Tina for a minute not understanding why people wanted to compare any future relationships to his first tragic love.

"I know that," he said shortly, diverting his eyes back to his object of interest.

"Have you told her yet?"

Ryan's attention was brought back to the compact little blond in front of him. "What?"

"Have you told her how you feel about her?"

Not believing this to be a subject he wanted to talk about with the biggest loudmouth in town, he shook his head. "I don't know what you are talking about."

"Oh, come on Ryan. That squirrel over there can tell you have feelings for the girl." She poked him rudely in the chest like a younger sister would. "You need to tell her. What are you waiting for?"

Ryan's silence sparked Tina's next comment.

"She won't leave if you give her a reason to stay." They stared at each other for a moment. Tina's point being well made, she punched him in the arm and said softly, "Ryan, you're like my brother. I just want the best for you. And if you ask me, I think she's pretty darn close to it."

$$* * * *$$

Lisa worked with the children for a couple of hours. Her arm ached mercilessly as the last little girl in the line sat patiently on her knee waiting for her to finish the kitty on her forehead. This was her third time in line after receiving a flower on one cheek and a ballerina on the other.

"How's that?" Lisa asked handing her the mirror.

"Purrrrrfect," the girl exclaimed animatedly. "Thank you, thank you."

The hug she received energized her enough to paint a thousand more kitties, birds, and tigers.

Turning, she expected to find another small child, instead she found herself staring midway up the legs of a very grown man. She recognized the firmly packed muscles in front of her and allowed her gaze to wander slowly up, letting out a soft sigh when she reached the green shimmering eyes she loved to lose herself in so often.

"What would you like big boy?" she asked with a laugh.

"Something you can't give with a paintbrush," Ryan replied, more serious than she had expected. He stepped forward and pulled her against him, the full length of his body pressed against her. Brushing a stray strand of hair from her cheek, his expression baffled her. "You are so beautiful."

His eyes never left hers. The kiss was light, hiding the blooming passion they both held. Although a man of little words, he sure said a lot in the encounters they shared. Lisa found herself moved by his few words, but more importantly his actions.

190

He raised his head, eyes glittering. "I guess I'll have to curb this for the time being." He quickly turned them both with his back toward any oncoming visitors. His laugh was soft and low, "I'm not sure how you do that, but you've done it again."

Lisa, felt the brush of his response to her kiss against her thigh and held back the giggle as Maggie came up behind him.

"Ryan, I need you to came help me with these chili pots. The judging is about to start."

"I'll be right there. Head on back and I'll catch up with you in a minute." He grinned at Lisa, who was having a hard time keeping a straight face.

"All right, then hurry up. I can't wait all day." Maggie peered past him to where Lisa broke out in a soft chuckle. She shook her head muttering as she turned to leave, "What has gotten into you two?"

* * * *

Ryan and Lisa sat across from each other at one of the picnic tables. She looked down at the enormous helping of chili that Maggie had dished up from her sixth time award winning entry.

"Well, she did it again," Ryan said dipping his spoon into the delicious mixture in front of him.

"Must be nice for her to know her cooking is recognized as the best from someone like Darla."

The mystery judge turned out to be the two time World Chili-Cook-Off champion, Darla Messing. The community event committee found out she'd be out on the peninsula visiting with her grandchildren this summer, and convinced her to bring the family out for the one-day event in Lake Duchess.

"She looks like she's on cloud nine," Lisa commented as Maggie said her goodbyes to Darla at the end of the judging tables.

"No doubt. She looks forward to this every year, but this year will be one she won't forget."

Lisa took another mouthful and glanced up to meet the glare of Angela across the picnic area. If the woman wasn't so obvious with her comical accusations, she might have to take a second look at her budding relationship with Ryan.

"Guess who came to pay me a visit at the Hut this morning," Lisa prompted Ryan as she stared back at the woman.

Ryan followed her gaze and gave a grunt. "Don't tell me, the wicked witch of the east over there. What did she want?"

The spot on likeness to the famous character of the Wizard of Oz made Lisa laugh. "She told me that you're taken, and I should keep my hands off."

He rolled his eyes and moaned softly. The grin he gave her was irresistible.

"Better not."

She smiled back, wondering if she dared believe in the feelings she'd begun to have for this man. The warmth he created in her flowed freely whenever he was around, making her crave his companionship. She couldn't help but think she wouldn't be able to keep her hands off if she tried.

Ryan raised his hand up and waived at someone behind her, and she turned to see an elderly woman being helped out of her seat. Lisa recognized her as the oldest person in town. She watched as several other townsfolk came up to say their goodbyes to the treasured individual. Marveling at the fact that everyone here seemed to truly love one another, she found herself yearning to belong.

What would it be like to live in a place all your life? To build a relationship with your fellow neighbors, and be treated like a member of everyone's family, was an image she hadn't allowed herself to visualize for a very long time. Though, now she'd begun to feel as if she were living that dream. She prayed for the vision to never end.

When Lisa turned back, Ryan's gaze was fixed on her, a strange expression in his eyes she wasn't sure how to interpret. He reached out to take her hand in his.

"Ryan…" she started to say, interrupted by Maggie, who'd come up behind her.

"Want some more of my chili?" Maggie smiled. "You heard it straight from the judge, best thing she'd ever tasted."

"I've been telling you that for years," Ryan replied with a softness showing in his eyes. He stood up to give Maggie a hug, then wrapped his arm around her shoulders. "Congratulations on another win."

"Thanks. There's plenty more," Maggie said raising her eyebrows at Lisa and holding her hand out to her bowl.

"No. But thank you." Lisa said shaking her head. If she ate any more today she would surely bust.

"All right then. If you change your mind you can come get some yourself. I'm going to sit down and take a load off and enjoy what's left of the day."

"You certainly deserve it."

As Ryan sat back down, Maggie started to walk away then turned around to say, "You two stay out of trouble."

"Not a chance," Ryan raised his chin in mock defiance with a smile on his face.

"Don't I know it," Maggie retorted and continued her walk to a seat not far away.

Lisa envied the affection she witnessed between Ryan and Maggie so often. What they shared was a mother and son relationship. The type of bond that had been ripped away from her before she'd been ready to accept her mother's failing memory.

"You are very fond of her. How have you two gotten so close?"

Ryan's eyes locked onto Maggie for a moment. He nodded his head, "She's actually my aunt from my father's side. Love her like my own mother though. She's my second mom really. I grew up in her house after my mom passed away."

Lisa realized her question had prompted the hard as steel glare to return, but this time she wouldn't let it slide.

"I suppose your father wasn't around then."

Ryan answered with the shake of his head.

"May I ask what happened to your mother?"

She sensed a gamut of emotion run through Ryan's head, expressed through his eyes alone, his face remaining motionless, like stone.

"She was beat to death in front of me by my alcoholic father. He passed out afterwards, and left me to deal with the whole thing."

Shocked, Lisa reached out and covered his hand with hers. "Oh my God, Ryan, that is horrible. I am so sorry." She wanted somehow to console him, but sensed he didn't want any comfort.

He returned his eyes to her and said, "It sounds heartless, but if I'd been old enough, I would've killed him."

She knew he meant every word.

"Is that why you became a Sheriff?"

"Partly," he disclosed. "I wanted to lock anyone like him away, to end the senseless pain and suffering of the innocent people around them. As I grew older, if I hadn't changed my ways I would have followed in his footsteps…at least in the alcoholic part."

"You must've been devastated as a child. To witness something like that is bad enough. But then being stripped of both parents at the same time would send any child into a tailspin."

"I struggled for a while. Maggie set me straight, real quick." He let a soft smile slide across his face. "She got me to understand we can't change what's happened already. We either, keep living in the past and continue to be miserable, or we move on to make a difference in what happens in the future. I guess you could say she saved me from myself."

Well, that explained a few questions she'd been pondering.

"Enough of my past skeletons," Ryan said switching subjects. "What do you think of this little community event of ours?"

It must be very hard to think about, Lisa thought watching him for a moment. His usual ease was restrained by where their conversation had taken them. She understood very well why he didn't like to focus very long on things of his past. She didn't either.

"It's awesome, I'm hooked. I can't believe you only do this once a year."

"Chili cook-off is only once a year, but we get together just about every holiday we can. Sometimes the weather makes things difficult though. Washington coastal weather can be pretty finicky," he said looking around. "It rains over six months out of the year. You've arrived during a pretty mild spell."

She nodded, imagining what it would be like to live here all year long. "I love rain. It makes everything so clean."

Ryan looked at her then, an odd curiosity in his eyes. He held her gaze with his as if he wanted to ask her something, but at a loss for words. There was a slight shake of his head when he looked toward a small scuffle that had broken out on the grass field between some of the boys.

They sat for a moment in silence. Lisa finished the last bite of chili and sat back in happy contentment. All of a sudden, she got a strange chill shivering down her back. The feeling of someone watching her every move trickled over her consciousness. The same one she'd gotten over the last couple of days.

She wrapped her arms around her body and sat straight up, shooting a glance from side to side. Off to the left, she thought she saw movement in the bushes. The hair on the nape of her neck bristled sending another chill down her spine. She was unable to move her eyes away, as if they were glued to that spot

"What is it?" Ryan asked right away, looking in the same direction.

Lisa swallowed hard and tried to will the feeling to go away. "Nothing really, I just got this weird chill is all. I thought I saw something."

"Do you want me to check it out?"

She was about to ask him to do just that when a soccer ball rolled out from under the brush and one of the boys ran up to grab it. She shook her head and pulled her gaze away and took a deep shaky breath. Although the movement had been explained, the sensitivity to being watched remained.

"No, I guess I'm just imagining things."

Or am I? She asked herself glancing around again, a creeping sensation traveling up her neck with a chill chasing not far behind.

Ryan reached out to grasp her hand. The gentle rub of his thumb on her fingers softened all other thoughts except for the two of them, there together, right now.

"What kind of plans do you have for this evening?"

"Hadn't made any plans at all really. Why?"

"I think you need to get away for a while. What you need to do is go into town with me to the movie theater, or maybe take a drive on the beach in the moonlight."

Oh, the beach! She hadn't been able to visit the ocean yet. This was a perfect chance to enjoy the roaring crash of the waves and swooshing of salty air against her cheeks that she'd dreamed about, hopefully wrapped in the arms of this gorgeous man. She gazed at him for a moment, taking in the fact he was for real and actually wanted to be with her. There was a twinkle in his eye and a smile on his lips that were too tempting to deny. How could she say no?

"I think I'd like..." Lisa was interrupted by Pat Hawkins' words from the table in front of them. She leaned in further to listen to what the group was discussing.

"They took the strangest things. Just like what happened to you, when we got up this morning, no mistaking someone had been rummaging around," he said to old man Beatty.

"Pat, did you call Sheriff Jacobs like I told you?" his wife accused.

Pat shook his head. "No, I figured he had enough on his hands today, helping Maggie and all. I thought I'd catch up with him later on."

"For gosh sakes, you should've called right away," Lucy exclaimed heatedly. "Why don't you tell him now? He's sitting right behind you."

Lisa hadn't taken her eyes off of Ryan. His face hadn't changed expression, though a flicker in his eyes resembled something akin to recognition of what they talked about. He turned as Pat came around to sit beside them.

Under his breath Pat said, "I'm sorry Sheriff. I wanted to wait until tomorrow. You're here with Lisa. I didn't want to disturb your day off."

"No problem. Tell me what's going on and I'll determine if I need to address the situation right away."

"Well, this morning when we went out to feed the chickens the door to the storage stood open. When I went in to check it out, I found everything had been tossed around. Stuff flung all over the floor, you know, like someone had searched for something in particular. The only thing missing is some old camping gear, the old rocking chair that's been out there for ages, a couple ropes, and some duck tape."

"Just like me. I tell you it's them damn Charlie's." Beatty's disgruntled grumble carried across the tables.

"Strange though, when I went around the side of the house to find out if anything else had been taken the only other thing missing is the propane tank off the side of the grill. Cut the hoses off too."

"Mine too. Why on earth would you cut the hoses? I told you Sheriff, you've got to catch 'em at night. That's when they're the sneakiest. I bet you they're building a bomb. They're going to blow this place sky high."

Lisa could barely stay still in her seat and not start running for the hills. Obviously, Beatty's conspiracy theories had been working overtime, but what he didn't know was the truth to the whole thing.

Matt is here, no doubt about it.

Suddenly, what Beatty said hit her hard. Ryan knew about this before, and he hadn't told her. By the look in his eyes, she couldn't tell whether he was aware of how wrong he'd been to hold this information back from her. What she saw was his full attention had been on her as soon as they'd started talking, which proved his guilt.

Unwilling to stand back and let someone else determine her fate, she made sure her anger was made known as she brought her glaring eyes to meet his cool calculating scrutiny. Nothing needed to be said. The significance of his actions passed silently between them.

Without taking his eyes from hers, Ryan said calmly, "Pat, I'll take a look in the morning. I'm sure it's nothing you need to worry about. Don't disturb the area before I get there, I'd like to check a few things out first."

"Yeah, you're right, probably just some kids fooling around, having themselves a cook out up on Hunter's Hill. You should go check out their favorite spot. I'll bet you'll find those tanks and stuff up there."

"Probably so," Ryan agreed.

His non-committal answer set Lisa off. She rose quickly from her seat, needing to get as far away from him as possible. He didn't care at all. He had no intention of doing anything to keep her safe. He hadn't believed a word she'd said.

"I need to go." She didn't care if she was rude. Nothing could be said to change how she felt at that moment. As quick as she could, she crossed the grass toward the road, stopping only once to say goodbye to a group of children who came rushing after her as she headed out.

Ryan immediately started to go after her, but Tina who'd been sitting close enough to hear the whole exchange, stopped him from making another huge mistake.

"You didn't tell her, did you?"

He shook his head.

"Idiot," Tina shot out at him. "I'll go after her." She shook her head with consternation. "After that you need to let her take a breather for a few minutes. She's not going to want to have anything to do with you."

"I know, I should've told her."

"You think?"

He stared at Lisa's quick retreat. "I thought she might leave."

"She still might." Tina never held back the truth to anything. "Let me go cool her down a bit. I'll bring her home, but you better not be far behind."

Ryan nodded his head. "I won't be."

Chapter 10

"Wait up," Tina yelled out from behind her.

Lisa turned as her friend caught up to her on the road. Tina bent over, her hands on her knees, out of breath from the fast jog. "Whew! You sure headed out fast. What's the hurry?"

Angered by the whole incident, Lisa began walking again toward town. "You heard what he said."

"Would you hold up? What are you a track star?" Tina caught up again, obviously struggling to keep up the fast pace Lisa had set for herself. "Why don't you wait? I'll go get the car and we can go more in style."

"I want to walk." After a few more yards, she stopped and turned to Tina. "What makes him think he has the right to not tell me? He thinks this whole thing is a joke, doesn't he?"

"Look honey, I'm not sure what he's thinking right now. I'm sure he has his reasons for doing what he did." Tina grunted as Lisa started walking again. "Give him a chance to explain himself."

"Hmm…" Lisa wasn't too convinced he would have anything she wanted to hear.

They continued to walk in silence, her thoughts deterred from anything but the need to get her things and get the hell out of this place. They'd made it back into town before Tina spoke up again.

"You're going to leave again, aren't you?"

What sense did it make to stay where you were in danger, and the one person you thought would protect you didn't seem to think it was such a big deal?

"I'm not sure. I guess if I'm not at work tomorrow you'll know."

By the time they reached Maggie's house Ryan had already arrived and stood outside of his truck, his expression filled with consternation, as if she'd been the one in the wrong.

How dare he?

Tina gave Lisa a quick hug at the driveway. "I'm going to head back home now. Just give him a chance. He deserves at least that much."

Lisa didn't believe he did. As she walked past him, he reached out to grab her hand, but missed as she pulled away from him.

"Wait, Lisa, I can explain."

Stopping as she faced the stairwell, she decided she really did want to hear what he would come up with as an explanation. Then she'd tell him exactly what she thought.

"You've got five minutes," she said, without turning as she started up the stairs to the entrance to her room. Ryan followed close at her heals.

All of a sudden, she stopped at the top step. Out of the corner of her eye, she caught the glint of something metal on the backside of the porch. She walked slowly over to examine the object. She didn't remember leaving anything out. As she got closer, to her horror a butane refill canister partially covered by a dirty piece of cloth had been discarded beside the galoshes Maggie left out for her. With a quick intake of breath, she motioned to Ryan the possible danger of going forward.

He came quickly to her side, and placed his body between her and the impending peril from behind the door. He glanced over his shoulder, to focus on what she'd found then with a nod of his head he reached down and pulled a short stub nosed pistol strapped to his leg. He took the keys from her and slowly opened the door, pistol raised in position, prepared to take down anyone who might have entered.

Scared, yet comforted by Ryan's actions, if Matt had been behind the door, surely Ryan would be able to stop him before any further involvement on her part. Not very many places existed in the small apartment for him to hide. She didn't find anything right away out of the normal. Following closely behind Ryan, they went from the open living area to the bathroom, and then a quick glance behind the counter in the kitchen.

Nobody was there.

Ryan turned toward Lisa, placing his gun back in the holster beneath his pant leg.

"Doesn't look like anything out of the ordinary happened here to me, do you?"

"No," she said, searching a second time. "No, it doesn't. But that doesn't mean he wasn't here."

"Other than the can on the steps outside, is there any other reason why you might believe he is here?"

Lisa remembered what had happened at the lake earlier. "I guess the missing propane tanks and the break-ins are just my overactive imagination."

"Don't go getting defensive now, I didn't mean that," Ryan said in a frustrated tone. "We don't know for sure all this is the result of this Matt being here. I have no proof yet he is to blame."

Lisa's blood began to boil. She walked back and forth in front of him.

"For God's sake!" she exclaimed. "What kind of proof do you need—a dead body?"

"Lisa, that's not going to happen," he began to say something more, but Lisa cut him off.

"Sure as hell will, if I don't do anything myself...Sheriff." Good, her snide reference brought a fire to his eyes. She wanted him mad. "You've known for days now he's here and you haven't done a damn thing about it. He could have killed me and been gone and you wouldn't have found out until it was too late."

She fumed now, the thought Ryan hadn't acted on the knowledge Matt had to be in town now raced neck and neck with the fact he hadn't told her. As she spoke, she began gathering the few things she would take with her, placing them at the end of the bed, ready to put into her trusty backpack.

"I've taken certain precautions..." Ryan began. Again she cut him off, not allowing him to finish.

"Admit it. You don't believe me do you? You think this whole thing is a farce. That's why you told everybody at the park you thought a bunch of kids were having fun."

She began stuffing the items into the backpack when Ryan grabbed her by the arm and turned her around to face him.

"Just shut up and listen for a minute."

Lisa started to speak her mind then snapped her jaw shut. He was angry, angrier than she'd seen anyone before. His face rigid with an impenetrable tautness, the brightness of his eyes had turned to an odd green flecked with heat from his fury. He pulled her to the front window and jerked it open. "Look over there to the west, what do you see?"

His forcefulness scared her a bit. Dusk had begun to settle over the land, and she wasn't able to make out much of anything, though she heard the distant commotion of the town's people winding down the day's events.

She hesitated then offered her answer, "An empty lot?"

"An empty lot, where every night either myself, or one of my deputies has been parked, monitoring your place to make sure nothing happens. I thought by now you would've figured out from the time you get to the Coffee Hut in the morning, to your time at the restaurant and back home, there isn't a time when you haven't seen me, or again one of my deputies, somewhere close. We've had a watch on you ever since Beatty told me about the missing tank."

Lisa had to think for a moment. He was right. There was usually someone first thing in the morning to get coffee, and then they would pull over somewhere close by. She thought they enjoyed their early morning coffee while attending to some important business. At the restaurant too, they may not have been in uniform, but she had to admit one of them had always been around. She'd marked it off to their patrol shifts, not that they'd been assigned specifically to her.

"I believe everything you've told me. There is no doubt in my mind he is here now. I didn't say anything at the park because I didn't want to stir up a big hornet's nest. I thought maybe you wouldn't want to become the main topic of discussion for the afternoon."

Ryan closed the window softly, his anger beginning to die down.

"Oh," was all she could manage. She felt so stupid for not seeing the obvious.

"And as for not telling you in the first place," he sat at the end of the bed, his eyes now showed something akin to sadness. "I didn't tell you, because..." he paused and stood again, searching her eyes with his. He reached for her, this time gently pulling her into his arms, "Because, well, because I didn't want you to leave."

His words were all it took. The tears started to well into Lisa's eyes. She wasn't sure whether she wanted to laugh with joy or cry with the emotion of the day.

"Oh, Ryan, I'm sorry I didn't trust in you. I don't want to leave either."

He buried his face in her neck and groaned softly as he began to nuzzle the spot where she'd put her perfume, the lasting power of the fragrance obviously still hard at work.

"You put that on to drive me crazy today, didn't you?" he mumbled as he began nibbling behind her ear.

"Uh-huh," Lisa responded, her legs going weak at the sensations he enticed.

He brought his lips around to claim hers. This time no subtlety came through. Gentle and soft didn't exist with the passion in his kiss. The heat poured into the simple meeting of their lips, enough to start a fifty-foot bonfire. Lisa pressed herself against his body, needing the length of him against her. Her physical response to him was unmistakable, a tension in her belly, and the urgent sensation of need centered quickly between her legs. She wanted him.

He lingered. His physical response she felt as strong as her own. Again, he stepped back. "Whew, if we keep that up I won't be able to pull my shift tonight. I'd better go."

Confused, Lisa asked, "You have to work tonight?"

"I let everyone off for the night. It's my turn to pull the night shift." Reaching for the door, he put his hand on the doorknob and looked back. "Don't worry about anything, there's no way he can get past me tonight."

Lisa struggled to understand. He meant to go out and sit in his truck all night, when he could be inside with her.

"You don't want to stay here with me?"

He shook his head, the grin she loved came to his lips. "I didn't say that. There's nothing I would like better than to stay here with you tonight. If I stayed though, we'd get into a lot more than me keeping watch."

"I know," she said simply. "Don't leave."

Ryan blew out a heavy breath as she sauntered slowly toward him intending to convince him to stay.

"I'd love to take you up on your offer, believe me I would. But there's something you need to understand," he said taking her by the shoulders.

"Yes?" She questioned as she began to unbutton his shirt.

"Stop that," he said pulling her hands into his.

"Why? You know I want you."

He held her gaze with eyes filled with desire, yet he held back - a silent war raging behind the scenes, a war she didn't understand.

"Up until now I would have taken you up on your offer without a doubt. I thought I knew what I wanted out of life - sweet and simple – no strings attached. Now, I have no idea what the hell I want." Ryan stepped back even further. "I'm not sure what is going on between us. One thing I am sure of is I don't think I can keep it simple. Not with you."

Lisa gave Ryan a blank stare then took in a deep breath.

Does he really mean what I think he means?

"So, if you plan on leaving soon, we might as well stop here. I won't have a casual one night stand with you," he continued buttoning his shirt.

She furrowed her brows, "I don't...I don't want simple."

"Really?" he asked, a disbelieving look in his eyes pressing his lips firmer together in conviction to his stance. "I can't take this any further unless you know what you're going to do."

Lisa hesitated. "Do...do you want this to go further?"

He took hold of her hands again. "Yes." He brought her fingers to his lips, his eyes closed, as if unsure of how to go on. "What do you want to happen, Lisa?"

If she'd learned one thing so far, she needed to take what had been granted and live life fully each and every day. Tomorrow may bring something different. Today there was no other place she would rather be.

What he wanted though, she wasn't sure she could promise. The idea of a lasting relationship was so far from the life she'd been living, the thought so foreign, she struggled to comprehend the full meaning.

Perhaps now there was a chance to do more than simply exist, but to actually live carefree, never to flee again. Desperate to find out what this would be like, she knew for sure the one person she wanted to dare to dream with was Ryan.

Wriggling her fingers from his, she stepped closer and began to unbutton his shirt again.

"I think I've never wanted anything so bad in my life." She trailed a finger down his chest through the open shirt, and gazed into his eyes, hoping he would see the seriousness in her own. "I'm thinking we need to explore the possibility of a very, very long relationship."

By this time she'd pulled his shirttails from his waistband. The glorious view of his chest stopped the breath in her throat, and she let it out in a small exclamation of joy. Better than she'd imagined in her dreams, his shoulders and pectoral muscles were perfectly shaped. Her eyes feasted on the tasty washboard stomach she'd imagined. She gazed into his expectant eyes and realized at that moment she'd been in love with him from the beginning.

She placed her hands on his chest. An excitement called out to her, and she closed her eyes to draw in a breath of pure man. She'd dreamt of this every night since they'd met. As if reading her mind, he pulled her against him. Her cheek pressed up against his chest, and she wrapped her arms around his bare torso, mesmerized by his strength. His arms grasped her against his warm skin, and the steady beat of his heart brought tears in a rush to her eyes.

"Does this mean you are staying – for sure?" He asked as he pulled her chin up to meet his gaze.

Even if it were just for this moment, she wanted to believe it could be true. She wouldn't think now of the probability of having to leave. To let go of the fear, to imagine no thresholds around her ability to love, was something she needed to grasp hold of and not let go. Not able to move away from him yet, she nodded with vehemence, the breath she held escaping in a soft sigh.

Nothing more could be said. His lips came down over hers with a fierceness she hadn't expected. Ryan pushed her up against the wall, his lips burning a trail of fire with every kiss. He stopped for a minute to catch his breath.

"I want you Lisa. Tell me I can make love to you." His eyes implored her to say 'yes'. "I don't think I can stand another minute."

Lisa needed to be loved, to experience again the basest of human needs. She had to feel him inside of her. She teased him for a moment by spreading kisses across his chest then lifted her eyes to his to whisper, "Yes."

The deep green of his eyes danced with elation, the sensation of his male energy sending trails of fire over her skin. Lisa pressed herself closer to him, her chin lifted, offering her lips to him. He lowered his head to hers. The kiss started sweet and soft but turned into wild abandon. Their tongues met in a dance of delights, each move providing the fuel to combust their smoldering heat. As his hands roamed carelessly over her body, his touch drew out a desire that stemmed deep from within her. She sought the feeling of his hands on her bare skin and began to push the sweater from her shoulders, her lips still locked on his.

"You're driving me crazy," Ryan groaned as he pulled the camisole over her head.

His urgent kisses covered every exposed part of her. He stopped briefly to explore the v-shape her bra formed against her breasts. Bent on getting her clothes off quick, with a flick of his wrist Ryan discarded her bra, the lacey item landing over the edge of the lamp in the corner of the room.

He stopped long enough to grasp her breast with his hand. Shards of heat drove down her spine to settle at her core as he brought his wet tongue across to bite ever so softly on her hardened nipple.

The moan that came from deep within her brought Ryan's eyes up to meet hers. His smile, she would remember forever, reminding her of the first day she'd seen him, standing virile and sexy in his uniform. As if he'd been waiting to rescue her and claim her heart for his.

"I can't believe how sexy you are." The tone in the roughness of his voice sent shivers over her uncovered skin, and she reached out to drag is mouth back down to hers.

She felt his fingers open the button on her jeans, his hand slipping beneath the cloth of her panties to clutch the firm globe of her behind in his palm. He pulled her against the rigid length of his thigh, pressing her belly against the growing bulge of his genitals, arousing her beyond reason. She wanted nothing more than to sink down over him, consumed by the feeling of fulfillment, and love— even if it was temporary.

Lisa helped with trembling fingers, but Ryan seemed to have everything under control. She in turn tried to loosen his belt to free him as well. As she stepped out of her pants, she stood naked to his roving eyes, trembling from excitement, yet not caring a thing about the decency of it all.

Words were unnecessary. Their need so strong there was no time for practicality. He shoved his pants to the floor, not taking the time to unfasten his ankle holster, or take off his shoes.

The minute he lifted her against the wall, the heat from his entire body against hers sent an unbearable urgency throughout her body. She made a trill of excitement as he slid into her, his girth surprising as he filled her completely.

The higher vantage point brought her level to his face, and she in turn smothered him with fiery kisses. His hands clasped firmly around her derriere, his fingers pressing the flesh of her inner thighs, sending rivulets of desire as he plunged into her. By wrapping her arms around his neck, she anchored herself to keep rhythm with his thrusts, each enticing a little moan from her.

She'd closed her eyes to the onslaught of sensations he'd unearthed. When she opened them again she found he had also closed his eyes. She gazed at the trickles of perspiration that formed at his brow, and reveled at the intensity of each lunge he made. Then he opened his eyes, their deep pools binding her in the swirl of love she now felt for him.

Lisa opened herself wide, arching her back as he changed his hold on her, one arm around her waist the other firmly under one thigh. She hadn't expected the first orgasm to hit as quickly as it did. Her body began to quiver and spasm in waves of excitement, yet built again for another as he changed his rhythm to a deeper thrust. Ryan gave her a grin, and bent his head to latch onto one of her nipples with his lips, suckling and massaging the responsive tip with his tongue as he drove himself into her repeatedly. She clung to him with her legs wrapped around his waist, her fingers of one hand curled in his waves of his hair the other fixed on the rippling muscles of his shoulder. She pressed him closer, encompassing the full contact of his heated skin against her body as the tension built to an explosive point. Overwhelmed by the power of the sensation, she threw her head back and groaned deep in her throat.

"Yessss," she breathed out with her culminating desire to let go.

"Hold it for me, Baby."

He pushed even deeper as her body began to convulse around him again, pulling her as far down as was possible over his pulsating penis.

"Oh, Ryan…ahhhhhh," she cried out, unable to hold back, releasing a volcanic like eruption inside her.

"God, you feel good," he exclaimed, as his long awaited climax came forth in a heated rush.

Her heart continued to beat wildly against her chest as he held her against the wall for the longest time, his forehead pressed up against hers, as if he too waited for the pounding of his heart to subside. Gently, as he brought her legs from around him, he held her in his arms and attempted to carry her across to the bed. Upon taking his first step though, it was obvious he wouldn't get very far.

Lisa peered down at his pants around his feet and began to laugh. "I think you better put me down before we both end up on the floor."

"So much for trying to be gallant," Ryan muttered, placing her on her feet.

She climbed into the bed and lay, watching him loosen the holster fastened around his ankle. It was odd, she wasn't big on guns, but he made her secure in knowing protection was so close at hand. She gazed at the man standing at her bedside and realized it didn't matter if he had a gun or not. She didn't feel the need to switch off the electricity panel, no reason to take the usual nightly precautions she'd adopted. She simply felt safe with him.

"Do you always have that with you?" she asked as Ryan lay the stub nosed .38 beside the lamp on the nightstand.

"Most of the time, when I'm off duty I carry some type of weapon, all depends on where I am and what I'll be doing. My duties as Sheriff never end." He'd turned to face her, his voice soft and concerned, he asked, "Does my wearing this bother you?"

Lisa thought for a moment and shook her head. "No. Not with you. It's part of who you are."

She lay back on the pillows and pulled the comforter over her. Ryan stood, appearing as if he waited for something. She raised the edge of the comforter and gave him a shy smile.

"Are you going to join me?"

There was no need to ask twice. He crawled into bed beside her, the full length of his frame pressed against her. She clung to him, not wanting to let go. She heard the strong pounding of his heart under her cheek and his arm came up around her to pull her closer. A sigh escaped from her. Something about being in his arms just felt 'right'.

A misting of tears came to her eyes. "I'm not scared when I'm with you," she whispered.

He placed his fingers under her chin and raised her face to look into her eyes. He studied her for a very long time and kissed her forehead.

"If I have anything to do with it, you never will be again."

Chapter 11

When Ryan woke, through the windows, a stream of moonlight drifted through the darkness of night with sleepy iridescent rays over the bed.

He rose to his elbow to gaze at Lisa's peaceful beauty. He'd become thoroughly enchanted by her in the conversation they'd had before falling asleep in each other's arms. Her aspirations were very much like his. She wanted a peaceful, comfortable life, doing something to make a mark in this life. Not on a grand scale, but a difference to the people she loved and cared for in her own little world. Charmed by her simplicity, and creativity, he found himself enticed by her hidden sexuality and eagerness for life.

Throughout the night, Ryan had made love to her, each time discovering his need to bring her to new heights. He couldn't seem to get enough of the taste of her sweet lips on his, the heat of their union, and the exhilaration of fulfillment. She was like a constant spark, lying in wait to be ignited into the blazing flame that happened as soon as he touched her. They lay there for what seemed like hours. Both too exhausted to do otherwise.

He watched her float out of slumber to open her eyes and turn to where the moonlight feathered a fanciful pattern across her face. She gazed up at him, the deep brown of her eyes dancing in mirth, seducing him with their secrets. If the warmth of her skin against his wasn't sexy enough, she brought him closer to her by throwing her leg over his body. The intimate contact sparked another immediate response of his manhood. He smiled, too satiated to do anything else.

For so long, he'd ignored the fact he really needed someone to fill the longing in his heart for a steady, comfortable relationship. What he hadn't realized was he'd been waiting for a certain woman to satisfy his every possible need. Someone to entice new feelings and desires, to fulfill the unexplored craving he'd disregarded for so long. Someone to bring the dormant joy back into his life while allowing him to bring the same fulfillment to her. It would take a special woman to fill those needs. That woman was Lisa.

"Hi there," she whispered snuggling into his arms, her warm torso pressed against his side.

Ryan glanced up at the clock. One in the morning wasn't such a bad time to be awake. "Morning," he murmured placing a kiss on the top of her head and pulling her even closer. Then the loud rumble from Lisa's stomach made Ryan chuckle. "Wish we had some of that barbecue now, don't you."

"Mmm…don't remind me," she muttered, kissing his chin and laying her cheek against his chest.

He never wanted to let her go. Her warmth soothed his soul. "You know of course the whole town is going to be talking."

"Do you care?" she asked anxiously. "I'm sorry, I didn't think about your reputation."

Endeared by her concern, he pulled her closer and kissed her on the top of the head. "I think my reputation can stand up to their gossip. I'm not worried."

From across the room Lisa's cell began to buzz. Both of them remained silent for the duration of the signal. Ryan watched Lisa's quick change of expression from startled surprise to a deep frustrated frown, upsetting her peaceful glow.

"Damn it," she muttered under her breath. The cell began to beep again, and again soon after. "I'm sorry. I forgot to turn the dumb ringer off. Sometimes that's the only way I can get any sleep."

Ryan rose to his feet and strode over to the phone. "May I?"

Hesitating, Lisa nodded her head.

"How long have you had this phone?" He turned the phone over in his hand, searching for the make and model.

"A couple of years now I think."

"Same number?" he asked glancing up to find her shaking her head.

"No, I know what you're thinking. But I've changed the number so many times I can't even keep the thing straight."

"Same company?" he questioned, trying to fill in the blanks to the puzzle of Matt's ability to find her so quick.

"Yes, I didn't think to change the company. Is that the problem?"

"Might be part of the reason…" Upon looking at the screen, eighty two calls were posted from the same number, all dating in the last 24 hours. "May I listen to these messages?"

"Go ahead, I have nothing to hide."

He listened to a familiar progression of aggressive messages, the increasing affect of the drug, alcohol, or inhalant in this case, causing a violent tendency in the user. They started out in an almost guilt ridden manner, Matt pleading for her to answer his calls. This soon moved to the blaming and threats, a familiar pattern of the addict.

The phone began to buzz again in his hand. He raised his eyebrow in question to her.

"Go ahead. Won't do any good, he doesn't listen."

Ryan brought the phone to his ear and pushed the 'talk' button to listen. At first, silence greeted him on the other end then the labored breathing of someone on the other end caused the hackles to rise on his neck.

"Lisa, damn you, I know you've got someone up there." A long pause, followed by what sounded like a hissing and a violent cough filled the receiver. "You cunt, I know you're fucking him, aren't you? Don't you understand, you're mine, you hear me? You shouldn't have left me. You'll pay big time for this. I'm going to mess you up bad. You need to be taught a lesson."

The words brought to mind a time Ryan would rather forget. A time when he'd been the one in danger, waiting to find out if the lesson to be taught would be a harsh one.

Ryan, tempted to tell Matt what he thought about his threats, knew if they were to catch him he didn't need to scare him off. Besides, he wanted to be the one to teach *him* the lesson. All of a sudden, the music playing in the background was turned up so loud he had to hold the phone away from his ear. That's when he heard the noise coming from outside as well.

He went to the windows to peek out. Across the street an unfamiliar gray van was parked haphazardly on the side of the road. The windows were fogged, but there was movement behind the wheel. If he worked things right there was a good chance they would catch him tonight.

Ryan clicked the cell off and brought his own phone to his ear.

"Bobby, I need you to get out here right away…Yeah, Maggie's place. A gray van is parked, facing west on Main Street. Don't use the lights. We need to come in quiet. Park at the Reynolds drive, I'll meet you there."

By this time, he'd put his pants on and pulled his shirt over his shoulders. Gun in hand he headed toward the door.

"Stay away from the windows, and unless you know for sure it's me don't open the door to anyone."

His orders were met with silence and he turned to find Lisa already dressed, her keys ready in hand, the same fear he'd seen before clearly in her eyes. He went to her and grasped her shoulders, bringing her attention back to him.

"We're going to catch him. Don't go anywhere unless you absolutely have to." He waited for her nod. "I'll be back. But if you do leave, make sure you call me and tell me where you are. Understand?" He hoped to God she wouldn't flee in spite of her promise to stay.

As he slipped out the door, Ryan made sure to stay in the shadows along the building side of the staircase. He couldn't see the vehicle from this viewpoint, but hadn't heard any indication the van had left yet. He followed the structure of the building then cut across into the trees beside Maggie's property line. He'd chosen the Reynolds' driveway because the streetlights didn't reach that far and their house sat far enough off the road their houselights wouldn't either.

He arrived as Bobby pulled up in the cruiser, headlights off and engine purring. Bobby got out, hand ready at the butt of his gun, the only noise being the gentle click of the car door closing.

Ryan motioned in silence for Bobby to back him up on the right, as he made his way toward the van.

Just as they reached the back fender, Ryan heard the loud snap of a tree branch coming from the other side of the vehicle. Suddenly, as if the towns own alarm system went off, Old Blue, the Reynolds' hound dog woke from his slumber on the front porch and began howling at the unexpected noise. With him, four or five other dogs began barking, the sound piercing the silence of the night.

The driver of the vehicle straightened up and looked to his rear view then to his side view mirror. For the briefest moment, their eyes met and Ryan saw the point of realization in the other man's eyes. Now, it was too late to catch him by surprise, but there was still a chance to get to Matt before he had a chance to react.

The engine started, and with a jump the man shoved the gears into drive. At that very moment, Ryan reached out to grab the handle to yank Matt out, missing by a sheer second. The van tore out spewing rocks and dirt in its wake.

Without question, both Ryan and Bobby sped back to the cruiser with Ryan taking the wheel. He peeled out knowing there was only a slim chance now they would catch him.

"Damn it Sheriff, I swear I didn't see that branch," Bobby exclaimed in frustration.

Ryan nodded, experienced enough to understand what the boy was feeling. "I know Bobby, sometimes things just happen that way. It's not your fault," he said without blame.

He wished now though he'd taken the chance to catch Matt without back-up. He would have gotten him.

Fresh skid marks at the entrance to the main highway veered left toward the mountains. Only if he was stupid enough to stay on the straightaway would they be able to catch up with him now. In the dark of night there were too many turn offs and directions to take that would afford a quick cover.

After a few minutes of speeding in the same direction, Ryan knew the van must have turned off somewhere along the way. No sign of taillights could be seen anywhere in the dark. Retracing their steps, they made a careful search of each of the turn offs into properties along the way. The other possibility was Matt had waited for them to pass in one of these dark holes and pulled out to go the opposite direction to his current hiding destination.

They sat for over an hour at the side of the highway near the entrance to Lake Duchess to wait for any passerby's that fit the description of Matt's vehicle. Frustrated, Ryan knew there was not much chance of them finding him at this point. They'd have to start fresh in the morning light to search the area again.

* * * *

Matt waited, knowing he'd found the perfect place to hide. They'd never find him here. He paced back and forth beside his van. The desperate need to pull out a new tank of propane, almost outweighed the need to stay conscious enough to escape, in case this cop turned out to be smarter than he thought.

When he drank down the last of a bottle of that foul tasting Gin he'd found at that cabin off the lake, he tossed the glass against the rocks, empowered by the shattering noise it made. They hadn't tracked him down for that yet. He was smart, and he knew how to get away with what he needed to survive. For damn sure wouldn't be made a fool of by some small town Sheriff.

He sank down beside the front tire and closed his eyes. The croaking of the toads and the chirping of the crickets reminded him of that night he and his friend had camped out by themselves, smoking weed and huffing their brains to an oblivious plane. He smiled at first, recalling the ecstatic feeling he'd gotten that night. Then all of a sudden, visions of the horrible charred bloody face of his friend popped into his mind. Matt's eyes shot open and he jumped to his feet.

"Go away damn you, leave me alone," he shouted into the darkness around him for no one to hear. "Leave me the fuck alone," he sobbed, dropping to his knees.

Reaching out he grabbed the last tank he'd left at the campsite. There still might be enough to destroy the images floating in front of him. He fumbled with the hose and flicked the lever open, sucking on the tubing as if his life depended on it. Thankful the familiar muted consciousness began to settle over him he sucked again and held his breath. The lights of the stars above wavered and the familiar darkness engulfed him.

Much later, Matt pulled his van as close to the little coffee hut as he thought was safe. There were no lights on in the apartment above the garage, but the truck he knew to be the Sheriff's was still outside.

He couldn't grab her if she wasn't alone. There was no way he could do this if the cop was close by. He'd just have to wait him out.

This was going to be tricky. Over the last few days there had always been someone close by, like she had people watching her or something. It wasn't going to be easy, but he'd figure out a way to get to her. He had to.

Matt stared up at the dark window with a hatred burning in his heart. Cops were the worst. They always took away what he enjoyed the most. His freedom to enjoy everything had been threatened in one way or another by every cop he'd known—weed, liquor, propane and now his woman. Thoughts of what might be going on in that little apartment flew through his mind. He kicked the floorboard of his van swearing as his ankle hit the side of the brake pedal. Why the fuck did it have to be a Sheriff?

What could he do to show this guy he would win? He couldn't rush in there. Fucker probably had a gun. He'd get shot for sure. He should have taken his dad's old service revolver out of the closet. Too late to arrange to get one now—he'd just have to figure out some other way to get her back.

He stared at the Sheriff's silver truck, all pretty and shining in the moonlight, and started to smile. He knew exactly what to do.

"Think you're going to get the best of me? I'll show you. Nobody takes my woman. Especially you," he muttered taking another hit off the starter fluid he held in his hands.

He didn't acknowledge the disjointed movements of his body as he got out of the van. He'd become immune to the abnormal affects the toxic substances had on him. After he'd opened the back door of the van he grabbed hold of the large plastic container at the

225

corner, gagging a bit as the lid popped off. He struggled to get the bucket out of the back without making any noise.

He snickered, "I'll show the bastard what's what."

He was glad he hadn't emptied the receptacle at the last stop he'd made before heading out to Lake Duchess. The contents would be put to good use—a testament to his superiority, a statement of things to come.

* * * *

"I think we need to tell the townspeople what's going on. They should be aware of what to watch out for." Ryan said as he slipped on his shoes.

Lisa had already gotten ready to go into work at the Coffee Hut, and sat quietly at the end of the bed. Ryan had come back to make her aware they hadn't caught Matt. She didn't ask, but Ryan stayed the rest of the night to give her the comfort and protection she needed. She was glad, because she wasn't sure what she would've done if he'd left her alone.

"You're right. It's not right to keep this from them."

"They can be a big help when tracking something down around here. They're like a network of busy bodies watching everything going on."

Lisa smiled as she remembered what Maggie said before about the town, though she raised her hand to her stomach and rubbed with an unconscious display of how tense she remained. The wrenching was almost painful.

Ryan came to stand beside her. "We'll catch him."

Lisa stood up and wrapped her arms around him, laying her cheek against his chest to try and pull the strength she needed from him. She wanted so bad to believe him, but until she was sure Matt couldn't get to her she wouldn't be able to rest. Though obviously impossible, she felt if she kept holding onto Ryan she'd stay safe in his arms. Nobody and nothing would harm her, as long as he was with her. The minute she let go, the fear she'd lived with for so long began to wash over her, goading her to make a run for it, again.

She straightened her spine, trying to be stronger. "When do you want to tell them?"

"I'll call everyone in to the high school cafeteria around lunch. Would be best to tell them all at once, otherwise the story gets a little jumbled as the message goes down the line, and nobody will know what's going on."

"I guess I'll see you there later on?"

She blinked her eyes to clear the blurriness away. Her stomach continued to churn, not letting up since the night's activity. When she did drift off to sleep, she'd had nightmares of looming figures chasing her in the dark, obviously incited by her fears.

"Let me walk you down to the Hut. I'll wait with you until Bobby gets down here to stand guard over you. I'd stay, but I need to check some things out first."

A sudden knock at the door made Lisa jump. Ryan set her behind him and went to the door. His hand went immediately to his unfastened holster, pulled out the gun, and yanked the door open.

Maggie stood a little like a deer in the headlights, slightly unsettled by the manner of greeting.

"Maggie, are you all right?" Ryan asked with concern.

She looked at him now with a hint of curiosity and peered over his shoulder at Lisa, sizing up the situation.

"I'm fine, but I think you might want to come see this," she said, gesturing toward the door. "You're not going to like it."

They followed Maggie out onto the small landing and down the stairs. Lisa followed close behind Ryan, afraid of what had happened.

"What the…" Ryan said with exasperation.

As Lisa came around to where they stood, a stench so strong hit her nostrils she couldn't help but gag. Smeared all over the windows and driver's side door of Ryan's truck was a brownish black mess, clumps of which were mashed into every possible opening.

"What the hell is that?" Maggie asked in disgust.

As she held her hand up to her nose to block the smell, Lisa recognized the substance by the familiar odor she'd once smelled. "I don't think you want to know."

Nobody needed to get any closer to confirm.

"How do you?" Ryan paused as he processed what she'd said. "Wait…Don't tell me, you had to experience this too?" Ryan asked, his eyes showing he didn't really need an answer.

"I found your truck stinking like this when I went out to the Hut to stock the cups. Who the hell would do such a thing?" Maggie asked as she placed her hands on either side of her hips.

"We had a visitor here last night before this happened. Lisa's ex came to pay her a visit. Since I was here he couldn't make his move on her."

"I thought I heard some activity earlier in last night, by the time I got outside nobody was around. Your truck was still here, but didn't want to disturb you." Maggie said making the point she was aware of what they'd been doing.

"Bobby and I went after him, but we couldn't find him. He must've snuck into one of the drives off of 101."

"Came back around to show you what he thinks about you, didn't he?"

"Obviously," Ryan said, the repulsed anger written on his face.

"He doesn't realize who he's dealing with though, does he?" Maggie said shaking her head. "If he had any sense in his head he'd take off for the hills and never come back."

"He won't get away. Not this time," Ryan stated firmly. "As soon as morning light hits we'll do a thorough search of the area. There's no way he's left yet. He didn't get what he came for."

Lisa shuddered at the thought and walked to the front of the truck as he spoke. She'd seen something odd through the window. Not visible from the other side, words were written in the muck on the front window.

"Ryan..." she said with enough tension he immediately came around to her side.

In big bold print the words 'SHE IS MINE' and 'YOU ARE DEAD' etched into the goo jumped out as a warning. Ryan put his arm around her shoulders and protectively pulled Lisa close.

"I think he has that a bit backwards, don't you?"

* * * *

Ryan and Bobby watched the first of the townspeople go through the entrance to Westlake High.

"That was just downright disgusting," Bobby said in hushed disgust. "Earl, down at the detailing shop, said you're lucky he didn't get the stuff inside. They had to take the door panels off to clean the window crevices. Told me he thought he might be able to get the stink out, but you should keep the truck aired out for a while. The vents may never be the same, so you might need to replace them."

Ryan gritted his teeth. He'd been seething since they found the mess.

"He's lucky all right. Must be smart enough to realize if I'd caught him in the act he wouldn't be around for another day."

"Tell me if I'm wrong, but that wasn't cow dung, was it?" Bobby asked with his nose scrunched up in offense.

Ryan's face hardened. "No it wasn't."

Helen from the market came past them as she grumbled, her gray hair flying in the wind. "This better be important. Pulling me out of the store at this hour of the day is ridiculous."

"Don't worry. This won't take long, Helen."

"Better not, I've got things to do." She shuffled off mumbling under her breath the absurdity of it all.

"What is this all about Sheriff?" asked Lucy Hawkins pausing as she and her husband followed Helen's lead. "This has to do with the new girl, doesn't it? I bet she has something to do with all this theft that's been happening."

Ryan wasn't surprised at the connection. The townspeople may be nosy, they weren't stupid.

"You'll need to wait to find out Lucy. We'll let you know soon enough."

Inside, everyone able to travel had answered the call to gather. Small discussions had erupted between friends and neighbors, all wondering what all the fuss was about. Why had the Sheriff felt it necessary to disrupt their day? Maggie thought best to keep Lisa out of the mix until Ryan was ready to address the group, because they would no doubt be swamped with questions by the well-meaning folks.

Ryan stood at the front of the group, in full uniform, his authoritative appearance strong enough to quiet them to a hushed whisper. Maggie and Lisa came out from the back and stood behind him, to allow him the opportunity to start the discussion.

"I'm sure you are all wondering why I've called you here today. As you all are aware, recently some rather unusual activity for us here at Lake Duchess has occurred. We are here to inform you what we know about these activities." He paused to reach out for Lisa to come to his side.

"Them damn Charlie's, isn't it? I knew it." Beatty yelled from the back of the group, and was immediately hushed by those around him.

"No Beatty, but this is someone we need to watch out for."

"Do we know who it is, Sheriff?" asked someone from the group.

"This isn't someone we've met before, but is someone I found out about recently. I think now would be best time for Lisa to explain a little more about this situation."

Lisa looked up at Ryan, unsure of how to tell these good townspeople she was the cause of what had been happening. She'd rehearsed what she would say in her head for the last few hours, now in front of everyone all words seemed to escape her.

"It's all right Lisa, we're all friends here," came the kind encouragement from her friend Tina.

Others joined in, with various urgings for her to tell them, all with a touching level of compassion. Lisa took a deep breath, and focused on Tina, her hand tightly clasped in Ryan's.

"I'm aware you've all wondered why I came here to your town. There's no doubt why I've stayed here though. I want you all to understand how much I appreciate your open hearted welcome." She looked around the faces of the people she'd grown to love.

Ryan squeezed her hand and Maggie came forward to stand beside her.

Lisa's heart pounded in her ears, her eyes darting away from the group, wishing she could just flee to avoid the embarrassment. Their expectant faces prompted her to go on and she knew they deserved the truth. Encouraged by these new people in her life, she felt her cheeks flush as she forced herself to tell them of the awaited admission.

"I came here by accident. For the last couple of years I've been on the run." She cleared her throat, pausing to find the best way to tell them. "A man has been threatening me, and he follows me everywhere I go. He's here now. That's who has been breaking in and stealing from you all."

"How do you know it's him?" one of the Crenshaw twins questioned.

Lisa looked up into Ryan's eyes and found the strength she needed. "We saw him here last night, and you've probably noticed the kinds of things being taken are rather strange. The propane tanks being taken was the first clue."

"He's building a bomb, isn't he?" yelled Beatty. "He's in cahoots with them other fellas."

Lisa wasn't sure if they would ever believe her. She wouldn't have believed it herself, if she hadn't actually seen what she was about to say.

She shook her head, "No. What he does is he inhales the fumes of propane to get high. He's been doing it for years. He's an addict."

"You've got to be kidding. Who on earth would do such a thing?" Helen stated in disbelief.

Ryan stepped in to take over. "There's no telling why the addict or alcoholic does what he does. The fact is they are everywhere. What we've got here is someone who has gone beyond an acceptable level, and is a danger to us here at Lake Duchess. I think you will all agree he can't be allowed to cause this woman more grief than she already has endured."

Various nods and verbal agreements spread through the crowd.

"Nobody's going to think they can get away with that in our town," Roberta chimed in.

"Tell us what you want us to do, Sheriff."

Reaching behind him, Ryan brought out a stack of copies of one of the pictures he'd sent out over the police network.

"Here is a copy of the likeness of the person we are looking for. If anything happens, no matter how strange, I want you to get hold of myself or one of my deputies. Don't worry about bothering us. Nothing is too small to be investigated. With your help we are going to catch this guy and put him where he belongs."

"Sheriff, I'm not sure if this is related, but the other day smoke was coming from the old state park that was shut down last year. I thought maybe some kids might be up there having fun."

"Thanks Pat, I'll go check that out first." Ryan raised his hand to get everyone's attention, his height lending to his authority. A hush came over the crowd. "He is dangerous. We're not sure how far he will go. So don't go getting all heroic thinking you can handle him yourself. Again, if anything happens or someone looks like this man, get hold of me. You all have my number."

The easy acceptance of these people touched Lisa's heart. She had to hold back the tears as they all crowded around her and Ryan, showing their support and agreement to help in any way they could. She felt a bit overwhelmed by their kindness.

"Come on, we need to talk," Maggie said from behind her. Placing her hand on Lisa's elbow Maggie led her away from the curious eyes and questions of the townspeople.

Chapter 12

Back at her office, Maggie eyed Lisa who sat wearily across from her. They wouldn't be disturbed in her office she knew that for sure.

"We haven't really had a chance to chat much, since you came into town. I figure now is a good time to talk about a few things." Maggie sat back in her chair, her eyes locked on Lisa.

Lisa moved uncomfortably in the chair, her expression showing she was aware of the impending interrogation.

"I have nothing to hide from you. What do you want to know?"

Maggie saw in the girls face, she would answer anything at this point. Now was an opportune time. She may not be so open to talk later. Though, Maggie intended to make some points of her own.

"First off, what the hell was that stuff on Ryan's truck this morning? And second, how did you know right away what it was?"

"You left before I had the chance to explain."

Lisa sighed deeply. Maggie knew she didn't have too long for this conversation. The poor girl was exhausted.

"And…"

"Matt spends extended periods of time in his van, sometimes not leaving for days at a time. He keeps in the back two containers. One is used for urination, the other for…well let's just say for the other. He smothers that one in used engine oil to keep down the stench."

"Jesus," Maggie made a face, definitely appalled at the thought. "How on earth would you know about that?"

"He showed me his van the first time I was able to get him to go to a drug counselor. He said he needed me to see what he was forced to live like—why he wanted so desperately to move in with me."

"Why the hell did you get involved with him in the first place?" Maggie's motherly side started to kick in. She immediately wanted to protect Lisa's obvious innocence.

"I ask myself all the time. But really, when I first met him he had this aura of spirituality surrounding him. I'd never experienced anything like it. He convinced me he was of a Christian spirit, and he followed the life of a good man. I admit I started to fall for him at that point. He had me so convinced when he finally revealed his addiction to me I thought I could help him to understand he had more to live for than his life as an addict." Lisa looked Maggie in the eye, "I truly thought I had been chosen to be the one to help him turn back around."

"Had you fooled, didn't he?"

"He pleaded with me to accept him and help him to stop. I tried everything to lead him away from his addiction. Then I discovered he'd been living this life off and on since he was about twelve and realized his whole character is formed around his addiction. No matter how hard he tries to be different, it pulls him back in to start again."

Maggie took a deep breath. "The only way change is possible is if they are the ones who want the change. Even then, it's an uphill battle the rest of their lives. Only a special person could stay with someone like that."

Lisa smiled halfway. "At first, I thought I was that person."

"Believe me, I understand wanting to be able to change someone's life for the good." Maggie spoke from experience, her own memories causing her to frown.

"I think sometimes if he'd made some different choices I might still be with him. I found out though, the compulsion to go back to the lifestyle he knew best won him over every time."

Maggie thoughts went to her brother, Howard. Although her sad experience with his addictions had turned out to be a blessing. She would never have had the relationship she had with Ryan if things had been different. He'd been the same way. Howard would plead with his family for forgiveness and say he would change. In the end he'd gone back to his drinking, which ultimately put him behind bars for murder.

"I'm not saying a person like that can't change for the good. People, no matter how good they are on the inside, sometimes get caught up in a need to forget their lives for a time. Despite what a lot of so called experts say, there's a lot more involved than just the addict's need to be accepted."

Lisa nodded. "We would talk, and every once in a while Matt would tell me about things that had happened to him, some of which I wasn't sure I should believe."

Maggie understood exactly what she meant. "They'll tell you what they think you want to hear one minute, then tell tall tales about things to help plead their case and justify their actions the next."

"Sounds like you've got personal experience with something like this," Lisa said sadly.

"I do." The grief residing in her heart surfaced for a moment then she pushed it quickly aside. "Howard, Ryan's father, is my half-brother."

"Oh Maggie, I am so sorry."

Maggie pulled herself together. "That's old history. There's no use in lamenting about things you can't do anything about."

She waved her hand in dismissal of the subject. There was no need to get all sappy and teary eyed.

"I suppose you're right," Lisa admitted.

"What we need to do, is concentrate on the current situation."

Lisa bowed her head. "Maggie, I should've left the day I came in. I'm so sorry I've brought all of this to your town. None of you deserve to be forced to defend yourselves against someone like Matt."

"Don't concern yourself. He's not going to last very long here. Not with Ryan on his heels." Maggie took another look at the young woman in front of her. The motherly instinct running high, this time for the one she may not have given birth to, but had mothered as a son, nonetheless.

"I'm so worried about Ryan. He needs to be careful. I'm not sure what Matt's capable of doing."

"I'm not too worried. Ryan can handle someone like Matt. What I'm not sure he can handle…is you."

Lisa raised her eyes, her brows furrowed. Maggie stared at her, needing to make her point abundantly clear.

"Ryan is very special to me. You and he have gotten pretty close to each other." Lisa nodded slowly, so Maggie went on, "My question to you is, after all of this is over, what do you think you will do?"

"Honestly, I really hadn't thought so far ahead. What I can tell you is exactly what I told Ryan last night. I would like nothing better than to explore the possibilities of a very long relationship with him."

"That's good to know. He deserves the best. He's a good man."

Lisa clasped her hands in front of her. "Yes, he's a very good man."

"I'm glad you realize that for yourself. Sometimes people can't see what they've got," Maggie said, shaking her head. "None of us deserve to be hurt the way either one of you have been."

"I guess this Tess really did him wrong. If I can help it, I would never hurt him that way."

Maggie nodded and sat back impressed the young woman understood what she referred to so quick. "I'll leave him to explain the details. But, I've seen him at his lowest, and I don't ever want to see him there again. If you do hurt him, you can believe you'll have more of us to deal with than just Ryan."

Lisa sat up straighter in her chair, her expression solemn. "If we can finally put an end to this nightmare of mine, I promise there won't be any reason for Ryan to be hurt because of me."

The two stared at each other for a minute, both wanting their point to be understood. A soft knock on the door brought their attention back to the world around them.

"Come," Maggie stated loudly enough for the person on the other side of the door to hear.

Ryan opened the door and stepped through quietly.

"Did the commissioned warriors go back to their lookouts?" Maggie asked referring to their inside joke about the nosey town folk.

"Everyone's gone back to life as it should be. I got them to promise not to harass either of you with questions, or hang about making the situation uncomfortable." Placing his protective hand on Lisa's shoulder, Maggie saw the immediate connection between them as Lisa raised her hand to cover his.

"I guess I should go back to the apartment, unless you still need me here?" Lisa asked, her eyes pleading Maggie to let her stay.

"Maggie, unless you need her, I thought Lisa might come with me to check out some things."

Maggie nodded her head, and stood in dismissal. "I think she's had enough for the day. I expect you to be bright and early at the Hut tomorrow. No reason for sloughing on your duties."

"I'll be there. Maggie, what I said about being careful, I meant that for you too." Lisa came forward and took Maggie's hands in hers. "Promise me you will take care of yourself."

Maggie's laugh was loud, "Are you kidding? He'd be crazy to mess with Maggie Travis."

* * * *

Silent, Lisa sat in the passenger seat of the patrol car waiting for Ryan to return. He'd told her because he had something special he wanted to show her they would bypass some of the other areas he'd planned on visiting, though first they would check out the lead they'd received from Pat earlier. He sent two of his deputies to check out what might turn out to be a resting place for the sought after Matt.

As they pulled into the recently closed state park, Lisa knew something didn't look right. The chain that should've been blocking the entry into the camp grounds lay on the ground allowing anyone to pass through. The lock appeared to be cut and discarded to the side. Even without this bold evidence, Lisa's untrained eye picked up on the recent upheaval around the chain's length. Freshly disturbed earth and fallen leaves showed bright against the weathered surrounding dirt where the chain had been dropped to the ground and dragged to the other side of the entrance.

After checking the abnormal entry to the park, Ryan got back into the car and started a slow progression forward, stopping at each camp area for a brief inspection of any fresh activity.

"Why did they close this park?" Lisa asked, looking around curiously. Just like the rest of the area she'd seen so far, this seemed like a beautiful place to take the family for a vacation.

"We had some trouble with rock slides at the eastern side of the park. The state has added this to the long list of needed repairs on the peninsula. We're not sure when they'll get around to installing the avalanche control that's needed."

"I bet that's affected your traffic from summer travelers."

"Yeah, put a dent in our usual summer revenues, but Lake Duchess is healthy and can stand alone without dreading any type of major impact."

Lisa gazed out the window to the cozy camping spots nestled here and there between the trees. She appreciated the fact Ryan realized she didn't want to be alone, and glanced up to his strong jaw and stoic expression as he focused his attention on the task. She didn't want to leave Ryan's side. He made her feel safe, but wasn't so sure she wanted to be present when he found Matt.

He slowed the car down to a stop when they came upon a site toward the middle of the grounds. Obviously, this one had been used by someone without much care to keeping the area clean. Trash was strewn across the grounds, blowing in the gusts of wind kicking up from the west. A small trickle of smoke came out of the fire pit, denoting recent use.

Ryan loosened his seatbelt and turned to Lisa. "Stay in the car. I'll go check this out."

Although she was warm, Lisa shivered at the thought of walking out in the open where anything might happen. The churning of her stomach rose closer to her throat, and she tried without much success to swallow the fear away.

"I'll be waiting for you," she said, trying to give Ryan a faint smile.

"Lock the doors, I'll be right back."

Lisa watched Ryan investigate the mess left behind. She didn't need the evidence. She knew who'd been the cause. Ryan rotated a propane tank tipped over on the side. He stood up and viewed the scene around him, and slowly walked back to the cruiser.

"He was definitely here. The tank has Pat's engraving on the side. Matt's still smart enough to keep moving around. He's got to be close by though."

Ryan laid his hand on Lisa's thigh as he started the car again. A tremble ran down her spine as she looked around, almost expecting Matt to pop up out of nowhere.

He squeezed her leg in his palm. "You're with me now. You don't have to be scared. You're safe."

Lisa leaned forward, her lips brushing his briefly to show her appreciation.

"Thank you."

"For what?" he asked, his brows furrowed.

"For being the one to try and end all of this," she reached up to caress his smooth jaw.

He caught her hand in his and brought her fingers to his lips. "I'll have to thank Matt for bringing you this far. I may never have met you if it hadn't been for him."

Lisa chuckled half-heartedly. "I'm glad I had the sense to stop for a sandwich when I did."

When they reached the highway, Ryan turned the car in the opposite direction of Lake Duchess.

"Where are you taking me?"

"Someplace not far from here I think you'll like."

A few minutes down the road, Ryan turned the car toward the mountains onto a gravel road. Before the turn, a small green sign read "Glacier Point – Next Left".

The road twisted and turned up the hillside for over a mile. A hazy fog gathered around the tree tops making it seem as if the giant trees jutted up, floating fearlessly over the steep depths of the hillside. At times, the drop on her right down the side of the cliff to the river below, made her a bit queasy so she closed her eyes. After a precariously sharp turn, the car leveled out, and she ventured to open her eyes again.

Ryan stopped the car in a small clearing designated as a parking area. Lisa looked around with curiosity. The underbrush had been removed from amongst this clearing of trees, and state park garbage cans were placed around the perimeter.

He came around to open the car door for her, and the powerful scent of pine and damp earth from under the thick carpet of needles washed over her as she took his hand and stepped out into the ambiance of the forest scene. Through the trees, the sunlight found crevices to sneak past the heavy boughs overhead, creating unusual warmth in the air. In the distance, the familiar sound of running river water was mixed with a constant crashing of sorts, accosting her senses with the unfamiliar sound.

"What's that?" she asked, searching around her for the origin of the noise.

"That's what I wanted to show you."

Ryan took her hand in his and led her toward the mountainside to a path leading up the side of a steep hill. Curious she followed him. All the while, the sound got louder. As they turned the last corner and reached the crest, Lisa exclaimed with joy at the sight she beheld.

Awed by the beauty of her surroundings, she rushed forward to experience the full view. To the left, the jagged mountainside shot straight up into the sky, hazed over by the steam from the moist rocks being heated by the sun. In front of them a rush of water cascaded through a gap in the hardened stone formed wall onto the river rocks some fifty yards below. Peering over the edge of the "View Point" site, the thunderous waterfall overtook all other sounds around her.

Precariously, even in the small fissures between the rocks of the cliff, plants and flowers had found a way to hang on to show their radiance against the hard bed they called home. Hardy bushes claimed their spots against the cliff in sheer defiance of the angle to which they needed to grow upright. Everywhere, life abounded— survived.

The air enveloped them in a blanket of cool refreshment, and Lisa breathed in deep to savor the moment.

"This is amazing!" she exclaimed and turned toward Ryan.

He stood behind her, his expression somewhat sad as he gazed behind her at the waterfall.

Sadness shouldn't exist in such a wonderful place, Lisa thought.

"Why such a long face? Don't you think this is beautiful?" she asked and raised her arms, twirling in a circle like a little girl.

Ryan moved forward and leaned out over the railing to the rushing water below. He stayed for a moment in his own thoughts then turned around to where Lisa had approached him with caution.

She was close enough for him to put his arms around her, and she wished he would.

"Beautiful, just like you," Ryan said as he ran his hands down her arms to grasp her hands in his. "I used to come up here all the time. There's a spot over there where I could be alone, to dream and figure things out. I didn't realize how much I missed coming here, until now."

She moved closer and pressed herself against his body, wanting to take away the despondency in his face.

"This is so close. Why on earth wouldn't you keep coming back?"

He frowned staring over her shoulder. Lisa recognized thoughts of a time when memories had not been so pleasant were clouding his eyes, something she'd seen in herself many times before.

"Last time I came here was right after Tess left me." Ryan's eyes came back to rest on her. "It was a very difficult time for me, and I haven't brought myself to come back."

Lisa's curiosity prompted a million questions, but she knew he needed to tell her in his own way.

"Tell me about her."

Ryan grasped Lisa's hand and led her to the picnic table set not too far from the glorious view. They sat beside each other, facing the waterfall, his hand on hers, his thigh touching hers, as if drawing from her a strength he needed.

"I've known Tess since we were kids. We didn't pay much attention to each other until high school. That's when I fell in love with her."

Lisa didn't need to say anything. She understood where this story was headed already. She rubbed his hand to let him know she was there for him. Ryan continued to gaze out into the distance.

"I wasn't handling things very well one summer, with my mom gone and my dad in jail. She helped me through some real tough times. Because she was so full of life, so motivated in everything she did, I couldn't resist her." He stared down at their connected hands.

"What happened?" She squeezed his hand and he squeezed back, his eyes coming to rest on hers again.

"We decided to get married after I went through law enforcement training to become what I thought was an honorable profession. I got a job in Cooper Point and worked as a deputy for a couple of years. I decided I needed to try my best to provide her all the best, so when the position here came up for elected Sheriff I applied. Luckily my mentor and friend, the retiring Sheriff Woodard, gave me the highest commendation a deputy can get. So, when all the election votes were counted, I received ninety-six percent of the votes and got the job."

"You must have been ecstatic to get a position like this so young."

"I was. A good job, a wife and a beautiful family was all I wanted. But Tess started talking about wanting more out of life. She was restless, and kept asking me to go with her to 'the big city'. She'd heard how we would be so much better off and live a better life away from here."

Lisa raised her eyebrows, "Believe me, my experience is the big city isn't better, it's just bigger."

He looked at her, but she could tell he wasn't seeing her. Gazing into his eyes she could almost see the distant past swimming in his mind's eye in a swirling eddy behind his green pools to the soul.

"Leaving became an obsession with her. She wouldn't talk about anything else. I told her once my first term was up as Sheriff I would think about applying to one of the larger cities where she could experience the city life."

"Sounds like you really loved her."

Ryan remained silent as he stared out toward the crashing water.

"I did," he said finally and continued. "We planned the wedding at the Chapel in Lake Duchess. Everyone in town was invited, and Maggie of course fixed this whole feast for us. Only it never got that far. When Tess was asked if she would love me and cherish me for the rest of her life, she stood there looking at me. She couldn't do it. She left me standing at the altar, with my heart torn to shreds."

Ryan's gaze came back to their joined hands. Tears stung the backs of Lisa's eyes and she wished she could say something to ease the heartbreak. This was a side of Ryan that Lisa hadn't seen before. The big tough Sheriff was actually a sensitive man who had suffered tragedies, discarded by the ones he'd loved. No wonder he was so scared of opening up to her.

"Used to come up here and wonder if life was worth all the sorrow it caused, and I decided I never wanted to experience that kind of pain again. I haven't gotten involved with anyone since then. I didn't want anything to do with a relationship. I'm still not sure I'm ready to get involved."

Lisa felt her heart leap in her chest. *What is he trying to tell me?*

His fingers pressed against her hand, rubbing against her palm. "I'm starting to have real feelings for you Lisa. All I ask is that you don't do the same thing to me. Just be honest with me from the start. I can't be blind sided again. If you don't want to find out what this thing is between us, tell me now. "

Overwhelmed, a single tear at the corner of Lisa's eye flowed over and traveled down her cheek. Ryan caught the tear with his thumb, brushing it away softly followed by a long kiss on her forehead. She wrapped her arms around his neck and held on tight. She needed to show him love did exist, and that life was precious. Above all she needed to reaffirm this belief for herself.

"Make love to me, Ryan," she whispered in his ear.

He pulled back from her, his eyes bearing a short lived scrutiny, as he scooped her into his arms. Their lips met in a feverish battle as she covered his face in kisses, drawing strength from his returned passion.

She knew she needed him. She already knew he was everything she'd ever wanted in a man. There was no turning back now. She would be the woman of his dreams as well.

Ryan was desperate to show Lisa what he was feeling inside. He wanted her in his secret place—a place where dreams were made. The legality of it all didn't even cross his mind.

He took her to his secluded spot and set her on her feet, unseen from the main walk, covered overhead by the giant boughs of the cedar tree he loved so much. It stood as regal and proud as he remembered. If cut down, the rings of time would show hundreds of years of standing against the coastal weather. This old tree may have seen many things, but he doubted the experience it was about to witness.

Clothes were flung this way and that as he and Lisa undressed in eagerness unmatched by the night before. The cool air against his bare skin reminded him it may be a little chillier than she may be used to, so he pulled her into his arms again and lay her down in the bed of grasses.

"I've never brought anyone here before," he murmured between kisses.

"Then I'll be the first to show you what you've been missing," Lisa whispered. Her lips tasted of sweetness, her zealous kisses of an unleashed passion he'd begun to crave. She slowly pushed him onto his back and rose up next to him. Unexpected, he gazed up at her soft sultry body poised above him, and wondered what pleasures to anticipate.

The twinkle in her eyes was enchanting, and he felt as if he were being drawn to her without any need to escape. Ryan couldn't resist the temptation, and he placed his hands around her waist and drew her up on top of him. He could see she understood exactly what he wanted. But instead, she leaned forward to tease him with the delicate brush of her breasts against his chest, her hardened nipples impressing upon him the need to capture one between his lips to titillate her with his teeth. Her long hair came down around her shoulders, tickling him as she made her way up his torso with hot wet kisses.

251

"Is this what you want?" she asked in a low breathy swoop as she brought her lips down to his. He sensed a tenderness where there hadn't been before, as if she savored the moment, testing the responses she evoked from him.

The game she was playing was a dangerous one. He didn't know how well he could hold back. As she gazed deep into his eyes, he saw a blazing heat stoked and ready to flare if she were to let go. For a second, he sensed he hadn't even touched the tip of her passions yet, and almost forgot to wait and let this play out the way it started. He wanted to take control and bring out the whetted appetite she'd begun to reveal to him. Yet surprisingly, her unleashed fever enticed him to wait for what she had in store for him next.

She brought her hands up to grasp the back of his neck and guided his return kisses where she wanted them. He granted her the unspoken requests while she in turn pulled him closer to his own power to ignite.

First, she drew him close to her ear, bringing his lips to brush her neck and pressed him closer to nibble at the spot where she'd used her perfume. The wonderful potion tantalized him still, the fragrance he would buy a boatload of for her as soon as he found out its name. When he trailed his lips back down her neck to the spot above her shoulder, her moan caused the blood to course through his veins quicker.

He brought his hands up to caress the curves she pressed against him, filling him with anticipation. Her thighs clasped around his middle, unmistakably taunting him with her wet heat against his abdomen. So close in vicinity to his straining manhood, he couldn't wait for her to sink down onto him and claim what he'd begun to believe would be forever hers. On a slight movement, she allowed him to tease her breasts with his tongue, and as she lifted up he took the opportunity to reach between her legs to find the spot to drive her equally wild. He felt as if he instinctively knew what she craved the most. She responded to his touch by pressing against his hand with an occasional gasp escaping between her lips. The sound was like a switch, turning his pleasure swiftly into a feverish need, one he had no doubt she could satisfy.

She pressed down hard enough he couldn't move his fingers any longer and whispered in his ear, "Not yet. Let me."

She rose up to sit on her haunches, her hair covering her shoulders like the picture of the Goddess Venus he'd seen once. He swore a glow surrounded her like in the painting. Barely able to contain himself, he waited, desperation beginning to set in.

Through her heavy rapid breaths, she smiled with mischievousness in her eyes. "But this isn't all you want, is it?"

He couldn't think of a word to say. So he shook his head.

She took her time as his hormones began to scream for satisfaction. Between her legs, she grasped his rigid penis in her soft hands and rubbed gently up and down, making his heightened sensitivity more intense. Then with a laugh at his throaty groan, she guided his entry, a feral sounding growl escaping as she sank down to the depths of his length. As the glorious warmth of her folds caressed him, her purposeful movements brought him to realize in her sensuality she expressed more than a mere physical need. Her actions spoke of things not yet said, of feelings not yet divulged.

He watched as she drew him into her very being with an emotional passion as deep as her physical need. A spirituality of fulfillment surrounded her every movement. Her need so great, Ryan's own arousal awakened a new realization within him.

He'd never really loved before. Not like this.

With a new fevered appetite, he drove into her. Grasping her hips, he pulled her down as she plunged over him. He wanted to show exactly how he felt, the elation too much to keep to himself, each stroke a testament of his discovery for her.

He felt her heat tensing around his penis as she threw back her head and called out his name. So with expertise, he grabbed hold of her and flipped her beneath him, never once missing a stroke in the rhythm they'd set.

Now, his strokes became gentler as he awaited her climb back up toward release.

"Lisa," he said softly. "Look at me. I want to see your eyes."

The erotic moment her eyes opened, bright with arousal and her cheeks flushed from the flow of the building orgasm, had his heart pounding with ferocious beats. His rhythm became faster, his strokes deeper. Her breaths came more erratic, and she reached out to grasp his shoulder. His own need to release came rushing forward, and an utter exhilaration flowed over him as they melted into each other in total ecstasy.

They lay, unmoving with nothing left to give. He moved far enough to gather her into his arms, the knowledge of his newest revelation replenishing his long lost sense of happiness.

Ryan wasn't sure how long they lay in each other's arms, but if it were up to him they'd never leave.

"Next time we come out we'll have to bring a blanket so we can stay longer."

He brought his hands up to pull her close to him, and his lips began to travel along her neck, amazed at how quick he was aroused by her kiss.

"Who needs a blanket?" she asked, eyes half-closed, reaching up to bring his head down to hers.

"My thoughts exactly," he laughed. He pressed her against him then started to pull away. "We need to be getting back. There are things I need to look into this afternoon."

Lisa smiled. "Always the Sheriff, aren't you."

He stood and swept her into his arms. "Admit it. You wouldn't want it any other way."

A sudden unusual static sound came bursting out of the radio clipped to his belt.

"Sheriff Jacobs…Sheriff Jacobs, this is Deputy Hines. Do you copy?" Bobby's familiar voice called out.

Without hesitation he released Lisa and reached down to grab his pants off the ground to pull the radio from his belt.

"This is Sheriff Jacobs. What's going on Bobby?"

"Sheriff, I think you should get back here quick. There's been an altercation in Lake Duchess."

Ryan had already started to pull on his clothes, Lisa not far behind.

"What type of altercation?"

"That crazy son of a…" Ryan heard voices in the background, and what sounded like a reprimand from Maggie about professionalism. "The person of interest was found breaking and entering at the Travis residence."

His stomach twisted in angst, relieved only by the fact he'd heard her voice. "Maggie? Is she all right?"

"She received an injury, but she's fine, just a little shook up."

"Did you catch him?"

"No sir, he'd gone by the time we got here."

"All right, secure the area. My ETA is 10 minutes."

"Roger that," Bobby responded.

Ryan hooked his belt as Lisa put on her shoes and held his hand out to her.

"Let's go."

Chapter 13

By the time they reached Maggie's house Lisa was a little shaken up herself. She understood law enforcement traveled at whatever speed they felt necessary, but didn't know if she wanted to ever experience *that* again, especially coming down off the mountainside.

Maggie sat on her front steps, a cold pack pressed against her left eye. Paramedics stood around her assessing any further need for medical attention. Both deputies stood as well, far enough away to not receive any more wrathful words from the fired up victim.

"No, I'm not going to the hospital. I've got a bump on the head. You said yourself I don't have a concussion. I've been through worse than this. I think I can handle a little headache. You over there...yes you, come here." Maggie shouted toward Bobby and the younger Deputy. "Don't you think you should be out searching for that maniac?"

Lisa almost smiled at the barking orders Maggie passed to everyone around her. The situation, however, was much graver than Maggie made it out to be. Here, an older woman had been attacked in her own home, by an intruder who could have caused her real harm.

As they reached Maggie, she appeared relieved Ryan had arrived.

"Finally, would you tell these people to go do their jobs and leave me alone?"

"Maggie, are you all right?" Ryan asked, gently pulling the ice pack away from her face. Lisa sucked in a quick breath. The beginnings of a black eye over Maggie's left temple had started to show red and purplish colors spreading from the eyelid to her hairline.

"I'm fine. This is only a bump on the head. It would take more than that little wimp to put a hurt on me. If he were here right now I'd show him a thing or two. Caught me off guard is all. But I gave him something he won't forget for a long time," she ranted raising the cast iron pan from beside her on the steps.

"What did I tell you about trying to be a hero? He could have killed you," Ryan said in frustration.

"I'm not going to let some whacked out maniac do damage to my property. Wiry little guy. He had to move pretty quick to get away from me though."

"Tell me what happened."

"Claudia burnt up one of my pans again at the diner," she claimed, referring to the lunch cook on the shift after Maggie's. "I came home to pick up another skillet, to bring back for the dinner crew."

Maggie adjusted the pack over her eye and drew in a deep breath. Lisa saw the trauma of the events beginning to catch up with her.

"When I came out of my house he was at the top of the stairs trying to break into Lisa's place with a crowbar. When I shouted at him to stop he came running down the stairs at me. He had this weird crazed look in his eyes and he kept screaming over and over again something like 'she's mine you hear me, she'll pay.' Smelled awful too, needs a bath," Maggie said, scrunching up her nose.

"What were you thinking? Didn't I tell you to not provoke him? Didn't I tell you to call me instead of trying to take things into your own hands?" Ryan snapped then shook his head and sat down next to her on the front steps.

"Took a swing at him with the pan, thought I'd get him too. He moved out of the way just in time. Didn't catch him square on the head like I wanted to, but he went flying against the wall. Only thing is, he took me with him. His elbow caught me at the temple here. But I caught the side of his head with the pan. Then as we went down I gave him a strong left hook to the nuts. Tried to get him in a headlock, but he squirmed out of it and ran into the woods screaming like a bunch of banshees."

Ryan bowed forward shaking his head with animated grief in his hands. All of a sudden he burst out in laughter, and Maggie joined in. Lisa, confused, watched the two of them laugh in a robust way making her think they had both gone a little crazy themselves.

"I wish I'd seen it," he exclaimed returning back to sanity. "Only you, Maggie, there's nobody like you anywhere."

Sniffling from the laughter's affect, Maggie took the ice pack from her eye, which had now bloomed into a full blown purple and blue splotch over her eye. Ryan reached over and gave her a big hug. He shook her a bit as he pulled back from her.

"Don't ever do that again, you hear me? I know you're tough, but leave the crime fighting to me. All right?" he said, making his point with the intensity of his glare.

Maggie nodded her head, and placed the ice pack back on her eye.

A police cruiser from La Push pulled up in front of them. A short round man in uniform wiggled out from behind the wheel and came toward them. Ryan stood and held out his hand in greeting.

"Hello John, come to help out?"

"I was down at the diner when the call went out over the radio about Maggie. Your boys here looked like they had their hands full, so I thought I'd do a quick search of the area to find this BOL of yours."

"Appreciate your help. Things have been pretty busy around here lately. He's upped his status to a B&E with an assault charge to boot."

"You sure this is the same guy?"

"No question about it," Ryan replied in assurance.

"You might want to look at what I found out at the Belamy's vacation spot. I know they aren't due to come in until the end of the month, but there's been some recent activity."

Ryan nodded. "Go on ahead and make sure he doesn't come back. I'll join up with you in a minute."

"You got it." John waddled back toward his car.

Turning back toward them, Lisa saw Ryan's professionalism written on his facial expression. He meant business, and nobody better get in the way.

"Ladies, I'm going to go check this out."

By this time, several townspeople were lingering in the background to find out what the flashing lights were all about. Ryan signaled to his deputies, gave them some short orders to follow in his absence, and came back to where Lisa and Maggie sat in silence on the porch.

"Lisa I want you to help Maggie pack up some things, and you do the same. When I get back I'm taking you both back to my house where I can keep a closer eye on you."

Maggie stood with authority, a small grunt on the way up, and pointed her finger at Ryan.

"Don't be telling me what to do here. Lisa can do what she wants, as for me I'm not going to let some half crazed dope addict chase me out of my home. Next time he comes I'll have my rifle handy and fill that scrawny butt of his with some buckshot."

Ryan stood back and didn't say a word. Lisa recognized he knew when not to argue with Maggie. He didn't agree or disagree.

"I need to go check out what John found. Lisa you need to be ready when I get back. Don't worry. Bobby will stay here until I return." He turned toward Maggie and pointed his finger right back at her. "You and I will discuss this later."

Lisa walked him out to his cruiser, her stomach churning again as it had the night before. She wished none of this had happened. Now she needed to worry about the people she cared about, not just herself.

It would be better if I left...she started to think.

Ryan turned to her and put his hands on her shoulders. "Try to talk some sense into her, would you?" Her non-response triggered his next statement. "You're not thinking about leaving, are you?"

Lisa wasn't one to lie. She didn't know how to answer his question, so she shrugged her shoulders, and made an indecisive sound, with brows furrowed.

"Dear God Lisa, are you going to run for the rest of your life? Are you going to let this idiot control every move you make?"

The emotion was too much to hold back, and tears began to stream down her face. "Maggie wouldn't be hurt if I wasn't here," she argued weakly.

"None of us would be hurt if everyone followed my direction. Maggie should have gone back into her house when she saw him and called the emergency number. The deputies would have been here in two minutes, and probably would have caught him in the act. He should be locked up right now. Instead she risked herself, and delayed our ability to catch him."

"She only did what comes natural to her," Lisa responded in defense of Maggie's actions.

"Yes, but she might have been hurt worse doing it." Ryan took a deep breath, glancing toward the sky and back before he continued. "Don't run on me now Lisa. Let me catch him so he won't be able to continue this pattern."

"But, if I wasn't here…" she started to say then he interrupted her in obvious frustration.

"Damn it, even if you were out of the picture, don't you think he'd be doing this to someone else? Thing is, whoever ends up with him may not be as strong as you were to leave him. What do you think would happen to them if they stayed with him?"

She'd never really thought in that manner. This picture was too horrible for her to imagine. She couldn't live with herself knowing she'd been the cause of someone else going through what she'd endured, or even worse. The tears continued to flow as defeat covered her either way she turned.

"Please, stay with me Lisa. Don't pull away from me now."

It was hard to look away from Ryan's mesmerizing eyes. They seemed to beg for an answer.

She'd thought she could be strong enough to stay and stand up against her assailant, but now she wasn't sure. By staying, she would be endangering everyone around her. She wanted to stay, to finally grab onto the freedom and love beginning to bud in her heart. But, would her selfish act cause her to lose the very thing she wanted to hold onto?

Ryan made an aggravated exclamation when she didn't answer. He walked back and forth in front of her then stopped and came back to place his hands on her shoulders again. He gazed into her eyes as if willing her to make up her mind.

"I'm so tired. I don't know what to do," Lisa rubbed her eyes vigorously, but no relief came from her action.

"I know you are honey. Let me do my job. I'm the expert here. Let me put a stop to all of this." He took her face in his hands and gently kissed both cheeks.

"Tell me one thing. Do you want to stay?"

The words wouldn't come. Lisa could do nothing but nod her head in response.

"Then you have to trust me. Stop running from your fears and let go of the reins. Trust me to make this right for you. Can you do that?"

She paused for only a moment longer, her heart torn between fear and love then nodded her head again. Ryan pulled her into his arms and held on tight. Lisa wrapped her arms around his waist to hang on as if he were her only life preserver.

"Now, I need to go check a couple things out." He pulled away gently and wiped the last tears from her eyes. "When I get back, you're coming with me."

Lisa looked toward Maggie, who was talking sternly to Bobby about something or other.

"What about Maggie?"

"I'm not sure we'll be able to talk her into coming with us or not. I can't force her. Knowing her, she'll stick to her guns and do exactly what she wants." Ryan brushed his lips across her forehead. "Maggie won't like it, but I'll have to continue the 24 hour watch, this time on her."

"Good luck with that."

* * * *

Unlike her normal actions, Angela stood off to the side of all the activity, cell phone glued to her ear. She watched everyone with a sharp eye, making mental note of Ryan's location at all times.

"No sweetheart, I don't know exactly what's going on. All I can get from these deputies is something happened between Maggie and this so called attacker. If you ask me, this girl's got something to do with it. I think she set this guy up to it so she could get some sympathy from Ryan."

Angela paused to walk a little closer to the conversation she heard from one of the other town members standing near.

"Wait, wait…hold on," she whispered into the phone, pretending to be looking at her nails as she listened to what the couple were saying to each other.

"That poor girl," said Lucy to her husband Pat. "To think, she's been living like this for so long. I don't understand why she never went to the authorities. Surely, they could have helped," she said shaking her head.

"We don't know what's gone on this whole time. Maybe she's looked for help, and Sheriff Jacobs is the first one to try," Pat responded. "Remember Molly Jenkins? You know, Ralph's widow. All she had to do was ask, and he was up on her roof putting up Christmas lights last year. He has a soft heart when it comes to women in need."

"You're right, Pat," Lucy agreed. Angela glanced up to see Lucy Hawkins eying her suspiciously. "Hello, Angela. Did you want something?"

Angela stepped back from her closeness to the private exchange. "Oh, no, no…just got carried away with all this activity," she said waiving her free arm in front of her.

She sauntered a few steps away and turned back to her cell phone.

"Tess, if you don't get yourself back here quick, you're not going have another chance to get in with the Sheriff. This girl's got her hooks in your Ryan and I don't think she's going to let go without a fight."

She watched and snorted as Ryan bent down to give Lisa a kiss.

"Don't worry, honey. Mommy will help you figure out a way to get him back for you."

After she hung up with her daughter, Angela continued to watch the activity. Ryan was putting the girl's bag in his trunk. Obviously she'd wiggled her way into making him feel sorry for her.

As if a switch had been flipped on, the solution came to her.

"Oh, you smart, smart woman," she said to herself. "He likes needy women does he? Well, I've got the perfect one for you, Sheriff Jacobs."

* * * *

Matt realized his van would be too recognizable, so he left the vehicle parked at the little cabin he'd found. He took the Taurus he'd jacked and switched the plates for luck. That had been one hell of a feat getting both vehicles in the same place at the same time without being noticed.

By the time he made it back into town, he'd found all the lights and activity focused around the house where Lisa lived. So, he parked in an inconspicuous spot to wait and see what would happen next. When he'd passed by slowly, Lisa had been coming down from the room above the garage and set down the bag she had in her hand to talk to the old woman. She was leaving. He was lucky she hadn't left yet.

Matt wished they would hurry up. The canister of starter fluid he picked up might be easier to carry around, but the damn thing didn't last very long. He craved the extreme euphoria the propane gave him, like nothing else he'd ever huffed.

He ignored the uncontrollable twitch of his hands on the steering wheel as he waited for Lisa and '*that dick*' to pack her things into the trunk of the cruiser. Impatience set in, and he whacked the car's dashboard with both hands, causing an unbearable tingle to shoot through his already sensitive nerves. Intense pain stabbed through his palms and seemed to go straight to his throbbing head. Swearing, he reached up to touch the lump that had formed after being clobbered with the iron skillet.

"Crazy old woman!" he muttered out loud to himself. "God, I need some propane right now."

The immense thirst for complete delirium was almost too much to handle. He knew he should wait to take another hit from the can of fluid on the passenger seat. The temptation to take a short trip and forget the here and now played with his need to stay focused. But if he listened, and took one now, Lisa might escape before he could function again. This might be his last chance. He had to follow through and work out a way to get her back this time.

Finally!

She was getting into the car. Matt watched in anger as Ryan opened the door for Lisa and gave her a long passionate kiss before giving her a hand into the cruiser's passenger seat. His heart pumped wildly when he started to imagine all the things he wanted to do to the son-of-a-bitch who'd stolen his Lisa.

Why does he have to be a cop? I hate those bastards.

They caused trouble for him all the time. None of them were worth their title. Only his father was worthy of the significance of wearing the badge of honor.

Matt started the Taurus's engine to wait. It hadn't been hard to steal. People out here were stupid. The car door had been left unlocked and the extra key he found in a magnetic box under the right front fender. Luckily, he'd found a detailed map of the area under the visor of the car. As he waited for the Sheriff's car to pull out of the driveway, he took another glance at the map. This would definitely help him keep track of where they were headed, in case he forgot later.

He began to cough, so he slipped a cough drop into his mouth to stifle the constant tickle he'd developed in the back of his throat. A pain shot through his swollen temple as he coughed again.

Matt glanced in the rear view mirror.

"Shit, shit, shit," he exclaimed and turned his face away from the window to act as if he were looking for something in the passenger side seat.

A black and white drove by without stopping, the driver obviously intent on something else. Ahead, the car pulled in next to the Sheriff's cruiser to communicate some piece of information, then parked next to the group of first responders still on the scene.

The Sheriff's cruiser pulled out to go the opposite direction from where Matt waited. He stayed stationary long enough not to be noticed by the Sheriff, and followed far enough in the distance to remain inconspicuous. This would be difficult to carry out. He imagined the Sheriff might give him some problems, but he would get Lisa back—one way or another.

This time he would make her stay.

Chapter 14

Intent on her surroundings Lisa sat silent looking out her half-open window, a strand of her hair blowing gently against her face. Ryan turned down the west side of the lake and veered to the left onto a long dirt driveway. Through the trees, a reflection of the late afternoon blue sky was painted on the glass-like surface of the water. Full alders and tall firs guarded the lake on either side of the drive, as if they stood guarding the drive and only allowed them access to their destination.

Ryan reached over and squeezed Lisa's hand. On instinct she griped his fingers and squeezed back. "Everything will be all right sweetie," he said with a smile.

She didn't know if she should believe him yet. In the back of her mind she kept seeing herself on the run again, fleeing for her life. The whole time they'd been driving she'd memorized directions and gauged the distance to the neighboring houses and main roads, in case she needed to escape.

Lisa gave a soft smile when he pulled her hand up to kiss the fingers that remained wrapped around his. She nodded, but continued her silence until they came into view of the house. Her eyes widened and she sat up straighter to peer through the windshield with awe.

"Oh," she exclaimed in surprise. "I didn't expect such a large place."

Ryan grinned with pride. "I was lucky. The couple who owned this lot before me moved east to take care of family. I'd known them all my life, so when I said I was interested in buying it, they offered me owner financing with a low down payment. Otherwise, I wouldn't have been able to afford something of this size."

She stepped out of the vehicle and gazed at the home of her dreams—an impossible dream she'd given up long before now.

The tree lined area around the house was in need of some landscaping, and paled in comparison to the resort fashioned exterior of the split level residence. Lisa's heart quivered as she took in the expanse of the fully surrounding porch, which screamed 'family' to her. She imagined a bunch of kids running and jumping, happily causing havoc, as she and Ryan sat on the porch swing to plan what appeared to be the start of a potting project along the west edge flower boxes. Her secret thoughts made her smile, and she caught Ryan's gaze as he caught her reaction. He grinned at her, his bright eyes sparkling with his own inner ponderings, as if he knew exactly what she was thinking.

Lisa shied away from him, and looked above her to see an architectural delight. Viewpoints were positioned on every side of the house through giant bay windows. These she imagined held the perfect place to snuggle up with an afghan and a good book. Something she hadn't done in a very long time.

The lake, at the far side of the house, rippled slightly with the breath of fresh air that streamed across the surface. Startled at first, she heard the loud quack of ducks, being disturbed by the loud barking of a dog. She walked a few yards to the right to see the lumbering chase of a redbone coonhound running around in a comical display of pursuit after the disarray of startled birds.

"Pluto," Ryan shouted through cupped hands at the preoccupied hound. The large head of the animal snapped around and he stopped dead in his tracks. In a matter of seconds, the huge canine's torso slammed up against Ryan's chest, paws on either side of his shoulders, with tongue happily lapping at his beloved owner's face. Taking Pluto by the collar, Ryan pulled him down to the ground, laughing the whole time.

"Looks like I have competition," Lisa said, the interaction between the two causing an odd joy in her heart. Such a simple thing, as the love of a pet, touched her in a way she hadn't expected. She had to stifle the sudden surfacing of tears.

Her voice brought the attention of the overly excited hound, and he vaulted toward her in the same manner. She tried to back away, which resulted in her back coming in contact with the car behind her. The dog effortlessly plastered her against the hood, his huge nose inches away from hers as he sniffed her with suspicion.

Ryan continued to laugh as he tried to pry the dog away from her, but the canine's curiosity was much more insistent, his neck straining against his owner's efforts to dislodge him. Then without warning, the warm wet dousing swipe of Pluto's tongue across her cheek made Lisa burst out in giggles. She wrapped her arms around his midsection, and buried her face in his neck, reveling in the unconditional love the dog had offered.

"Pluto, you big goof," Ryan exclaimed as he succeeded in pulling the dog back down to the ground. "Sorry. He's just a big baby. He wouldn't hurt a fly."

Lisa continued to laugh as she wiped the drool off of her cheek with her sleeve. "No problem. He's just such a surprise." The dog plopped his butt down, but continued to sniff her fingers as if waiting for a surprise.

"Welcome to my home, Goofball and all," Ryan indicated the steps up the front porch with one hand, his other hand ruffling the red fur on the top of the dogs head in affection.

Once inside the wide entryway, Lisa looked around with a curiosity more fitting to a future homeowner than a guest. To the left, a see-through fireplace wall had been crafted at the far end of the huge great room, separating leisure from the indulgence of the dining area that faced the lakefront. The open high-vaulted ceilings of the two rooms created an appearance of grandeur. Yet, when she walked into the area, comfort surrounded her in a blanket of warm brown and orange colors. The occasional splash of blue and green showed her what she thought would be a picturesque view of the lake at fall.

Ryan proceeded to show her around the house, no doubt proud of his accomplishment. Here and there, she found his heritage revealed in the furnishings and décor he'd chosen for each room. His den held what he described as an old Quinault tribal floor mat fashioned out of tightly wound cedar bark, the design indicative of his cultural ties. Beautifully crafted pots, baskets and vases, set in strategic places picked up the light from the afternoon sunlight filtering through the massive windows in every room of the house.

Lisa held his hand as they walked through each room, her heart thudding, her need to belong increasing in exponential bounds. She'd dreamt of a home like this—a man like this—and wondered again whether she would be able to stay. The thought of leaving now devastated her.

Not really knowing if God listened to her, she had to believe that he did, and prayed silently, asking again for an end to her nightmare.

Please Lord, make this possible. Let me have a real life. You know the desires of my heart. Let me love and be loved by this man forever.

Upstairs not all rooms had been decorated. A guestroom in clean and simple décor, sat across from Ryan's room. She was more interested in the masculinity pulling at her as it flowed from his room with rich brown, rust and evergreen colors, surrounding the sturdy wood framed bed and dresser. Lisa felt as if she belonged there, and was torn whether to ask if she would be sleeping in his room, or in the only other room ready for occupancy.

He hadn't offered to show her the room off to one side, the door slightly ajar. Curious, she placed her hand on the doorknob. As she glanced up into his face for acceptance, she saw an almost stone-like coldness in his eyes, so unlike his usual demeanor.

"May I?" she asked, her inquisitive side peaked by his sudden change.

He nodded without words, not offering to supply any further information.

Lisa opened the door and stepped into the cool darkened room. Boxes, taped and ready for storage sat along one wall, others, in the process of being packed, sat open in the middle of the floor. She moved toward one and peeked inside.

The remnants of some type of craft project gone horribly wrong caught her attention. She reached in and pulled out what appeared to be a large yellow sunflower potholder. The shape resembled a big round yellow dot with half embroidered seeds in process, the leaves a misshapen cornstalk. Underneath, various other kitchen decorations of the same motif were thrown in haphazardly. Not something she imagined Ryan wanting in his kitchen. She turned and raised her eyebrows at him in silent question of the source to such an uncharacteristic item.

"Not much for crafts?"

Ryan shrugged his shoulders and said without any hint of emotion, "Tess had a thing for sunflowers."

"Oh," Lisa responded, realizing she was tiptoeing on shaky ground.

"I haven't had a chance to send that stuff back to her. Don't know if she even wants it." The male tendency to not divulge any information unless asked showed through in his answer.

Still very curious, Lisa turned and pulled out a picture frame from an adjoining open box. The image of a younger Ryan up close and personal with a young, blond haired girl struck her in an odd way. She studied the faces of the two young people, obviously in love with each other. This must be Tess. She peeked up at Ryan's rocky expression and decided to leave any further questions until later.

Lisa placed the photo back into the box and turned to him. She didn't like him to be this way. Upon impulse she grabbed him around the waist and pulled him toward her. She pressed her lips to his, encouraging his stature to relax, coaxing him with kisses as she molded her fingers around the back of his neck to pull him closer.

"What are you doing?" he asked in surprise.

"You need to loosen up a bit," she said smiling up at him. "What do you say you show me where I'll be sleeping, and then I can scrounge up something for a late lunch?"

She continued to place little kisses along his jaw line, moving slowly down his neck, stopping at the base of his throat where the pulse beat with heated arousal.

Snapped out of his candor, Ryan scooped her up into his arms and brought her out into the hallway. He moved into his room closing the door behind him with his foot, and dropped her onto the full king sized mattress, his eyes burning a trail of fire into her with his desire.

"You'll be sleeping here with me. But, how about I show you the pleasures of said inhabitance, and then I fix you a delicious barbecued steak for an early dinner?" he replied pulling his shirt out to unbutton the first few buttons.

"Hmmm…" Lisa said in exaggerated consideration. "I have to tell you, I think I like your idea much better."

"I thought you might." Ryan lowered himself over her, and began a luxurious exploration of her neck, and collarbone with his lips and teeth. She felt the hardening of his virile manhood against her thigh, his warm breath against the sensitized skin of her breasts. "I want you," he breathed against her ear.

"I want you too," she whispered back.

You have no idea how much I mean that, she thought in desperation and pulled his head back to plunder his mouth with kisses.

* * * *

The night air brushed past Lisa's cheeks, the unique scent of the surrounding woods enveloping them while she watched Ryan place the steaks on the grill.

He came back to the patio table and picked up the half empty bottle of white chardonnay. She smiled at the inquisitive look he gave her as she lifted her glass for a refill. This was her second glass before dinner, and she didn't care.

"I'm glad you're finally relaxing," Ryan commented as he sat down next to her.

Pluto had settled himself under the table, his back end against Lisa's foot, his nose resting on his huge paws. Lisa laughed when she looked down at him, his big brown eyes staring right back at her. Then he would glance toward Ryan and back again, apparently waiting for a taste of the scrumptious smelling beef that sizzled on the grill.

She reached down to pet his head, loving every minute of the returned affection in the lapping of his tongue against her palm.

"There isn't much else to do but relax out here. You have such a perfect life. I'd give anything to share something like this."

Lisa grimaced at herself and glanced up at Ryan. She had no idea why she said her thoughts out loud. At times his face could be very expressive, this time she saw she'd sparked some curious thoughts in him and wondered what he could be thinking. Though, his silence bothered her.

"It's not as perfect as it seems. It can be pretty lonely at times." His low saddened voice made her tremble in recognition of his solitary circumstances. So many times she'd felt the same way.

"Not possible. You've got the best friend possible here. There's no way you can be lonesome when he's around," she said reaching down to pet the dog again. In awaited expectation, Pluto rose up quick to meet her hand, in the process knocking his head on the rim of the glass top table.

"You goofball," Ryan laughed as he reached out to steady the table. "Food isn't done yet. Settle down."

They sat for a moment gazing out over the setting sun on the lake's surface. Lisa continued to scratch behind the ears of the coonhound, his nose resting on her knee as he continued to stare up at them.

"Tell me about your mother."

The out of the blue question startled Lisa.

"Oh. What would you like to know?"

"Do you miss her?" His question brought a bundle of guilt and loss to her mind. She'd never had a chance to share with anyone about her mother before.

"I do. I can't tell you how much." Lisa traced the floral pattern of the tabletop with her finger. "There isn't a day goes by I don't wish things were different."

"Have you been able to visit her at all?"

"I tried once, but somehow Matt knew I was there. He was waiting outside the Marshall Center when I got there, holding a pitiful bunch of flowers in his hand. By the looks of him, he'd been using and still living on the streets. I couldn't take the chance. I thought maybe he'd try to lure me close enough to grab hold of me. I told the cab driver to take me back to the airport."

"When was that?"

"Let's see…must be about two years ago," she said sullenly. "She doesn't deserve this. I should be there for her."

"Are you anything like her?"

The tears sprang up quick, and she brushed away the one that escaped. "Funny, my Dad used to say we were twins." The smile on Ryan's face made her want to tell him all about her mother. "Here, you want to see a picture of her?"

"Sure," Ryan said getting up to flip the steaks.

Lisa came back with her wallet in her hands. She waited until Ryan sat back down to open it up.

"This is when I was about five years old," she said turning to the front of the credit card sleeve. She pulled the wallet size photos out and began showing the few favored pictures of her youth she still had, going into detail about each one. It felt so good to be able to open up and enjoy a real conversation about the life she used to know.

"He's right. You two look very much alike." Ryan held the close up shot of her mother next to her face.

The heated blush rose to Lisa's cheeks. She believed her mother to be the most beautiful woman she'd ever seen. To be compared to her was flattering.

"You really think so?"

"Without a doubt," Ryan muttered as he brought his lips against hers for a quick kiss.

The breeze kicked up and blew some papers from the open wallet on the table.

"Oh, shoot." Lisa scrambled to grab them as they flitted about on their way to the deck.

Ryan helped by picking up the ones that flew toward him. He started to hand them back to Lisa then pulled his hand back. He stared at the receipt on the top for a minute, his gaze coming up to meet hers.

"You used a credit card at Roberta's?" Ryan's eyes narrowed.

"Well, it's a debit card, but yes. I use it every once in a while when I need some things."

Ryan's expression confused her. Why would he care where she used her card?

"How often do you use it?"

"I don't know. There's a monthly deposit from my father's trust fund for my mother. It's just a small amount to help me take care of the business end of things for her. I use it every couple of months I guess."

"Would you say, maybe once or twice, before you start getting calls from Matt?"

Lisa stared at Ryan for the longest time. The realization of what he suggested sinking in slowly.

"You mean that's how he's following me?"

"Since this whole thing started, did you ever change the account?" He asked as he started flipping through the rest of the receipts he held in his hand. "These cover about a year, and there's no change in the ending account numbers."

"No, I've never needed to." Lisa shook her head, still not quite comprehending the evidence. "Wait, how would he be able to track me that way? He doesn't have access to my accounts."

"Do you have online access to your account set up?"

"Well, yes. That's the only way I can take care of certain things."

"Was this account set up when you and Matt were together?"

Lisa thought for a minute. "Yes. But I still don't understand how he would get access to my accounts."

Ryan held out his hand toward her. "May I?"

She handed the wallet she held over to him, still baffled as to what he inferred. Ryan searched around in a couple of the wallet pockets then pulled from the back a small piece of paper. When he unfolded it, at the top she'd written: Passwords. Underneath she'd listed her bank, phone, and e-mail accounts.

Lisa gasped. "I forgot I even had that. How did you know?"

"This is the favorite hiding place for most people, and the worst. Every good thief can find them."

Lisa sat suddenly, her knees weakening under her.

How could I be so stupid?

"You must have left your purse out when he was at your place."

She buried her head in her hands, shaking miserably back and forth. "Why didn't I realize how he did it? That is so idiotic."

Ryan pulled her against his chest. "The important thing here is we know how. He doesn't have some outrageous insight, he's just lucky you haven't changed your passwords."

Still used to her old way of thinking, Lisa pushed away from him. "I need to shut down the accounts. Then go someplace he will never find me. Maybe then I'll finally get some peace of mind." She began to pace, her mind rushing to her next moves to gather up her belongings and disappear.

Ryan stood with his arms to his sides. Lisa paced back and forth. It was his silence that brought her back to the present moment.

"Is that what you want, to just disappear again?"

The calm question struck her hard in the chest, her breath flew out of her, in a swift swoosh. She slowly started to shake her head in a negative stance. Their eyes locked, and she immediately regretted her words.

His eyes were a stony mass of guarded feelings, and she knew how wrong she'd been to even think that way again. He pulled her against him again and plundered her lips with his. Her heart beat thunderously in her chest when he released his grip on her and stepped away.

"Where will you find what you've been dreaming of for so long? Where can you finally be with your mother and settle down to live the life you are meant to have without looking over your shoulder waiting for the next attack? Where is that place, Lisa?"

Lisa had no hesitation, "Here, here with you."

"That's right." As if needing to hear confirmation, Ryan asked, "Are you leaving?"

"No." Her answer sounded weak even to her own ears. "No, I'm not leaving. I'm staying here with you," she said with more strength, a new conviction breathed into her by an unknown power.

The hardened edges of his jaw returned to the smooth planes of the face she loved. She stepped back into his arms and wrapped hers around his neck to pull him down to her. The passion just under the surface begged her to be released. Their kiss was unbridled by any imaginary constraints. He may not have told her, but there was something more in his kisses now—love.

"I'm so sorry. I've been escaping for so long it's all I know how to do anymore."

"I'm trying to understand that, but I promise you, we will catch him. Pluto and I will protect you. You have no reason to be scared," he said pressing his cheek to her forehead. "Do you believe me?"

Pluto wanted in on the attention and nuzzled his way between the two, his eyes peering up between them. Lisa couldn't help but laugh and bent down to give Pluto an aggressive hug and kiss on the top of his head.

"Yes, I believe you," she said in an animated manner to the loving canine. The tears were close to coming forth again, with Ryan's strength and Pluto's protectiveness she had more than she'd ever expected. She couldn't help but feel safe.

"Good. Now if I don't get these steaks off the grill they won't be more than a delicious chew toy for the dog."

* * * *

It had been three glorious days of rest and relaxation. They sat on the deck to enjoy a drink with the remaining light as the sun began to disappear behind the trees to the West.

"Looks like it's going to be a beautiful day tomorrow," Lisa commented looking toward the beautiful reddish haze to the evening sunset.

"How do you know that? Washington on the peninsula is unpredictable. You never know what to expect," Ryan replied standing from his comfortable position.

"Something my mother used to tell me, what was it? 'Red sky in the morning, sailors take warning, red sky at night, sailor's delight'." She rose and wrapped her arms around him, reluctant to waste any part of this time she had with him. "I suppose, since you've again cooked such a wonderful meal, it's up to me to take care of the dishes."

Ryan drew her close to him and rubbed his lips along the curve of her jaw, nipping and licking on his way to her neck.

"Mmmmm…I think I have a better idea." He continued his arduous kisses. Lisa made a sound of welcome luxuriate encouragement. "I'm going to take you upstairs and show you the best purpose of having a house out this far. Nobody but the ducks and Pluto will hear you yell out my name in ecstasy."

His grin was precious. "Why Sheriff, are you going to take advantage of me?" Lisa said coyly placing one hand up to her heart, the other on his chest. He laughed and pulled her into the house leading her toward the stairs.

This time was different. Before, the mad rush to fulfill their fiery needs had ruled over their union. Now, Ryan was playful, his loving soft and sensual. Each touch of his hand brought a new meaning to her experience from a lover.

As she lay beside him he gently touched the curves of her body, watching every quiver his fingers brought forth, as if treasuring the moment. Anticipation intensified her sensuality, an immense test to her control. Her breathing became shallow and rapid, and she thought she was about to explode, and he hadn't done anything more than touch her.

She watched him as his eyes traveled with his fingers, followed by a few light kisses over her highly sensitized breasts. The green opulence of his eyes reminded her of a cat about to devour its prey. She tried to pull him to her lips, but he stayed steadfast in his path.

"Please Ryan, I can't take much more of this," she pleaded with him breathlessly. "Make love to me, now."

"Ah, but I am," he said with a hoarseness that replicated the urgency in her own voice.

He rose above her and clasped her hands above her head, the length of his body mere centimeters from hers. She could feel the heat pouring from his skin, and the strength of his muscles as he remained just beyond her reach. He kissed her eager lips with the same gentle strength. She tried to free her hands and wrap them around his neck, but he held them tight with a glint of mischievousness in his eyes.

In her sexual frenzy, she began to writhe beneath him, arching her back, in hopes to find some type of contact.

"You want more?" he teased and positioned himself between her legs. He hovered over her, the muscles in his biceps flexing as he lowered himself over her to lathe her nipples with the hot wetness of his tongue. He pressed his erection against her, hard enough to make her plead for him to go further.

"You're driving me crazy," she whimpered, her body aching for release.

"If you ask me, turnabout is fair play in this game," he chuckled, and she realized he referred to her antics in the park. Leaning forward he began to kiss her fevered lips, pushing himself closer and closer to enter her core of desire.

"Now, Ryan, please."

When he didn't respond right away, she became frantic and made a move that even surprised her.

At just the right moment, Lisa wrapped her legs around his midsection and pulled him swiftly inside her, arching her back and making the connection as close as she could manage, a gasp releasing between her lips.

"Well, aren't you the feisty one," he kidded then his eyes became serious as he began to stroke in and out.

Each time he stroked in, she would use her legs to force him further inside, reveling in the extreme exhilaration of his hardened penis taunting her to release what was sure to come soon.

Suddenly, he changed his rhythm, and pulled her legs from around his waist to wrap them around his shoulders. This brought an angle she'd never experienced before. He drove deeper than before, caressing her innermost folds, compelling sensations to roll forth that made her cry out with elation. As he pulled out, he would pause long enough for her to yearn and whimper for more. Then he would drive his penis down hard and deep, eliciting a glorious fusion of stars to rush across her vision. And he did it again and again until she thought she would pass out.

Then, with a mere movement of his hand, he pressed his thumb against her swollen clitoris. In rolling the hardened area, he maintained his thrusting force as the orgasm grasped her quick.

"Yesssssss!" she screamed as her body began to buck beneath him, the orgasm hitting her with such force she thought she would pass out. Her contracted muscles continued to grip his manhood like a vice, as he continued to titillate her sensitivity.

When she finally released him he pulled out as he lowered her legs to the bed, still hard and ready for more. His readiness brushed against her leg and she wondered why he hadn't released as well.

"What's wrong?"

"Shhhh, nothing baby, I just want to give you as much as you can take. It's all about you tonight." The glimmer of a smile in his eyes tantalized her, as she wondered what more that could possibly entail.

The kisses that followed began in a subtle manor and grew to a fiery stream of passion. From her lips, he moved down her neck and to her highly responsive nipples again bringing her to crest toward a new sensual experience. The warm wetness of his tongue soothed then he would nip with his teeth causing the core of her being to burn with desire.

Having allowed enough time to calm slightly, he moved down to grasp her still engorged clitoris between his lips, the heat from his mouth breathing fire into her smoldering sexual response to him. Then with his tongue he made the same movement he'd done earlier with his thumb to bring about a totally new string of sensations. Her urgency resumed, assembling for another release.

As he began to suck with his lips and tongue she could think of nothing but her own need to press for quicker movement in an attempt to attain the awaited goal. His next move surprised her as his fingers were inserted into her wet folds, the length curved forward to massage her sensitized g-spot.

"Ryan," she screamed out, as he brought her to the point of explosion then relented his onslaught of passion, just seconds before she came. Her heart beat furiously, her body wound up like one of those toy tops waiting to be released.

This time he didn't wait, he rose up and drove his rock hard penis inside of her, again and again. The difference in sensation took only a minute before her orgasm rumbled forth to be completed. Sweat beaded over his skin, glistening in the moonlight. He looked like a warrior at battle as he grasped her hips and brought her down over him harder and harder, until the need to give in took over.

"Baby, I can't hold on," he gasped through his teeth.

"Ohhh, yesss," she exclaimed as her body began to pulsate around him.

"Ahhhh," he roared as his climax overtook him. His explosion deep within her, triggered yet another onset of orgasmic sensations, and she succumbed to her body's liberation to his sexual storm. Ryan remained, unmoving from his powerful stance over her, and Lisa felt him continue to throb within her as the length of his orgasm let go of its last hold over him.

Lisa stayed coherent long enough for him to collapse beside her in a heap of well satisfied contentment.

Chapter 15

Ryan couldn't help but stare at Lisa as she cooked him breakfast the next morning. The long sleeve button down denims shirt she'd chosen from his closet all but engulfed her body, making her to look like a nymph from the woods, as her thighs peeked out from under the hem line.

He tilted his head sideways, his heart picking up speed when she reached for the syrup, kept high on the top shelf, and the shirt rode up to the edge where the curve of her buttocks shadowed the tops of her thighs.

Just a little higher, he pleaded to himself, amused by the glimpses of body she was showing.

He was hungry in both ways. The aroma she'd created in his kitchen was mouth-watering, but the thought of Lisa's shapely legs, leading upward to the body he craved to satisfy took precedence. Amazed by her ability to tantalize him to the point of forgetting his rumbling stomach, he began to rise from his chair, fully intending to succumb to his growing need for her.

The plate of pancakes and bacon she set in front of him brought him to the present. Before he could satisfy his desire for her his body needed nourishment. As he took a bite of the bacon, a warm pleasant awareness drifted over him. She provided him with everything he could want, beyond his expectation. This was that little something he'd been missing, the satisfaction of being cared for—surrounded by love.

Love? He questioned himself, could it possibly be. *Is that what I'm feeling?*

Lisa smiled at him as she sat across the table. He couldn't help but analyze her every movement. Like him, she seemed happier, as if she didn't have a care in the world to weigh her down.

But he knew better.

The darkened circles under her eyes spoke of the constant fear she carried around with her. She continued to toss and turn all night long. Her days filled, as if waiting for something to happen

Until he eradicated the cause of her life-threatening plight, neither one of them would be able to rest.

He watched as she drank her coffee, gazing out at the late summer morning. There was a nagging thought he couldn't let go of though. The argument still existed. Was what she said before true? Once they finally caught up with Matt, could he trust she would stay with him?

Or is she going to run off and break my heart like Tess did? The possibility brought a frown to his face.

Yet, his intuition told him she'd meant it. There was no question he wanted her to stay, what he needed was for her to want it as well. He realized he needed her companionship, more than he ever had with Tess.

The clink of his empty mug against his plate caused Lisa to jump up to bring the coffee pot around to pour him another cup, her glance rising up to meet his eyes.

"What?" she asked with concern, as she looked down at his half-eaten plate of food. "Aren't they any good?"

"They're perfect." He laughed, not yet ready to let on what he'd been thinking.

He stuffed another mouthful of pancake into his mouth, and the maple syrup dripped down his chin. Before he had time to wipe the drizzle away, Lisa came forward and kissed his lips, licking away the tasty treat.

"Mmmm, you taste good," she giggled and gave him another quick kiss, running her tongue across her own lips as she tried to step away.

Ryan pulled her back to him, and she stood between his legs, fresh from the shower her damp hair curled enchantingly around her face. He gazed at her for a moment, unsure of what he needed to do next. The words seemed to come out of his mouth without thinking.

"You're perfect."

"Silly. It's the pancakes talking," Lisa exclaimed.

He brushed a hand across her cheek, hoping his next words would come out more romantic. "No, you really are perfect for me. What would you say if I asked you to stay with me?"

Lisa frowned a bit. "I thought I was staying with you. Isn't that what I'm doing?"

"No, that's not what I meant. Why don't we…" he paused for a second, the words sticking in his throat.

A sudden loud rap on the glass door shook them both. The unexpected noise made Lisa jump and Ryan felt her stiffen as she glanced from side-to-side for an escape route. The immediate need to protect kicked in and he stood, pulling her behind his body, out of harm's way. Lisa raised her hand to Ryan's forearm and he reached over to grasp her fingers in reassurance and squeezed.

"No worry, it's just someone at the door," he told her as he saw her head come around to peer past him at the unwelcome guest.

Ryan could tell the intruder didn't appear to be a threat from Pluto's point of view. The massive dog didn't bark, but he'd rushed up with his usual greeting, his large muddy paws propped up against the stack of wood at the door, his nose pushed into the woman's face. She shoved him off her, as she muttered what appeared to be a rude response. Apparently, she didn't like dogs.

"I'll take care of this," he said assuming the woman had lost her way and needed directions.

The woman was of average height with a cap of unnatural bleached blond hair, and sported a short miniskirt, the scant coverage of her butt prominent as she turned to shove Pluto away from her again. As she swiveled back around, their eyes met, and Ryan had the oddest feeling he knew her. She waved at him, almost jumping up and down with excitement.

He padded toward her, not really wanting to open the door to the untimely intrusion. He didn't think he knew her, but the peculiar note of recognition hovered in his memory. When he reached for the handle, it hit him square in the chest. He did know her. She didn't look the same, but her features he would never forget. They were the ones he'd memorized in his dreams from long ago.

As he slid the door open, the woman rushed in and threw her arms around him, planting a big kiss square on the mouth. Ryan remained stiff, refusing to return the hug.

"Ryan sweetie, it's Tess," she squealed, backing up far enough to view his face, her body still plastered against his, arms wrapped tightly around his waist. "Aren't you going to greet the love of your life?"

He stood silent for a moment then politely removed her tentacles from his body. Tess stepped back and glanced toward Lisa. Her eyes traveled from head to toe, as her lips curled in a snarl of sorts. Out of the corner of his eye, Lisa's uncomfortable reaction caught Ryan's attention as she tried to pull the shirt tails down to cover herself.

"Well, isn't this cozy? Hope I'm not interrupting anything." Tess tossed another glaring look over her shoulder toward Lisa, and puffed out her glossy red lips.

"What do you want Tess?" Ryan hoped his flat inquiry would let her know she wasn't welcome.

Tess reached down to lift the bag she'd flung on the floor to place it on the chair Ryan had vacated. She dug through her purse and pulled out a tissue for a dramatic dab at her eyes.

"Tess missed you so much, baby. She can't believe she was stupid enough to leave you."

"No argument there." He recognized her third person phrasing as a way of distancing herself from a difficult situation. It had always irritated him, and did so even more now.

She came forward to grab Ryan again, the odor of cigarette smoke drifted from her clothes, and he looked closer at the woman he'd once treasured. Her face had aged, now lying under an unappealing thick layer of foundation. Unusually light for her skin tone, the makeup made her appear sickly against the other dark colors she'd chosen for her eyes.

"She lost her head for a while. You must know how much your Tess loves you," she cooed, reaching out to grasp the collar of his shirt.

Ryan's stomach did a sudden lurch, almost sickened by the thought of taking her back into his life. All of a sudden, the subdued questions he'd harbored for some time fell away to reveal the truth. His gut reaction to her exposed the fact she no longer held his interest.

Seeing her like this, he couldn't believe he'd ever been in love with her. Maybe in his youth she'd been his first love, but in her absence, he'd matured and she'd remained the same—a game player with obvious hidden agendas. Astute enough to know she was after something, he perceived her eyes still held the lies so common to her in the past.

Lisa cleared her throat and tried to brush past them. "Excuse me. I'll leave you two alone to talk."

Ryan didn't want to be left alone with Tess, but had no choice. He moved forward so Lisa could scoot past behind him, in the process giving Tess the chance to grab hold tighter. He took Tess by the shoulders and pushed her as far away as possible

"Thank you," Lisa whispered, her eyes averted, and she darted up the stairs.

Ryan hated the fact he'd caused the troubled expression in Lisa's eyes. He needed to talk to her, as soon as he found out what Tess wanted. He didn't need to cause Lisa any more stress than necessary.

"Now, drop the cutesy talk and tell me why the hell you're here. And don't give me anymore bullshit." He crossed his arms across his chest and stared at her, observing a slew of potential answers roll beneath the surface of her dark smoldering lidded eyes.

Tess threw her arms up in the air, a harrumph sounding from her throat. She paced back and forth in front of him, and turned with a perfect angelic expression pasted across her face.

"Baby, I came back for Angela's sake," she said referring to her mother like a friend. "She told me how much she was missing me, and how she mopes around the house all day waiting to hear from me. So I dropped everything to come see her. But you have to know, I really came home for you." She batted her eyes at him and tried to reach out to touch him again.

Ryan blew out a breath in exasperation and stepped back. "Stop that."

Moving away, he put the safety of the kitchen table between them. Tess stuck out her bottom lip in a pout, and dabbed at her dry eyes again.

"I'm not stupid. Angela's been off to Hawaii again, she just got back a couple of days ago. Try again."

Tess walked back and forth then plopped down in one of the chairs. "I should've realized I couldn't fool you."

"That only happens once with me." His heart marbleized with the memory of how she'd treated him, an impassive attitude washing over him in a rush. He didn't care if he was being rude, this surprise visit wasn't settling well with him.

Tess grimaced. "You have every right to be mad at me Ryan, but I wasn't sure what else to do."

"Why are you here?"

She placed her forehead in her hands and shook her head. When she glanced back up, tears now streaming down her face – real tears.

"I need your help, Ryan. I have no place else to go."

He stood still for a minute, unsure if he wanted to get involved. Ready to throw her out, he struggled with the right and wrong of that action. Sometimes he wished his need to protect would take a break. Instead of acting on his anger, he sat down across from her, and took a long look at the woman he once loved.

"Tell me what's going on."

Tess sat silent for a minute. Ryan sensed she struggled to tell him the truth.

"You remember I wanted to make something of myself?"

Ryan simply nodded.

"When I got to Los Angeles I had to find some way to pay my bills. I finally found a job at the cosmetics counter at Macy's. They said if I wanted to further my education they'd help pay my tuition if it benefited the company."

He remained silent, waiting for her to go on.

"Which is a pretty good deal, right? So when the time came, I enrolled into cosmetology school." She gazed into his face, innocent to the fact her tears had created a real mess of the foundation and mascara she wore. "I really think I've found something I'm good at, don't you?"

Not wanting to laugh, Ryan did the next best thing and pretended a small cough to cover up the noise bubbling up into his throat, and raised his head slightly in feigned acknowledgement.

"Yes, well, have you completed your certification?"

"Not yet. I thought everything was going smooth enough, but it's really hard work to go to school and hold down a job at the same time. I missed a few classes and ran late at work a couple days out of the week, and they fired me."

"Did you try to explain?"

"Yeah, but my manager said some policy about tardiness kept her from making any exceptions. She said if she didn't hold me to the rules, she'd have to let all the other worthless employees stay too," she said obviously not realizing she'd insulted herself.

"I'm sorry to hear that," he said truthfully. He'd never experienced her work ethics, but didn't think she meant to be a bad employee. He believed she meant well. "So, what happened?"

"I didn't know what to do. I was afraid I would be kicked out of the apartment. Rent was due and my electricity would be cut off if I didn't come up with the full amount. My neighbor Rosa told me she had a way to make some good money by going out to parties and stuff with lonely older single men."

This is trouble, Ryan thought.

Tess looked up into Ryan's face and rushed to retreat with a vigorous shake of her head.

"It's not what you think. She said I would act as a companion and these guys would pay me to make them look good for their friends and acquaintances."

Ryan suspected where this story headed, and couldn't believe she'd been dumb enough to fall for into their trap.

"George said I would be perfect for the job. Said I was just the type he'd been searching for in his business. He started me out at $200 a gig. That's great money for one nights work."

"Prostitution is a pretty lucrative business," Ryan stated, his eyes set hard on her face.

Tess jumped at his words. "No, no, you don't understand. It wasn't like that. I just went to parties and kept the customers happy, no funny stuff," she said refuting the reality of his words.

She turned her face away from him, her silence dragged on, and Ryan wished she would get to the point and fess up to what he suspected she'd done. When she turned back, the tears had welled up, causing her eyes to appear larger than before.

She hesitated then revealed the truth, "That's all it was, at least at first."

Ryan didn't want the details, but his cop's intuition needed proof of what he'd already deducted. "What happened?"

"George was really good to me. He paid the rent for me and my phone. Then he bought me all these nice clothes, and had me go to the spa to have my hair and nails done."

Ryan followed her gaze as she looked down at her long air brushed nails, the stark green color a bit over the top for his taste.

"Did he tell you why he did all those things?"

"He told me he wanted to take care of his girls."

"Tess, you understand what he is, don't you?" Ryan's incredulous question was unmistakable. He truly couldn't believe she didn't realize the man was a pimp.

She nodded and glanced away again. "I do now. But I didn't at first. I just thought he was really nice."

He shook his head, unsure if she was just stupid or truly that innocent. "Okay, what changed your mind?"

She got up and paced back and forth a few times and sat back down.

"He asked me to go out on this weekender run with one of his best clients. He told me things might get a little weird, and the guy would ask me to do some really kinky things, but it didn't matter and I should keep him happy. When I told him I wouldn't do that kind of thing, he told me if I knew what was good for me I'd do what he told me to do. He said I owed him. That's when I knew…" she trailed off, her eyes darting away.

The whole time she'd been talking, Ryan noticed she kept looking away from him then back again, as if putting the story together as she went. He realized he'd seen that look before. Back in high school, she'd been notorious for getting out of trouble by the stories she would tell to justify her actions.

What was she up to now? Had she come up with this grand scheme to get his sympathy?

Something in her eyes bothered him. As if she tested his belief in her. One thing for sure, he knew she was smarter than she was making out to be. She wasn't so naive as to not know from the beginning what she'd gotten herself into.

What does she really want from me?

298

"I went that first time because he paid me really good money. I got over two grand. But I swore I wouldn't do it again."

"Did you stop?"

Tess shook her head, embarrassment written all over her face. A well rehearsed emotion he felt she'd practiced many times. He decided to continue to play along.

"How long have you been doing this, Tess?"

"A little over two years now," she whispered.

"Why didn't you leave?"

"George told me I could come and go as I please. I tried Ryan, I really did, but it's hard out there. Jobs don't come easy. I thought I would be able to stop, but I couldn't make it work."

Ryan studied her face. No matter how he looked at it, he was astonished the woman he once loved was pretending to be a high priced prostitute. Or was she? He couldn't tell what level of truth to apply to this story.

"Why didn't you call Tess? I would've helped you."

"To tell you the truth, I didn't want to have to tell you about any of this. You're right. Life is better here."

"Life is what you make for yourself. Anywhere it takes you."

The mascara had begun to run down her cheeks with the tears. She wiped at her face with the tissue she had in her hand, making the mess worse.

"I figured after what I'd done, you wouldn't want anything to do with me," she said with a laugh as she looked out the window.

"Have you told your parents?" he asked thinking this might smoke her out.

She nodded. "Earl threw me out," she said of her stepfather.

Ryan didn't know her stepfather well enough to know how he would act in this situation, but he knew him to be a fair man. Perhaps if he spoke to Earl he would change his mind.

"I wouldn't blame you if you threw me out too."

Ryan stared at her. That he wouldn't do, but he had another issue to deal with that had higher priority.

Lisa.

"What I am going to do is bring you back into town. I'm sure we can find you a place to stay," he said glancing toward the stairs.

"I just need to stay until I can get a job and get back on my feet again. I thought maybe I'd dye my hair black and go out to Forks to try my hand at wannabe vampire make-up. Shouldn't take too long," she said flouncing her now almost white curls.

Ryan raised his eyebrows, but tried not to be rude. "Oh, that should be interesting."

Tess was an opportunist, but did she seriously think she could make a living providing occasional tourist cosmetics?

"Please, Ryan. Can I stay here with you? I don't want to have to tell anyone else about what happened. You can say I came to visit."

Ryan shook his head and glanced toward the stairs again. "You can't stay here, Tess."

"Oh," she said, her glance following his to the stairwell. "It's serious?"

Ryan nodded slowly, his thoughts racing to the woman upstairs. "Yes."

Tess sighed softly. "You're a good man Ryan. I hope she realizes what a lucky girl she is to have you."

He smiled across the table at her. "Thank you." He still didn't trust her, but felt safe enough now to come around to where Tess sat. He bent down to put an arm around her shoulders. "Don't worry. We'll figure out a way to get you out of this mess you're in."

"I hope so, Ryan. No joke. I really hoped you would change your mind when I got here. No matter what you think, I do still love you." Tess took the opportunity to wrap her arms around him and kissed him soundly again on the lips.

He should have figured she'd try it again.

The python grasp she had on him was difficult to loosen. It took only a second in her arms for him to know for sure he no longer had feelings for the woman.

"Would you please stop that?"

At that moment, Lisa came around the stairs and stopped. Ryan watched the hurt in her eyes swell up and he cursed himself. Tess held on for a second longer then dropped her arms to her sides. Thankful he didn't need to make a scene, he stepped away and approached Lisa, hoping she would understand what was going on.

"We need to take Tess back to town. I was going to take you with me later to drop off the cruiser and pick up my truck anyway, and there are a couple of files I'd like to pick up at the office." He looked down at her bare fee and the shorts she'd slipped on. "You might want to change your clothes though."

Lisa looked at him then behind him to where Tess stood and an odd look crossed over her face, as if having met up with something disagreeable.

Tess piped up and said a little too quick, "Surely you can't expect her to go traipsing around town on my behalf. Maybe she should stay here."

Lisa raised her eyebrows for a second then nodded. "Honestly, if it's at all possible, I think I'd rather stay here," her words were clipped short and the cynical expression when she brought her gaze back to him told him exactly what she thought of Tess.

He glanced back at Tess, who had a sickening sweet look on her face, then back at Lisa, and could tell it would be a very unpleasant trip.

"If you're sure," he questioned Lisa, uncomfortable with leaving here there. The decisive nod she gave him told him he probably wouldn't be able to change her mind. "Then I'll call Bobby and have him come up."

"Yes, please."

He hesitated. It shouldn't take him long. By Lisa's description of past events, Matt wouldn't try anything during the day hours anyway, so he felt fairly content she would be all right for the short time away from him.

"Okay. I'm going to go up and shower first. Bobby should be here before I'm done."

He bent down and kissed her forehead, not wanting to tarnish the taste of her lips with the memory of Tess's kiss.

Turning, he caught the tail end of Tess's begrudging glance toward Lisa. A look he didn't trust.

He definitely needed to get her out of his house, the sooner the better.

"Tess, I think there might be some breakfast left over, if you're hungry. I'll be right back," Ryan offered on his way up the stairs.

As Lisa put the dishes in the dishwasher Tess ate a healthy helping of bacon. Lisa could feel Tess staring at her as she chewed each bite in a slow pondering style. The squint of her eyes, and the smirk on Tess's lips unnerved her. She wasn't sure what Tess was thinking, but it looked as if she were weighing the chances of winning a prized fight.

"So, you and Ryan have a little thing going, do you?"

Lisa turned pulling her eyebrows together in question.

"A thing?" she asked.

Tess nodded.

"Well, I can't blame him. He's a virile healthy man. He needs some type of release, doesn't he? I suppose you're as good as anyone else." Tess rose up and came into the kitchen to place the plate into the sink in front of Lisa. "But I'm back now. I don't think he'll need you much longer."

"What…what are you talking about?" Lisa stuttered, surprised by this new angle.

Tess sashayed to her purse, grabbed a tube of lipstick and smeared a healthy amount across her lips. Lisa knew the bright red shade was meant to be empowering. All it accomplished for Tess was to make her face appear unkempt and uneven, the cat like slant to the smoky eye makeup she'd freshened up unnatural and overdone.

"He told me he's missed me something fierce…and wants me back," Tess drawled in a theatrical southern manner. "He always did like the sex. He might try to keep us both going for a while."

"He…he said that?"

Lisa put her hand up to her throat to ward away a sudden constriction. This couldn't be true. Could it? Was what Ryan and she shared only about sex?

It only took Lisa a second to think about it. No, definitely not. This woman was trying to psych her out.

Tess nodded and tossed the lipstick back into her purse with unnecessary force. She came back to stand with hands on hips in front of Lisa. Not intimidated, Lisa stuck out her chin.

"I don't believe you."

"Well, believe it missy, 'cuz pretty soon your heart's going to be broken, and I'm going to be havin' me a good time."

The smile Tess shot at Lisa was daring and somewhat creepy. Lisa realized Tess actually thought she would be successful in winning him back.

"Believe me when I say, I'll stop at nothing to get him all to myself again."

Lisa shot Tess a grimace through raised eyebrows, and muttered, "In your dreams."

"Unless you want to fight for your man," Tess said as she stepped toward Lisa again like a tiger having spotted its prey.

Lisa stood her ground and glared at Tess as she straightened her spine in her own form of defiance. The front doorbell rang, but they continued to stare at each other a moment longer.

"Excuse me," Lisa said, and as she brushed past Tess she stated point blank, "You want a fight, I'll give you fight."

"Ooohh, I'm scared," Tess retorted with a laugh.

Lisa couldn't believe the gall of the woman to barge in and claim stakes to what she'd begun to believe was meant to be hers. She loved Ryan, and this witch of a woman wouldn't have a chance of taking him from her. He hadn't said it, but she felt down to her bones he loved her too. Indignation boiled under her skin and she almost opened the door without thinking.

She took a deep breath. "Who is it?" she asked with her hand on the doorknob.

"Bobby, Miss Lisa. Sherriff called me over to sit with you while he's gone."

Recognizing his voice, she opened the door. Bobby wasn't in uniform, but she saw the cruiser out front as he stepped into the entry and she closed the door behind him.

"Hey Bobby, how's it going?" Tess shouted from the other end of the room.

Bobby turned, shock pasted across his face. "Tess?" he asked, squinting across the room for better focus.

Tess bounded across the living room and threw her arms around Bobby. His breath swooshed out when she grasped him, and his face burst into a bright shade of red. Lisa wasn't sure if it was embarrassment or the limited amount of air left in his lungs.

"I can't believe you're still in this little Podunk town. I thought for sure you and Susan would have made it out of here by now." Tess laughed as she slapped him on the back.

Ryan came into the room and Lisa caught the stone cold glare he gave Tess.

Bobby glanced back and forth between the three of them then gave a low whistle of astonishment. He shook his head and glanced at Lisa again. No need for words, Lisa felt his whistle summed the whole situation up.

"Bobby, I need you to stay until I get back. Understood?"

Lisa sensed the silent communication between the two, appreciating the fact Ryan didn't go into the details in front of Tess.

"Tess, Bobby will take your bag to the truck. I'll meet you there in a minute."

As the door closed behind the two, Ryan turned and pulled Lisa into his arms. "I'm sorry you had to meet Tess like that, she's a bit of a drama queen at times."

You have no idea, Lisa thought, holding him tight against her. She wasn't sure if she should let him go.

"I'm going to drive Tess into town and get her a place to stay. She's gotten herself into some trouble, and I can't turn my back on her." He bent and their lips met in a brief kiss. "I'll be back soon. You don't have anything to worry about. Bobby will be outside monitoring everything. Between him and Pluto, nobody will get in here."

Lisa hung on a moment longer wondering whether there was any truth to what Tess said.

When Ryan looked into her eyes, she swore she saw love shining behind his striking green eyes. He pulled her back to him, his lips devouring hers as she clung to him. In the sweet taste of fresh mint mouthwash whetting her lips from his, she felt a personal strength come from his arms, and knew this was where she belonged.

"I promise I won't be long, sweetheart."

"Don't let Tess steal you away from me," she said half-joking.

Ryan rolled his eyes at her as he turned to open the door. He groaned and threw back a smile that swelled her heart.

"Not a chance."

* * * *

"You won't believe who is back in town!" Bobby claimed to his wife Susan on the other end of the cell phone. He leaned against the cruiser and took a swig of the soda in his hand.

"Terry?" she asked in excitement, referring to Bobby's older brother.

"No." he said, shaking his head. "Not even close."

A few minutes before, he'd walked around the house and hadn't seen anything out of the ordinary. He couldn't hold back any longer. He had to tell Susan. She'd never forgive him if he didn't tell her first.

"Come on Bobby, I hate to guess. Tell me."

"You'll never guess anyway," he said, triumphant he knew something before his wife did. "It's Tess. She was here at Ryan's when I got here."

"Oh, my God, are you serious?"

"I swear. She was standing there acting like she'd never left."

Bobby heard the baby in the background who'd woken from his nap and was hollering something fierce.

"Oh, hold on. I can't understand you over the baby." He heard the commotion as his wife picked the toddler up and tried to quiet him. "Shhhh, sweetie, I've got you."

"Let me talk to him. He needs to hear his Daddy's voice," Bobby said with pride.

"All right, hold on." There were some shuffling noises and then the loud whimpers of his son came across the receiver. "It's Daddy, sweetie. Daddy's on the phone," Susan said encouraging the boy to listen.

"Hey, Josh, it's Daddy." The immediate quieting of the little boy pleased him immensely. "What's all that crying about? You don't need to be making all that noise."

"Daddy?" Joshua sniffled.

Bobby grinned. His little man was the joy of his life.

"That's right. Now you be good for your Momma. I'll be home in a little bit. I promise we'll play ball when I get home, all right?"

"Ok, I get my ball." The little boy shouted, followed by the sounds of his son clambering off his mother's lap to search for his favorite ball.

"You certainly have a way with him," Susan said, her voice thankful. "Now tell me everything that happened with Tess."

Bobby heard a loud noise behind him. He twisted, hand reaching for his pistol. A sharp pain pierced his skull. Then everything went black.

Chapter 16

It had been about an hour since Ryan left. Even though Bobby was outside, Lisa had begun to feel a little unnerved. She'd found an interesting book on the American Indian culture, and settled herself on the couch to wait for Ryan's return. She wasn't much of a history buff, and after a bit her head began to swim with so many dates and names all at one time.

She needed to do things to take her mind off the eminent problem hanging over her head. Lisa pulled the sketchbook out of her backpack and wondered what she should attempt to recreate. Images from the book she'd been reading flashed through her mind, and her eyes finally came to rest on the intricately designed basket that stood in the corner of the room.

Pluto lay at her feet in a dream land far away, his feet twitched and his nose wiggled at the invisible prey he chased. Lisa laughed at the display, and tucked her feet underneath her to create a pseudo table on her lap for her sketchbook.

The noise at the back door made her jump. Not loud, but the sound was definitely a glass door sliding open and closed.

"Bobby?" she called out.

No answer.

"Bobby, is that you?" she called out a little louder now, pulling her legs from underneath to rise to her feet.

Her heart thumped heavily in her chest.

Matt was there.

Several entry ways into the long living area were accessible from other parts of the house, and she wondered desperately which direction to take.

Ryan had showed her where his extra weapons were kept, and the location of the keys to the four-wheeler locked in the garage. She cursed herself for not putting the keys in her pocket when he'd left earlier.

The closest weapons were in the rifle case against the wall in his study. If only she were able to get to them, she'd be all right.

A loud crash sounded in the hallway to the right of her, as if something had been knocked over.

Damn, that's where I need to go.

The smashing of the pottery against the wood floor woke Pluto out of his sound sleep and he sat up, eyes blinking furiously to clear his mind from his slumber. Suddenly alert he stood still, waiting for Lisa to give the command to attack. Lisa had begun a silent path to the other end of the room, and she pointed toward the hallway hoping he would understand what she meant. Trained to follow the direction of his master's lead, he moved slowly toward the opposite direction.

Matt appeared in the entry, the crazed look in his eyes scared Lisa to death. In one hand, he held a large branch from one of the downed trees outside. Around his shoulders, a rope was looped awaiting its next use, and to her horror, a pistol was shoved into the front of his pants.

"Now," she shouted at her now growling protector.

Pluto ran and jumped at Matt, his ferocious bark muted as Matt swung the branch and connected with his head in mid air, knocking him out cold.

Lisa didn't hesitate, and ran toward the back door, grabbing the keys off the hook on her way through the kitchen. The click of the safety release sounded like a bomb in the recesses of her mind.

"Don't make me shoot you Lisa. You know I will." Matt shouted from behind her, wheezing from the effort of the chase.

Lisa turned hesitantly around to face her assailant, knowing she couldn't outrun the bullet from a pistol. Even if he was a bad shot, there was no way he would miss this close.

The stench coming from Matt stung her nose, bringing tears to her eyes. He stood a few feet away, pointing the gun directly at her heart.

"You're coming with me now. You belong to me," he rasped out easing the rope from around his neck. "I didn't want to have to do this, but you made me."

He seemed calm. She stared at him, trying to calculate the best way to outwit him. If she got the chance to get the gun away from him, maybe she would have a chance.

"Don't do this Matt. I'm not worth your being put in jail. Just let me go and I'll let you get away," she said.

Although, she knew Ryan would never let it go and he'd search until he found Matt.

Matt's face turned a bright shade of red and he screamed, "I'm not letting you go. You're everything to me bitch. I'm going to show you what you've done to me, and prove to you why you belong to me."

The quick mood switches she feared the most. There was no telling what he was capable of when he worked himself into a frenzied state. She had to keep him calm.

"All right," she said softly. She'd once been told if there was no other way out, the only way to survive was to agree and not fight the offender, watching for any chance to escape later. She could see now the truth to that statement.

She needed to change the subject, get his mind off the direction he'd taken.

"Where's Bobby? What did you do to Bobby?"

Matt sniffed loudly. A small trickle of blood appeared at his nostril, and he wiped at his nose with the back of his hand, smearing the dark red across his lip. She recognized the stage of damage she'd learned his inhalants would take. His tissue weakening had begun to appear, and the red splotches on his face were another sign of his cell's atrophy.

"He's all right. I just knocked him out is all, and tied him up real good." Lisa watched him closely as he pulled the handcuffs he'd taken from Bobby from the back pocket of his unwashed jeans, obviously stained by urine and other bodily fluids. "Here, put these on."

He threw them at her clumsily, but continued to hold the pistol to her face.

"I'll go with you Matt. I don't need these," she hoped she could convince him she would go willingly.

He laughed aloud. "Yeah, right, and I'm Princess Leia." He indicated with the tip of the gun for her to continue as instructed. "Hurry up. We have to get out of here."

He was losing his patience. That wasn't good either. If she wanted to stay alive, she'd better play the game.

She fastened the handcuffs with her hands in front of her, thinking if he didn't recognize the mistake she might be able to use this to her advantage later.

He didn't.

The end of the rope he'd fastened into a lasso and now slung the restriction over her head, tightening the knot around her midsection. He must have planned this method before having the good fortune of getting access to all of the officer's resources. Now it was just an added precaution.

"Turn around in circles," he ordered, motioning with the tip of the gun the direction she should go. He held the rope tight as it wound around her making movement almost impossible from her elbows up.

When she'd finished, he stuffed the pistol into his pants and came closer to wrap his arms around her, grasping the end of the rope with his free hand. She attempted to grab hold of the handle, but the gun was just out of her reach. She morbidly thought her attempt appeared like she'd reached out for him as he tied the knot in front of her in a secure sailor's knot. Thank God he didn't notice.

Another mistake, she realized. If given the chance, loosening a visible knot would be easier than one behind her back.

From the living room she heard Pluto's loud groan as he came out of his stupor. He must have picked up the scent of Matt because he began barking then she heard the noise get louder as he rushed toward the back of the house.

Matt shoved the back door open and pushed her through. As soon as she stumbled over the threshold, he slammed the door with a bang just as the dog was about to attack. She turned and saw the welt that had risen on the side of the dog's head. The blood seeping over his swollen eye and down his muzzle made her sick to realize Bobby was probably in the same shape. Pluto lunged toward them misjudging the door's closed status and knocked himself backward.

"Dumb dog," Matt mumbled as he took hold of Lisa by the neck. "Move it."

He shoved her toward the lake, following close behind.

"Where are we going?" Lisa tried to keep a level head, and ask the right questions.

"The car is over there," he said pointing toward a tree-covered alcove to her right.

"Where?"

"See that big maple tree? Head toward it," he panted, out of breath, as he thrust her along further by pushing her at the back of her neck.

The best tactic would be to go as slowly as she could. Maybe Ryan would come back in time to find her before she was whisked away to who knows where.

"I said come on," Matt yelled as he came forward and began pulling her with him by the rope, causing her to stumble and fall to her knees. He yanked her to her feet.

"You're hurting me," she yelped, hoping to connect with some type of compassion in him.

He jerked her forward so that their faces were mere centimeters apart. The blood had rushed to the vessels in his face with the exertion, his eyes bulging out in a horrid manner.

"You think I give a shit if you hurt? You're lucky I don't show you whose boss. I should just get it over with right here and now."

* * * *

Ryan looked back toward the table where Angela and Tess sat discussing something in detail. Their close proximity accompanied by their whispers and conspiratorial glances toward him verified he was correct. Something was definitely wrong with the story Tess had told him earlier.

"I'm sick and tired of being played the fool around here," he mumbled, not too interested in finding out the truth about the ruse. He had better things to worry about.

"You're nobody's fool," Maggie said as came up to stand beside him. They watched the two for a moment. She jerked her head toward the two women. "What's going on over there?"

"Frankly, I have no idea. Tess came to my house moaning and crying about not having a place to stay because Earl threw her out of the house. Angela says he's known to have a temper, but it doesn't sound much like Earl to me. I'm not sure what to believe."

"Hard to tell," Maggie commented nodding her head.

"If she needs a place to stay like she says, will you put her up for me?"

Maggie nodded in answer.

"Look, I've got to go pick up the truck and get back to the house. Find out what you can for me would you?"

"Sure thing, I'll give them a word or two of my own," Maggie let slip. Ryan shook his head and headed toward the door. He knew she would do exactly that.

As he parked his cruiser outside the office, he could see his truck gleaming in the sunlight from Earl's Auto Mechanic and Detail Shop lot across the street. It looked brand new, but he knew different. Probably would never be the same.

"Hey Earl," he called out as he walked closer to the shop.

Earl stepped out of the garage, wiping his greasy fingers on a worn blue shop towel. In his usual manner, he nodded his acknowledgement.

"Come to pick up your truck?"

"Is it ready?"

"Barely," Earl said with a grimace. "The person who did that should be shot, if you ask me."

"No argument here," Ryan agreed wholeheartedly.

They stood for a moment staring at the truck, neither saying a word—sort of a male bonding thing.

"So, I hear things got a little heated at your house," Ryan said, trying to ease into asking him about Tess.

Earl raised his eyebrows. "Heated?"

"Well, with Tess and her lifestyle and all."

"Lifestyle?" Again, Earl raised his brows, clearly not understanding what Ryan was talking about.

Ryan stood staring, unsure of how else to ask. He'd learned it was better to be clear and honest than not. "Did you, or did you not, throw Tess out of the house because of her being a prostitute for the last couple of years?"

It was as if Ryan had punched Earl in the stomach—hard. All of the air swooshed out of Earl's lungs and he started to cough in violent spurts. Ryan reached out to pound him on the back a couple of times, hoping he hadn't caused the man to hyperventilate.

"Easy there, Earl."

The man wiped the sweat from his brow, leaving a dark streak of engine oil across his forehead. "What the hell are you talking about?"

"Tess told me about her life in Seattle. She told me she'd told you. Obviously not," Ryan determined Tess was going to be in more trouble than she expected when he saw the look on Earl's face.

"I don't know what she told you. All I know is she couldn't pay her bills, so she came back home to live for a while."

"She seems to think she can't come back to live with you and Angela for some reason," Ryan was beginning to see that it had all been a big story, like he thought.

Earl shook his head. "She and Angela have been keeping something from me since she got back. I don't know what it is, but I'll find out. Are they at Maggie's?" With Ryan's nod he turned to toss the shop towel into the closest bay. "You coming?"

Ryan shook his head, but the ringing of his cell phone cut off his response. He pulled it from the clip on his belt. He recognized Bobby's home number right away and connected.

"Sheriff Jacobs."

"Ryan, something is terribly wrong. Bobby isn't answering his cell. We were talking a few minutes ago, and all of a sudden, he went away. At first, I thought this lousy reception up here was causing problems. But then he would have called me back right away when he found a spot that works," Susan rattled off in her quick speak fashion.

Ryan's heart did a tumble in his chest. This wasn't good.

"Did you hear anything strange?"

"Well, I'm not sure. There was kind of a crunching sound. I thought maybe he'd dropped the phone. Oh God Ryan, is he all right?"

"I'm going to check this out Susan. I'll call as soon as I find out what's going on."

"Hurry Ryan, if that crazy man did anything to my honey I'll hunt him down myself," she claimed.

"I'm on my way."

Ryan pressed the button on his communications device at his shoulder, hoping the malfunction was with Bobby's cell phone. "Deputy Hines, this is Sheriff Jacobs, do you read?"

Nothing but silence came in return.

Ryan turned as he clipped the phone back onto his belt. "I've got to go. Something's wrong at the house."

Ryan left Earl heading toward Maggie's for a battle with his daughter, one he wished he could see. Dirt and gravel spewed out the back of his truck as Ryan sped out of the drive onto solid pavement. The faint stench of crap floated toward him from the vents, but he didn't notice. Cursing himself the whole time, he gripped the steering wheel with an iron fist.

"I shouldn't have left her. I knew it. Damn it, I should've had Bobby take Tess into town," he shouted in rage at himself.

The truck tires ate up the distance quicker than usual. In a mere fraction of the time the trip normally would have taken to arrive at the turnoff to his house he shot past the mail boxes and wheeled into his driveway. As he got closer he had a sickening feeling in the pit of his stomach. When he peeled around the last curve, Bobby's cruiser was in the drive, the doors open and the trunk popped open, his body next to it on the ground.

Skidding to a stop Ryan jumped out and rushed to Bobby's side to assess the situation. Bobby had been tied with hands behind his back, the goose egg above his eye proved Ryan's fears that he'd been knocked senseless, incapable of helping Lisa. His eyes were glazed over, but he struggled to come alert.

"Where's Lisa?"

Bobby began to shake his head and groaned with obvious pain. "I don't know. She might still be in there," Bobby croaked out. "Sheriff, I'm sorry. He's got my revolver."

Through the pain, Ryan recognized the shame eating away at the young deputy. He would've felt the same way.

Ryan cursed under his breath and checked the car to find out what else was missing. Matt hadn't taken the shotgun, but all the ropes and latches attached to the rescue climbing gear were gone. He returned with the shotgun in hand, and reached down to cut the ropes loose giving Bobby the ability to defend himself. He reached into his ankle holster and pulled out his snub-nosed .38 and handed it to Bobby.

"I'm going in." Shotgun in one hand ready to fire, Ryan crouched down beside Bobby. "Sit here, you aren't much good to me if you fall over. If the son of a bitch comes out...shoot him."

Ryan figured Matt would go out the back, knowing Bobby was still out front. There was no other vehicle in the drive, so either he'd already gone or he'd parked in the hidden alcove to the west of his house.

If he had, then he might still be inside. He could only hope.

Plastered against the side of the house, Ryan made his way around to the back. The screen hung loose, barely connected to the upper groove and the glass door was shut. Through the smudged glass, Pluto lay patiently at the opening, nose pressed up against the corner. Ryan knew if he was at the door, Matt had already gone.

Blood and drool smudges covered the lower half of the window, turning Ryan's stomach because he didn't know yet whose blood it was.

Pluto jumped up excitedly at the sight of his master. His whine was that of a canine who'd waited his turn for an expected action. As soon as Ryan opened the door, the dog leaped out and attempted to run straight toward the lake. He grabbed hold of his collar, scarcely able to keep the animal from breaking loose. Pluto began barking the howl of a canine on a mission.

Ryan pulled him back into the house.

"Hold on boy, is Lisa here? I have to find Lisa."

Ryan's stomach rolled at the residual stench permeating the air. He'd seen the blood on the dog's head, but he had to make sure Lisa wasn't lying somewhere, bleeding to death. He ran from room to room and found only her beloved belongings in the living room, strewn across the floor. The pool of blood on the carpet caused his heart to flip.

Had he shot her? Was she wounded?

Pluto remained at the door, ready to bolt. Ryan knew he would lead him to where Matt had taken Lisa.

"Ok, take me to her boy," he said as he opened the back door again. Pluto shot out streaking toward the lake, nose down to the ground. Ryan followed in close pursuit. "Where is she boy, where'd he take her?"

The dog stopped for a moment and shook his head as if to clear the muddiness he must be experiencing from the blow to the head. He looked up at Ryan and whined. Ryan reached down to reassure the dog.

"It's ok, boy. I think I know where they went." He started toward the little alcove again, and the dog rushed past him, barking again with vehemence.

They reached the maple tree where cars were able to pull in off the road, but there was nothing. In the distance, he heard the roar of an engine being pushed to the limit, and through the trees he saw the missing Taurus jumping over the bumpy pit filled path.

"Damn it." They would reach the highway before he'd be able to get back to his truck. As he began running back toward his house he reached down to his belt for his cell and hit Speed dial 3 to reach his officer on duty at the office in town.

"Doug, I need you to high tail it out to 101 and head south. We're looking for Belamy's old Taurus. The suspect's got Lisa, and he grabbed Bobby's revolver. If you spot him, just follow and find out where he goes. I don't want any shooting going on, okay?"

"10-4 Sheriff, I'm on my way." Doug had good sense. He was one of his long time deputies. Ryan knew he could trust him.

His next move was to call for the emergency crew to get out and check on Bobby, and have them take Pluto to the vet.

By the time he reached the house again Bobby had gotten to his feet and was standing fairly steady.

"Did you find her?" Bobby shouted out as he came around the corner of the front deck.

"No. He parked out at the end of Old Perkin's Road, and took off before I got there."

Bobby's face, streaked with the blood dripping from his head wound, was sickeningly white. He tried to walk toward the approaching Sheriff, but stopped and returned to the side of his car.

"I'm sorry Ryan. I didn't mean to let that happen. He came out of nowhere and whacked me upside the head. You gotta believe me. I didn't hear a thing until too late." The concern in his eyes touched Ryan's heart, but he also knew the young man had been on the phone, which was a problem he'd have to deal with later.

"We'll talk later. Right now, I'm headed out to see if I can spot where he's taken Lisa. I called the EMR. They should be here in a second. Make sure they look Pluto over too, would you," Ryan said climbing into his truck, already outfitted with everything he needed, which might come in handy if he had to do some four wheeling.

"Yes sir, I will," Bobby replied taking hold of the fender of his cruiser and sitting slowly on the rim of the trunk taking hold of the loyal canine's collar, both of whom didn't seem to mind resting to wait for further help.

The sirens in the distance indicated Ryan wouldn't need to worry about Bobby anymore. In a spew of grass and gravel, he spun around and took off down his long driveway, halfway down meeting up with the ambulance. Without hesitation, he drove to the side, through the bushes past them, so as not to lose any more time.

He grabbed the radio from the bracket on the dash and dialed in the open channel for the area.

"This is Sheriff Jacobs from Lake Duchess. This is an APB, repeat an APB, on a 207 in progress. Victim is one Lisa Roberts, age 28, brown eyes and brown hair. Suspect is driving a 1989 Ford Tempo, license plate VGF979, heading either north or south on 101." Ryan stated from memory of his local residents records. "Vehicle may be abandoned to switch to a 1970's gray van, with out-of-state plates. Suspect is armed. Repeat suspect is armed and dangerous."

He hit the main road and careened to the right toward the highway entrance. Almost without stopping, he wheeled to the left onto North Highway 101.

Static from the radio came blasting through his speakers and he recognized the gravelly voice of John Lawson responding to his request for help. "This is State Trooper #507, what's your 10-20 Sheriff?"

"I'm headed North on 101 about two miles out of Duchess."

"I just passed mile marker 5, headed south out of Forks. Do you think they've made it this far?"

"Negative, John. If they're headed north they're only about 8 minutes ahead of me."

"I'll keep my eyes open and meet you half way."

"He's armed John. Don't take any chances."

"10-4."

* * * *

Matt drove recklessly around the curves in the highway. Then to Lisa's surprise, they veered off onto a side road. His other mistake had been to not cover her eyes. She made a mental note of every direction and length of travel, in hopes she would get the opportunity to use the information to her advantage.

They drove this road for a little over five miles and turned onto a gravel road to the left, just past a Weyerhauser forestry company's sign that read 'Hedges Plot #516 - 40.3 Acres of Timberland - Planted in 1989.'

The dense coverage of trees indicated to Lisa it would soon be time for them to come back in to clear the land and plant again, and she began to wonder if they would find her body when they did.

Matt slowed the vehicle way down when they hit the dirt and gravel road. Lisa felt as if they were crawling along, but figured he was aware of the dust that would rise from the dry road if he went too fast. As they drove around a curve, a few hundred yards from the cut-off, they passed through an open gate. She saw the broken chain hanging from the enclosure similar to the one she'd seen at the state park.

"Where are you taking me?"

"Doesn't matter, you're with me now."

Silenced, she watched the curves of the logging road pass her by, the upward angle increasing as they drove up the side of the foothill. They finally came to a leveled area where she saw his van parked in front of a small box like structure.

Matt laughed. "I had a heck of a time getting both these vehicles here. During the night I had to drive a short way with each one and walk back to get the other. Back and forth like that took me over four hours." She noted the change in mood. He spoke as if in a normal conversation with a friend, his countenance light and jovial.

"What is this?" Lisa needed to be able to describe this later on if she got the chance.

"I don't know. I figure the logging company built it for the workers when they come in to work. Nobody's been here for a long time. They must not be up here very often," Matt said, popping another of his cough drops into his mouth and pulling up beside the dirty gray van.

Lisa hoped the dust rising up from this viewpoint would be seen from down below. Matt jumped out to come around her side of the car. He bent over to pick something up off the ground and she gauged her success at trying to open the door and make a run for it. She let out a huff of air, resigned to the fact this was not going to be easy. As tight as her arms were against her sides, she couldn't grab the door handle before Matt would realize what she was doing. Besides, he still had the gun tucked in his pants. Even if she were able to escape, he no doubt would shoot her before she reached safety.

He opened the door for her and reached in to grasp her around the waist. His potent smell made her gag a bit and she turned her head away from him. Lisa's hand brushed against the cold steel of the gun and she tried to grab hold of the weapon.

"Whoa," Matt said jumping back from her. "What are you doing?" She'd managed to knock the gun out of place and she swore to herself as the clunk of cold metal dropped to the rocky ground. "Come on Lisa, don't try anything. I don't want to hurt you, but I will if you make me."

Jamming the barrel back into place, Matt reached in this time not so gently and pulled her to her feet from the front of the rope.

This high up, the sun beat down on her shoulders, and the air was thick and humid with summer heat. The sharp rocks under her feet reminded her she hadn't put on shoes yet. A small breeze kicked up to brush past her bare legs. She still wore Ryan's shirt over the pair of shorts she'd slipped on after breakfast that morning. She'd told herself to wait to change her clothes until after Ryan returned. She hadn't wanted to be caught unaware—a lot of good that did.

Matt forcefully pushed her toward the building's door into a darkened room.

"There's no electricity, so we'll have to make do with what we've got."

It took a minute for Lisa's eyes to adjust to the difference between sunlight and the shadows of the enclosed area. As Matt busied himself with something in the corner, her eyes slowly focused to make out the sparse furnishings of her surroundings.

A bunk bed against one wall had an uncovered pillow that looked like it had seen better days. The small square metal card table in the middle of the room sported three mismatched chairs. Oddly enough, a rocking chair stood next to the small woodstove at the far end of the room. A makeshift kitchen in the opposite corner contained a standalone sink and an old-fashioned icebox. Apparently, loggers were not meant to stay for long periods of time.

"Here, sit." Matt pulled her to the rocking chair and forced her down.

Behind the chair, he pulled out more rope and began to bind her legs together. Then he pulled the climbing hooks from his pocket to hook her feet to the chain fastened around the woodstove foot pedestal.

Lisa searched the area to find anything to get loose from this well thought out arrangement of bindings. The hooks she could easily loosen, if she could get her hands free. She spotted a knife lying across the sink rim, and she prayed she would reach it somehow to cut the ropes.

"Isn't this nice? I got the rocking chair just for you. I thought you'd like it." He tucked a dingy quilt on the side of the chair and tossed the ratty pillow into her lap. Lisa flinched at the thought of where these items had been.

Matt looked around the room as if searching for something more to comfort her.

"I know," Matt shouted and dashed out the door.

A few minutes later he rushed back in, a sprig of bright yellow flowers from the Scotch Broom bush she'd seen outside and a couple of the stems of wild Foxglove that grew in abundance around the area. Grabbing an empty glass from the windowsill in the kitchen, he ran outside again. When he returned, the glass was filled to the top with water and he stuffed the ends of the flowers in, water pouring over the rim onto the floor.

"We're lucky I found a barrel of rainwater out there," he said, totally unaware of his peculiar behavior, as he set them down on the table in front of her. "You like those don't you?"

Lisa didn't know what to say. She only nodded her head in agreement.

Matt ran back out to the van and carried in a plastic grocery bag with some food items, and laid them on the table next to the flowers.

"Thought you might get hungry later on, so I stopped to get something for you," he spoke in a nervous almost boy like quality. "Can I get you anything right now? Do you need anything?"

Perplexed by his actions, Lisa shook her head and continued to watch him move about the area. He acted as if he were on a first date, wanting to make everything perfect. Only she was his captive, not his girlfriend.

Matt came to the table and emptied his pockets. A ratty old wallet, falling apart at the seams bulged out with his most important belongings, a wad of keys to who knows where, the gun from the front of his pants, and to Lisa's surprise a cell phone.

Lisa recognized the style as the ones used by Ryan and his deputies. She figured Matt had taken it from Bobby when he'd tied him up earlier. The screen was black, but she hoped to God there would be some battery life left.

"Sometimes I wish I had a purse like you women carry around. All this shit gets to be too much sometimes." As Matt sat down he pulled out a carton of cigarettes from the grocery bag. "I've been dying for one of these all morning."

She closed her eyes as he lit the lighter, half expecting him to blow himself up one of these days. His tissues must be so entrenched with the toxic substance he huffed, it was inevitable. She definitely didn't want to be around when that happened.

With no loud noises, she opened her eyes again as he took in the first long drag from the cigarette and blew it back out. They sat in silence, him facing her, slowly pulling in the effect of the tobacco into his lungs. His eyes squinted through the smoke spiraling from the tip, as if studying her every line.

"You sure make things hard." He took another drag from the cigarette and stubbed the end out on the edge of the table. "Why do you keep running from me?"

Lisa stared at him in disbelief. "Because you've tried to kill me," she cried out.

"I never did." Matt rubbed his hands on his thighs, the vehement shake of his head tossing his tangled red hair in his face. "No. I wouldn't do that. Why would I want to kill you?"

The confusion in his eyes so evident, Lisa wondered if he could possibly believe he was innocent.

"You even described the ways you were going to do it in your messages," Lisa exclaimed.

He got up and paced the floor. "I don't remember doing that." Then sitting back down in front of her, he pleaded, "You've got to believe me. If I did I didn't mean it."

"Sounded like you meant it to me," she muttered.

"You know I get a little hyper sometimes. I do things that don't make sense to other people. But I never meant to kill you."

The look in his eyes brought a smidgen of forgiveness into her heart, but the past few years of experiences were too much to forget. He couldn't possibly have forgotten all he'd put her through. He was only trying to win her trust back. He'd known what he was doing.

She shook her head. "I don't believe you."

"You have to. You have to forgive me. I didn't mean any of it. I say those things while I'm high. But I'd never go through with them."

Lisa couldn't even begin to believe him. "I don't understand. Why have you kidnapped me?"

Matt reached out to grab her left hand, yanking so hard on her fingers they cracked with a sharp shooting pain.

"Where's the ring?"

Oh, Lord. Now what am I supposed to say?

"I...I don't have it with me."

He jumped up and started pacing back and forth again. "Shit, shit, shit. I can't go back without that ring."

"Why not?" Lisa asked as she realized the significance of the ring to Matt, was much greater than she'd thought.

"Don't you understand anything," he whirled around and glared at her with bloodshot eyes. "I've got to have you by my side and that ring on your hand. That's the only way they're going to believe in me again."

"Who?"

"My parents," Matt frowned. "My dad."

He went to the door, grabbed the pack of cigarettes from his pocket, and shook one out with force. He looked at it, swore and flicked it outside, unlit.

"I hate it when those fuckers get broken." Matt began to pace again in front of her, glaring off in the distance with unseeing eyes. "Now I'll have to go back to get that damn ring."

Lisa thought maybe this could be a chance for her to escape. "Take me with you, Matt, I'll show you where it is."

He stared at her then started shaking his head. "No. See, I know what you're doing. You're not going anywhere until I make you understand."

"Understand what?"

Matt shook another cigarette out and lit it. He stood up and walked back to the open doorway. He squinted as the smoke drifted up into his face.

"What do you want from me?" she asked, dumbfounded by his professed ignorance.

"I want it to be the way it was before. You mean everything to me." He stared out at the trees blowing in the wind a minute longer. Then turning he fixed his gaze on Lisa. "You're mine. You promised yourself to me."

This was absolute craziness. Could he really believe she would forgive and forget how tortured he'd made her feel? Afraid to show her face in public, scared to make friends, the time she'd lost with her mother? Anger began to bubble up, and she wished she could stand up to release some of the emotion through movement. She wanted to knock some sense into him.

Instead she took a deep breath and let it out slow. If she wanted to escape, she needed to remain in control of herself.

"Matt, we're over. We can never have what we had with each other again. Your huffing is not something I can endure. I can't stand by and watch you kill yourself with that stuff."

Lisa wasn't sure where this would go. Calm as he seemed to be now, there was no telling when he'd fly into a rage. She had to be careful in choosing her words.

Matt threw the cigarette out the door, and dropped to his knees in front of her. He grabbed her fingers that lay limp in her lap from their encased state.

"I'll stop for you. I promise. I'll do it for you. Just give me another chance."

"A chance for what?" she asked incredulously.

He rose up on his knees and wrapped his arms around her. The stench of his unwashed body and the fumes from his engulfed clothing made her cringe and attempt to shrink away.

"I want you to love me again, Lisa. Everything was good when you loved me. You made my life bearable."

He tried to kiss her, but she turned her head sharply to the side, and his lips landed at the side of her mouth.

She made a negative sound of disagreement, and Matt pulled away from her. The look of disgust in her eyes must have been enough to change his approach. He rose to his feet and lit another cigarette, his back turned to her.

"Okay, okay, I know you might take a while to remember. But I swear you'll love me again," he said as if convincing himself.

"No, I won't," she said as firm as she could, hoping if she were able to convince him otherwise he would understand his errors.

He flew around, the quick fury bubbling beneath the surface of his eyes. "Yes, you will. I'll make you."

Trying another angle, Lisa softened her tone and said, "You can't make me love you. I can't love you Matt. I love someone else."

Rage flew up to the surface as Matt's face turned red, his blood-shot eyes straining to their limits.

"No!" Matt screamed and reached out and threw one of the chairs against the cabin wall. The flimsy wood shattered into pieces when it hit the floor in a crash.

Obviously, that's the wrong approach to take, Lisa thought.

"You will love me, damn it!" He rushed forward, his arm pulled back as if to strike her across the face. She sucked in air, in full expectation of the foreboding violence.

"Please, don't hit me," she pleaded, fear sweeping through her, as she inward waiting for the contact of his fist to be made with her face.

Matt pulled back and glared, his eyes shooting venomous darts into her. Then he turned and shoved the table away, knocking the flowers to the floor.

The last thing she heard as he headed out the door was an unintelligible grumble about the 'fucking cop.'

Through the open door, Lisa could see him head for his van. From the inside, he pulled out a propane tank and threw it beside the vehicle, causing a cloud of dust to rise up around him. He sank to the ground and leaned against the front wheel, his head bowed down over his knees and his hands fell to the gravel below.

He stayed in this position for a short time, as if drained of all energy. Then she heard him cuss zealously at the gods above as he grabbed the nozzle to the tank and raised it to his lips. The first huff didn't seem to make a difference, and she watched as he breathed in the toxic fumes over and over again. He shouted obscenities from time to time, and finally wilted to the side, his grip on the nozzle loosening as it fell beside him.

She'd done the wrong thing. She should never have told him she loved Ryan. Now she may never get away alive. The only thing to do was to wait for him to come back around. In the meantime, she needed to figure out another way to get him to let her go.

Chapter 17

Ryan strode to the map in his office, poking pins into the areas he and his deputies had already searched, cursing himself with every pin inserted.

He and Trooper John met northbound on Highway 101, about fifty miles out of Lake Duchess. Neither one spotted the vehicles in question on the main highway. Doug and one of the other troopers from an adjoining area hadn't come up with anything southbound either. Roadblocks were set up north and south, and so far had turned up nothing.

That meant they must still be in the area—somewhere.

"Nothing here Sheriff," Bobby said turning the last page to the reports he'd been going through. "No stops or arrests for any out of town vehicles, or the Belamy's Taurus, in a hundred mile radius."

Ryan had hoped they would be in luck with spotting a location if they'd been stopped in an outlying area. No such luck.

Grabbing his hat from the hook on the wall, he headed toward the door.

"I've called on some of the authorities in the area to meet me at Glacier Park in about a half hour. We'll spread out and search for any signs of Lisa and this Matthew Caine."

"You want me to come with you?" Bobby implored.

Ryan stopped for a minute and stared at the young man. The large bump had subsided into a mass of discoloration against the right side of his face.

"No, you'd better take things easy for a while longer. Stay and make sure nothing happens here at Lake Duchess," he instructed, protective of both the deputy and his township. "I'll be back."

As Ryan took the steps down to his cruiser, a few of the townspeople caught sight of him, and hurried across the road toward him, forming a small crowd.

"Let's get the sucker," old Beatty shouted out from the edges of the crowd.

Helen, from the market, stepped forward to speak for the group. "Sheriff, we've all been talking and we'd like to form a search party to help you."

Ryan surveyed the crowd, appreciative of their willingness to get involved. He held his hand up to quiet the crowd.

"Look, I know you all well enough to understand how you feel about what's going on. You can't help this time. This is a very dangerous situation and without training or authority, you'd only end up getting hurt."

"We all own some sort of weapon. Hunting rifles, army shotguns, and the like. Heck I'm a pretty good shot with this thing." Helen pulled out a B-B Gun from behind her skirt. "Scared off a few predators in my day," she said looking around her at the accepting nods.

"Yeah," Beatty shouted out again, this time holding up his army pistols. "You can deputize us Sheriff. We want to take the bastard down."

Beatty's overzealous ways started several of the other people loudly discussing various ways they would apprehend their subject.

Lord, if I don't stop this now I'll have a riot on my hands, he thought recognizing the signs of vengeance in the eyes of his loyal townspeople.

"All right, let's settle down now," he shouted, over the crowd.

"Quiet, everyone quiet," Maggie's booming voice rang out from where she stood beside Ryan. "Let the Sheriff talk."

Everyone immediately quieted to face the Sheriff and wait for him to speak. This wasn't the first time, but the quick response Maggie could get from a crowd never ceased to amaze him.

She is one of a kind, he thought gratefully.

"At this point let's not go too far. I've got a crew of troopers meeting me in about..." He glanced down at his watch. "Ten minutes. We are going to form an in-depth search over the area for Lisa and her abductor. Right now, all I need you to do is keep your eyes open for anything out of the ordinary."

The disappointed rumblings of the crowd concerned him, his brow furrowed. He hoped they would take heed to his directions. There wasn't enough manpower to conduct a search, and control their feisty actions. They'd probably end up shooting each other.

"Above all, I want you to be safe. There is no reason for any one of you to get hurt."

"If the son-of-a-bitch comes at me with that stick of his, I'll show him where he can shove it," Beatty yelled out again, always ready for action.

The stick wasn't what they needed to worry about. Ryan had to think fast. He couldn't very well tell them Matt was armed with Bobby's stolen pistol. They'd lose faith in his ability to protect them.

"That's one thing I don't want you to do. We have reason to believe he may be armed. If you see him, or Lisa, immediately call me on my cell, or Bobby at the office. I do not, I repeat, do not want you to get involved in a confrontation."

Disappointment rose up again from the crowd. Maggie stepped out and shouted, "Enough. You heard the Sheriff. Now, go on about your business."

Like little ducklings following their mother's orders, grumbling in discontent, they all turned and dispersed, talking quietly amongst their fellow cohorts traveling in the same direction.

"I wish you'd teach me how you do that," Ryan frowned. "But really, Maggie, be safe. I'm not sure what I'd do if I lost you, too."

He gave her a hug, a heartfelt twinge rising up to sting the backs of his eyes, so he turned and got into his vehicle before his emotions got the best of him.

Ryan tore out of the parking lot onto the main thoroughfare, focusing his mind on the next steps they needed to take to find Lisa.

* * * *

Lisa awakened the next morning with the rattling of plastic and Matt's short hushed curses coming from the direction of the

339

kitchen. When she started to shift pain shot through her spine, her neck so stiff she wondered if she would ever be able to move again.

Dawn had broken, and the softness of daylight streamed through the open door. During the night, she'd attempted to spread out the quilt Matt had left for her, but only succeeded in covering one leg. She shivered in the chill of the early morning dampness creeping over her through the open door.

She'd watched Matt into the late summer evening hours until she could no longer see him through the dark haze of night. He'd come alert from time-to-time only to grab hold of the nozzle and suck again on the demonic fumes, to pass out in his induced state of unconsciousness.

He moved about now in a methodic rhythm, slapping peanut butter between two pieces of bread, then he opened the icebox and took out what looked to be a slab of lunchmeat and a jar of mayonnaise. The putrid smell of something rotten drifted out and made her cough and the sneeze from the cold came swiftly behind.

Matt turned. His face smeared with dirt, his hair an odd shade of dirty gray on one side, where he'd laid his head on the ground during the night.

"Oh, good, you're awake. How did you sleep?"

Lisa stared at him. She couldn't believe his nonchalant attitude, like nothing at all was wrong.

She wanted desperately to cover her nose, as the smell wafted past her, but she couldn't.

"What the hell is that smell?"

Matt turned, his dazed eyes resembling glassy marbles. He blinked once or twice then gave her a crooked smile.

"Oh, that? Some fish I picked up a couple days ago spoiled. I threw it out this morning, but the fridge still stinks. Ice is gone and no electricity means stuff starts to go bad."

The necessity to move her legs overwhelmed her. She felt as if her bones were about to crack and crumble to the floor in a pile. Lisa groaned to herself as she moved her hips back and forth to loosen the joints.

"What are you doing?" she asked to keep him talking. He seemed to be in a fairly good mood. This might be a chance to talk some sense into him.

"I'm making you some breakfast. Bologna still smells good. Sorry, can't start a fire though, might catch somebody's attention."

He placed the two sandwiches he'd made on the table, and she stared at their unappealing contents. She didn't want to eat anything in this hellhole, but at some point she'd need to eat something to keep up her strength. If she had to, she'd pick the peanut butter one. The bologna no doubt would give her food poisoning.

All of a sudden, the need to relieve herself made her almost cry out in pain.

"Matt, I've got to go."

"You're not going anywhere. Not until we talk," he said firmly.

"No, you don't understand. I've got to go pee," she pleaded with him.

He stared at her, the realization of what she meant taking a minute to connect. "Oh, yeah, I thought about that."

He came around and unhooked her from the chain he'd used to attach her to the wall.

Lisa glanced around in desperation. "Where's the bathroom?"

"There isn't one. The only thing is the outhouse about twenty yards down the hill, or my handy-dandy makeshift toilet," he said stepping from in front of the improvised beverage cooler he'd created for use in his van. "I'm not sure though. I don't think I should trust you to go outside. You might try something funny. I think you'd better go here."

My God! Is the man crazy? I'm not using that thing, she thought to herself.

"I promise. I won't do anything stupid. Untie me and let me go."

She tried her best to sound convincing, although the minute she had a chance she would bolt. She couldn't help but take a quick glance around and caught sight of the gun sitting on the table next to the cell phone.

Something in her voice must've tipped him off. He started shaking his head.

"Nope, no can do, I'm not stupid." Matt lifted the lid to the cooler. He presented his ingenuity with a proud smile, "See, all empty and ready for your use."

At that point she didn't care where she had to go. The pressure on her abdomen was unbearable. If she didn't, she didn't want to think what would happen.

"All right, all right, just let me go," she yelped.

He started to loosen the ropes then must have realized his mistake. He reached back, grabbed the gun and shoved the barrel into his pants.

As he finished the release of her leg restraints, he rose back up and Lisa pushed past him to where the container sat. Now what? With her arms still tied to her sides, how was she supposed to get her pants down?

"Matt!" she pleaded again.

"Oh yeah, guess I'll need to help you with those."

Repulsed by the thought, she turned her head as he pulled her shorts down, disturbed by the smirk he gave her as he rose back up.

"Turn around," she ordered him.

The leer on his face made her stomach lurch, but he turned as directed and she quickly squatted over the opening of the cooler. Her eyes shot from one place to the other trying to find something else she could use as a weapon.

Damn. The knife is gone. Where'd he put it?

"Shake a little. Sorry, I forgot the toilet paper for you," Matt called out over his shoulder. "You finished?"

In disgust, she allowed him to pull her shorts back up. The feeling so nasty she prayed to God she would get out of this soon to take a long hot shower.

He wobbled a bit and lost his footing as he stood up, the chemicals still present in his system. Lisa had to take the risk. She shoved him as hard as possible with her body and ran for the open door. If she hadn't stepped on the sliver of wood sticking up out of the floor, she might have made her escape.

"Aghh," she cried out in pain, still trying to escape through the door on her wounded foot.

Cursing, Matt leapt up from the floor where he'd landed and grabbed her around the waist. "Shit Lisa, I figured you'd do something like that."

He whirled her around and threw her into the chair again, her head coming square against the backrest. The room swayed for a second, but the blow to the head wasn't strong enough to knock her out. By the time he'd finished tying her ankles to the chair legs again, she began noting the things she'd done wrong.

As he sat back in the chair across from her, panting from the effort she'd caused, he grabbed the almost empty pack of cigarettes. The most recent use of propane didn't seem to concern him. The flick of the lighter again prompted Lisa to shut her eyes, unable to watch his impending explosion.

"Don't do that again Lisa, or so help me God I'll shoot you in the back."

She had to figure out a different way. Maybe if she could win his trust, he might remove the restricting ropes. She needed to do a lot of sweet-talking to get past the little stunt she'd tried.

"I'm sorry Matt, I'm so scared."

"You don't understand do you?" His eyes still held a glassy, uncaring expression from the night's indulgence.

"Tell me what I don't understand." She needed to stall him and think fast for another way to get out. This switching back and forth between moods was hard to deal with effectively. How did you talk to a crazy person?

"I don't want to hurt you. I want to love you. You and I were meant to be together."

His expression was of true innocence. He had no idea what he suggested would be impossible. She had to get him to understand. "Matt…" she began.

"When we leave here we're going to visit my parents back home. Then you'll see I'm not such a bad guy." A wistful smile came across his face. "My mom is going to love you. She's always wanted a daughter-in-law."

At that moment, Lisa saw a young man, eager to impress his parents with the girl of his dreams. The truth was he had no idea how wrong his actions would be perceived, if they knew what he was truly doing.

He looked down at her captive hands and shook his head. "It's not going to work right if you don't come willingly. They wouldn't understand if you're tied up like this."

Matt got up and walked to the door, the cigarette hanging from his lips, then turned all of a sudden a light flashing in his eyes. "I know. We should get to know each other better. Maybe if you did, you'd love me again."

"I think I know all I need to," Lisa muttered.

"Wait. Before you say anything else, I've got to tell you how much I love you," he said swiftly.

She started to shake her head but remained silent as he held his hand up to stop her from responding.

"I realize you don't think you love me now."

She shook her head, watching his every move, waiting for another explosion. Matt's eyes were fixed hard on her, and Lisa couldn't imagine the effort it took for him not to get worked up over what she'd said the day before.

"I think you'll start to believe in me again before too long. We just need to spend more time together. That's why I think we should talk. Ask me a question, anything you'd like."

Lisa eased herself into a more comfortable position, which wasn't easy. "All right, why do you huff propane?"

Matt's eyes shot out a sharp irritated look. "You don't play around do you?"

"You said ask anything."

"If you must know, I tried a couple hits with some friends of mine when I was about ten or eleven. Way cool, but I didn't really get into it then 'cuz the stuff was so hard to get back then. Gas was a lot easier to get. Just crack the lid on the gas tank of any car, and you had yourself a good time."

"So, why did you switch to propane again?"

Matt stared at her, his emotions shuttered behind glassy eyes. "I guess 'cuz propane lasts longer and doesn't give me that blasted headache I get with gasoline."

He stood at the open door gazing out at the early morning light, the bright green leaves of the maple trees fluttering in the breeze around them.

"Did you ever really try to stop?"

This is good, he's talking. Maybe I can lead him into wanting to let me go.

His head whipped around, he stared at her with eyes dark and accusing. "What do you mean by 'really try'? You don't think I've tried to stop?"

"I just meant you're still using, so you must have a reason why the rehab you told me about before didn't work."

"Rehab never works. There is no treatment that deals directly with huffing. It's not the same as alcoholism, but they treat all addictions the same. I've tried so many times I've stopped counting. Nobody understands what this is like."

"Tell me," Lisa prompted.

Matt blew out a breath and continued to stare outside. "If I had to describe what huffing is like, I'd have to say it's an obsession of sorts. Like the stuff calls out to me in the night, begging me to come back."

There was a long silence, and he turned to sit down in front of Lisa again. He reached out to grasp her fingers. She stared down at their hands. She immediately wanted to pull her hand back, but couldn't. His long fingers were in need of a good washing, the nails unclipped and blotched with dirt and grime, his palms sweaty.

"Like a woman, a beautiful woman like you, telling me she will give me pleasures beyond anything I've ever known. As if it cares about me and wants to take care of me and make me feel good."

His eyes came up to meet hers, the blue spheres surrounded by the reddened vessels irritated by the chemicals he'd inhaled.

"Until I met you I didn't think I could ever find anyone to give me the same feeling."

Lisa realized how badly Matt needed help. If anything, he had a distorted vision of reality. He wasn't an evil man. If there was any way to help him, she had to understand why.

"You kept using, even after I pleaded with you to quit."

"When we met, that was the longest I'd ever gone without the shit. Pastor Williams and I had been talking for a long time, and I'd thought all his quotes and spiritual crap was finally starting to work."

"But you didn't stop."

"I couldn't stop. Not the way you wanted me to. Huffing is what I do to get by. I know I should stop, but every time I try, the shit keeps tempting me and I want it even more."

"If you were to let it go, I'm sure you would find what you are looking for again." Lisa caught something fly across his beseech filled face, a panic of some sort.

Matt jerked his hands away from hers and stood over her for a minute, then moved back to the open door. Lisa wasn't sure what to say next. With his back turned to her, she couldn't tell what he might be thinking.

"You just don't understand, do you? I can't stop."

"Why?"

"Because, I need to forget things," his voice rasped out as if his throat had constricted, challenging him to say any more.

"What kind of things?"

Matt glanced back at her, and she could see his hesitance in opening up to her. He came back into the darkened room, blocking the light from the door, his features hidden by the shadow. He stood staring at her, his breathing intense as if gathering the courage to admit his innermost thoughts.

Grasping an unopened pack of cigarettes, he turned and walked out the door. Soon after, he came back in with one half-empty and one full bottle of clear liquid in his hands, and slammed them down on the table. A cigarette still hanging from his lips, he grabbed a coffee cup from the sink and proceeded to pour the contents to the brim.

By the looks of the bottles, Lisa thought this was probably the gin Old Beatty had whimpered about losing that day at Maggie's. In silence, Matt began to slurp down the liquor, staring across at Lisa as if he hated her.

She'd learned that his drinking on an empty stomach lead to a sure path for a quickened effect, one she dreaded. If the huffing wasn't bad enough, the short time she'd been with Matt, she'd found out he was a mean drunk. She'd tried to talk him into getting help for that too, but he'd acted as if she were an overly sensitive woman, with no experience of a real man before. That was the point she'd known there was no hope for the relationship.

After knocking out the partial bottle, he sat back, the chair back creaking with the additional weight. For the longest time he sat with eyes closed, his breathing shallow, almost as if he'd fallen asleep. Then he suddenly sat forward, and squinted as he looked directly at her.

"Why the hell do you want to know?"

Lisa already understood trying to reason with a drunken individual was never successful, and would only get her in deeper trouble.

"I thought maybe I could help."

"Oh, now you want to help," he yelled as he stood, stumbling forward, but he caught himself in time. "Where the hell have you been all this time?"

He got up real close to her face, his rough breath seeping over her with its thick alcoholic stench.

"You've been out here fucking some asshole's brains out, haven't you?"

Oh, no. He's going there again, she thought entrenched with new fear.

Matt shoved her back from him, causing the chair to start rocking violently. At first, Lisa thought she would tip over, her inability to block her fall frightful. The sickening movement began to cease, though her alarm to what would come next remained.

"I should kill you - right here and now." His slurred speech drove his words in deeper into Lisa's awareness of how bad this could turn out. "Why the hell shouldn't I?"

He turned and grabbed the pistol from the table, pointing the tip of the barrel at her forehead. Lisa's heart pounded mercilessly in her ears. This was it—this was the end. She closed her eyes, waiting for the blast, the air clogged in her lungs.

The length of time seemed to loom over her, and she finally had to gasp for air. Her eyes flew open to find Matt still standing over her, the gun drooping from his fingers.

She took a long breath. "Because you don't have it in you to kill someone," she whispered, hopeful to have hit the truth.

He grabbed the unopened bottle of cheap gin and twisted off the cap. Taking a long pull from the inebriating liquid, he began laughing uncontrollably.

The heightened emotion, resulting from his intoxication, caused him to dart his eyes wildly about the room, making him look like a wild man.

"Fuck. Why not? I've done it before," he gasped between roaring breaths.

Lisa stared at him. She might not have believed him before, but at this moment, she had no idea what to believe.

"What do you mean?" she choked out.

"You want to know?" His voice came out in a raspy whisper, and he looked from side to side as if ensuring they were alone. Matt brought his face up close to hers, his breath slamming into her face as he struggled to steady himself on his feet. "One night, my buddy

Harlan and I were huffing out at the abandoned warehouse on Fifth Street, and the sparks from the fire lit the fucker up. Harlan knows. He knows just how bad I can be. Poor bastard burnt to a crisp right there in front of me, and I didn't do a damn thing about it."

The effort was too much for him, and he slumped back down into the chair behind him. Lisa was at a loss for words, so she let him ramble on by himself.

"He screamed and he screamed," Matt whispered, his own face contorting in his memories. "He kept screaming at me to help him, but I couldn't…I just couldn't move."

The picture Lisa imagined was horrific. "Oh my God, Matt."

Matt grabbed the bottle and drank down a couple more swallows, gasping as the harsh fiery liquid went down. "It burns baby, burns."

His rasp turned into a scream, mimicking what she thought he must have heard that night. Teetering out of the chair, he repeated the phrase over-and-over as he stumbled toward the doorway, bottle in tow.

Chapter 18

Exhausted, Ryan went back home to change clothes and make sure Pluto was all right. The passing of over 24 hours turned up no clues as to where Lisa had been taken. He knew the longer the length of time, the colder the trail would become.

A shower refreshed him a bit, so he decided to make some coffee and sit down to plan out his next moves. Pluto followed him into the office and lay down at Ryan's feet, the faithful canine's eyes tracing his every movement.

He pulled out a detailed map of the peninsula from his drawer and spread the unfolded page over his desk. The roadblocks he'd set up north and south on the highway were strategically placed, before any possible cut-off intersection leading away from the area. He'd cut up the area in four sections, each assigned to a group of troopers from surrounding districts. He and his group of officers took Section 3, centering on the Lake Duchess sector, and had ended up with nothing. So far neither of two other group leads had reported anything unusual, nor any contact with the subject. If he didn't hear back from the last group in the next hour he'd take that section himself.

Taking another sip from his coffee mug, he scoured the map in front of him hoping something would pop out shining a light on where she'd been taken. They had to be close by – but where?

The gnawing frustration in his gut was about to tear him apart.

Where the hell is she?

His gaze caught the picture of his mother he kept on his desk in both offices, in town and here at home, a constant reminder of the loss he'd suffered so long ago. He reached out to pull it closer to him.

"I may not have been able to save you, but I'll be damned if I let some addict take her away from me," he exclaimed to the memory of his mother. "If he does anything to hurt her, I swear I'll kill him."

His eyes became cloudy, a display of emotion he didn't often let himself experience. Rubbing the tears from his eyes with the back of his fisted hand, remembering all too well the pain and heartache he would feel if he were to lose his newly found love. He may as well just rip his heart out himself.

He had to find her.

"Damn it," he said scooping up the map to shove the frustration back into his desk.

A white envelope dropped from between his fingers and lay on his desk prompting his attention. The strong bold lettering was addressed to: Ryan Jacobs, c/o Maggie Travis, with the state penitentiary return address stamped in blue across the top.

Ryan picked the cloaked message up and turned the offensive item over in his hands several times, not sure if he really wanted to know the contents. He'd had a nagging sense of obligation to read the letter since Maggie gave it to him a few weeks prior. Opening the sealed envelope slowly, he pulled out the single folded page and stared at the introduction.

'*Dear Son*' wasn't the opening he'd expected.

He couldn't remember a time when his father paid much attention to him, so why would he address him in this manner now?

'Dear Son – I don't expect I will ever hear from you, but there have been some things in my heart I've needed to tell you. I've had a lot of time to think about the things I've done in the past. There are no excuses to give for my being the bad father that I was, and the cause of your mother's death. I only want to tell you how sorry I am. But, I want you to know that your mother and I loved each other. You may not remember her much, but she was the sweetest woman I'd ever met. At that time, I didn't realize the evils of alcohol and my sinful nature would take her away from us. You both deserved so much more from me. It's taken me a long time to understand why I did what I did, and hope that through the ministry here I can help others to change their lives to become the men God intended them to be. I will never be able to atone for my sins and only hope someday you can forgive me - Your father, Howard.'

Ryan sucked in a breath and slowly folded the letter into the envelope, shoving it again where he'd kept it hidden in the desk drawer. He couldn't deal with this now. He sat staring at his mother's picture, the significance of his father's words not yet able to sink into his cloudy brain.

Not able to comprehend the evilness of his father from the past could ever change he didn't know if he had the ability to forgive his father for what he'd done. He rose and went to the window, wondering how so many crimes could be committed within the home, right under everyone's noses.

"That's it," he exclaimed reaching for the phone. "Doug, get all the deputies together. We are going to form another type of search party. I'll meet you at the office in fifteen."

Under their noses – Matt had to be in someone's home, maybe holding them hostage, too.

* * * *

Some hours later, the sun had begun to set in the West. Lisa's bones were crying out from the length of time in a sitting position, and she tried to loosen them with any type of movement she could achieve. Matt must have slept off the inebriation, as she watched him drag himself back into the room unsure of what to expect next.

He sat down, another bottle of gin at the ready swinging from his hand.

"God, I wish I had another tank, that shit gets used up way too fast."

Slamming the bottle down on the table he sat back, staring at Lisa. The drift of the cigarette he lit this time swirled toward her, and she coughed at the forced inhalation of second-hand smoke.

He moved his hand toward the door. "Sorry."

She watched his movements carefully. His hand shook a little as he brought the cigarette back to his lips. He seemed to be fairly sober, maybe she could get him talking again before he started drinking again.

"You wanted me to get to know you better?" She waited for him to acknowledge he connecting to what she said. He stared at her then nodded slowly. "Tell me about your parents. What is your mother like?"

The smile that came across Matt's face struck a chord in her heart. He obviously loved deeply, perhaps too deep.

"She's the best. So sweet, always willing to help and the greatest cook I've ever known. She's been a life saver for me. That's for sure. You're like her in a lot of ways."

"Sounds like, she's a wonderful woman. What about your father?"

A frown skittered across his brow. The question caused him to reach out and grab the bottle of gin. He held the container unopened, just staring into the clear liquid as if his answers would come floating to the top.

"He's a good man. The best cop you'll ever meet." His eyes came up to challenge her to say something derogatory.

His words did not match up to his actions. Lisa wasn't sure if she should push the subject or not.

"Do you get along with your father?"

Matt jumped up, looking as if he were ready to fight.

"Why wouldn't I? I have nothing against him. Just because he gets cranky, I don't blame him, just that blasted metal leg he's got."

He grabbed another cigarette and shoved the end into his mouth, dragging on the fumes as if they would solve all his woes. Lisa had obviously hit a sensitive note.

"How did he loose his leg?"

357

"Went out one night to pick up some ice cream for me and mom at the Quick-Mart," Matt's voice quivered with the memory. "Walked into a burglary and some asshole blasted the damn thing out from under him."

Matt sat back down and started to rock in the chair, back and forth as if to calm down, tears coming to the edges of his eyes. He cut a glance at Lisa and wiped the one that began to trickle down his cheek. "He went because of me. It wouldn't have happened if I hadn't made him go."

Lisa's heart broke for him. He believed he was responsible for his father's injury. Nothing she could say would ever wipe the memory from his mind.

"How old were you?"

"I was about ten. My mom took the call from the station and broke down crying. We rushed to the hospital, next thing I knew I'm staring at this space on the bed where his damn leg should be—really freaked me out."

"I'm so sorry." Lisa didn't know what else to say.

"My Dad is honored as the best cop around. He can take anyone down. He got that fucker right back too. Showed him whose boss and blasted his brains across the store." Matt sat up straight and puffed out his chest in obvious respect. "You should see all his medals and stuff. He's a hero. You'll see for yourself when we go out to see Mom and Dad."

Lisa felt his grasp between past and present faltered somewhat.

"What happened then?" She questioned not sure if she was leading him in the right direction.

"You know, we used to pal around all the time. Throw the ball around in the park, go fishing and stuff. Then after the leg thing, he just sort of clammed up, like life wasn't worth living."

"I'm sure that must have been so hard for all of you."

"You have absolutely no idea."

He shoved the carton of cigarettes away from him and grabbed the bottle of gin in his hands, rolling the cylinder back and forth as if contemplating his need to start drinking again. Lisa watched carefully as he set the liquor back down on the table with a concerted effort, and began to clasp, and unclasp his hands together in his lap.

"Mamma is so strong. I only saw her cry that one time, but I know it tore her up. Dad changed. He wasn't the same after that. She's never said anything, but I know he started to smack her around some. She takes care of us like nothing ever happened."

Lisa saw a troubled teenager still present in his glassy eyed stare.

"What about you?"

"I don't know. It was like I lost him that night—like he died." He shoved another cigarette in his mouth and lit it up. "I'm sure he blames me."

"Did he ever tell you that?"

"No, but you know he had to."

She knew no matter what his Dad felt, Matt would always take the blame.

"After that, I used to try so hard to get him to notice me. Got good grades, and took honor roll in high school. But nothing ever works, it's never enough." Lisa immediately picked up on his cross between past and present.

"Were you using back then?"

"Sure. I mean, huffing is the only way I can get through the day sometimes. I'd come home and he'd be yelling at me. Mom and I knew better than to talk back to him. She'd just stay in the kitchen and I'd go out back to the garage."

"Has he ever heard you play the guitar?" Lisa thought maybe she could sway the conversation to something more positive and help him to see that the past can never be changed, but the future was what he needed to concentrate on.

"Naw, he says it's not worth the effort. He doesn't see the band as anything more than a time waster. Tells me I'm a looser and I'll never be anything worthwhile."

She pulled her brows together. Finally seeing the whole picture didn't make this any easier.

"He's wrong Matt. I know. I've seen you play. You are an awesome musician. I'm sure the other band members tell you the same thing."

Matt reached over and grabbed one of the sandwiches he'd made that morning and offered her some. Lisa tried not to grimace visibly at the thought of eating either one, but especially the bologna.

She shook her head and smiled. "No, thank you. Go ahead."

Lisa watched as he hungrily shoved the sandwich in his mouth and downed it with a couple of loud slurps of water he'd brought from outside.

"Actually, they kicked me out. Robbie said some bullshit about not meeting deadlines for the recording. But it wasn't my fault. They were the ones that got me started. In fact, they were all using meth the night before. I tried the stuff again, but it just wasn't doing it for me, so I switched to my tank in the van. It's not my fault what I use takes longer."

Lisa hated to think it, but she'd seen this coming from the start. "I'm sure if you were to talk to them they'd give you another chance."

Matt rose to his feet and paced to the door and back. "Nope," his conviction was steadfast. "Not going to do that. They had their chance. I'll show them. I'll just find me another band to join up with, and they'll see the mistake they made losing me."

Lisa was running out of directions to take with him. Music was really all he had left.

"That's what you should be doing. You need to start looking for other bands to play in," she said with a slight groan as her leg started to cramp up on her. "If you let me loose we can start looking together. Would you like that?"

Matt's eyes widened considerably. "You want to start helping me again?"

"Of course I do. You just have to find the right place to be is all." Lisa said in truth.

"We make such a good team Lisa. That's all I've ever wanted, for us to make everything work together."

Lisa sat still, not wanting to jinx the moment. He looked as if he were about to loosen the ropes for her as he bent, coming to rest mere inches from her face. Then he tried to kiss her again. It was all she could do to hold back from spitting it back into his face. He tried to deepen the kiss by prying her lips apart with his tongue, and that's where she couldn't handle it any more. She turned her face away in disgust.

Matt rose back up his eyes glaring into hers, the heat of anger rising quickly to the surface.

"It's that fucking cop again isn't it?"

She didn't dare say a thing to refute the truth. Her voice would surely give her away. She shook her head and looked down into her lap.

Matt sat back down across from her, she could feel his eyes boring holes into her and the trust she'd tried to build with him. She looked back up after a long period of silence. He grabbed the gin bottle and twisted off the cap, and tossed the metal object across the room. He lifted the bottle up to her as if in a cheer, and the long gulp he took at first caused his eyes to water a bit, as it went down.

"What the hell does he have that I don't?"

Lisa decided being silent was the best route to take this time. Any words she could say would only start him to flare up again.

"Is it romance? Hell, if you gave me a chance, I could romance you 'til death do us part," he exclaimed his voice cracking at the end.

His reference to the marriage he'd once offered her surprised her, and she raised her eyebrows slightly.

"Yeah, I bet your lover boy hasn't popped the question yet has he?" He took another long pull on the contents of the bottle. "Well too late, I already have. We're getting married. So you better just get used to it. I don't care if I have to keep you locked in the trailer. You're mine and you can't do anything about it. Understand?"

Lisa nodded out of fear for what he would do next.

Matt slammed his fist down on the table and raised the bottle again to his lips. He'd consumed almost half the gin already.

"Damn it, talk woman. Don't give me that silent shit."

"Yes, I understand."

Where the hell is this conversation going?

He rose from his chair and stood over her, bottle still in hand. The remainder, sloshing from side to side, he swallowed in a matter of seconds, tossing the empty bottle to the floor.

"I know what you need," he grumbled, his words slurred, and a leer surfacing to his eyes.

Lisa knew exactly where this was going.

Matt reached down and tore away the top portion of her shirt, as far as it would go behind the ropes around her waist. Lisa felt the chill of the evening air swoosh past her, carrying with it the stench of the drunken man in front of her.

He sunk down to his knees and pulled her to him, mashing his lips against hers and forcing the kiss to sink in. He mumbled something she couldn't make out as he tried to clasp her breast in his mouth.

"Please Matt, don't do this," she cried out. She couldn't push him away.

"Shut up. You know you like it. You just need me to show you what you've been missing. I've got everything right here for you, baby, and I'm going to give it to you right now."

She could feel his engorged penis rubbing against her leg as he crushed her lips again with his. The air had backed up in Lisa's lungs and she wasn't sure if she would pass out. God, how she wished she would.

"Damn ropes," Matt grumbled as he rose to his feet again.

Reaching into his pocket, he pulled out the cell phone and tossed it to the table, followed by the gun and the keys. Lisa watched where everything landed.

This was her chance. If he was about to do what she thought, there was no way around it. He needed to take the ropes off to get to her.

That would be his fatal mistake.

"Take them off Matt. I need to be able to move for you," she cooed hoping to resemble encouragement for what he was planning on doing.

Matt weaved as he stood back from her for a second, his glassy eyes trying to focus on her.

"I knew it. You want me to fuck you, don't you?"

The term sickened her, but she made sure not to show the offense in her eyes.

"Yes, oh yes, quick Matt. Get these ropes off me quick."

In a matter of minutes, he'd loosened the ropes and she was able to stand unsteadily on her legs that were half asleep. The ropes around her body dropped to the floor, her arms finally free. Hoping to get some blood running, she moved her joints and back in a way Matt might have thought was seductive, but in reality, she needed as much agility as possible. If she was going to do this she'd better do it right.

"Get these handcuffs off me Matt. I want to feel all of you," she almost choked on her own words, the disgust boiling in her stomach about to come up.

"Right, right," Matt slurred feeling around in his pockets. He turned them all out, but nothing was there. "Shit, shit, shit. I can't find the keys."

Lisa figured if she had to, she could get away without the use of her hands. The next move would be the most important one. Gauging the distance to the door, and his position between her and the escape route, she had to make sure he wouldn't be able to chase after her.

"Hurry Matt, I can't wait much longer."

"All right, all right," he began to chuckle. "If I'd known it was this easy I wouldn't have waited so long."

"Me too," she played along, the escape foremost on her mind.

"We'll just have to do it with the cuffs on. Kinda kinky if you ask me." He thrust her against the bed frame and onto the mattress. "Take your clothes off."

She hesitated then pretended to begin unbuttoning the rest of the shirt as she smiled up at him. Hurriedly he pulled his pants down to his feet and began to climb onto the bed, pushing her backward as he went. With one swift movement, she brought her knees up to her chest and kicked out as hard as she could.

Matt went flying out with a grunt and landed hard against the steel woodstove behind him. She saw his head connect with the rim as she gathered her balance and ran straight for the table. The gun fell to the floor when her hip hit the edge, but the phone and keys remained in reach.

Struggling to grab the items in her cuffed hands, she succeeded and bolted for the door. She then realized she hadn't heard anything more from Matt. It might be her doom, but she turned to see if he was all right.

He lay still on the floor next to the rocking chair, his head close to the stove he'd hit. She slowly went over, afraid that she'd killed him, but his foot moved and a groan came from his throat. That was enough. She sprinted out the door raising her cuffed hands to the moonlight to find a key that would fit the door of the Dodge. The keys slithered out of her fingers and dropped to the ground.

Shit, I can't go back and get them now.

Running at full throttle down the gravel road, she decided her best cover would be the woods to either side her. If Matt was able to get up he would surely be able to find the keys and head after her.

She hushed a yelp as her foot connected with something sharp on the ground cover under the trees, the pain causing her to double over. In the distance, she heard the shouts from Matt, cursing and threatening to dominate over her.

Lisa kept close to the ground crouching, and all but crawling in one direction, the dark shapes along the side of the road she hoped were the ones she'd seen on the way in. Branches and rocks dug into her bare legs and tender feet, but she knew her survival depended on her ability to stay hidden in the darkened forest floor.

She got as far away as she thought was safe and covered the glare of the cell phone screen with her body as she attempted to make a call.

'Low Battery' displayed across the top of the phone. God, she hoped there was enough power left to save her life.

Ryan's cell number showed in the number one position of contacts, and thankfully, she pressed the 'talk' button to dial his phone. She brought it up to her ear and got down as close as she could to the ground.

Please, please, please work for me, she prayed.

Holding her breath Lisa waited for it to ring. It felt as if it took too long to start ringing, but finally she heard the faint ring, faltering slightly with the bad reception.

"Lisa. Lisa is that you?" The hurried voice of Ryan came across the receiver, the strong, smooth voice she loved so much.

Lisa kept her voice to a whisper so as not to give her location away.

"Ryan, oh my God, you've got to help me."

Chapter 19

A few minutes earlier, Maggie had poured coffee into Ryan's mug and sat down across from him. Ryan's hunch hadn't panned out. In a short time they found everyone safe and sound in their homes, no intruders in sight.

"How are you holding up?"

Ryan shook his head. "Rigby called in and said they didn't find anything in Section One. Maggie, we've got to have missed something somewhere."

"What's the next step?" Maggie asked as they watched a family come through the front door for dinner.

"I'm going to start the search over, this time by myself. I'm not going to stop until I find her, Maggie. I can't."

Maggie nodded her head. "You won't." She reached out and covered his hand in hers. "I've got to get back to the kitchen. You be safe."

He looked up into her tender eyes, full of love and compassion. "I'm always safe," he gave his standard answer back with a half smile.

Tess strolled up to the table, hips swaying and a smile he knew she *thought* was sexy dripping from her lips.

"Hey, big boy, where you off to?" she asked, in a breathy voice.

"I'm headed out to find Lisa." Ryan pulled a couple of bills out of his wallet and placed them over the ticket on the table.

Tess sat down with a heavy sigh and leaned forward, her ample bosom pressing hard against the black spandex encasement she wore.

"Don't you think it's been long enough? If you ask me, she wanted to get out of here. Maybe that Matt fella's her excuse to vamoose."

Anger bubbled up and Ryan had a hard time not expressing what he thought of her assumption out loud.

"Not everyone is like you, Tess," he said quietly.

"You'd be surprised, Ryan. She told me how she's been waiting for her true love to come save her."

Ryan narrowed his eyes at Tess. She fiddled with the edge of a napkin, her long nails now black in color. If his training was worth anything, her demeanor and the slithery snakelike glaze in her eyes was an indication she was lying.

"If you know what's good for you, you'll stop right now," he said.

Tess sat back with a harrumph. "Why are you so stuck on finding her?"

"First off, it's my sworn duty to uphold the law in my town, and a grave injustice has been committed here. I will not allow for any illegal actions, including kidnapping. Second, not that this is any of your business, but Lisa is the kindest, most loving woman I've ever met. Neither she, nor anyone else, deserves the treatment she's endured."

A smile of derision slowly glided over Tess's face.

"If you ask me, I think she likes it rough."

"Tess," Ryan warned. He swore if he didn't have any sense he'd haul off and smack her.

"When are you going to realize she left because she wanted to? I'm here for you now." She batted her eyes at him.

Ryan sat back to stare at the woman he had once loved, wondering why.

His brows came together in a frown. "You know, if you'd come back a couple months ago, I'm not sure what I would have done. That's how confused I was after you left. But I have no question now."

Tess's silky smile reminded him of the snake again, slithering toward its prey.

"Let me take you home and I'll give you what you need."

Ryan stood, disgust seeping into his heart. "Not now or ever again. Tess, leave me the hell alone."

He strode off, leaving Tess to chew on his words.

Ryan stood beside his truck filling the tank with gas, ready to head out to scour the land again, starting with the last section called into him. The cell on his belt clip began to ring.

"Sheriff Jacobs," he said, his shoulder propping the cell up to his ear while he inserted the gas nozzle back in place.

"Sheriff, this is Deputy Foster from the Forks area. Trooper Rigby thought I should tell you when I started the search on the northeast end of our assigned section I got called back into Forks to deal with a dispute at the Red Bone Tavern. We didn't turn up anything in the area we were able to investigate, but you might want to head out and take a look in the area yourself."

Ryan swore silently. "Roger that, Foster. Thanks for the help."

Shoving the phone back into the clip, he yanked the door to his truck open and got in. He'd known it. In his gut, he felt something was still missing. What did Section One have that was different from the others?

Nothing but trees out there. Think, where is the best place for them to hide?

He peeled out of the station and headed toward the highway. His cell rang again as he reached the Coffee Hut. Glancing at the incoming call, he jerked the wheel to the right and pulled to a dead stop at the side of the road.

The call coming in was from Bobby's cell number—the stolen cell. Ryan's heart began to thump in his chest.

"Lisa. Lisa is that you?"

He barely made out the answer, but knew it was her.

"Ryan…help me." She was saying more, but the reception cut in and out.

"Where are you?"

Silence.

He moved, hoping to get a better connection. "Can you tell me where you are? Lisa…Lisa."

Lisa's voice was faint. "Cabin…Hedges," was all he heard, but it was enough.

"If you can hear me, I'm on my way."

Of course! Why hadn't he thought of that himself? The old forestry cabin would be a perfect place to hold up. With a swift yank on the wheel to the left, Ryan tore off again toward the highway. He punched in the radio channel to the office on his dashboard.

"Lake Duchess Sheriff's office," Bobby answered the call.

"Bobby. Get Doug and head out to the Weyerhauser cabin at the Hedge's plot, North 101 at milepost 60. I'm headed that way now. Suspect Caine to be apprehended. Remember, he's armed and dangerous, proceed with caution."

"10/4 Sheriff," Bobby responded.

Ryan drove as never before toward his destination. The temporary light he'd placed on the roof of the truck swirled red beams against the trees and oncoming cars pulling off to the side of the road as he sped past. Each car he checked to make sure wasn't either of the two vehicles they searched to find.

As he pulled onto the cut-off to the Weyerhauser plot, the lights from his fellow police officers came into view behind him in his rearview mirror. He turned on his search lights to the side, in hopes to catch sight of Lisa.

* * * *

372

"Damn it, Lisa. Where the hell are the keys?" Lisa dove further down to the ground as Matt screamed at the top of his lungs. "You're dead. Do you hear me? That's the last time you get away from me."

Between the trees, she saw movement outside the cabin as he used the dome flashlight to search for the keys. She needed to get further away. Sooner than later, he would either find the keys, or come searching for her with the light. She didn't dare take off the bright blue denim shirt she wore. The blue of the shirt and the paleness of her skin would both be easily sighted against the trees and groundcover, and she preferred not being caught half-naked against the trees by anyone.

Lisa crawled on her hands and knees over fallen trees along the ground. Leaves and branches brushed her face, tearing at her clothes, as she tried to make as little noise as possible.

She prayed Matt was too drunk to find the keys she'd dropped in the gravel. If he were able to start the car, the headlights would surely pick up her attire in the bushes.

Thank God, Ryan had picked up the phone. He would come get her soon. She only hoped he'd heard what she said. The phone had beeped the low battery warning while she waited for him to answer, shutting off right after she'd told him where she thought she was located.

She had to keep going. If Ryan hadn't heard her, then she was still on her own. The best thing she could do was get as far away as possible.

Her hand came down on something slimy, and she jerked her hand back and stopped. She held back the scream that gurgled in her throat. Movement below her wriggled off to the right as the moonlight picked up the tail end of a reptile slithering away from her. Thank God, no rattlesnakes were found in Washington, at least not in this part of the state. She wasn't sure what kind of snake that was, but at least it had the decency not to turn around and bite her.

Off in the distance she picked up the roar of a motor vehicle engine.

Or is that more than one?

At first, she couldn't tell from which direction the noise came. She feared it came from behind, which meant Matt had found the keys. Then all of a sudden the bounce of headlights in front of her made her breathe a sigh of relief. Hopefully she was still headed in the direction she'd started out. So, someone must be coming in from the highway. A second set of headlights came into view behind the first, both travelling at a tremendous speed along the gravel, pothole spotted road.

Ryan!

Pulling herself up from the ground, Lisa ran straight for the oncoming lights, waving her arms over her head to attract attention in the darkness. Rocks and twigs dug into her tender feet as she leapt over a broken log onto the side of the road. The bright lights blinded her. She had a hard time in judging distance in the dark and the beams of the headlights kept coming toward her. She stopped in the middle of the road, closing her eyes in hopes they would spot her in time.

The tires of the oncoming vehicles ground to a stop and she opened her eyes as the driver of the first threw open the door and rushed toward her.

"Lisa," Ryan's voice rasped out her name.

His face came into view seconds before she let herself be swallowed into his arms as he wrapped them around her with the protective warmth she'd been craving. She felt the rapid beats of his heart against her cheek as she held on tight, his breathing shallow and quick. She buried her face in his neck, his familiar musky scent washing over her in a wave of relief.

"Baby, it's all right. I've got you now." She let out a small whimper when he started to pull away from her. He brushed the hair from her face and glanced from side to side. "Where's Matt?"

"At the top of the hill…looking for the keys," Lisa whispered, her parched throat tightened by the tears rushing into her eyes.

Ryan hesitated only a moment longer, his grief filled eyes searching hers. "Are you all right?"

"Yes," she managed to say.

He reached into his pocket and pulled out a set of keys. Stepping away from her, he lifted her hands up to remove the cuffs still encasing her wrists. He held on firmly, his eyes fixed on the purple welts where the metal had dug into her flesh.

"He hurt you. What else did he do?"

Lisa shook her head. Words froze on her lips as she witnessed a change come over Ryan. The concern in his eyes shifted to a hardened vengeful stare, scaring her a bit, as he looked up toward the cabin.

"Bobby," Ryan shouted and picked her up off her feet. He strode over to the cruiser behind his truck and indicated with a movement of his head for Bobby to open the rear door. As he gently placed her on the seat, she held onto his neck, not wanting to let go yet. "You have to let me go, Lisa. I've got to take care of this now."

She released her hold unwillingly and he stood to exchange words with Bobby. Lisa caught only part of what they said.

"Please, let me go with you Sheriff. I promise I won't let you down this time."

Ryan shook his head and barked out an order, which made Bobby stand stiffly to the side to allow Ryan to pass by.

Doug came over to receive his directions from Ryan. Lisa sensed Bobby's intense uneasiness, confirmed by the frustrated curses from under his breath, as he bent in to help her with the seatbelt.

"What's he going to do?" Lisa asked.

"By the looks of it he's going to make sure this guy won't ever do this again to you, or anybody else."

Ryan returned to the open door. "Lisa, Bobby is going to take you back to the house and stay with you until I get back. The EMT's are going to check you out to see if you need any further attention."

The merciless attitude remained, but his eyes softened slightly when Lisa reached out to touch his face.

"I'm not hurt, I'll be okay."

"I'll be back as soon as I can."

The roar of an engine pierced the night. Matt had found the keys.

Ryan's eyes turned cold as granite as he turned to close the door.

"Don't...don't hurt him," Lisa stuttered. "He needs help, Ryan. Please, he just needs help."

Ryan stood still momentarily, answering only by the half nod of his head, then shut the door securely and marched to his waiting vehicle.

Bobby wheeled the car around and took off back toward Lake Duchess. Lisa wrenched her neck around and saw Ryan's tail lights disappear over the hill in a spew of gravel.

"He won't hurt Matt, will he?" she asked Bobby, unsure of Ryan's intent.

"I wouldn't bet on it."

* * * *

Ryan skidded to a stop as he turned the truck to block the roadway. No way would he let this asshole escape again.

The van remained unmoving in front of them. The headlights glared into his eyes, the engine roaring, as the driver was forced to make a life changing decision with his next move.

Escape was impossible from either direction to the side, the trees too close together to allow for a vehicle to pass through. The only way out would be back the way he'd come, and even that was fruitless as Ryan knew the road ended a short distance past the cabin.

Ryan rammed the steering wheel of his truck to the right, to head back up the hill when he saw the van jerk into reverse.

Stopping in a flurry of dust, Matt flew out of the van and ran with wild abandon back to the cabin and disappeared.

"Cover me," Ryan shouted at Doug as he jumped out of the cruiser behind him. As he chased the unwieldy man, he reached the threshold of the cabin door, blocking any escape on either side, and pointed his revolver directly at the back of Matt's head.

"Stop, police, hands in the air," he shouted, spotting the blood dripping down the back of Matt's neck, a huge welt peeking through the hair on the right side of his head.

Way to go Lisa! Ryan thought appreciating her apparent ingenuity.

Matt swung around pointing Bobby's stolen pistol right back at him. Ryan eyed him, never swaying from his target. Sweat poured down Matt's face. Ryan couldn't be sure if the unnatural dilation of his eyes was due to drugs, or perhaps the concussion from the whack on the head. Matt's hands shook as he pointed the gun at Ryan, looking from side to side for some kind of escape.

There was none.

"N...N...No, you'll shoot me."

"Give me the gun Matt and I won't have a reason to shoot you."

Ryan held his hand steady, pointed straight at Matt's forehead. In his peripheral vision he had a clear view of the chair surrounded by the ropes and chains that must have secured Lisa for the last few days. The bed in the corner was bare, except for the crumpled pillow in the shadows of the dim light.

His mind skipped across the possibilities of what might have happened on that dingy mattress. His index finger on the trigger began to tighten and he had to force himself not to squeeze to complete his mission of putting an end to this scum in front of him.

Doug sidled up behind him, and held his pistol on the shaking criminal in front of them. Ryan sensed his deputy's tense control, and almost wished he didn't have a witness as he envisioned beating Matt to an inch of his life before turning him over to the proper legal process.

"Drop the gun, Matt."

Matt had begun to waiver his focus between the two men.

"I didn't do nothing wrong. Don't shoot me?"

Adrenaline rose to the surface as Ryan's stomach rolled with the indignation of Matt's refusal to acknowledge what he'd done.

"Maybe I should."

"What?" Matt's chin dropped.

Matt's grip loosened on the handgrip just enough that Ryan took the opportunity with quick assurance. Stepping forward, he wrenched the pistol out of Matt's hand to throw the weapon across the room, thrusting the smaller man into the rocking chair with a tight grip around the flailing criminal's neck. The muscles in Ryan's arms raged against the loose control he retained, as he shoved the barrel of his pistol against Matt's head, and brought his face up close and personal to the now frightened young man.

"Maybe I should give you a little of what you did to Lisa. Scare you to death. Make you feel small and incapable of defending yourself."

Matt shook his head violently, his hands grasping the arm that held him captive. "No," he managed to gasp out.

"No?" Ryan jerked him up out of the chair and shoved him against the bed frame, knowing he indeed was out of control, but didn't care. For once he wanted to get revenge for the pain he'd suffered watching his mother's painful murder, and the now vivid image of Lisa's suffering. "Maybe I should kill you here and now."

The straining terror-filled eyes of Matt, surrounded by purple veins about to burst, made Ryan pause before following through on his threat. There was fear, real fear – and he'd caused it, and despised the feeling that washed over him.

Yet, in one last burst of anger, Ryan raised his engulfing arm high above his head, the body of the struggling captive dangling then he threw him against the wall. Matt crumpled to the floor like the pillow in the corner.

The subtle clearing of his deputy's throat shook Ryan out of his vengeful state of mind. He took a deep breath, suddenly realizing his anger was so deep, he'd allowed himself to become no better than the abusers he hated. Unsure if he would have been able to stop himself, from mutilating the now unmoving individual if he'd been alone, scared him.

Ryan's deputy placed his hand on his shoulder, and he knew he'd gone too far. Disgusted with himself, he jerked his head at Matt to indicate Doug should take over. He stepped toward the door, his back turned against the unfolding scene.

He'd wanted to kill Matt. The fierce urge to do so had almost taken control of him. That feeling he would never forget.

Behind him, the shuffle of feet, and the distinctive clink of handcuffs being fastened around Matt's wrists helped to ease Ryan's need to bring justice to the victims of this world. Taking a deep breath, he turned around slowly.

"My father's a cop too, and he's got a lot of control. He won't let you get away with this."

The blood surfaced quickly again. Ryan stifled his anger with a hard swallow. "Not in my jurisdiction he doesn't."

"I bet he does. He's Captain Caine of the Columbus, District 4 Police force back home and he'll put you in your place," Matt puffed out his chest and held his head high with false self-importance. "He'll get me out of this."

"Not a chance," Ryan pulled him close again, his eyes boring into the now self-righteous rage of Matt's watering blue spheres. "I'm going to make sure you pay for what you've done to Lisa."

His choice of words suddenly struck Ryan square in the chest. Had he really just used that phrase against someone?

"What for? I didn't do nothin' wrong."

There's where you're wrong, Ryan thought.

"Among other things, you're being charged with two counts of burglary in Lake Duchess, breaking and entering, assaulting an old woman and an officer, cruelty to animals, kidnapping, and rape."

"I…I never did," Matt stuttered, shaking his head. "She wanted it. I swear."

The only thing Ryan could see was this dark cloud of red engulfing his sight. He started to haul off and knock the lying words

381

out of Matt's mouth then halted in mid air. Lisa's pleading words came back to him. *Don't hurt him. He needs help.* The raging anger lowered to a slow simmer. He knew better than to use his position and his strength to hurt someone, no matter how disgusting and wrong they were. Loathing his own actions, he slowly lowered his arm to his side.

"Read him his rights, Doug."

The Miranda was recited to Matt without fault, and Doug forced him out the door toward the cruiser.

Ryan turned one more time to survey the area. The blood on the concrete blocks surrounding the wood stove would prove where Matt had hit his head. He saw from the angle of the blood splatter, he'd been shoved hard from the direction of the bed, the indentation in the mattress showing where Lisa must have laid on her back.

The rumble in his ears made Ryan take a forced breath to clear his mind. He had no proof of what his mind began to conjure up.

He turned and shouted out the door for Doug to bring him some collection bags. There was a job to do now, and collection of evidence from the crime scene was his main priority.

He couldn't kill Matt, but he'd make damn sure to put him away for a very long time for what he'd done.

Chapter 20

In the soft afternoon light, the colorful bruise across Lisa's face showed vividly next to the stark white pillow her head rested against. As hard as Ryan tried to refocus, his thoughts remained on the fact he wished he'd inflicted at least the same amount of pain to her captor. The muscle in his arm flexed involuntarily with the need to grasp Matt's neck and squeeze the life out of him.

He set the prescription bottle back down on the dresser and glanced back at Lisa's peaceful slumber. The night before, Doctor Hughes' concern over her agitation with the activities surrounding her rescue had warranted him giving her a mild sedative. Other than the rope burns on her wrists and ankles, and minor injuries to her legs and arms, the doctor said exhaustion and dehydration were the most prominent needs to be addressed. Solid sleep would be the best medicine he could give her.

Lisa had responded to the prescribed sleep aid within minutes, falling into a deep sleep nestled against the soft pillows of Ryan's giant bed.

She looked so small—so abused.

For hours Ryan watched over his love, watching her face as she slept without movement, an occasional murmur the only indication she was still with him.

Overwhelmed by the need to protect, he'd wanted to crawl into bed next to her and pull her into his arms, but knew she needed her rest. Instead, he sat with his back to the wall, grasping the green quilted bed roll against his chest. His fixation on the excruciating futility he'd experienced with every action he'd taken to find Lisa drifted in and out of his consciousness followed by a previous time, forever imprinted in his life.

Memories of his past when he was a small boy, hiding in the cupboard, watching in fear as his mother shielded him from harm, flitted with sporadic bursts through his mind. He'd possessed no control over what happened then, or now. He realized the feeling was the same, as if he'd been pulled back into that cupboard, incapable of stopping the cruelty around him.

Ryan refused to acknowledge the uselessness that had seeped back into his thoughts. His chest tightened, and he banged his knee with his clenched fist, blaming himself for allowing this to happen to Lisa. He should've done more.

As he slid in and out of sleep, his mother's figure, standing firm against his father, mixed with the nightmare he'd created of Lisa being held captive by a crazed monster. His dreams comingled into one, the mental picture of the two women he loved the most coming together as they ran from the abusive terrors they feared. Somewhere just out of reach, he felt as if he were there, encased in the same fear they evaded. He woke, drenched in sweat, heart beating thunderously in his ears, and he knew this was how they must have felt.

In the dim moonlit room, Ryan gazed at the woman he loved. He knew the love coursing through his veins for her was not just physical. He'd found she filled him with so many feelings. Things he'd never known could exist in his path of life. He loved her without question, and needed her beside him, now and forever. There was nothing he wouldn't do for her, and vowed never to let anything bring the look of fear he'd seen in her eyes over the past few weeks again.

As if being dropped into a cloud of knowing, he wondered why he hadn't seen it before. He would ask her to become his wife—to be his friend, and his lover, to bring happiness and exhilaration—to be the core to his universe.

The thought soothed his aching head, and he leaned against the wall to figure out how he would propose to her. He considered sneaking under the covers to press his body against hers, to whisper in her ear the love he had for her. A gust of cool air through the cracked window caused the curtains to flutter letting in a bright stream of light, and the bruise across Lisa's face glowed in opposition to his line of thoughts.

Now was not the time. Soon enough she would be his. He had no doubt in his mind. He settled again, to watch his love silent in sleep.

Finally, in pure exhaustion, he too fell into a deep sleep. His head drooping to the pillow he held, total darkness blanketing his feverish thoughts.

* * * *

The constant ringing of a bell brought Ryan out of his dozing state. Then it stopped. Before his mind had time to engage, he came alert, ready for immediate action. He threw the pillow to the floor and stood, listening for any unusual sounds. The ringing began again, with annoying consistency, and he realized it was his front doorbell. The nuisance was some fool trying to get his attention.

For a moment, he waited in hopes they would go away, not wanting to leave Lisa's side until she woke. He watched her, and as the ringing continued and she started to move her head back and forth at the irritating noise.

He'd made sure his instructions were clear. No one was to bother them, no matter what. Incensed at their persistence, he slipped out and quietly closed the bedroom door behind him.

Whoever this is better have a damn good reason.

Swearing under his breath, Ryan trudged downstairs to the front door and swung it open quick and hard, ready to give the visitor a piece of his mind.

Tess stood, eyes wide open, the vivid blue of her eye shadow standing out like a neon sign. She held in her arms a bag of groceries, a bunch of yellow and pink flowers sticking out of the top.

"What the hell do you want?"

"Do you greet all your visitors in such a bad mood? Especially when they've got goodies," Tess giggled, stepping through the door without invitation.

Ryan followed her into the kitchen and glared as she emptied the contents of the bag onto the counter.

"What is this?"

"I'm here for you, baby. I've come to help you out with your poor little Lisa," Tess said, the emphasis on her words and pout of her lips disturbed Ryan. "You probably haven't eaten yet, so I thought I'd fix some steak and eggs for you."

Food—he hadn't thought of food for days. He actually began to feel weak at the thought.

"I can take care of everything here. I don't need your help." The unsuspected growl of Ryan's stomach deceived his stance of independence.

"See now, you're hungry. Just go sit down and I'll have this ready in a jiffy. I'll be out of your hair in no time."

Unable to do otherwise, he sank down onto the stool at the breakfast bar and inhaled the tall coffee she'd set in front of him from the Coffee Hut, feeling a haze come over his ability to refuse as Tess quickly made use of his stovetop and skillets.

When did I eat last? Two days ago?

He stared at her over the rim of the cup. She was saying something, her lips moved constantly in some mindless chatter that made no sense.

Ryan didn't care for Tess's type of generosity. Her motives were obviously jaded by her relentless belief they would get back together. But he had a hard time convincing himself to throw Tess out when she'd caused his stomach to overrule all other thoughts. Besides, he wasn't sure he had any food in the refrigerator. Sooner or later Lisa would need to eat too.

Dulled by the sudden need to eat, he found himself watching Tess with an odd fascination unable to stop her exuberant actions. When the sizzle of the succulent steaks hit the cast iron skillet, their savory aroma wrapped his senses into overdrive, and his stomach took over. Sadly, he knew he'd lost the turbulent war being fought in his brain.

Lisa won't be up for a while yet. Food first, then I can take care of her better, Ryan tried to convince himself.

Tess busied herself with making toast and scrambled eggs. Within minutes, she placed the most wonderful smelling food in front of him. He dove in without hesitation. His knife and fork hardly stopped moving as he worked his way through the meal, disturbed only by her ceaseless babbling.

"I've been thinking," she said as she sat down next to him, folding her hands on the table in front of her. "You told me how you feel about this Lisa, but what I don't think you realize is these are just misplaced emotions."

Ryan stopped eating and raised his eyes to Tess's serious expression. Oh, this had to be good. He had to hear more.

"Really?"

"You see, someone else cares very deeply for you, and you've shared something with her you can never get back with this Lisa."

"Please, go on."

Tess scooted closer to Ryan and placed her hand on his, batting her eyes in the way that annoyed him. She'd always been superficial. He realized now, her blatant personality had made him laugh before, but now her whole nature seemed to bother him.

"You shared your first love with this woman. Although, she got confused for a short time, she's loved you all her life. She knows you love her too, you just need to be reminded of what it was like."

Ryan figured her use of the third person wouldn't hurt her so much when he put her in her place, again. So he obliged her pretense.

"You're right. I loved her for a while, but she's no longer the one I love. We may have had our time, but she and I weren't meant for each other, not really. As for the two of us getting together, there's no chance of that happening. She needs to leave and let me get on with my life."

He had no doubt he'd loved Tess at one time. Unlike her though, he'd moved on. His love for Lisa was stronger than his love for Tess had ever been. Defeat hovered over her expression as she peered up at him with pitiful eyes. One last time, he took his former love's hand in his and gave it a little kiss.

From the corner of his eye, Ryan saw Lisa at the foot of the staircase. He jumped up from his seat and gently led her to one of the kitchen chairs.

"Lisa, you should've called out to me. I would've helped you down the stairs," Ryan said, a bit uncomfortable at being found with another woman's hand to his lips. "Tess was just leaving."

Lisa was pale—too pale. Her large brown eyes were shadowed by the dark circles underneath, the bruises strangely colorful against the white skin of her cheek.

"How are you feeling?" he inquired, unable to tell what she needed at that moment.

"I'm fine. A bit hungry though. It's been a while since I ate last. I knew you had company, but I smelled the food and couldn't wait any longer." Her voice sounded small, as if she were a child having woken from a nap.

Tess stood and walked into the kitchen, the unkind glance Ryan saw her give Lisa undeserved. "I didn't cook enough for the sick one. I guess I can cook up some scrambled eggs for her."

Ryan noted the slight movement of Lisa's body stiffening against the back of the chair. "I'm not sick."

"No, of course not," Tess agreed as if pacifying a child. "But you sure don't look well."

Ryan rolled his eyes and let out a sigh. Lisa didn't need this attitude around her. Tess needed to leave, now.

He walked into the kitchen, grabbing Tess's purse handles as he went by, and took her by the arm attempting to lead her out to the front door.

"Thank you for stopping by, but you don't need to stay. I'll fix Lisa something," Ryan said sternly in hopes she would leave without further discussion.

Instead of a negative response to being shoved out the door, Tess moved closer to him and gave him a quick hug. He caught sight of the begrudging glance she tossed Lisa before she plastered on a huge smile for him.

"Of course, you need to do this on your own, don't you? I'll be out of your hair," Tess twittered snatching her belongings from him.

Ryan followed her out onto the porch. Tess turned and gave him a sassy little grin. She reached up and placed her hand on his chest, peering over his shoulder at Lisa.

"You make sure to call me when you're ready for me to come back."

"Not going to happen," Ryan replied.

Tess scrunched her nose at him then blew a kiss his way when she got to her car. He shook his head dumfounded by her actions.

Good Lord, is she ever going to get it through her head I don't want her anymore?

Lisa didn't catch how Ryan responded to Tess, but she'd heard enough of their earlier conversation to know what was going to happen.

She wouldn't stay where she wasn't wanted. In fact, she needed to get out of there as soon as possible. A queasy, faint feeling began to surface again. She needed to eat something first. Then she'd be gone.

Rising to her feet, Lisa took a few steps toward the kitchen and had to grab hold of the breakfast bar before tumbling to her knees.

"Whoa there, what are you doing? I said I would fix something for you," Ryan's deep timber tickled her ear as he grabbed her from behind and forced her to sit back down at the table.

Shivers ran up and down her neck, tempting her to turn and wrap her arms around his neck to prove the words she'd heard were wrong. He came around to the front and gave her a quick kiss on the cheek, moving on to the kitchen as if he were trying to get away from her.

"Can you believe that Tess?" he asked shaking his head. "Quite a character, isn't she?"

Lisa remained silent, wishing she'd been able to leave when she'd stumbled upon the two of them together. She watched his nervous actions, and realized what she heard must be fact. He didn't want her around anymore. She couldn't tell whether the churning of her stomach was because of her hunger or the impending doom of what she'd thought was the perfect relationship.

"Really, tell me, how are you feeling?" Ryan asked, his eyes averted, as he busied himself with the task of scrambling eggs.

"I'm fine," she said, not knowing what else to say.

"That's good. Ummm..." She had never seen Ryan at a loss for words before. "Yeah, that's good."

Ryan set a cup of coffee in front of her, along with some milk and orange juice. Their eyes met for a brief moment. It felt as if they'd never been lovers. He was a stranger to her. She glanced away first, unable to keep the connection.

Who is this man? How could he pretend to love me when he really loved someone else? Was I really so stupid?

Lisa watched him while he finished the meal he'd created for her. As he set it in front of her, he knit his brows together as if worried about something.

He can't think of anything to say. The only thing we had in common was Matt. Now he's out of the picture Ryan doesn't know what to do with me.

He sat down in front of her and stared down at his coffee cup. He twisted the mug this way and that way. When the cooled coffee sloshed over the side onto his hand he swore under his breath.

Standing up to get a paper towel to wipe up the liquid, he gave a small laugh.

"I guess that was pretty stupid."

Ryan sat down again and laid his hands on either side of the mug. "Lisa…" he started out again, his voice dropping off as if he was unsure of what to say.

She couldn't take this. He obviously wasn't sure how to tell her he wanted to get back together with Tess. He stared into the coffee as if looking for something to say. His silence so thick, Lisa felt smothered by the effect it had on her.

They sat in an awkward silence as she tried to swallow some of the eggs he'd cooked. She took a deep breath and realized she could get through this too. Ryan had been right about one thing, she was stronger than she'd believed herself to be before all of this happened. She needed to thank him for being the support she needed.

"I want to thank you for rescuing me last night. I appreciate everything you've done."

"Looks as though you saved yourself, all I did was take the bastard away," Ryan said, meeting her eyes again with his.

"Where is Matt?"

Ryan's eyes were deceptive as they rose up to rest on her. She couldn't tell if he was angered by her asking or not, but she had to know what was happening.

"He's being transported this afternoon to the Olympic Corrections Center up north. We don't have enough room here at Lake Duchess to house him while he awaits sentencing." His voice was unusually gravelly, unlike the calm cooling sensation she had grown to love.

"What's he being charged with?"

"In addition to the charge of kidnapping and attempted rape, the citizens of Lake Duchess should be charging him with breaking and entering, burglary, and assault. I'm going to need you to sign a statement of your charges against him, but that can wait until tomorrow morning, and I'll fax it over to the county courthouse."

"How long will he be in jail?"

"We won't have a determination until after he's gone to court. Depending on his priors, the burglary alone would get him a couple of months to a year. With the assault, kidnapping, and rape it'll be a very long time before he'll see possible probation."

"Ryan, he didn't rape me."

She thought she saw a look of relief cross over his face as he glanced at her.

"Oh," he responded with, "Attempted rape, then."

Lisa merely nodded in acknowledgement. She looked out beyond Ryan's shoulder to Pluto's antics in chasing after the ducks. Her decision to something she'd been struggling with for some time came to her all of a sudden. She understood now what she needed to do.

"I've been thinking this over, and it might not seem right, but I'm not pressing charges." She felt strong about this, and her voice spilled out solid with conviction.

Ryan sat up straight in his chair. "I'm not sure I heard you right."

"I'm not pressing charges on Matt for what he did. All I ask, is they force him to stay in one of those programs that can help him."

He pushed away from the table and stood, the iciness of his glare piercing her skin. Then he turned abruptly to stare out at the same peaceful picture Lisa had been watching. His silence was worse than the look he'd given her. Tension along her shoulders traveled up her neck and pulsated at the base of her skull. She rolled her arms back and forth to ease the pain that remained from being tied up for so long.

"I read about a clinic once, real close to our hometown. Apparently, they have very positive results with both alcoholics and drug addicts. I'm sure they must deal with his type of addiction from time-to-time."

Ryan turned back to face her again. His brows were pulled together and he stared at her, his analysis unwavering.

"What makes you think he'll stay in one of those programs? I'm sure he doesn't have the money, and the state definitely doesn't have the funds for any type of extended stay assignees. At least not without his being incarcerated."

She straightened her spine with dignity, and said with determination, "Because, I'm going to pay for his treatment myself."

Lisa could see what she thought was anger boiling under Ryan's icy stare. "Where the hell are you going to get the money?"

"I still have my part of the trust fund my father left for me and my mother when he died. I've always thought I should do something special with it, and I'm choosing this as my gift to Matt's recovery."

Ryan raised his eyes in disbelief and stared at the ceiling. She could tell he wanted to say exactly what he thought of that idea, but he remained silent.

Lisa took a deep breath, let it out slowly then continued, "I think he should go straight from the detention facility to the program where he can be assessed by a professional. Maybe that way he won't have a chance to skip out again. He's done it before."

"What makes you think treatment will work this time?"

She looked down to the floor, unsure if she was making the right choice. There was no guarantee, but she had to try to do something to help the man. He'd pleaded for help, in his own way, the whole time she'd been his captive.

"I don't know. But I am sure putting him in jail is not the answer. He told me some things that made me realize he's got some real psychological issues. I don't think he's ever seen anyone about these problems before. If he did, maybe he would be a better person."

Ryan shook his head. "You know he could get through that program with flying colors, then turn around and do this again. Are you willing to live your life not knowing what is waiting for you around the corner?"

Lisa knew he was right. At the same time, she couldn't help the need to offer some type of assistance to the man she once cared about.

"I guess I am." The frown sitting on Ryan's brow was exactly what she'd anticipated. "I can't expect you to understand. But, if I do one thing in this life, I'd like to feel as if I've been of service to my fellow human being. I can only tell you, if I were in the same position I'd want someone to reach out to support me too."

Ryan's skepticism overflowed into his expression. "You are one special lady," he said finally. "I don't believe anyone is quite like you."

He began an impatient tapping of his fingers on his pant leg. "Lisa, we need to talk."

Lisa remembered his words 'she needs to leave and let me get on with my life.' He wanted her out of there, and apparently didn't know how to ask. She couldn't bear the thought of hearing him tell her he wanted her to leave. She wouldn't make him. She'd make it easy for him, and for her.

"Are you going into town soon?" she asked, taking the last bite of her toast. She forced a smile onto her face and glanced back up to meet his concerned gaze. She needed to act nonchalant, like none of this meant a thing to her. "I need to get all my belongings together and make sure my car is ready for the trip out to the closest airport."

"Airport?" Ryan asked. He lifted his eyebrows, the clear green of his eyes emotionless.

"I figure now Matt isn't trailing me I should go back home to my mother."

"I see."

Lisa tried to keep her face straight, though she could feel the tears bubbling up. "She needs me. I want to take care of her now."

Damn it. I can't read his face. What is he thinking?

The granite surface of his face hid everything. She found herself glaring into eyes that had narrowed and turned into a frozen subarctic pit of unmoving molecules.

Can't he express some type of emotion? I've just told him I'm leaving and I'll never see him again.

"Right." Though his abrupt agreement was expected, it angered her.

Why should he argue?

"I won't be a bother, will I? I'm going to go pack up my things now." She waited, hoping he would say something— something that would prove he still wanted her. He glared at her with those cold analytical eyes so long she wanted to scream to find out what was wrong with him.

"Well I should go into the office anyway. I've been gone too long," was all he said.

Ryan stood and grabbed the dishes off the table and set them down with force, a fork tumbling off the plate to clatter against the metal sink bottom. He remained with his back to her for the longest time, then turned and placed the heels of his hands on the counter behind him. The blank glare on his face tore her heart from her chest.

Lisa wouldn't let him see her cry. She needed to get out of his sight before she broke down totally.

"Then I'll go pack my things." She bowed her head toward her feet so he wouldn't see the makings of tears about to spill over. "I'll be ready in a few minutes."

She turned and started toward the stairway.

"Lisa."

The sound of Ryan's voice, almost too low for her to hear, made her go even faster. She couldn't take the apologies, or any more lies for that matter. She just needed to get out of there.

"Lisa," he called out again, louder but this time with more urgency.

She stopped and turned her head enough to see he was standing at the bottom of the stairs. There was a pained look in his eyes, one that if she'd let herself believe could be interpreted as heartbreak.

They stood staring at each other.

The crunch of gravel under the tires of a vehicle on the driveway reverberated in the pregnant silence between the two. She saw Ryan flinch and glance toward the front windows, yet he continued to stand at the staircase. The knock on the door didn't prompt any movement either. The sound of radio static followed by an official response came from the individual at the other side of the door.

"Lisa, we should talk," he said in a hurry, as he glanced toward the door and back at her. He appeared to be waiting for her answer, so she nodded quickly, but as he turned to answer the door, she ran up the remaining stairs to lock herself in the bathroom.

Chapter 21

Ryan didn't get a chance to talk with Lisa like he'd hoped. His deputy's arrival brought a need for him to commit his full attention to an altercation at the other end of town between a drunken Beatty and one of the truckers that had ventured out to the park for a little down time.

When he left her at Maggie's diner he'd told her to wait for him to come back. But she'd acted as if she couldn't wait to leave.

Beatty had given his deputies a rough time of it, and would only listen to Ryan, just as it had always been. Settling him down took a little longer to deal with this time, and Ryan worried Lisa would take off before talking with him. Her leaving was tearing him apart. Did he imagine all of the feelings they had shared over the last few months? He had to at least find out whether she'd felt anything at all for him.

He couldn't let her go without knowing. If he did, the mysterious relationship they'd shared would drive him crazy.

After he pulled into the parking lot, he sat for a minute to gather his thoughts. Should he ask her to stay so they could find out if they belonged together? Or, maybe just suggest she think about making Lake Duchess her home?

Shit, either way makes me sound like an idiot!

He got out of his truck and looked around the empty lot. The early evening crowd hadn't arrived yet, but the regulars would be gathering soon enough.

As he walked into the restaurant, he was greeted by silence, the creak of the door and the sound of his boots on the wood floor sounding oddly loud to him. Something was missing.

"Maggie?" he called out.

"Over here," she responded from the far side of the dining room, behind the half wall supporting the cash register.

Maggie sat at one of the tables by the windows, feet propped up on an opposite chair, tickets from the lunch period spread out in front of her. Her pencil lay still beside the silent calculator on the table in front of her.

Tina sat at a table across from Maggie uncharacteristically silent, wrapping the clean silverware with green linen napkins and gently placing them in a tray for the next shift's use. She looked up at him and shook her head, the glare she gave him reminiscent of a mother's disapproval.

"Where's Lisa?" he asked, not sure if he wanted the answer.

"Gone," Tina spouted, as she jerked her head toward the door, a frown pasted across her face.

Ryan stood still, unable to breathe.

"She left?"

"Appears so," Maggie responded with a nod. "She asked for her last check and cleared all of her open accounts in town. She's got a red-eye flight out of Sea-Tac to Columbus."

Ryan didn't know if he wanted to cry or swear. Doing neither, he shoved his hand into his pocket and balled his fist around the keys. He pressed hard, not caring that their sharp edges dug into his palm. His heart raced like the rush of a herd of mustangs scared by the shot of a gun.

Life had done it to him again. The woman he loved was gone, and there was nothing he could do to hold her back. She'd said it herself, she belonged with her mother. If she didn't want to stay with him, he'd have to accept her decision.

Damn, that decision hurt.

"She didn't let me say goodbye."

Maggie stared up at him from her seat for a moment then jumped to her feet. Tina followed suit, the remaining napkins in her lap falling to the floor.

"Goodbye? What the hell are you talking about?" Maggie all but screamed at him.

Confused by Maggie's outburst, Ryan stepped back, his brows rising up. He studied the two women and truly did not understand their anger.

"That would have been proper manners, wouldn't it?"

"Proper manners?" Maggie shouted. She glared at him, her face scrunched into an angry version of her usual intensity. "Hell boy, you can be so stupid sometimes."

"You tell him Maggie," Tina encouraged. "I never thought he'd be stupider than the men I've dated."

"Stupid?" Ryan asked, somewhat offended.

"Why the hell would you choose Tess over Lisa? You've got to be stupid to do something as lame-brained as that," Tina said punching him in the shoulder.

"Stop that." Ryan rubbed his arm. That one actually hurt. "Wait, what are you talking about?"

"She left because you broke her heart you idiot." Tina came close enough to stick her face close to his. "She said you didn't need her messing up your life, and something that sounded like you and Tess are getting back together."

Ryan took Tina by the shoulders and stepped away from her, which allowed Maggie in to shove him hard and stomp her foot. She shook her head and said a few frustrated words under her breath that Ryan couldn't understand, but knew were directed at him.

"Is she right? Better not be," Maggie barked.

"No." Ryan immediately shook his head.

They were teaming up on him. Ryan felt as if he was twelve again, being scolded for some idiotic thing he'd done—reprimanded yet strangely loved.

"Where'd she get that idea?"

"From you," Tina and Maggie said at the same time.

"That's ridiculous. She knows how much I care for her. She knows I want her to stay."

"Does she?" Maggie squinted at him. "Does she, really?"

He stood, unmoving, staring out toward the lake, and remembered a time not long ago when he'd been faced with a similar situation. The person he'd thought would be his forever, left him to find new adventures and make a new life, without him. This replay of a bad movie irritated him.

"Maybe she never meant to stay and this is just her excuse to leave," he said remembering the conversation he'd had with Tess. Maybe he'd misjudged her—wouldn't be the first time. He'd thought she was different. He'd thought what they'd shared meant something real—apparently not.

Maggie's attitude softened and she lay her hand on his arm. "I like to think I know people pretty well. Lisa loves you. You two were meant to be together. She wouldn't feel the need to leave if she'd been given a reason to stay."

"Aren't I a good enough reason to stay?" Ryan mumbled.

"Have you asked her yet?"

His brows came together as he thought hard about the answer to that question, and began to realize every time he'd tried to tell her of his feelings they'd been interrupted. Intimacy was one thing, but they hadn't had a chance to share their dreams and feelings for one another.

"You haven't, have you?" Tina asked heatedly. "Of course not, look at him Maggie, dumb as a doornail. Have you told her you love her?"

"Well, not exactly," he had to admit.

Of course she would leave. They were right. Maybe she didn't know how much he loved her. Maybe if she knew she would change her mind.

God, I hope she loves me too.

"Go tell her," Maggie said. "You'll never rest until you do."

Ryan looked into Maggie's stern but loving face and nodded. She'd been through it all with him. She knew him so well. He wouldn't rest. If nothing else, he needed to know if Lisa loved him. He glanced down at his watch, gauging the time it would take him to get to Sea-Tac.

"Which way is she headed, North or South?"

"She asked me if there were any charter flights nearby she could catch at such late notice. I told her about Ziggy's Fly-on-the-Fly service. I think she said she was in luck and was headed out to Port Angeles." Tina offered.

"How long ago did she leave?" He knew about Ziggy, he'd go anywhere, anytime, and it wouldn't take him long to get ready to fly out.

"About half-hour ago," Maggie said, grinning from ear to ear.

He grasped Maggie by the shoulders and kissed her soundly on the cheek, and did the same to Tina. Promptly, he headed toward the door. He twisted toward them as he kept walking and waved his hand at the two women.

"Wish me luck. Thank you. You guys are the best."

From the road he punched the Fairchild Airport into his GPS and headed North on Hwy 101. It would take the normal driver about an hour and a half to get there. But he wasn't your normal driver. He reached into the glove compartment and took out the siren. He didn't abuse his position as a Sheriff, but this situation warranted immediate action. If needed, he could use this as his excuse for employing speed in his favor to catching up with the one woman he wanted to share the rest of his life.

* * * *

Lisa sat on the uncomfortable row of seats in the waiting area of the airport, facing the windows that overlooked the runway. She watched as a Cessna taxied, bouncing and swaying a bit down the rough concrete slabs.

She'd never flown in a single engine airplane before, and heard the flights were quite bumpy depending on the weather patterns. She hoped today would be free from any turbulent air pockets. The way she was feeling, she prayed they would have some type of receptacle on board, just in case she lost it.

The pilot told her not to worry. He could fly in a tornado if necessary. His self touted ability didn't do much for her trust in him. She felt a little queasy at the idea of being propelled across the sky in such a small contraption. Somehow, the thought of the upcoming larger commercial plane ride to Columbus didn't make her as uneasy.

Ziggy was more than agreeable to take her across the peninsula to Sea-Tac International. She could almost see the dollar signs glaring in his eyes as he quoted her the price for such a short notice flight. This was one of the times she would use a large chunk of the funds her father had left her. Otherwise, as far as she was concerned, the rest of it would be set aside for the housing and treatment for Matt.

She heaved a long sigh as she stared out at the blue sky. A few puffy white cotton-ball clouds off to the west floated happily in the air, without a care in the world. The recent events hadn't cleared yet, and her exhaustion still hung gloomily over her like a darkened cloud ready to let go a wet monsoon downpour.

She was finally going home. She should be happy about that, but she wasn't.

As she lifted the tissue to her bleary tear blotched eyes the limp paper fell into her lap in pieces, and she realized she'd been shredding it as she sat waiting for her flight. She reached into the bottom of her bag searching for another tissue. Unable to find one, she used the edge of her t-shirt sleeve to sop up the wetness.

She couldn't stop thinking about Ryan. His rich green eyes shimmering in the moonlight, the sexually taunting grin, the longing to feel of his arms wrapped around her seemed to haunt her every thought. No use in crying. That wouldn't change the situation. No matter how much she cried, her tears wouldn't bring him back to her. The sad thing was, no matter how much she loved him, that wouldn't bring him back either.

It would be different if he loved her the same way, and the only thing she had to battle was that self-indulged arrogant Tess. That she could deal with—and win. But she'd heard it straight from his lips, she needed to go and leave him to get on with his life. What they'd shared hadn't meant a thing to him.

Tears sprang forward and she reached for her sleeve again. From out of nowhere a tissue appeared over her shoulder, the hand holding it somewhat familiar. The scent of clean clothes and Irish Spring bath soap caught her attention.

"Ryan?" she asked hopefully as she turned around.

"None other," Ryan responded. "Why are you crying?"

She stood to face him, the tears rushing up like a faucet being turned on to a steady trickle. She grabbed the tissue out of his hand and wiped at her eyes in frustration.

"Just happy to be going home is all. What are you doing here?" She forced her voice to be level and unaffected by the emotion of seeing him again so soon.

"I might ask you the same thing." Ryan stood, stone faced, as she tried frantically to think of the right answer.

"I told you, I'm going back home to be with my mother." The turbulence she had in her stomach right now would outshine anything she might experience on the small plane.

He nodded silently as he stared at her. "When I left you at Maggie's I asked you to wait for me to come back. The least you could have done was let me drive you up here, to give us a chance to talk."

"You're right, I know, but I didn't want to be in your way," she said with the lump in her throat causing an unexpected raspy hoarseness.

"You've never been in my way, Lisa." Ryan cleared his throat twice before he started again. "You know…you could stay."

Lisa almost choked on her response.

Why on earth would he think I'd want to stay when he's with Tess?

"Thank you for the invitation, but I think I best be getting back to my mother in Columbus." She willed the building tears away, unsure of how long she could continue this ruse of polite conversation.

Ryan breathed out a deep breath as if he'd been holding it a while.

"You know, if that's the only reason you're leaving, Hannah Mullins is a nurse at the assisted living center up north. She's got that huge house off of Alder Street. I've heard she wants to work locally with the residents of Lake Duchess. She's been remodeling her home to take in three or four elderly people that need care. Maybe you could bring your mother out here to be her first tenant?"

This was the strangest line of conversation she'd ever had with someone.

"Why would I want to do that?"

"That way I can keep my eye on you and make sure nothing happens to you." Ryan's gaze shot out to the windows as a small plane's engines readied for take-off, then back to her. "And because then you could stay—if you wanted to that is."

Frustrated, Lisa glared at him in silence. What the hell was he talking about? He made no sense at all.

"Tess might have a problem with that."

"I don't give a damn what Tess wants." Ryan's quick movement surprised her as he came around to wrap his arms around her waist. Lisa pushed at Ryan's hold, his words totally illogical to her.

"Oh, is that why you told her I just needed to get out of the way and leave you to live your life in peace? I heard you say there's no chance of us getting together anyway, so why do you want me to stay?"

Ryan scrunched his forehead then rolled his eyes toward the sky.

"Wait, you thought I was talking about you? I didn't realize you heard that."

"Well, I did. So you can drop the game you're playing. I don't know why you're here. I'm not staying any longer than I have to." Lisa tried to stiffen herself against the hold Ryan still had on her, without much success.

"Tess talks about herself in the third person. It's really strange, but I got used to it a while ago. I forget others may not understand." He shook his head at her. "She has this idea that we should renew our relationship. When I said that, I was trying to let her down as easy as possible. She still can't seem to get it through her head she needs to leave me alone."

Lisa tried again to pull away. "That makes no sense at all." Although, she had to admit she remembered hearing Tess speak that way before and thought it odd.

"Then tell me, does this make sense?"

Ryan shoved his hand against the back of her head and dragged her lips up to meet his. The kiss started out rough as if Ryan was trying to prove a point. Then it began to melt into her as a sudden heat traveled through her body with the intensity of a hidden message. Her response to him was uncontrollable. She parted her lips at his insistence and felt as if an elixir of love poured through the warmth of his kiss.

Ryan's head rose above her, the significance of the kiss to her still not sinking in. She lifted her eyes to gaze up into the beautiful green pools of mystery she'd fallen in love with, the secret to their depths she still didn't understand.

She slowly shook her head. "No."

"Damn it, I love you, Lisa. I've never been very good at expressing my feelings, and I know I'm not easy to understand." He took a long breath in as he gazed into her eyes, then let it all out as he continued, "But, I hope to God you love me, too. If you leave me now, I'll lose all faith in what I feel. I know I'll never love again, not like this."

Lisa couldn't get herself to speak. A few minutes before, she'd thought the world had dropped out from under her. Now it seemed the one thing she'd dreamed of all her life was coming true.

She raised her hands up, grasping the back of his neck she pulled his head down for another kiss. When their lips parted, they were both out of breath. This time Lisa smiled at the dazed look on Ryan's face. Then he became quite serious, never loosening his hold on her.

"I need to hear you say you love me, Lisa."

"If you don't know that by now, I'll just have to try harder to convince you," she laughed, feeling a bit light headed. The grave look on Ryan's face lightened only for a moment. "I love you more than I'll ever be able to tell you."

"Marry me," he whispered as he buried his nose in her neck, his hot breathe tickling her ear. "I can't lose you again. Please be my wife."

She didn't need to think about it at all, and nodded her head vigorously. Ryan pulled back far enough to gaze at her, his eyes still holding a question.

"Was that a yes, or a no?"

"Yes," Lisa's smile broadened. "Yes, yes, yes, yes, yes!"

Ryan crushed his lips against hers. Lisa felt as if her heart were about to explode. Finally, her heart was at peace, her world was right again. Love and laughter, the two most important things in life, had come to stay.

EPILOGUE

Lisa sat on the porch watching Ryan dig the hole for the new dogwood tree he'd brought home to commemorate their third anniversary. Each year he'd produced a decorative tree to add to the landscaping in honor of the strength of their growing love for each other.

He pushed the shovel into the soft ground and stopped, his foot poised on top of the foot rest above the blade. As if sensing her focus, he turned toward her and flashed the smile that melted her heart every time.

This gorgeous man is mine. All mine, she thought as the small infant began to stir in her arms.

"That man sure loves you," Tina said, smiling across from her, while patting the bulge of her eight-month pregnant belly. "We're both so lucky to have found these men of ours. Michael said because he loves me so much he'd clean the whole house while I'm gone. Can't ask for more than that can I?"

Lisa chuckled and lifted her son to her shoulder. "Yes, we are definitely blessed."

She snuggled the top of her newborn son's head to her nose, and gave him a kiss on his rosy cheek, the cooing sound he made causing her to beam with a mother's love. Pluto sat devotedly at her feet, his nose propped on Lisa's knee, a protective eye on both her and his newest best friend.

"Are you ready to get back to the kids in your class yet?" Tina changed her sitting position with a groan.

Lisa smiled. She did miss them dearly. Nothing could take the place of a room full of excited children ready to create the next best art project for their mom or dad. Nothing except the treasure she now held in her arms.

"No, I think I'm going to enjoy the three months of maternity leave added to summer vacation."

"You won't be able to wait to get back to them. I know, I've seen how much you love it."

"Not more than I love this little guy," Lisa said giving him a little squeeze against her chest.   "Evan and I are going to go see grandma this afternoon. Hey, do you want to come with us?"

Her mother's condition had improved immensely since they moved her to the home in Lake Duchess. She had her good days and bad days, her long term memory continuing to fade. Lisa took every opportunity she had to bring the baby to visit. Ryan joined in when he could get away.

"Sorry, sweetie, I've got to go back home to that man of mine and see if he's blown up the house yet. You know how he gets when he focuses on too many things at once."

"Yeah, he can get a little obsessive," Lisa agreed.

Tina laughed as she struggled to her feet. "Hey, Hercules, come help this Prego down the stairs," she called out to Ryan.

He held up his hand to her briefly, dug one more shovel of dirt then swung the root ball of the tree into the hole. Shoving the blade into the ground he started toward them. The grin on his face

414

grew wider, his gaze fixed on Lisa and his son, but his face changed quickly when an unexpected sputter of tires on the long gravel drive grew louder. He stopped and turned around to acknowledge the newcomers.

Pluto jumped to his feet and ran out to Ryan, wagging his tail and bouncing around at the car's approach. Ryan grasped hold of the canine's collar to keep him in check.

The older white Olds Cutlass that came into view was not one Lisa recognized. It stopped not far from where Ryan was standing at the side of the drive and a man got out from the driver's side. All of a sudden, Pluto began barking and lunging at the man, which was unusual to say the least. She could see that it took all of Ryan's strength to hold him back.

The man looked familiar, but Lisa couldn't place him right off. He wore a bright paisley shirt over worn jeans, his red hair blowing in the wind. Ryan stood straight as an arrow. Somewhat blocking her view, his shovel within reach, he looked like an armed soldier getting ready for battle. The two men exchanged words and Ryan shook his head and pointed back toward road where the man had come from, as if telling him he needed to leave. The man in the paisley shirt appeared apologetic but didn't back down right away.

"Oh, my God, is that who I think it is?" Tina asked.

As Ryan looked back to her, Lisa caught a full glance of the man's face and took in a sharp breath. Her heart pounded in her ears the way it used to, but this time was different. She knew she was safe.

"Matt," Lisa responded in a hushed whisper.

"What the hell is he doing here?" Tina sidled up to her protectively.

"I don't know." Lisa said a little shaky. She stood and held the baby out. "Tina, would you please help me change Evan's diapers and get him ready for our visit with grandma. Warm up a little afternoon snack for him, would you? I need to find out why Matt's here."

"I'll be watching from the window," Tina claimed taking Evan from her, kissing his soft velvet hair as she snuggled him into her arms. He turned his head side to side, his mouth wide open taking in quick breaths, in search of his awaited snack. "What shall it be Sweetie, steak and eggs or a monster taco? No? I think you're absolutely right, warm milk it is."

As Tina walked away with the gurgling child, Lisa took in a deep breath and started down the stairs toward the two men. She needed to do this. She had to do this.

Ryan met her halfway in between the house and Matt, who waited at the car door.

"He says he wants to talk to you for a minute."

Ryan's disapproving stance was more than obvious to her, but she'd known this would happen sooner or later. Now was no different than later. Either way it would be difficult.

"All right, we'll give him a minute," she consented.

"You don't have to do this. I can have him out of here on trespassing charges in a heartbeat," Ryan offered.

"No. It's all right. Take Pluto to the back yard to settle down."

416

"I won't do that, Lisa. We'll wait right here for you." His stern voice, she knew was not one to be argued with, as he positioned himself in protective mode and made Pluto sit beside him. The dog continued the low growl, his eyes glued to the whereabouts of the offending human.

Lisa had to appreciate his stance, as she was still a bit unsteady about confronting her abuser. She gave Ryan a kiss on the cheek.

When she got closer to the car she saw Matt impatiently drumming his fingers on the top of the door frame, a characteristic she recognized from before. He discontinued the activity when she stopped a few yards from where he stood.

"Hello Matt, how are you?"

His ever present energy came out in movement, so he walked back and forth in front of her for a second then forced himself to stop.

"I'm good, really good, how about you?" His strong response indicated that he meant what he said.

"I'm glad," Lisa said a bit uncomfortable. "I'm good too."

Matt paced again then turned with a sheepish look on his face. "I suppose you're wondering why I'm here."

"Well, yes…"

He jumped in, cutting off any more of what she may have been about to say. "I wanted to thank you."

"For what?"

"For not putting me in jail, I would never have lasted in there," Matt said, his brows coming together into a puff of red fluff across his forehead. "I would have been dead within a month or two."

Lisa could understand why he thought that would happen. He wasn't a fighter, never had been. The ruffians in those places would have eaten him alive.

"I also wanted to let you know they told me you chose and paid for the program I went into." He began pacing back and forth again, then visibly made himself stop. He glanced up at Lisa and blew out a breath. "You didn't have to do that you know."

"I know that. I just hope it has helped you," Lisa said softly.

"Oh, yeah, it's a really awesome counseling center with support groups I go to every week, every day if I need to. Still facing those demons of mine though, but as we learned in the center, take it one day at a time."

Grateful to know her decision had been right, Lisa said with all sincerity, "I'm so glad to hear that, Matt."

"I've been clean and sober for over two years now. It's a daily battle sometimes, but I'm hanging in there. " He gave her a grin, reminiscent of when she'd first met him. "Course, I never would have made it without Cindy."

Lisa raised her eyebrows. "Cindy?"

"Cindy's my sweetheart. I never would have met her if it hadn't been for you," he said grinning with obvious love. Lisa watched him, seeing the change in his face as he started talking about Cindy. He really loved her. "We met at the center. She's been a volunteer there for a year now. She keeps me on track and doesn't let me get away with anything."

Speculating on what a new love could do for him Lisa gave him a simple smile. "That's good."

"I've got a job now, and I'm learning to take care of business."

"I'm so happy to hear how well you are doing."

"Yeah, you too," Matt offered nodding.

There was an awkward silence then Matt reached out toward her, but Pluto's immediate barking caused him to hesitate. Ryan could be heard restraining the hound from bursting forward to attack. Lisa recognized Matt's fear, yet he pushed forward to grasp her hand in his.

"Lisa, I had to come see you again to show you how well I'm doing. I would never have been able to get here if it wasn't for you. And…" he began, his voice drifting off. He stared down at their joined hands for a moment. "And, I wanted to apologize for what I did to you."

He glanced back up to Lisa, his eyes somewhat watery around the edges. She remained silent, unsure if she should so readily accept his apology.

"I should never have chased and kidnapped you like I did. It was the way my mind was messed up from the chemicals. At the time I really believed you were mine, because that's what I wanted to believe."

Lisa already knew this, but appreciated he had finally come to understand the truth for himself. She squeezed his hand in response to let him know she acknowledged his confession.

"Besides my mother, you were the only one that ever treated me right. You never made me feel like I was less of a person than everybody else. There's no excuse for what I did. I know that now."

She reached out to place her other hand on his shoulder, and made sure she had his full attention by looking directly into his eyes.

"Apology accepted. I just want you to take care of yourself and this new relationship of yours."

"Yeah, I will. Hey, thanks for getting that ring back to me. I might have a use for it here soon." The smile that came across his face was priceless. New love wasn't a guarantee he would succeed in his attempt at normal life, but it obviously gave him a foundation on which to build his sobriety. Lisa prayed silently it would be enough to keep him away from the temptations of addiction he would face from day to day.

He began to pace back and forth, an added force behind his disquieted spirit. He looked down at his feet then back up to Lisa's face.

"I…I need to know, can you forgive me for all the shit I put you through?"

Lisa smiled. "Matt, I forgave you a long time ago. I know what you were doing wasn't who you really are on the inside. I'm so glad you've finally found some help with your struggles. After you told me about some of them, I realized how hard it must be. You need to look at what you've got now with Cindy."

"Yeah, well, I've got a real reason to stay out of that stuff now."

"Make sure you do, she deserves the best from you," Lisa agreed.

Matt stood for a minute, his eyes locked on Lisa's then he nodded again in agreement.

"All right," he said glancing over her shoulder at back at Ryan and Pluto. "I've got to get going. Cindy's waiting for me back at the motel in Ocean Shores. She's got some crazy idea about building sand castles on the beach."

Matt got into the car and said happily, "Hey, I've been playing with a band called 'The Rocks'. If you're ever down in Columbus again, come catch the band at Ronnie's Bar and Grill on Saturday nights. You'll have a blast."

Lisa felt as if a weight had been lifted from her shoulders. The unknowing of whether Matt had taken the opportunity to improve himself, or if he'd returned to his old addictive ways, had been weighing on her subconscious. She hadn't known how badly she needed to know until she'd seen his face.

She waited for Matt to turn the car and head back out to the main road before turning back around to face Ryan. He and Pluto stood still, the granite expression still glued to his face. At peace in her soul for having done the right thing, she sauntered back toward them.

"Are you all right?" Ryan asked, still sheltering her every need.

She smiled up into his eyes, loving him that much more.

"Yes, I'm glad Matt stopped to talk. We both needed to have that happen. Thanks for being here for me."

Pluto began to push his big wet nose into her hand and she bent down to give the still hyped dog some well deserved attention.

"You are such a good boy, Pluto." The following wet laps of his tongue against her cheek made her giggle. "I know, I know, you are here to protect me, aren't you?"

Ryan let the dog's collar loose from his hand, and Pluto proceeded to monopolize Lisa's attention by plopping down to the ground and presenting his belly. She bent down to indulge the canine's craving for love with a good belly scratch, cooing encouraging words to his over the top reaction to her touch. Glancing up, Lisa found Ryan smiling down at her with the same look she'd fallen in love with, his bright eyes twinkling in the sunlight.

"What about me? I was here too," Ryan said with playful dejection.

She stood and rose to her toes, wrapping her arms around his neck. Ryan's arms came swiftly around her waist and held her tight against his body. As always, shivers of joy raced down her spine. From the first time she'd laid eyes on him, she'd known he was the only one for her. She began planting little kisses up and down his neck, causing him to groan with pleasure.

"I have something much better planned for you."

The End

Author Bio

Analiesa Adams is an author who enjoys reading and writing about the many nuances of life and romance through her insight from both personal experience and careful observation. Her lifelong dream to express the intrigue and revelation of her many interests, using contemporary romance, suspense, and light paranormal themes, has motivated the creation of over 100 plots. Though challenged by her professional occupation, she will never give up the freedom of creating through writing.

Away from work, she lives on the beautiful peninsula of the Pacific Northwest with her two best friends, kitties by the name of Loca and Bebe, both of which give her constant joy and love. Soon to have the companionship of her mother, who will be moving in sometime this summer, she revels at the chance to spend more time in her elder years. Visits with her adored son are also treasured, and she takes every chance she can get to spend time with him as well.

Freelance and technical writing, of various types of composition have been an aspect of her licensed personal business services for over 19 years. As a member of various writing groups since 2008, the abundant opportunity to grow in the craft of fiction writing, and the chance to meet with others who share her love of writing has inspired her to continue her dream.

To keep updated on the next adventure in the writings of Analiesa Adams, visit her website at:

AAdamsBooks.com.

Drop a note on the contact page and let her know if you would like to be added to her E-mail list for updates, or follow her through Twitter at:

#AAdamsBooks

Made in the USA
Middletown, DE
07 July 2018